BOOKS BY D. L. RICHARDSON

SCIENCE FICTION
Earth Quarantined
Earth Arrested
Earth Reclaimed coming soon

The Apocalypse Games - Pandora
The Apocalypse Games - CyberNexis
The Apocalypse Games - Chrysalis

YOUNG ADULT
The Bird with the Broken Wing
Resident Spy
One Little Spell

THE APOCALYPSE

GAMES

PANDORA

BOOK ONE

D L Richardson

The Apocalypse Games - Pandora
www.dlrichardson.com

First electronic publication: November 2016
First print publication: November 2016

Smooth seas do not make skilful sailors.

AFRICAN PROVERB

1

Jack

Jack Minnow grabbed a brochure off the rack and read the back page. "It says here that rule breakers are ten times more likely to survive an apocalypse. They're adaptable and they rely on cunning and instinct."

Jack was five foot eight, and the woman behind the counter, called an operator, was easily six foot tall. Gazing up at her was like looking at a marble statue atop a pedestal. She was all white – her hair, her tight-fitting jump suit, her face, neck, and hands, painted to resemble a computer generated character. He allowed himself to imagine that the stage make-up covered places he couldn't see.

She gave him a polite hostess type of smile and pushed a plastic tray towards him, the kind handed out at airports to slip under x-ray machines. "It also says that rule breakers are ten times more likely to die within the first hour. They're reckless and often act without thinking."

Jack dropped his wallet, phone, and car keys into the tray and flashed a smile. "So it's a win/win situation for a guy with a superhero complex."

His mother used to call him Superman whenever he brought home a stray dog. "Can't help but save things," she used to tell the ranger. Even as a boy, Jack knew what happened to the mutts who were taken to the pound, but he still brought dogs home for one last night of fun. His superhero complex was the reason he'd entered *The Apocalypse Games*. Save everyone. Save the world. Nobody dies except the virtual characters.

The operator removed the tray, and he stood there waiting for a voucher. When none came, a warning flared up into his brain. What did he really know about this operation?

"Seriously, about those odds," he said. "Exactly how much testing has gone into the program? I mean this *is* opening day. There must be kinks to iron out."

"We use the same technology as NASA," she said. "The nutrient tubes and mist emitters feeding into the simulation pods are the same as those used in space travel. The structural integrity of the pods was tested by NASA engineers only last week." She tilted her head to the side. "We'll take good care of you, Mr Minnow. I'll see to it personally."

He didn't know her name, or anything else about her, but he felt he could trust her. He *had* to trust her; he was placing his life in her hands.

He shook his head to rid himself of the doubt. His life wasn't in any danger. The game was harmless. He could exit at any stage. It said so on the brochure.

She stepped out from behind the counter, slipped her arm through his, and guided him toward a set of doors where he caught flashes of shiny surfaces and bright lights. A sign above the door read: Launch Pad.

"How will you see to it personally?" he asked, dragging his gaze back to her dazzling blue eyes. They had to be colored lenses. Eyes didn't sparkle like hers. "Will you be in the game with me?"

She shook her head. Pity. He liked the way she flirted with him.

"You've got a good crowd here for the opening," he said. "How many players you reckon? Eighty? Ninety?"

"There are one hundred and five players taking part in today's auspicious event."

Jack's mood sank a little. "Won't it get crowded?"

She gave his arm a gently squeeze. Others might have found the gesture too friendly, but not him. Attention from a beautiful woman – genuine or as part of a customary service – warmed his insides.

Not all operators were female. At least a dozen men were painted white: their hair, faces, hands, and they wore all-white bodysuits. Every pair of operator eyes was a brilliant hue of blue, and dark makeup accentuated their eyes and lips so they resembled life-like ghosts of the machine. It was like being at a comic book convention where every character was the same.

"There are many apocalyptic scenarios on offer," said the operator. "Some players have chosen to be placed randomly, in which case we'll load them into scenarios that other players haven't pre-selected. It's highly unlikely you'll all be playing the same game." She stopped at a machine that was similar in size to an ATM, and ran a laminated pass across the scanner. "I understand you'll be teaming up with two other players, Reis Anderson and Kelly Lawrence."

"Kelly's my sister." Jack didn't want the woman to get the wrong impression. "I'm being a good brother and chaperoning her."

The operator nodded. "Have you chosen an apocalypse to survive? Or will you opt for the random selection?"

"I don't mind surprises, but Kelly... let's just say she's a novice at this. We've decided to play—"

Her fingers swiftly landed on his lips. "Don't tell me. If I don't know then I can't reveal any spoilers."

She slipped the laminated pass around his neck and continued ushering him towards the Launch Pad. At the doorway, she pried her arm away and her azure-blue eyes twinkled. "I assure you, Mr Minnow. You will be in the greatest of care. Please make your way inside and enjoy your complimentary champagne. It won't be long until you're taken to the simulation pod."

A course of doubt niggled at him. "So when we die in the game—"

"You're body is perfectly safe."

"Yeah, but when we die in the game, what happens? Will we remember it?"

She looked off to another player signing up at the desk.

"Miss... Operator?"

At last she turned around and smiled, revealing dazzling white teeth. "I assure you, you'll be safe. Everything is virtual."

"But it'll feel like death. That's what the brochure says."

"Yes, it will feel like death," she said. "So I suggest you do everything to stay alive."

2

Reis

Reis Anderson spied the overly-chatty operator who'd signed him into the system hovering around. Her furtive glances reminded him of a woman he knew, so to avoid further conversation he headed towards a group of guys who pumped their fists and flexed muscle like they were about to head into a boxing ring.

One of them turned and gave Reis a derisive look up and down. "You sure you're in the right place, Mr America?"

He'd tried to avoid people recognizing him. He'd even tried registering under a false name, but at the last second the operator had updated the database. Now everyone would know the Senator's son had signed up to play a video game. All right, not quite a video game. *The Apocalypse Games* was far superior. But to the eyes of the media, he might as well be playing with action figures.

He turned to focus on the stage where banners with images of zombies and aliens hung from the ceiling, but they only confirmed his reason for avoiding the attention. *Why had he come?* He felt a presence in the room and twisted his neck to spy Kelly Lawrence standing in the entryway, as if deciding whether to stay or go. Her eyes met his, and for a second a spark of determination entered her gaze. Then she glared at him and skulked her way into the room, getting swallowed up by the crowd.

He had the answer to why he was here.

An operator in a military-style costume stepped up to a microphone. "Players, welcome to the apocalypse. Soon you will be entering your stasis chambers to enjoy twenty-four hours of simulated terror."

A small cheer rose from the front. Reis suppressed a smile. Half the people here would crap their pants at the first sign of simulated terror.

"The Apocalypse Games is a game of skill and chance," said the operator. "Inside these virtual worlds you will gather items for survival, go on quests in lands of the unbelievable, hunt monsters, and kill the enemy. Some of you will even take journeys of self-discovery. Some of you are here to fulfill your fantasies of being warriors. Whatever the reason, there is something for everyone inside this game. As with all games, there are rules. Rule number one. You cannot kill another player. It is immediate disqualification. Say goodbye to five thousand dollars, no refunds. Rule number two. You cannot target or hunt other players. That is also immediate disqualification. These are the only two rules. The rest you will need to decide for yourselves. After all, the fate of mankind is in your hands."

If this lot was the fate of mankind, Reis pitied mankind.

"While you cannot die inside the game," said the operator, "with the neural hook-up allowing you to touch, taste, smell, and feel your surroundings, your body will experience virtual pain. The key is to stay alive. No refunds for early exits."

Reis let his gaze travel over the crowd. He spied Jack Minnow up the front, eyes wide and his neck craned to inspect the setting. A display simulation pod stood off to the right. Reis noticed that Jack went over to lift the glass lid a few times. He cast a glance again to locate Kelly, saw her glaring at the stage, and he thought that maybe he and Jack should have signed up to play this game on their own. Like, totally on their own, with no other players at all. It wasn't like he couldn't afford it.

"You may assist other players," said the operator. "In fact it is encouraged. Aiding assistance will count towards bonus points which you may use at the gift shop or accumulate for another game."

A murmur swept over the crowd, heads nodded, players conferred with other players, some nudged each other, and Reis's neck muscles started to relax. He hadn't realized until now that his body was as tightly wired as the guys in front of him, because maybe, if the temptation to help other players was on offer, this virtual game wasn't the worse place someone without any gaming or fighting experience could be. Say, someone like Kelly.

Music started up and images played on the screen behind the operator: people in combat gear, digital images of heads-up display data, images of chaos and destruction.

"The game lasts for twenty-four hours," said the operator. "The mind can handle this amount of stimulation, but since player safety is the first priority, the mainframe computer will be constantly monitoring your vitals, and should a player suffer undue stress or too much pain, you will be transmitted into a virtual waiting room which will be a pleasant and safe experience. No refunds for early exits. As you may have guessed, the aim is to stay alive."

The guy man in front of Reis nudged the guy beside him. "I thought kill or be killed was the point of the game."

The second guy nodded. "I'm counting on it."

Screw the rules, thought Reis. He'd gladly throw away the five thousand dollar entry fee to take out these two jerks.

"You will receive instructions for each game via your heads-up display units in the simulation pods," continued the operator. "Some of you will be preloaded into a game wearing appropriate attire. Other games will allow the players to choose clothes to wear, merely by picturing them in your mind. The neural linkup will do the rest. However, all players will enter the game empty-handed. You must find weapons. Find the enemy. Find safe zones. Find survivors. These games are not just about killing the enemy. It's not just a game of the fittest and mightiest. It's survival of the human race. And since this is the survival of the human race, try to do your best, not your worst."

3

Kelly

Kelly Lawrence lay inside a glass casket. Her handsome prince wasn't going to rescue her because he was dead. In one week's time it would the first anniversary of her husband's death. That she was taking his place at the launch of *The Apocalypse Games* had as much to do with honoring his memory as with attempting to extinguish the inextinguishable grief that burned in her veins.

"You must know how to meditate." The operator's voice came over a tiny speaker in the wall of the simulation pod. "You're incredibly calm."

Kelly didn't answer. Small talk was one of the first basic human functions to desert her. Next to go had been the desire to shower, eat, watch TV, read books.

"Yoga?" inquired the voice.

She cleared her throat, because it seemed the operator wasn't going to accept silence as an answer. "I don't meditate or do yoga."

"Well, the other player's heart rates are beating off the charts."

One needed a beating heart for it to operate erratically, thought Kelly. The idea of entering a virtual world of apocalypses should have terrified her, instead, she'd been somewhat comatose since Matt's death. With no specific end date to her grieving, she could be numb inside forever. It seemed fitting that she should enter a world of undead creatures, in this case vampires. It also seemed as if she ought to feel a sense of belonging with the undead, but as yet she felt nothing but her own loss.

The simulation pod was made of glass, it had a domed lid, and was about the size of a tanning bed. The head gear and body suit kept Kelly prone, so she saw the operator in her peripherals. A different operator to the one who'd signed her in, and yet Kelly hated her as much as the rest of them because they were another reminder of Matt's absence. As a member of the graphics design team creating the non-character players for the games, Matt had designed the features of the CGI women. He'd joked one evening about his excitement at having one of these 'come to life' fantasies hook him up to the simulation pod. Kelly had tried to cover the sting that his fantasy woman looked nothing like her by voicing her opinions about sexism and chauvinism on the way into the bathroom. When she'd returned to the bedroom with her long brown hair hanging limp and lifeless, her slightly pear-shaped body swathed in a dressing gown, a toothbrush wedged inside her mouth, her gentle giant of a husband had chosen that moment to say she had nothing to fear. To him, she was the most beautiful woman in the world.

Matt Lawrence had taken something more precious to the grave than the location of the keys to the luggage. He'd taken the ability to make his wife smile.

"Are you all right?" asked the operator. "Is the helmet too tight?"

Kelly couldn't stem the flow of tears, and she couldn't wipe the tears from her eyes even if she wanted to; her hands were encased in metal skeletons with wires and tubes poking out, much like a patient in the intensive care unit of a hospital. Wires and cables and neural augmentation devices – NADs – were necessary for the symbiotic hook up with the game's mainframe computer.

"I'm good," Kelly said.

The operator's face loomed into view. Then her eyes looked off to the right and her lips pursed together, as if considering whether or not to continue with the hook up.

"I'm *good*."

"Okay," the operator said. "But you've still got a few minutes to change your mind."

Kelly's counselor had told her she might never get over Matt's death, but she would eventually return to living and working at full capacity as a paralegal, although she would most likely never be the same person. The problem was that Kelly missed her old self. Everyone did. She could see it in their faces, the way people's eyes brightened as if today might be the day she showed up at after-work drinks. This weekend might be the one she danced like a princess. She might return to partying or shopping or doing anything other than moping around the house in unwashed clothes.

It was while sorting through Matt's desk that she'd decided to take his place at the launch of the games. An email to CyberNexis at two a.m. to indicate her intentions, they'd replied first thing the following morning with heartfelt condolences and a promise of an invitation. It had taken the year after his death to build the facility to house two hundred computers and almost that many simulation pods. It had taken her all that time to get over the shock of yet another day Matt would never be a part of – her twenty-sixth birthday, his thirtieth, their first date anniversary, their wedding anniversary. Every day was filled with moments they would never again share.

If this was his final triumph, then no, she couldn't change her mind.

Time had lapsed anyway, indicated by the blue mist that swirled around inside the pod. It was the purest oxygen Kelly had ever breathed. Yet, like most things now, she couldn't find anything pleasurable about it. Green fog seeped in next. It was cold, wet, and designed to reduce the body temperature by ten degrees and drag it into a state of deep sleep, commonly known as hypothermia. Next came the pink fog; nutrients to keep the player hydrated and fed for the next twenty-four hours.

For those twenty-four hours, Kelly could, if she chose, be whoever she wanted to be. Even her old self. If she could remember who that was.

She clenched her teeth as dozens of NADs pierced her flesh. It felt like thousands of ants attacking her. Sparkling atoms ripped across her vision in a hurry to crash into one another. She closed her eyes but it didn't stop the fireworks. The NADs were designed to work even with her eyes shut. She had come to learn that most things worked even with her eyes shut. No matter how dark the night, no matter how hidden the path, no matter how deep the wound, life went on if only to spite the people who wanted it to stop.

The built-in heads-up display unit in the glass lid switched on, speeding up the zipping atoms until all the colors merged into a giant ball of white light. Kelly was about to enter a virtual apocalypse. She wasn't scared. Surviving anything in a virtual world would be a million times easier than surviving another second of real life.

A computer generated voice came over the tiny speaker. "Player thirty-one has chosen vampire apocalypse."

It was with mild interest that she found herself watching the presentation of the game as it rolled across the heads-up display unit.

"Welcome to the apocalypse," said the female host, Command Leader Stephanie Gey, a Californian blonde with pretty features and dressed like a flight steward. "Having reduced the number of humans considerably, the vampires may have begun to feed off animals though this isn't practical. Vampires need human blood, and since they are half human they will resort to feeding off each other."

The camera switched to show the face an older man with silver tips on his hair and a George Clooney smile. The name appearing on the monitor was Command Leader Jonas Barrett.

"Despite folklore stating that bloodletting between vampires is common practice," said Jonas, "dead vampires no longer produce palatable blood. It's like poison to another vampire. Insanity amongst them is prevalent."

The tips the two Command Leaders provided afterward were rather ordinary. Find items for a panic bag. Get to a safe zone. If you couldn't get to a safe zone, make one. Hide until daylight. Source food and water. Burn fires. And let no vampire live.

The computer generated voice returned. "Player thirty-one will enter the game in ten seconds. Ten... nine..."

Kelly's equilibrium shifted. She felt her body rolling up then down, her jaw clenched, her stomach dropped, and then, with a jolt like the lurch of an elevator about to do a nerve-wracking descent, she emerged from the ball of showering atoms. She expected to see scenes of rotting corpses, buildings and cars on fire, tanks in the street; instead she found herself standing on a quiet suburban sidewalk. Jacaranda trees in bloom lined the empty street and the purple flowers carpeted the sidewalk. Birds flew high in the sky, too far away to be heard. There wasn't another person in sight and she could imagine herself stuck inside a computer monitor, except the waning afternoon sun and breeze gently kissed her cheeks.

She already knew sight and sound would be activated in this world, Matt had told her so, yet he'd also told her that other sensory perception might be limited.

"The system uses forced feedback to transmit touch sensations," he'd said. "Much like the vibration in a steering wheel of a virtual racing car game. I won't get my hopes up. Touch and smell are the hardest to replicate in a virtual world. I could probably cut my hand off and not feel it."

She was glad now that she'd sat in his office while he'd worked his magic on the computer. Not to understand the details of the game – she truly didn't care if she won or lost. He'd run his fingers through his sand-colored hair then he'd reached for a Coke. She'd tell him he shouldn't drink too much caffeine and remind him that he needed a haircut, and he'd laugh and say that he liked the hyper-hippy look. She'd wake at two a.m. to a cold bed and get up to make him a grilled cheese sandwich because it was the only way to get his brain to shut down. He'd never once learned how to empty the waste basket in the office; instead he'd let his scribbles of his prototype CGI women pile up till a forest's worth spilled over and became a trip hazard. Traits she'd once considered annoyances were now endearing qualities she'd give anything to be real.

Feeling the gentle breeze on her cheek, she closed her eyes and made a wish. Maybe dead was dead, but dreams were dreams and nothing could have stopped her from wishing it was Matt's lips she felt against her cheek.

***

Other traces of Matt were noticeable in the game. Blue shutters, movie posters, pizza and donut stores. A white Hummer sat parked on one side of the street, a black Hummer on the other. The billboard for the animal rescue shelter caused a stagger in her step. Had Matt designed this town with the intention of one day bringing her here?

The idea that NADs were sticking into her flesh caused her to roll her neck and kick her legs to stimulate blood flow. Inside the pod her actual legs were kicking, but the pod and mass of wires connected to her cyber suit would restrict movement. She waved her hands in front of her face, expecting to see a crack in the imagery. Lastly, she stared up at the sky, feeling like a zoo exhibit. The operator would be staring down to check her vitals. Nobody stared back.

Immersed in the game's mainframe, she sensed Matt's presence and turned.

Nobody was there. The flicker of light must have been her imagination.

***

The day Kelly's brother, Jack, had discovered she was taking Matt's place he'd purchased a ticket. Jack operated Quest, an adventure tour business. He'd said this was an opportunity to test the game but Kelly knew it was an excuse for him to keep up his suicide watch. Her brother was two years older, and they'd been close growing up, yet this past year Jack had excelled in his sibling duties. She couldn't have coped without him. He'd taken control of everything, refusing to let anyone else help. He'd paid her bills, forced her to eat, filtered the calls from friends, organized the funeral, pushed her into the bathroom and told her to brush her teeth and hair. He'd swept in like Superman and prevented her from falling off the cliff.

Now, a car-sized ball of atoms appeared across the road, and Jack emerged from the center.

"Stay there," he yelled. "I'm coming over."

A second flash of white light appeared, and from the center came Reis Anderson, Jack's friend and business partner. She couldn't dictate who could enter the game, but Matt's death had sent her world imploding until the only central people in her life was her immediate family – herself, Jack, and her parents. A ball of resentment settled in her stomach at Reis's presence. But it could have been nausea from the sudden jolt into the game.

As the two men crossed the street, white light exploded in front of her. When it dissipated she was standing on a different street. Jack and Reis were gone. She waited for them to show up, and after a few minutes, she accepted that she was alone. Good. She hadn't wanted them to follow her anyway.

A poster on a store window warned residents of the vampire plague. At least she was in the same game. But why had she jolted to another street? They'd signed on as a team and the idea was they'd play as a team.

The street was deserted, quiet, no signs of life. The poster flapped in the breeze as if to draw her attention to it. She read that a plague had swept through the country, killing or turning millions of people. National Security had imposed quarantines and curfews while thousands of vampires were hunted and slaughtered. This town was at Stage 5 – containment. People were not allowed to return to their homes and places of business until after Stage 6 – annihilation.

So this is what a world devoid of humans looked like.

A world devoid of humans was a world without animal cruelty, rape, sexual slavery, human trafficking, live stock exports, drugs, strip clubs, fur coats, puppy farms, hunting for sport: matters that had manufactured misery in Kelly long before Matt's death. But a world without people meant something else rising up to rule the planet and humans becoming the prey. So Kelly walked a little faster until she came to a boarded-up 7-Eleven. Tearing off loose boards, she slipped inside and piled a load of goodies into a carry bag. The aim of the game was to collect items to survive the apocalypse, and since she didn't care about fighting vampires, she stocked a bag full of wine and junk food. Not the panic bag the game inventors had in mind, but so what. She had her own reasons for being here.

When she stepped out of the 7-Eleven the sun had dipped an inch lower in the sky. The vampires wouldn't attack until night. Pity.

"Are you lost?"

Kelly jumped at the voice from behind. She spun to see a tall, black man in a trench coat smoking a cigar. He had gray stubble on his face and a rifle in his hands. The weapon wasn't aimed at her. The warning from the operator jumped to mind. Players weren't supposed to attack other players. Didn't mean he wasn't the enemy sneaking up on her.

"Who are you?" she asked.

The stranger reached a hand inside his shirt – her hand went to her bag where a can of Mace sat on the ready. Around his neck was a laminated pass attached to a lanyard. It contained a passport-sized photo of his face next to a series of icons – lightning bolt, mushroom cloud, skulls and crossbones, biohazard sign.

"I'm a player," he said. "Ash Brogen." He lifted himself up to his full height. "You look like you could use some help Miss..."

Her mouth went dry. "It's not Miss. It's Mrs Kelly Lawrence."

"I'm Special Agent Ash Brogen. Do you require escorting to the safe zone, Mrs Kelly Lawrence?"

'Special Agent' went a long way to explaining the trench coat. Admittedly, she could have imagined any outfit and the game's computer would have created it for her. Yet she had no idea what to wear to an apocalypse. It wasn't like they had a fashion show for it, or if they did she wasn't on their mailing list. So she'd settled for the regular clothes she'd worn to the complex – black jeans, cream leather jacket, red top, black ankle boots.

"You tell me," she said. "Is it safe to go to the safe zone with you?"

"Of course it is. I'm a Special Agent." Ash's whole demeanor deflated before her eyes. "Please. This is my fantasy. Can you help an old fool out by playing along? I wanna win a free game and helping strangers is the only way."

"Thanks, but I don't need your help."

He let the tip of the rifle fall to the ground. "Yeah, I don't reckon many players need help. That's probably why they were eager to offer the bonus points. But you seem different to the rest of the players."

Tears nipped at her eyelids and she forced them away. It was stupid of her to come. Maybe she *should* go to a safe zone and sit this game out. "Fine. Can you please escort me to the safe zone?"

He surveyed the street and started walking. She followed in silence. As she looked around, it occurred to her that she ought to at least explore this world, seeing as how Matt had designed parts of it. Except she didn't have any weapons, any skills, or any clue about what to do if she stumbled across a vampire. The list of reasons to stick with a player who could keep her alive was long.

Yet her plan didn't call for her to stay alive.

"These games are damned expensive," Ash said, stopping at a corner of a building to scan to street.

"I guess."

He gave her a quick look up and down. "You a VIP."

"No."

"Won a ticket?"

"No."

"Sorry. I don't mean to pry. Leanna, she's my wife, she's always telling me that I meddle too much. She's always saying I don't know when to shut up. Hell, I'm just the curious type."

Ash stepped out onto the street. Kelly's feet were planted firmly on the ground. She suddenly couldn't move because an invisible hand was squeezing her heart.

"What is it?" Ash asked, his eyes widening. "You psychic? Can you sense them?"

She shook her head.

My husband died. He worked on the game. I'm taking his place. None of this information was his business. And the words wouldn't come anyway.

Ash gave her a knowing smile. "It'll get dark soon," he said. "We've gotta hurry if you want to make it to the safe zone."

"You should go and have fun. I'll be fine."

"No can do. It's no longer about the bonus points. You clearly don't belong here and my wife would kill me if she found out I'd left you on your own."

"Nothing can hurt me," she said. "Not in here."

He nodded. "That may be so, but I've still got a conscience. I'd like to keep it clear if you don't mind."

***

The rest of the walk was completed in silence and Kelly let her mind drift where it wanted to go. Mostly it landed on all the things Matt would never be able to do. Like walking through a virtual world where millions of people had been killed or turned into vampires.

"Well, here we are," Ash said. "The safe zone."

They'd stopped at an area that was cordoned off with a ten foot high chain-link fence with barbed wire on top. She peered through the fence. Inside the compound, dozens of people were huddled around camp fires, rubbing their hands, laughing and talking as if nothing was wrong. It didn't feel safe. It felt stupid. Ash was right. She didn't belong here. But she didn't belong anywhere else.

"Darkness is coming," said Ash. "You'll be fine inside."

"Aren't you coming in?"

He clenched the cigar between his teeth. "The action ain't in the safe zone. It's out there, where the freaks of nature are hell bent on wiping out humanity. It's my job to prevent them."

He lifted up his rifle to stare through the sight as if taking aim at an unseen target. He didn't look in a hurry to go into the battle zone. He looked like he didn't want to leave her side.

She didn't want a babysitter. Not in the real world. Not in this world either.

"Thanks, Ash. You can go now."

"On second thoughts, I can wait for them to come to me."

"You paid five thousand dollars to kill vampires, not to make friends."

His eyes narrowed. His jaw tightened. Had she said something to offend him? Maybe he wasn't here to kill vampires, after all. Maybe he, too, had other reasons for entering this fake world.

"This isn't a game for me," she said, her voice low and husky, surprising herself with this admission.

Ash nodded. "This isn't a game for me either. It's a chance to be more than I really am."

She knew it. He wasn't really here to 'kill or be killed'. He didn't belong. He was kind and caring, and even though neither of them had entered the game to make friends, her heart told her she had found one anyway.

"Everyday Ash Brogen is fine as he is," she said. "Thank you for everything."

He glanced away, as if embarrassed. "If only everyone thought like you. Good luck, Mrs Kelly Lawrence. Oh, I've got something for you." He reached into his coat and placed something in her hand. "You can probably use this more than me."

She looked down to find a string of rosary beads and fought back tears. She knew all about making the sign of the cross, then saying the Apostle's Creed, then the Lord's Prayer, three Hail Mary's and a Glory Be. When Matt had failed to walk through the door she'd accepted that the days spent repeating prayers had been wasted ones.

She held the beads out to him. "Thanks. But I don't believe in God anymore."

"It's to keep the vampires away."

Trusting that he knew more about this stuff than she did, she stuffed the string of beads in her jeans pocket and stepped inside the safe zone.

The sun had dipped further in the sky. She was one minute closer to her impending death.

***

The safe zone. It looked safe. Tall fence. Brick huts. People were carrying items into the huts. Silhouetted by the falling sun, Kelly watched a group of people setting up tents. The steady whack of metal spikes being driven into the ground reverberated across the air. Fires were burning bright. The orange and pink sky overhead was turning dark purple. A small group of children ran around a large fire. She knew this was a ruse of the game, using children to provide the illusion of security. This deception drove a spike of disappointment into her; maybe the kids would keep the danger away. She was relying on danger for her plan to work.

She headed further into the compound. Lit up with a spotlight was a sign almost as big as a billboard. ALL SURVIVORS MUST READ RULES OF THE COMPOUND was written in large black lettering. The rules were simple. Keep the vampires out. Kill any that came in. She hadn't quite known what to anticipate, but she was a little disappointed about the lack of activity so far. No bloodshed, no overturned cars, no ambulances, no sirens, no people screaming. The end of the world was rather insulting. *To think that Matt had died for this lackluster event.*

She headed for a picnic table to take the edge off boredom with a slug of warm white wine from her panic bag. Midway through her second mouthful, she heard a growl. Looking over her shoulder, she saw two dogs the size of wolfhounds baring their teeth and skulking towards her. They weren't normal dogs; they had leathery skin, red eyes, and emaciated bodies. She scrambled up on the table, her heart beating inside her chest. Wishing for death was one thing. Wishing to be torn apart by rabid dogs was a sick fetish she wanted no part of.

"Go away," she hissed. "I'm not playing your game."

The low guttural growls only urged her heart to race faster. It was a given that someone would be monitoring her vital signs, yet it occurred to her they must be monitoring her brainwaves as well. These dogs had *appeared* just as she'd thought about the lack of danger. It was illogical to believe that a computer could tap into her mind to read her thoughts. No. This was just a coincidence. A horrid coincidence that would bring much pain if they attacked.

Curling her hands into fists, she banged them in the air as if hitting the glass lid of the simulation pod.

"Change the channel," Kelly said to the sky.

Why had she let Jack talk her into vampires? There were so many more ways to die that didn't involve sharp teeth and the draining of one's blood. Death by chocolate. Shopping till she dropped. Drowning in champagne.

The dogs continued growling, yet they still hadn't attacked, and the sense of being watched from outside hit her once more; perhaps the reason they hadn't attacked was because *she hadn't run*. Maybe her movements were being monitored, just not in the way she expected. What if surviving the apocalypse was a ruse? What if watching players survive the apocalypse was the game?

Finally, the dogs lunged and her reflexes kicked in. She threw her panic bag at them. A bottle of wine hit one dog on the head. It yelped and backed off. The other dog jumped up onto the table, snapping at her jeans as she launched herself into the air.

By no means was she a sprinter, nor was she able to run a marathon, yet hooked up to the cyber-computer, physical difficulties became actualities. She was running faster than the dogs, but they were close behind.

"Kelly!" someone shouted.

It was a miracle she could hear anything over the noise of her blood pumping in her head.

"Kelly! Go left."

She recognized Jack's voice. He'd said to go left and so she swerved left. From behind came a *thunk* and then a squeal. One dog down, but she didn't dare slow down. From behind came a second *thunk*, but no squeal. She'd forgotten what a klutz her brother could be. He had a weapon aimed in her direction and he was likely to take her down instead.

"Go right," he shouted.

Side-stepping to the right, she jarred her ankle but kept running. Don't look back, and keep running, she told herself. And pray it was just a strained muscle in her ankle and not a product of Jack's inaccurate aim. From behind came another *thunk* and a yelp, and she ran full circle till she came to a stop in front of Jack.

He had a tight grip on a crossbow. "Are you all right?" He looked her up and down. "Were you bitten?"

"I'm good."

Reis appeared, dragging the body of a dead vamp-mutt with him. He dumped it at Jack's feet and bent down to inspect it.

Jack stepped back. "For Christ's sake, what are you doing?"

"I want to check it out." Reis poked and prodded the body, lifted a leg, opened its jaws. "It looks real."

"It's gross. Leave it alone." Jack turned to Kelly. "What happened? You just disappeared."

She shrugged her shoulders. "I don't know where I went. But I met another player." She told him about Ash and how he'd helped her to this safe zone.

"It's hardly safe." Jack pointed the crossbow at the dead dog. "We'll have to stick together."

Kelly's plans didn't include her brother chaperoning her. In fact, she'd spent much of the three hour drive from San Diego to Arizona preparing for Jack to say exactly this. But now that he had, she wasn't sure she had the energy to argue.

Reis stood up. "We're here to test the game for our clients, not stay out of danger."

She recognized the harsh tone of his voice. He didn't want Jack's little sister tagging along, just like he'd never wanted her tagging along when they were growing up. He was always ready with the disapproving look whenever Kelly emerged from her bedroom to follow Jack on some adventure. She could no longer remember if he ever smiled.

"We will test the game," Jack said. "Kelly won't get in the way. It'll be like old times."

Kelly shook her head. "Jack, I don't want to go with you. I want to explore this world on my own. Besides, nothing bad can actually happen. It's a virtual world."

Jack's gaze narrowed. "If you die, it will look real enough to me. You're coming with us."

Perhaps when she was her old, un-emotionless self again she'd win an argument, but right now she followed them into a white sedan that was parked near the front gate of the compound. She sat in the back, her hands in her lap and her eyes on the road, not interested in sightseeing. Reis drove, occasionally glancing at her through the rear-view mirror. She didn't mind copping his dark-eyed glare. It felt good for a change to be on the end of an angry look instead of a pitying one.

In the passenger seat, Jack ran off a list of things they'd need in town for their panic bags – garlic cloves, sharpened wooden stakes, crucifixes, holy water – as if this was a shopping spree. She didn't need her sibling sixth sense to know he was excited. Her sibling sixth sense also warned her that her melancholy would do major damage to his enthusiasm so she stayed quiet.

They drove past a supermarket and Jack pointed through the windshield. "Pull over. We need garlic gloves."

"I'm not wearing garlic around my neck," said Reis.

"You're no fun. I'm putting that in your next performance review."

"Fine. While you're at it, you might as well add theft. Yes, I stole your yoghurt."

"You blamed the cleaner. I almost fired him."

Kelly felt a smile tug at her lips. She missed this playful banter, and even though a part of her longed to join in, a bigger part was too broken to care.

A few blocks away, a church loomed into view. Jack pointed at it and Reis pulled over. Kelly followed them inside like a docile donkey. At the front door, she expected to feel a sense of loss. And she did. Grief slammed into her chest, knocking the breath out of her so hard she had to sit on the pew while Jack and Reis filled empty water bottles from the baptismal fountain. She stayed seated facing the front, and when the urge to demand from God why He had taken her husband came over her, she got up and headed for the door.

"I'll be in the car," she sang out.

"Kelly—"

"I'll be in the car!"

She stormed outside and fell into the back of the car, where she curled up into a ball and covered her face with her hands, trying to breathe, trying *not* to breathe. This was too much too soon. Why had he died? Well, Matt had told her one *why*: missed flight, desperate to come home, hired a car. The coroner had told her another *why*: fatigue from overwork and the inability for the human body to withstand impact with a tree and losing that much blood.

If only she hadn't insisted that he hurry home...

There was a slam as the trunk opened and shut. The car shook as Jack and Reis got in the front. Neither of them asked her how she felt, and she would have punched them if they had.

A short while later, the car stopped, the engine was turned off, yet she remained curled up on the back seat. Someone shook her leg.

"You can't stay here," Jack said gently. "We might need your help."

"You don't need my help."

"Humor me."

They were at a hardware store, and once inside, every tool and implement reminded her of the jobs around the house that Matt would never get around to finishing. Never mind that he wasn't any good at fixing things around the house, he should have had first option to screw up.

Jack snapped her out of her reverie when he dropped a pile of wooden stakes on the ground. Added to the pile was a garden weed spray bottle which they'd filled with the holy water, and a crucifix which Reis had stolen off the church wall.

"We're battle ready," Jack said.

***

The battle came with a crash as paint tins toppled to the floor and rolled towards the cash registers. A bloodied figure burst out of the shadows from where Jack and Reis had earlier been working. The creature ran towards them, fast and agile. Jack and Reis scrambled to pick up their spray bottle and crucifix. Jack released the trigger and a steady stream hit the vamp in the face. Reis held the crucifix at arm's length as if he was pushing through an invisible wall. The vamp kept charging.

Kelly had watched the opening presentation with mild interest. It had played on the heads-up display unit of the simulation pod. These methods to repel the vamp should have worked.

"Maybe it's upside down," Jack said to Reis.

"It's the right way up."

"Then maybe you need to speak Latin."

The vamp was female, or what was left of a female. The only confirmation of gender came from the clothing. This one wore a tattered floral dress. The creature's eyes were milky white, its blood-red hair was a bird's nest, its mouth was caked in congealed blood, and a dark stain ran down its chin.

In order for one of these things to kill me, Kelly thought, it will have to bite me.

Fear crept up into her throat. She was out of her league here. She'd never played a video game, never shown any interest, and she certainly had never shown interest in having her throat torn apart.

Her hand reached around for the latch to open the pod. Nothing. She was immersed fully into this virtual world. Perhaps if she stopped and stayed very still, she would touch the glass lid or the metal hinges or even feel that her fingers were inside metal skeletal gloves.

"Kelly!" Jack shouted.

She opened her eyes in time to see the vamp spring at Reis and knock him to the ground. Hissing and snapping its jaws, it lunged at his throat as if dunking for apples.

Reis struggled to keep it at arm's distance away. "Get it off me."

Jack kicked at the vamp with his boot, but it didn't lessen in its endeavors to sever Reis's head from his neck. Jack gave it a second kick, and this time it hissed at him and swiped at his leg with its claws.

Her heart pounded. Her mouth was dry. Strange that the sensations felt so real.

"Jack, you'd better do something," she said, her heart speeding inside her chest. Would this be the sign the computer took as undue stress? Would the computer transmit her into a virtual waiting room?

Jack reached for a garden stake, but his hand hesitated, hovering over it and clenching into a fist.

"What are you doing?" Reis shouted. "Kill the thing."

"Killing dogs is one thing," Jack said. "This is a person."

The 'kill or be killed' mentality had been established the moment this creature had launched itself at Reis. Either this vampire would kill them, or they would kill it. It was easy to ignore the consequences in a life or death situation. Or so Kelly thought. The moment she picked up a stake to attack, she understood her brother's uncertainty. Could she drive a stake into the vampire's back and think there wouldn't be repercussions?

Jack finally took action. Holding the stake high above his head, he brought it down. Hard. It pierced the vampire's chest. No blood. No explosion. Just a few shudders and then the creature fell to the floor.

***

Outside, Jack struck a match from his panic bag collection. With no wind, it burned steadily all the way to his fingertips. Kelly smelled sulfur. Matt would have been impressed to know the programmers had mastered the art of smell and touch.

As well as sulfur, she smelled blood. Looking down at her hands, they were covered in red patches. She'd gripped onto the wooden stake so tightly that the splinters had bitten into her flesh and caused her hands to bleed. Still feeling the pinch of splinters, she buried her fists into her armpits to hide them from sight. She shouldn't have felt like she'd taken part in a murder but she couldn't work as a paralegal and *not* think this was wrong.

Jack struck a second match, and then another. It was like he was developing a nervous tick burning matches and she was developing a nervous tick watching them. A trauma such as this could reverse the healing she'd managed to date. It might scar her forever.

She had to start treating this as a game.

"The dogs back there," Kelly said. "It was like they were waiting for me to run. Like I was being forced to play."

"Maybe you were," said Reis.

"You're supposed to tell me I'm imagining things."

"Okay, you're imagining things."

She turned her attention back to Jack. Now she couldn't shake off the feeling that they were being used as a form of entertainment. It made sense. Reality shows were a profitable and inexhaustible venture. Activist groups were targeting people who exploited animals for entertainment, but exploiting humans in this manner was more than acceptable. Perhaps there was something about this on the registration form, though she had read through it with her legal mind and hadn't found anything to indicate her consent to being videotaped.

Reis snatched the matchbox out of Jack's hands. Then he said to Kelly, "Thanks for helping back there."

"Hey, *I* wasted the vamp," Jack said. "And why am I acting like a teenager about it?"

"You're probably having a reaction to the electrodes forcing your brain to work." Reis gave a nod in Kelly's direction. "If this were a real apocalypse, I'd rather have your sister on my team."

He smiled at her, yet she felt nothing. It wasn't his fault. If there was anyone she would have feelings for, it would be Reis. She'd had a crush on him when she was thirteen, as did all the girls in school. He was even more handsome at twenty-eight now that his tall, lanky body had filled out. He'd taken to wearing a close-cropped beard on his face, which she had to admit suited him. And she really didn't mind his dark, angry stare that had a temper to match. His temper was a sign that he was alive. She envied him this.

"Let's get into position," Reis said. "It'll be dark soon."

They got back into the car and drove to the center of town. Kelly was still picking splinters out of her fingers when the sky turned indigo-blue then darkened to black. Dark shapes emerged from the alleys and from the rooftops. Then more shapes, until this new darkness erased every speck of the overhead darkness.

The mass of vampires numbered in their thousands. Darkness rushing toward her at one hundred miles an hour with fangs and teeth was the most frightening sight.

"Change of plans," Reis said. "We find a place and fortify it."

"Shit." Jack pulled at the door handle of the car, peered in through the window. "I've locked the keys inside."

"Run," Reis said. "Run!"

He grabbed Kelly by the arm, which she shook off in order to sprint down the street. Single-story shops and businesses were situated on both sides. Up ahead was an intersection. They stopped there, panting to catch their breaths. On each of the four corners were a church, a library, a gym, and a gas station respectively.

"What do you reckon about the gas station?" Jack asked.

"We have weapons," Reis said, "and the place will have enough food and water for as long as we need."

Jack gave Kelly a nudge toward the gas station, and she glanced over her shoulder, confirming that she was still averse to the idea of becoming vampire fodder. They hurried through the scattering of abandoned cars. At the entrance, the automatic sliding glass door stood wide open. Jack went in first to make sure the place wasn't already inhabited.

"Clean," he yelled out. "But it needs a few modifications to make it safe till we can work on a plan of attack."

In a cage beside the entrance were bags of split wood used in log fires. Reis located a half-filled jerry can which he poured over the split logs. Jack sprayed holy water around the outside of the building. Then they moved shelves in front of the windows and managed to push the glass doors closed.

Kelly would have offered to help, but she didn't have a clue how.

"A bunch of vamps just ran around the back," Reis said.

Jack nodded. "I'll check the door is locked."

At the front window, vampires pressed faces up against the glass. Some banged their fists which caused a hollow rumbling sound to echo throughout the building. *Why would anyone want to pay money to have the life terrified out of them?* Perhaps someone without a beating heart that needed a jolt in order to get it going again, she thought. Someone like her could benefit from this environment; she had to admit, the sight of vampires was making her feel emotions she'd repressed – fear amongst the top contenders.

"You okay?" Reis asked from behind.

She wished everyone would stop asking her that. He had a stick of gum in his hand which he held out to her. She just stared at it. Some days it was unbearably difficult to be part of normal conversation.

"I think it's a nice thing you did," he said.

"What thing?"

"Taking Matt's place at the launch. I liked him."

"Me too."

He gave her an apologetic look and she squared her shoulders, ready to defy him to utter something that was designed to cheer her up but wouldn't.

"To be honest," Reis said. "I was convinced you wouldn't last ten minutes in the game."

She almost smiled. "Yeah, me too."

He nodded and looked towards the back room. Sometimes people didn't know what to say around her, and sometimes they expected her to make it easy on them by doing all the talking. That was the other thing she missed about her old self. She had liked to talk. Could have stayed up all night drinking wine and chatting about the rights and wrongs of the world. Now, the rights and wrongs were blurred and at times completely insignificant.

Jack returned from the back room. "Have we come up with a plan yet?"

"We can make flame throwers from the insect sprays," Reis said.

And just like that, life went on whether Kelly Lawrence wanted it to or not.

She moved over to the counter and idly flicked through the magazines while Jack and Reis noisily rummaged around the gas station shelves to make flame throwers. Tears bit at her eyelids. Months ago, as part of the healing process, she'd started a list of all the things Matt would have missed. Not just the usual stuff like anniversaries, birthdays, Christmases, but the once in a lifetime stuff. The new Star Wars movie, the pod of dolphins that came into the harbor, the lunar eclipse. And now this. Making flame throwers from insect spray canisters and firelighters.

"Come on," Jack said, grabbing Kelly around the elbow and guiding her towards the front door. "And stay close."

She must have closed her eyes while they battled the vampires, because one second she was being jostled out the door, and the next she was in the back of a large sedan. The car stank like something had died in it.

Jack got in behind the wheel. Reis took the passenger seat. The engine clicked and whined the way it did when it wouldn't turn over.

"It'll be low on gas," she said, though without any of her usual derisiveness. Her inner voice had wanted to throw logic in their faces. The tanks would be empty because they were *here to fill up*.

While vampires banged on the hood of the car, the engine finally kicked over and it lurched forward barreling over them. Then they drove in silence along the road for a few miles. They passed turnoffs to unknown interstates, chains of motels, industrial areas. Since this wasn't a place they knew, Jack could have been driving into something worse than what they'd fled.

It occurred to her that terror was, in essence, one purpose of the game. And she was scared, but not babbling-like-a-lunatic scared. She suspected the pod was releasing mood stabilizer drugs along with oxygen, water, and food. Or perhaps her deadened heart could not be kick-started by the NADs. In which case she felt a little saddened that despite her efforts, she wasn't getting any better after all.

Just as they drove past an intersection to the airport, the car slowed down to a crawl. It rolled to a complete stop a few feet away from a sign telling them the next gas station was five miles ahead.

"Great." Jack slammed his fist against the steering wheel. "We're miles out of town, miles from the next gas station, vampires are on the loose, and our stolen car has just run out of fuel."

A loud noise to the right made them all jump. Kelly stared out the window to see the rotor blades of a helicopter chopping through the air. A single beam of light scanned the area below, while above the chopper a halo appeared. It moved off and left them once more alone in the dark. She looked out the window to a sky aglow with orange from a fire somewhere to the south; maybe a nearby city was aflame. Up ahead came the sound of gunfire and sirens. It appeared that they were not lone fighters in this war. An army of *us* was fighting the army of *them*. Just another thing Matt would have missed.

"Maybe there's fuel in the trunk," Reis said, getting out of the car.

Jack shook his head. "Yeah, because I always keep a jerry can of fuel in my trunk." He spun in his seat to face Kelly. "You okay?"

A groan escaped. "Will everyone stop asking me that?"

"You know I can't." He gave her a goofy grin. "But I meant are you handling the game okay? Is it meeting or exceeding your expectations?"

She sighed. "I'm handling it. Thanks for shadowing me, but I don't need you to keep up your suicide watch. You should be enjoying yourself."

"I am enjoying myself."

"Will you get a load of this," Reis called out from outside.

Jack and Kelly got out and found Reis staring into the trunk. Inside was a military grade flame thrower, a rocket launcher, and a couple of AK-47s.

"Whose car did we steal?" Kelly asked.

Jack let out a whoop. "Who cares? You know what this means? It means we're gonna blow up a gas station."

4

Kelly

Of course I'm not a princess, Kelly had said. *Let me help carry the weapons*, she'd said. Idiot. Her spinal discs were crumbling beneath the weight of the rocket launcher. Her shoulders ached no matter how many shifts she gave each one. And her feet were killing her. Matt had been wrong to suggest that the effects in this game would be half of normal sensation. Right now they felt doubled.

Reis wandered over. "You should let me carry the rocket launcher."

Putting aside her hard-won feminism, she hoisted the device onto his shoulder and rubbed hers back to life. Even Reis, who was six foot tall and physically fit, strained under the weight. Jack's eyes begged her to carry his weapon for a spell, but she was done being a martyr. Besides, they'd arrived at a tall chain-link fence that ran in two directions, one along the road, and the other off to their right. The safe zone. Only now there were about a dozen military vehicles and Kelly hoped one of them was unmanned and fully fueled. She didn't want to stay inside the safe zone, since it wasn't exactly safe.

They found a black Hummer and she slumped into the seat, feigning exhaustion from carrying the rocket launcher. The truth was she'd wanted to connect with her late husband, yet there was so much of his imprint that it was starting to overwhelm her.

Jack drove at full speed back towards town, and he stopped a few hundred feet from the service station. From here, they could see the vampires, although they were a small part of the carnage that had happened while they'd been gone. Traffic lights, running on emergency power, blinked red-amber-green-red-amber-green. The sky above glowed orange from distant fires. Helicopters hovered and shone bright lights. Overhead, a jet flew so low it rattled the windshield and echoed inside Kelly's chest. The library raged with fire, and non-player characters – NPCs – gathered outside to wail about the burning books. More NPCs huddled inside the church praying for salvation. Gym equipment had been tossed out the windows and now littered the lawn, perhaps to entice the enemy to exercise in an effort to overcome the urge to eat flesh.

She'd been in this game a few hours yet it felt like weeks.

"This is too close," Reis said. "Back up or we'll cop the blast from the rocket launcher."

Jack slammed the car into reverse and floored the pedal until the Hummer slammed into the pole of the traffic light. He drove forward enough to get the rocket launcher out of the back. The three of them stood on the street to stare at the gas station.

It was filled with the same vampires or maybe different ones. They all looked the same to Kelly which meant, that as the enemy they didn't stand a chance. Matt's words returned to her. "When the enemy looks the same, the psychology of killing comes into play. Soldiers may shoot, but they don't always kill. They shoot to intimidate, to warn off. It's much more difficult to kill someone if you can hear their breath, smell their odor, see their eyes." The war-expert consultants had told him this. Matt enjoyed video games but was actually anti-war and would never have otherwise considered military tactics as a topic of conversation. She didn't know why she was remembering all this.

Jack stood with the rocket launcher balanced on his shoulder. Distance would provide him with the appropriate emotional detachment. But it was wrong to be detached. She ought to know.

"Have you ever fired a WMD before?" she asked.

"No. I'm not even sure it's pointing in the right direction."

He was subdued as he aimed the weapon at the building and she was pleased he was at least considering his actions. You could see war all around, but until you were forced to pull a trigger that would decimate the enemy, you might find you had more courage inside you than you thought. Or not. Seconds later there was a whoosh of air. Immediately afterwards came the explosion. Flame followed. Then debris. The explosion was deafening. For almost a minute she'd lost all hearing and all bearing due to the backblast. She couldn't tell if she was standing or lying down. Her temperature rose from the hot gasses expelled. She was sure her body had been lifted off the ground a few inches.

She felt herself being rocked back and forth. Someone was rolling her – she couldn't tell who because her eyes were squeezed shut from the smoke. Then she was dragged across the road and onto the cool lawn of the library. When she opened her eyes, Reis was swatting flames off her jeans.

He began to rub her leg. She pushed aside his hands. "Thanks. I'm good."

In silence, she watched the service station get obliterated as underground gas tanks exploded. Balls of flame and smoke reached up into the sky. Most of the vampires were now chunks of scorched flesh flying through the air, although a small number had displayed a level of intelligence by fleeing the immediate blast zone and retreating into the darkness. From the sounds of gunfire, they were being taken out by unseen assailants attacking from the rear.

Her leg burned, and as she bit down on the pain she wondered why a virtual game would allow a player to experience something as horrific as third degree burns. What sort of world had she entered?

***

"What now?" Jack asked.

"At five grand a ticket," Reis said, "it had better not be Game Over."

The two men were staring at the carnage with awe and wonder, and Kelly couldn't understand why. This game was many things – surreal, a glimpse of a possible future, a waste of time and money – but most of all it was a lie. Apart from a few glimpses here and there of Matt's personal tastes, she wasn't connecting with him on any level. She was supposed to see more of *him*, and less of whatever this was.

"I want to head into town to see more of the action," Reis said.

Jack turned to Kelly. She could see the lust in his eyes. Then it faded.

"I'll stay here," he said.

"Go with Reis," she said.

"No."

"Yes."

"You sure?"

She nodded. "I want to be alone for a little while. Now will you go and stop fussing over me?"

He seemed to falter, but a helicopter appeared over a building, and even in the dark she could tell that his eyes were lighting up with glee.

"Go," she said, showing him the rosary beads that Ash had given her. "I've got protection."

***

She watched Jack and Reis run down the street looking in the car windows to check for keys, which they must have found because they got into a car and drove away. Alone with her thoughts, she was free to be swept up by memories, painful and pleasant. The moment she closed her eyes she heard Matt's voice.

"The players can't actually die," he'd said.

"But what happens when they get shot or stabbed or blown up inside the game?"

"You just keep playing till the game ends. You get transmitted in again and again. Though I did hear the programmers talking and they put in a virtual waiting room for the idiots who can't stay alive. The mind can only handle *so* much abuse. They designed a waiting room for the player to experience the virtual world without the violence. They call it a death dream."

"Like a place to heal," she'd said.

Matt had given her a quick kiss. "You're sweet. No. It's so players don't demand their money back."

An explosion off to the right brought her back to the present. She should have moved off to a safe place, yet she stayed sitting on the lawn of the library rubbing the rosary beads out of a long-dead habit, tempted to say a prayer but deciding against it. Long before her husband had died, she had lost her love for the world. He had come into her life and he'd made the darkness go away. While ever she breathed, he would be her only light. That was another thing she hated people saying to her. That she was young, she'd meet someone else. She didn't want anyone else. She wanted Matt to be alive so that *she* could be alive.

She once again heard his voice in her head:

"Babe, you'll never guess what they let us do today."

"What?"

"I can't tell you till I get home."

He'd been away from home for two weeks and she'd been missing him. But CyberNexis was afraid they'd miss the deadline so they'd ordered all staff to work onsite instead of working from home, and they'd put them up in hotels. Her body ached for him to return to her bed.

"When are you coming home?"

"Tonight. Wait up for me. Aw, I'm too excited to wait till I get home. It's awesome, babe. CyberNexis has let the graphics team integrate their voices and images into the mainframe. Can you believe it? I'm going to be *part of the game*."

***

Ten hours later, dawn arrived and she was still on the lawn of the library. Nobody had come to kill her. And she hadn't found the courage to kill herself in an attempt to transport herself into a death dream where she could search for Matt. She had survived the end of the world, she hadn't seen Matt as she'd planned, and now it was too late. It would be game over, go home, and get on with living like a ghost. Perhaps she could return here to work as an operator. Better yet, what would it be like to be a permanent fixture in this world?

The NADs would keep her fed and hydrated. They would also keep her comfortably numb. She would experience pain but not really be afflicted by it.

Perhaps Matt had created the perfect world for her, after all.

Dawn erupted across the sky in a blaze of smashing atoms. The NADs pierced her flesh. She screamed in pain. If this was the end of the game, then the 'unhook' was far more painful than the 'hook up'.

The ground shook as if the simulation pod was plummeting to Earth. She reached around for the latch but felt only air.

A ball of white light enveloped her, and when it disappeared she stood in a parking lot of a shopping center. Beside her stood Jack.

"Jack, shouldn't the operators be unhooking us?"

"That'd be my guess."

"So why aren't they?"

"I have no idea."

"I was okay before, but now I'm a little worried."

And when he didn't give her a reassuring smile, she knew he was a little worried, too. And that was when the panic set in.

5

Reis

"Player twenty-two will enter the game in ten seconds. Ten... Nine..."

The heads-up display was wrong. It couldn't be the start of a new game. Reis was only booked in for one. He should have been wrestling his way through the gift shop by now. Instead, he experienced the short freefall and sudden stop, and then he emerged from a ball of white light to stand on a street. Above was a bright blue sky. Same game, different day? Hard to tell.

He stood in a parking lot. There were tall apartment blocks on three sides and alleys running between. The road ahead went in a straight line to the horizon. A short way off to the right stood a multi-story building with large glass windows. The rest of the landscape was pretty sparse, much like the Arizona desert where CyberNexis complex was located.

He looked carefully to make sure this wasn't a real setting, but the truth was, the special effects inside *The Apocalypse Games* were exceptionally good; he couldn't tell if this reality was genuine or virtual.

He hadn't assisted anyone in the previous game to earn bonus points, and even if he had, shouldn't he be unhooked from the pod so he could spend his credits or register for a new game? Instead, it appeared as if he was getting a free game. And he suspected why. The update to his profile at registration would have led a diligent staff member to realize that Reis Anderson was the son of Jewel and Stafford Anderson. Jewel was a socialite and Stafford was a U.S. Senator. Which meant Reis was a VIP and VIPs got special privileges. Although, this sort of publicity was something Reis liked to avoid. He was copping enough flak from Stafford about his current career. Stafford had taken to phoning him every day to pester him into working in politics, even threatening disinheritance if Reis didn't come home where he belonged.

A whirl of dust in the near distance caught Reis's attention. Something was moving along the road; too far away to tell if it was coming or going, too far away to tell if the dust was from vehicle or people movement. A gust of wind swept the dust ball aside and he noticed legs and arms. Since he'd received no presentation, no warning, he knew nothing about this particular apocalypse. Yet in this world, a crowd of people running usually meant players or non-players escaping a disaster. He looked around for the source of terror but found none. Unless *he* was the reason the crowd was running.

He wore the same clothes he'd worn when he signed up – blue jeans, khaki-colored button-down shirt, hiking boots. The boots were brand new, and they'd been stiff to walk around in. It seemed as if he'd projected this trait into his virtual outfit because he could feel the pinch around his toes. Or the pinch might have been a result of the NADs in the simulation pod digging deeper into his flesh.

He studied the crowd, indecision rooting him to the ground. Friend or foe? Did it matter? Did he care? He was here to trial the virtual game for his business clients. He and Jack operated a tour business called Quest. This should be a one-day, in-and-out operation to verify that *The Apocalypse Games* were everything the creators claimed it to be. A trial run had been the plan but he couldn't say he was sorry to be given a free game. He could use a break from the outside world.

The way the crowd moved triggered a groan from Reis. The awkward way they ran, the way they limped and flailed their arms, the way their guttural cries and shouts carried across the air. Zombies acted like this. Quest clients would expect a unique experience, not the overdone formula of zombies and vampires. He shook his head, mostly at the way he'd allowed Jack to convince him to enter a Level 1 game because Jack had wanted to chaperone Kelly. It was the least they could do, Jack had said. Reis agreed because picturing Kelly's sad face caused a knot in his stomach. She'd once been the queen of fun, albeit a tad bossy and vocal when drunk, and she once used to tag along to test activities for Quest. Those moments used to be the highlights of his week. Now, her haunted gaze and downturned smile meant he could barely look at her without it hurting.

A woman's scream cut through the air and he ran toward the sound. Instead of being thrust in the middle of a rescue-Kelly mission, huddled on top of a dumpster were a man and a woman. The man wore tie-dyed jeans, sandals, a black t-shirt. He was fending off the handful of zombies by waving his denim jacket through the air. The woman had pixie-blonde hair and wore a bloodstained shirt, slacks, and low-heeled shoes. It would only take one zombie with enough residual gray matter left in his head to play tug-o-war with the jacket and the couple would be brain chowder.

For a split second, Reis wondered if he should just watch what happened. For all he knew they were non-player characters and this was a scene he wasn't meant to interrupt.

Every ten feet or so along the alleyway was a door leading to a business, and the closest door lay wide open and hanging off a solitary hinge. Without knowing what waited inside, Reis stepped through the opening. He found himself in a commercial kitchen. Hanging from the ceiling were frying pans, mostly stainless steel, but there was one cast-iron pan which he grabbed before stepping out into the alley. Creeping up on the nearest zombie, he smashed the frying pan against its head. It dropped to the ground as quietly as he'd crept up on it.

He smashed the skull of the next nearest zombie. This creature didn't drop as easily as the first. Its knees bent but it managed to stay upright. Then it growled and started shuffling toward Reis. He smiled and beckoned the zombie with his free hand. The zombie accepted the challenge, tapped the zombie next to him on the arm, and together they grunted, licked their lips, and started moving towards Reis. Tightening his grip on his weapon, Reis vowed he'd prove to everyone that if he could survive growing up with Jewel and Stafford, he could survive anything.

The zombies made garbled noises as they advanced. Language was lost, but their eyes spoke plenty. Reis felt his heartbeat quicken as the sense of 'kill or be killed' overwhelmed him. He knew which outcome he wanted.

He kept his gaze fixed on the creatures but spoke to the man and woman. "Get out of here. Find weapons. Anything you can smash their brains in with." The woman began to whimper. "Lady, you need to stay quiet. Zombies have short term memories. They'll forget all about you as long as you stay quiet."

His plan called for him to taunt the zombies and lead them away from the couple so they could flee. So far so good. When he backed up until he stood in the parking lot, he turned and ran, hearing their grunts. Adrenalin and years of tennis lessons easily put distance between predator and prey.

A block away, Reis stopped and turned to wait for the enemy to catch up. But the zombies were gone. Disappointed, he dropped the frying pan.

"Ouch," a voice said from behind.

He spun and found the couple from the dumpster standing a few feet away. They'd either snuck around the alleys, or they'd materialized from out of nowhere.

Dammit. This wasn't a rescue. He'd inadvertently activated the programming for the non-player characters to engage players they encountered.

"We wanted to say thanks," the guy said.

Reis turned to leave.

"Wait," the woman cried out.

"Look, it was nice to meet you," Reis sang out over his shoulder, "but I've got to go."

The woman was quick. One second she was behind him, the next she stood in front of him holding her arms out to make his stop.

"We're glad you came along when you did," she said in a rush. "We've managed to avoid them all morning. We thought our luck had just run out. I'm Casey Novak. This is my brother Zeus."

Maybe if Reis stayed quiet their programming would deactivate and they'd leave him alone. He wasn't here to socialize. He now regretted helping them.

"Those dead dudes have gotten smarter," Zeus said, slipping into his denim jacket. "Developed real predator skills. One half of the pack broke off and circled behind us while the other half drove us towards the other. Clever."

"Awesome," Reis said absently. "I'd love to debrief about this, but I've got to find my friends."

He'd signed on as a team with Jack and Kelly. It stood to reason that if Reis had advanced into a free game, so had they, although he wasn't fussed if he played alone. He'd felt their cold shoulder several times during the vampire game.

Casey's eyes widened. "You can't leave. You saw what they were going to do to us. We have to stick together. Safety in numbers. What if they come back?"

In order for Reis to offer his clients a complete experience, he'd have to provide as much research as he could about the scenarios so his clients would take full benefit of the twenty-four hours. In all of his research on surviving an apocalypse, he hadn't found *any* evidence to suggest the survival rate of humans increased by sticking together. If anything, the opposite was true. In a catastrophe, team members often argued for leadership, stole or depleted resources, or panicked and got other members killed. The pep talk at the launch about working together to save humanity was a load of crap designed to avoid law suits. When it came to it, everyone would adopt the 'kill or be killed' mentality.

"You'll be fine," he told Casey. "Just get some weapons."

"At least take us with you."

Reis bent down to pick up the frying pan. It had proven to be an effective weapon, but the urge to do further damage coursed through his fingers. Already his mind was running through a range of weapons to source: baseball bat, crowbar, sledgehammer.

"Dude, what do your friends look like?" Zeus asked, interrupting his train of thought. "Maybe we've seen them."

Reis glanced at the hippy. There was no expression on his face to suggest that he shouldn't be trusted. But looks were often deceiving.

"Who are you really? You're not one of us."

Zeus flicked his gaze to Casey who answered. "I told you. I'm Casey. He's Zeus."

"Show me your player passes."

Zeus patted the pockets of his jacket, his pants, then he began muttering to himself and shaking his head.

"Show us yours," Casey said.

Reis shook his head. "I asked you first."

"You're the one with the weapon. How do we know you're not going to attack us?"

"I saved you. Why would I attack you?"

She planted her hands on her hips and glared at him. He actually felt sorry for her, he didn't know why, but this unforeseen empathy was enough to cause him to reach inside his shirt and produce his laminated pass. It was the only item of clothing that carried from the real world into the virtual world since it doubled as a tracking device to monitor vital statistics.

Zeus and Casey scrutinized his pass, far longer than necessary. At last Casey nodded and reached inside her shirt. She waved her pass in Reis's face. Zeus did likewise.

Reis studied each of their passes. They contained the same information as his: name; photo; symbols of biohazard sign, mushroom cloud, lightning bolt. The passes appeared genuine. Yet something about these two didn't sit right with him.

Zeus slapped him on the shoulder. "Dude. You thought we were non-player characters. That's so funny. But no way would we get stuck on a dumpster just to trick you."

"Now Zeus," Casey said with a matronly stare, "Reis has every right to be cautious." She gave Reis a warm smile. "What do your friends look like? We saw a few players running past us."

"None of them stopped to help," Zeus said with a scowl.

"Jack's five-eight with brown hair, needs a haircut," Reis said. "He's wearing regular clothes. Though, he really could be wearing anything. He could even be a giant turtle for all I know."

At least that was how the CGI imagery of the virtual world was meant to work. Hooked up to the pods via cyber suits and cables, a player only needed to imagine an outfit and they could run around in combat gear or a tuxedo. Reis didn't care for costumes, but during the three hour drive, Jack had gone on and on about his indecision over which superhero to turn into like he was fourteen instead of twenty-eight.

"And your other friend?" Casey asked.

"Kelly has long brown hair and sad brown eyes." His voice became trapped in his throat. It was a struggle not to take hold of her and tell her that everything would be all right. But she'd made it clear a long time ago that she wanted nothing more than friendship from Reis.

He cleared his throat. "She's wearing regular clothes. Black pants, leather jacket, red top."

His mother would be proud of his inability to recall these crucial details.

"I think we saw them when we were trapped on the dumpster," Casey said. "They went into an apartment block. It's this way."

She took off down the alleyway. Zeus shrugged and ran off after her. Reis hung back since he had no intention on wasting a free game by teaming up with *this* brother and sister duo. Wasn't one enough?

"You'd better come, dude," Zeus sang out, pointing behind Reis.

A group of about twenty zombies were making their way down the alley. The frying pan was handy against a few but it was hardly adequate to battle an army. So Reis jogged to catch up to Casey and Zeus.

"We were making our way to these high rises when we were confronted," Zeus said. "We wanted to search the apartments for clothing, food, weapons, that sort of thing. Dude, it's good to have another pair of hands."

Casey stopped at a red-brick building and jumped up to grab the bottom rung of the fire escape ladder. Like a squirrel climbing a tree, she made the ascent look easy.

"We'll be fine inside this building," Zeus said. "Zombies can't climb. That's why we jumped up onto the dumpster. But the tricky little monsters were figuring out how to use tools to get us. Necessity breeds invention. Did you know that, dude? Most of the products in the civilian world are a product of necessity in the military world. It doesn't make sense how the wellbeing of the general population comes second to warfare."

"You'd like to meet my father," Reis said.

Picturing Zeus and Stafford sitting down over cognac to debate the necessity or evils of war brought a rare smile to Reis's face. It would be fun to watch Stafford's cheeks grow a brighter shade of red for each minute a hippy was in the house. Then again, Reis would have to contend with Jewel thinking Zeus was 'just the cutest thing' and fawning over him as if he were a piece of jewelry.

Casey continued to lead the way up the stairs, testing the windows as she went. On the fifth floor, she sang out "Bingo" and disappeared through the opening.

Zeus followed her inside. Reis hesitated on the landing. A chill had settled on his skin. The feeling that something wasn't quite right with these two nagged again. They made him want to approach CyberNexis about designing an exclusive Quest package so his clients wouldn't have to mingle with the regular crowd.

Inwardly he slapped himself. The Minnows were the regular crowd and Reis would be a mess if it weren't for them. No waiting on him hand and foot – you wanted something from the fridge or pantry you got it yourself. No special treatment – you got up on the roof and cleared gutters like all the suburban home owners did. If it weren't for the Minnows, Reis wouldn't have lived to blow out the candles on his twenty-eighth birthday cake.

"Are you sure they went inside this building?" Reis asked.

Casey popped her head out the window. "How do you think we knew about the fire stairs? We saw two people getting chased by zombies. They probably came through this very window. Now, come on."

Reis leaned over the edge, and the group of zombies gathered at the bottom had doubled in size. They stared upwards and pointed at the ladder. Too late to pretend he'd escaped them. It wouldn't be long before they figured it out. Not because they were advancing in intellect, as Zeus had suggested. They'd figure it out because the programmers would have made it so, just like they made everything else in this world. It would be skewed in favor of the players to avoid complaints.

He should have realized the full implications of being hooked up to a computer. How many times a year did he need to take his laptop to the store for repairs? What if his presence in a second game had nothing to do with a marketing ploy, and everything to do with a computer virus?

He shook off this ominous thought and searched the apartment for his new friends. He found Casey in the bedroom going through the wardrobe, holding dresses up against her body and tossing them onto the bed.

"What are you doing?" he asked.

"Sorry." Casey gave him a sheepish look. "Dresses are prettier than pants, don't you think?"

"They're not practical. It'll get cold at night. Grab a sweater. And we'll need blankets. Plus leather clothing for protection if you can find any."

Reis stormed out and found Zeus in the kitchen pulling food out of the pantry.

"You do understand that we don't *really* need food," he said.

"Not me, dude. I'm starving."

Zeus carried a box of cereal and a carton of milk to the dining table. He poured both into a bowl and began to cram spoonfuls of the breakfast cereal into his mouth.

"We don't have time for this," Reis said.

"Sorry, dude, but I haven't had milk before. It's amazing. And chocolate flavored milk at that. I mean, wow."

"What do you mean, you haven't had milk before?"

Casey entered the kitchen, carrying two large suitcases and a dozen dresses in her arms.

"I'm sorry," she said, "But I'm not leaving without these."

Zeus resumed feeding himself.

"What the hell is wrong with you two?" Reis said.

"I'm crazy with hunger," said Zeus.

Casey dropped the suitcases and clothes. "You're angry. I can tell. Please don't leave us."

"We're pacifists," Zeus said as if reading his mind. "We don't want to fight. We just want to live."

"So what are you doing here in the game?"

Zeus shrugged. "To be honest, I don't know."

There was a noise from the bedroom and Reis went to look. When he came back to the kitchen, Zeus and Casey were gone. Other than the kitchen, the apartment had two bedrooms, a bathroom, and a living room off a small foyer. The place wasn't big by any means, but Reis searched each room anyway and couldn't locate Casey and Zeus anywhere. He checked the landing up and down, giving the ladder a good shake. It clanged like a fire truck. The noise would be heard inside the apartment, so if they'd bailed this way, they'd been super quiet and super fast about it.

It wouldn't be the first time he'd offended people and they'd walked out of the room, but the sudden disappearance of Casey and Zeus hinted of something else. He raced to the front door; the safety latch was on. Nobody could exit through this door and put the latch on from the outside. They'd disappeared into thin air.

***

Reis's temper rose steadily, bubbling to the surface. Various techniques to control it usually worked, but he couldn't be bothered applying those techniques now. He wanted to be angry. And now that he realized he'd been tricked by non-player characters whose role was obviously to lead players down a merry path, his blood boiled. His anger demanded that he destroy items in the room. He kicked a chair, threw items off the sideboard, picked up a painting and hurled it across the room. He found a baseball bat and smashed photographs and décor.

Calm down, his inner voice said. *Do you want them to hear you?*

He didn't want to calm down. He wanted his anger to grow until it ballooned inside and burst. He'd always had a temper, and as a child nannies had quit because of it. His mother would tell them that he was simply acting out for attention and then she'd offer to double their hourly rate. But they always quit, eventually. Even his music tutor, Eddie, the only person he considered a friend, had left when Reis was twelve to return to Spain to care for his sick mother. Reis had reckoned it was madness that drove anyone to *want* to take care of their mother.

The only people who had refused to give up on Reis were the Minnows. First Jack and Kelly had befriended him, and soon afterward, their parents, Daniel and Kim Minnow, had taken him under their wing. Thinking of the Minnows was the key to cooling his ferocity. If Jack hadn't come into his life when he had, Reis was certain he would have ended up dead in a gutter.

Locating a baseball bat in a planter by the front door, he gripped it tightly and stepped out into the hallway. A zombie stumlbed out of the apartment across the hall, dripping with flesh and blood. This creature was swiftly, if not messily, disposed of. A second creature was patrolling the corridors. It stopped when it caught sight of Reis and charged down the corridor. It, too, ended up with chunks of his brain and skull smeared across the carpet.

The internal fire stairs were clear as Reis made his way down to the ground level, but he was disappointed that nobody attacked him. It didn't sit well with him to be played by decoys. His anger hadn't abated by the time he came out in an alleyway.

Yet when he spied Jack and Kelly running towards him, his rage finally simmered. His mind returned the years not long after college, to a time before Kelly had met Matt. Her smile used to be the last thing Reis pictured before he fell asleep. He'd found himself becoming infatuated with her. She wasn't smiling now. And even though Reis had personally liked Matt, he loathed the man responsible for turning the once beautiful and spirited woman into a miserable shadow.

Jack, however, seemed happy to see him.

"Did you pay CyberNexis to keep you in the game longer?" Jack asked.

Reis took offense to that. He'd never bribed anyone. He gave Kelly a reassuring smile but her scowl only deepened, and he flinched at her hostility. It was the same cold shoulder treatment he'd copped in yesterday's game. He could dish it back.

"Maybe you didn't do it on purpose," Jack said. "I'm still betting you're the reason we're in Zombieland. But let it be known, I'm not complaining."

"I am," Kelly said. "This was a waste of time. I want to go home."

Home for Reis was a two bedroom apartment in San Diego with a pet turtle named Angus and a handful of vintage electric guitars. It might not have been of a standard acceptable to Jewel and Stafford, but it was his sanctuary. At least it used to be. With Stafford and Jewel both phoning him every day, home was becoming a place to avoid.

"Is that blood?" Kelly asked, pointing at the baseball bat in his hands.

He shrugged. "The only way to kill a zombie is to smash in its skull."

Beneath her reproachful look he suddenly felt like a wicked child caught with a firecracker pointed at a Ming vase.

"I'm out of here," she said, turning to walk away.

"Earth to Kelly," Jack called out. "There *is* no way out of here. Not from this side of the pods anyway. You know, they never did tell us how to exit the game."

"I meant out of this vicinity," said Kelly. Her features twisted with concern. "Do you really think the computer's broken?"

"No, he doesn't." Reis shot Jack a harsh stare. "I'm sure we've been given a free game."

"You're sure?" Her eyebrows were raised. "How can you be sure?"

"I can't." He sighed. "But it's the best explanation."

She turned her back on them and started walking down the road.

"Kelly, come back," Jack shouted.

She seemed pissed, which was a step up from miserable. Reis jogged to catch up with her. "I'll help you get through this," he said. "The game, I mean."

She stopped abruptly and studied his face. Searched it for something, he had no idea what, but she didn't say if she'd found it or not. She just turned her head and stared at Jack who was still standing where they'd left him. A half-smile broke out on her face and she shook her head.

"Look at him," she said. "Like a dog that doesn't want to stop playing with its ball."

She waved to Jack and he came jogging over. Reis knew that as siblings they were close, but it hurt to be excluded when for so long they'd called him their other brother.

"We need weapons," Jack said. "I think the building on the highway is a shopping mall. It'll have a sporting goods store."

It turned out that Jack was right about the shopping mall, but there were no cars around so they'd had to walk. The mall was further away than it appeared. Reis's boots pinched his feet and he might have complained except that he was awed by the level of sensory detail inside the virtual world.

As they entered the parking lot of the mall, he calculated backwards. Each game was meant to represent twenty-four hours, so they'd spent one day inside a simulation pod hooked up to a machine. Despite the claim by CyberNexis that the body could handle more than three days of stasis, the research he'd done, in order to assure his clients that they'd be safe in this environment, indicated that a player should spend no more than three consecutive hours in a virtual world. Any longer and players tended to become distracted with real life. He could appreciate that. It was a symptom he hoped to inflict upon himself.

There were symptoms of prolonged inactivity that he wasn't too keen to explore. Muscle atrophy, bone degeneration, bedsores. His research had led him to discover that bears were able to overcome these issues when they hibernated. They also didn't eat or drink, yet they didn't starve. They emerged from their den after months of inactivity, thin but healthy. But Reis was not a bear.

The worst symptom of this unexpected stay was that people would notice his absence, namely his parents, and they'd be frantic. He'd probably emerge from the pod to be greeted by the FBI, the CIA, the Secret Service, a press conference, and a wall of psychiatrists.

***

The three of them stopped fifty feet from the entrance. Blocking the way in were four teenage zombies. Their stance was one of defiance – necks bent low as if giant antlers weighed down their heads. They clumsily held onto unlit cigarettes and cans of Coke. Some human instinct still functioned and Reis wasn't sure if this should deter him from killing them or not. The teenage zombies eyed them with caution. They hadn't automatically charged like the zombies in the alley. Maybe these teens were smarter and waiting for the humans to walk into their trap.

The taller zombie had bloodied legs and arms. It had once been a girl judging by the short skirt and tank top. It wore a wedged sandal on one foot and nothing on the other. Zombie Girl's attention seemed to be focused on Kelly's feet. The zombie looked at her own feet, then at Kelly's, then once more at her own.

"I think she wants your boots," Reis said.

"She can get a job and pay for them like I had to."

"If you *don't* give them to her," Jack said, "she might tell her boyfriends to attack."

"And if I *do* give them to her, I will be walking around in bare feet and totally useless if I have to run anywhere."

"You could try imagining new boots," Jack said. "The game is meant to be a projection of our imagination."

Kelly's voice came out flat. "Wishing doesn't work. I've tried it."

Reis tried imagining wearing an armor-plated combat suit. It didn't work. Was this a malfunction the game creators had to work on? It should have been tested before allowing one hundred people to suit up. Because if this feature wasn't working, what else might not work?

Reis had been keeping an eye on the teenage zombies, and the boys now appeared to getting restless. He tore his attention away from the zombies to study Kelly. Another symptom of long term stasis that he hadn't factored in was mental anguish. She was already in a poor state of mind. What if *The Apocalypse Games* worsened it? Should he demand his clients undergo a psychiatric evaluation before they participated? And now that the idea was in his head, why hadn't CyberNexis elected to do this? *Anybody* could be lurking inside this killing ground.

Kelly removed her leather jacket and handed it to Jack. "She can have this."

"No," Reis said. "It's leather and will offer protection. We'll find something else to trade."

He reached inside his shirt and ripped off his player pass. He swung it through the air and Zombie Girl's eyes were immediately attracted to the shiny plastic.

"Wait a second," Jack said. "That pass stores our vital signs. It acts like a GPS. What if someone on the outside needs to know where you are?"

"They know where I am. They put me here. Plus the things are useless as identity."

He quickly related to Jack and Kelly about his run in with Casey and Zeus and how they had replicated a pass just by looking at his.

"Decoys?" Jack asked.

"What else could they be?'

Jack smiled. "The plot thickens."

Zombie Girl was still ogling the pass. Since it was plastic, it wouldn't reach her when thrown, so Reis looked around for something to tie it to. He found a piece of broken fence paling, wrapped the cord of the pass around it, and hurled it into the air. All four zombies watched it sailing through the sky. When it landed, the girl reached it before the boys. She grasped it like it was the golden ticket that won her a tour of the chocolate factory.

Reis took this as the cue to walk briskly into the mall. At the door, he flicked a glance and saw that Zombie Girl was fighting with the others to hold onto the item. He hoped she won. Something about her touched his heart.

Inside, it was a clear route from the entrance to the stores. In some places there was broken glass and Kelly gave Jack a told-you-so look. The directory guided them to a store that stocked sporting gear, which was on the same level and only halfway inside the large mall. Electricity was usually the first casualty in a mankind depleted environment, and it was true in this case. But sufficient light streamed in from the overhead glass ceiling for them to make their way through the mall. They reached the store; the window and door were both intact and locked securely. Reis and Jack both took turns at busting through the door like the cops did in the movies, but they only managed to hurt their shoulders.

Reis spied a pot plant with a heavy base. Noise would attract zombies, but they had to get inside. It took three attempts to get the planter to smash through the door. Once inside, Jack and Reis changed into padded pants, jackets, and gloves. Kelly already had the protection of a leather jacket, and she didn't seem interested in gathering weapons. She stood by the counter, looking into the display cabinet. She bumped into a DVD player on the counter and it sprang to life.

"Greeting players and welcome to the apocalypse," a voice sang out.

"Power may be out but the battery is still charged." Jack ran towards the counter. He turned the DVD player around so it faced them.

The two Command Leaders appeared on the monitor. CL Jonas Barrett sat in an armchair, with his back straight and his left leg hitched up on his right knee, wearing a navy blue suit and jacket with a white shirt and red tie. His silvery hair was neatly styled, reminding Reis of Stafford.

"If you are watching this presentation," CL Barrett said, "humanity is under attack by zombies. It's likely zombies outnumber human survivors ten thousand to one. They are mindless and insatiable killers who need the flesh and brains of their victims to survive and will stop at nothing to get it."

The camera panned to his co-host, CL Stephanie Gey. She was young, with blonde hair and large, wide-set brown eyes. Her uniform consisted of a red jacket and short skirt, and instead of a tie she wore a red scarf. Her white shirt had the top buttons undone, and her hair was neatly coiled on top of her head.

Reis saw that Jack was riveted to the screen.

Stephanie turned to face the camera. "Having reduced the numbers of humans considerably, the zombies will turn to feeding off animals, mostly livestock and pets. Do not leave your pets behind to bear this suffering. We believe that without a source of living bodies the number of zombies will gradually decline, though we have no scientific evidence to prove this. All it takes is one bite to turn a human into a mindless creature. As with all apocalypses, proceed with caution."

Jonas stared into the camera the way news reporters do. "If you find yourself in the midst of a zombie apocalypse, you will need to prepare a panic bag before making your way to the nearest safe zone. Your panic bag should contain the following items. A blunt object such as a baseball bat, a crowbar, a sledgehammer, or the blunt end of an axe."

"Guns won't work," Stephanie said. "Zombies can only be destroyed by pulverizing their brain."

"I love it when she talks dirty," Jack said. "I could watch her brush her teeth."

Kelly scoffed. "If you met her you'd end up moving her furniture or watering her house plants while she slipped off to Rio with her lover."

Reis bit down on the smile. It was true that Jack couldn't resist helping others, to the point of ending up a doormat. He'd once spent a summer doing errands for an ex-girlfriend who'd broken an ankle. He wouldn't explain why he aided her, and no amount of ribbing from Reis could get him to quit being taken advantage of.

While CL Stephanie Gey lectured them on how many pairs of socks players needed to gather, Reis studied Jack and Kelly. The three of them were born and bred in the same city yet they were from different worlds. Reis had wealthy parents, a mansion, a chauffeur and maids. He only had to snap his fingers, make a wish, and he got what he wanted. Or so people thought. All his life, he'd wanted parents who adored him. He'd eventually gotten his wish; the trouble was the parents belonged to Jack and Kelly.

"I don't care what you think of my beloved Stephanie," Jack said turning up the volume. "I want to hear what she says."

"...Crackers, nuts, dried fruit, energy bars. Pantry items such as tinned food, pasta, flour, sugar, and rice. Torch and spare batteries. Boxes of matches, fire lighters, and newspaper to burn. A pistol. There is no cure for a zombie bite. You'll need a pistol to end your suffering or the suffering of a loved one."

The camera panned out so the two hosts were in the single shot. In the background was an image of a military boot resting on a bloodied and crushed head.

Jonas stared into the camera. "We at Simulated Military And Recreational Training – SMART for short – have designed this program because we are committed to the survival of the human race. And because we are serious, SMART has put together the following tips for players encountering a zombie apocalypse."

A series of thumps came from the front of the store. They grew louder and Kelly started to retreat into a clothing rack.

"Don't wander off," Reis told her.

She ignored him, disappearing into a rack of camouflage pants and shirts. Reis wandered over to the camping section and returned with an axe which he thrust into the rack for her to take.

"Jesus, Reis." She stepped out and glared at him. "Do you know what I do for a career? I help put murderers away."

"This isn't murder. It's self defense."

"I still won't do it."

Jack started swinging a baseball bat. It slipped out of his hands, landing ten feet away.

"Give it to him," she said.

"Stop being stubborn," Reis said, although that would be like telling a bird to stop being a bird. Despite the comforting feel of the baseball bat, he handed it to Kelly. "If you'd rather use a blunt object—"

"I said no!"

She brushed past him and stood beside the front counter again. The loud *crack* of the front door splintering made her jump and he gritted his teeth. Kelly shouldn't be here, she shouldn't have felt obligated to honor Matt's memory. More importantly, Matt shouldn't have been able to affect Kelly from beyond the grave.

Two zombies pushed through the opening. They were male, possibly middle-aged by the style of their slacks and shirts. The stench of rot was overpowering. Scraps of gray flesh hung off their faces. Their eyes were bloodshot and jaundice-yellow. Reis would take pleasure in destroying these two, but he caught a glimpse from the corner of his eye. Kelly's eyes were wide. She wasn't acting pig-headed. She was terrified.

One of the zombies spied her and lunged. Reis came in swinging the bat and the creature staggered a few steps then went down, but the handle had broken.

Shit. He reached for an axe, then he and Jack came at the zombie together. It went down, but two more appeared. This time, when Reis swung the axe, the zombie ducked and snatched it out of his hands. These movements were too fast for typical zombies. Zeus had said that they were advancing in intellect. Reis hadn't believed him. But here he was, facing a zombie who was as nimble as a ninja.

It swung the axe, slicing the air, and Reis had to twist and jump to avoid being cut in two. He caught glimpses of Jack who was busy battling the other monster. This creature kept swinging at Reis, forcing him to back up to where he'd soon be trapped. Reis fumbled around for a weapon, keeping his attention on the axe. Things fell on the floor, he almost tripped over them, and the axe swung relentlessly, missing him by mere inches. *Damn this creature for overpowering him.*

Reis threw everything his hands landed on to slow the zombie down.

All of a sudden the zombie's body contorted, its eyes widened, and then it dropped to the floor.

An axe was wedged into its back. Reis looked up to find Kelly staring at the creature she had just killed. Her face was turning green. He scrambled up off the floor and pulled her into the office out the back. He got her a drink of water from the dispenser. He and Kelly weren't actually *here* and this wasn't real water, but the gesture still worked to take her mind off what had just happened.

She gulped down the water and held the empty cup for him to refill it. By her third glass, color had started to return to her face.

"Kelly—"

"Don't say it, Reis."

"Don't say what?"

"You want to know what I'm doing here. I can't answer that question because I don't know myself. Well, that's not entirely true. Before Matt died he told me that the employees were allowed to imprint their images and voices into the game. They're meant to be in here somewhere and I think I have to die in order to find him. Please don't tell Jack about this. He'll try and stop me."

"And I won't?"

"Not if you know what's good for you."

It was bad enough the dead man still held front row seats to her mind and heart, but to have a digital copy of him running around inside the computer caused a jealous rage to sweep over Reis. And for the first time in his life, he directed his anger at Kelly.

"Matt's dead," he said. "Why can't you leave him alone?"

He stormed out of the office and found Jack wiping brains off his weapon.

"Where's Kelly?" Jack asked.

"In the office."

"Is she okay?"

"How the hell should I know?" Reis regretted his harsh tone but damned if the woman didn't mess up his head. "Can we focus on getting out of this situation alive?"

He indicated to the teenage zombies hovering around the door, muttering to each other but staying outside. One of the boys reached into a pocket and pulled out a cell phone. Its face contorted as if it struggled to remember something from its human life. Zombie Girl snatched the phone from him and lifted it to her nose. She sniffed, put it in her mouth and bit down. She must not have found the taste to her liking, because she hurled the phone into space.

"Please don't piss Kelly off," Jack said. "I need you two to be friends."

As Reis watched the teenagers fight over the phone, he put thoughts of Kelly out of his head and instead opened himself to ideas on how to end this game.

"How much battery does the DVD player have left?" he asked Jack.

"Let me check." Jack fiddled with the controls. "Maybe an hour."

"Pass me that skateboard, will you? I want to test something."

The three teens continued to hover outside. The zombie boy held the broken phone to his ear. Perhaps in life they were banned from this store and the memory of it remained, much like the memory of putting the phone to the ear.

Jack pushed a skateboard along the floor and the kids eyed it with morbid desire. Reis then placed the DVD player on the skateboard and pushed it towards the door. Zombie Girl reached in and snatched the player. A smile lit up her mangled face and she clutched the device close to her chest. Compassion for this creature tugged again at Reis. He had quite possibly found someone he felt sorrier for more than himself.

6

Reis

Undead creatures wandered around the levels above and below, yet Reis wanted to track down Zombie Girl. Perhaps he could cure her, save her from the players who would hunt her and kill her. She wasn't human but she wasn't a brain-munching zombie either. A misfit, stuck in between two societies. He could appreciate that.

Kelly appeared at his side. "Please don't tell Jack what I said. He'll just worry I'm going to do something stupid."

"Are you?"

"I'd like to. I'm not sure I can."

He was satisfied with that answer, but still angry at her; misdirected, since he was mainly angry with himself. It hurt more than he realized that she still loved Matt. It meant he didn't stand a chance. He opened his mouth to apologize for his early outburst, but Kelly had wandered over to stand beside Jack who was poking his bat at the corpses on the floor.

"I'm all for battling these things," Jack said with a sigh, "but we should try to get out of the game."

"I want to stay," Kelly said.

"Ten minutes ago you wanted to go home." A mixture of emotions flittered across Jack's face. "Kelly, we don't know why we're in a new game. There could be a problem with the pods or the computer."

"The brochure says we can stay inside the pod for three days," she said. "It's perfectly safe."

Reis had figured she'd be the first to cry foul and demand they search for a way out. Now that she'd confessed her true reason for being here, he wasn't sure she should stay. But he was in no hurry to leave either. Nobody believed that Reis Anderson could have any problems in his life. Nobody ever truly pitied the rich. It was his mother who'd taught him this lesson. He hadn't fully grasped the intent until recently when he'd tried to tell Jack about his most recent difficulty. A woman named Candice whom he'd dated in college for a month had shown up out of the blue a few weeks ago, claiming Reis was the father of her ten-year-old boy.

"So marry this woman," Jack had said.

"He's not my kid. And I don't want to marry her."

"You don't want to marry anyone." Jack's disapproving tone hadn't escaped Reis's notice. Neither had the hypocrisy, since Jack was also single.

Now, Reis followed Jack and Kelly out of the mall. At the entrance, they discovered the zombie teenagers had returned to their spot. When Zombie Girl spied Reis, she waved at him.

"Did she just wave at you?" Jack burst out laughing. "Only Reis Anderson could convert an enemy into a fan."

"She does seem happy that you gave her that DVD player," Kelly said. "Makes you wonder if they're really the bad guys."

"Oh, they're the bad guys," Jack said. "And if you want proof, try to take it off her."

They hurried to the parking lot. Reis was determined to find a car with keys inside, but he had no such luck. He refused to believe the computer was smart enough to manipulate the game, but after ten minutes of searching he had to admit defeat and walk in the hiking boots that he'd forgotten to change out of. He wasn't even really *here*, so he couldn't figure out why his feet were hurting. He had to wonder for a second if *here* was the real world and somehow they'd emerged from the pods into the middle of a real apocalypse.

After a mile of walking they came across a public swimming pool. The thing about parents objecting to peeping toms staring at their children meant that many fences around public swimming pools were made of solid walls of metal or brick. This fence was brick and over six foot high. They walked around the front and were denied entrance by the coin-operated turnstiles that went from the cement floor to the roof. Ideal for keeping out cash-strapped zombies, but the three players had no coins either.

Jack used the grooves in the brick to climb over the wall. Reis gave Kelly a boost, and finally Reis followed. The place was deserted. The chlorine in the pool meant the water had not yet turned green. Alga was forming in the corners and frogs and insects occupied the lawn that had grown to knee height. Weeds appeared in the cracks of the pavers around the edge of the pool. Too rundown to be a real end of the world, since they'd only been in the game for about thirty hours.

Jack turned to Reis. "You ever been to a public pool?"

"Once or twice." It was a lie. He'd never set foot inside one, yet around the Minnows he always felt the need to shake off his privileged background. His mother called it the pedestrian syndrome. During some of her rages she would phone Reis to accuse him of resenting her because she refused to spend her days elbow deep in baking dough.

"Give me the beach any day," he told Jack. And to deflect the topic he said, "Want to raid the candy store?"

He headed for it anyway and soon heard footsteps following. Once his pockets were full, Reis spied the life guard's high chair. He'd always wanted to climb one and so he did. Movement on the metal indicated Kelly and Jack had followed, but when he looked, only Kelly had climbed up.

"You don't seem worried about being stuck in the game," she said.

He shrugged. "Like you said, it's perfectly safe."

"Reis, have I done something to upset you?"

He could ask the same of her.

He forced his attention away from Kelly's quizzical face to what was happening over the fence. From this vantage point he could see a few hundred yards in all directions. Just like in the mall, zombies shuffled aimlessly around the streets and parks. Some carried severed limbs. Turf wars erupted when one gang of zombies got too close to a particular stretch of street another gang had decreed as theirs. Other undead hobbled with their eyes downcast as if nervous. Social clicks had formed and a hierarchy had emerged in death just like it had in life.

"Reis?" Kelly prompted.

"I've just got a lot on my mind."

"I haven't been much of a friend lately. Even before Matt's death I pulled away. I know Matt didn't like us spending time together." She sighed. "I guess I thought it wouldn't matter if I never had another friend. He and I were supposed to be together till the end."

Reis said nothing. It was true that he missed his friendship with her. What Kelly didn't seem to realize was Matt had every reason to be jealous of Reis.

"Incoming," Jack said.

The scaffold shook as Jack climbed to the top. Then he pointed out over the fence. Four zombies had banded together and were ripping a picnic table out from its ground fasteners. They were going to move it against the fence to climb over it.

"So what's the plan?" Reis asked.

"We could fireball our way through," Jack said.

"We did that yesterday."

"It worked."

"It worked on vampires," Kelly said. "Since I have an aversion to smashing in the heads of monsters, I say we use Reis's distraction technique. The DVD player worked on the teens at the mall. It should work here as well."

"Except we are hiding out in a swimming pool," Jack said. "Not a department store."

"Should we even bother?" Reis asked.

As he gazed out across the field he saw more undead creatures heading towards the wall, and the question answered itself. If they were to be stuck here till the end of the game, then yes, they should bother. So he told them of a plan to battle the zombies. Once Jack heard it, there was no putting a stop to it.

They scrambled down from the diving board and hurried to the office. A door led to a work shed crowded with floats, ropes, flags, chlorine, tools, and a pickup truck. The car keys sat on a hook on the wall. Reis's plan called for two stops in a land he didn't recognize but maps in the office told him was named Whittlesea. Pinned on a notice board was a business card for a hardware store that, according to the map, was four miles away on the north side of town. He reckoned they'd locate an appliance store nearby, unless the game had other plans for them. Either way, they'd firstly have to get out of the grounds via a metal roller door. Power was out, so the metal door had to be lifted by hand which meant the potential for flesh coming in contact with zombies.

"I'll volunteer to open the door," Jack said.

"You'll trip and get swarmed by zombies." Kelly shook her head. "I'll go."

"In the real world I'm a klutz. But in here I'm Superman. You drive the truck and Reis and I will sort out these idiots."

Jack had made a good point. Inside the game, their minds were in control of their bodies, so it stood to reason that they could outrun any danger and overcome their enemy using superhuman strength. Still, Reis didn't want to risk this notion not working, since they were able to imagine clothing of their preference and hadn't yet managed it.

"Drive the truck," Jack told Kelly, handing her the keys. "I'm not going to be eaten alive. And Mom and Dad would kill me if I let that happen to you."

Minutes later, Reis was crouched low in the back of the pickup. He heard the creak of metal on metal as the roller door was opened. He felt the jolt as Kelly floored the gas pedal, and poked his head up in time to see Jack swinging a bat, causing brains and gore to splatter everywhere.

A dozen zombies ran to swarm around Jack. Reis jumped out of the truck and raced over to help him. Kelly plowed through a handful then swung the car around, crushing more with the bull bar. Jack finally managed to get the roller door down. As soon as the truck was within range, Reis and Jack launched themselves into the back.

Kelly sped off. None of the zombies were smart enough to figure out how to open the door. But they were smart enough not to give chase. Getting in would be harder than getting out because they had just lost the element of surprise.

***

The town center resembled the aftermath of a natural disaster. Store windows were smashed. Rubbish was strewn about. Cars sat with doors opened, abandoned for safety. With the dead reanimated, at least there were no corpses lying on the ground.

The hardware store had been cleaned out of power tools and axes and other blunt instruments. Reis's plan didn't call for weapons. It called for bags of cement and the loading dock was filled with the stuff. They piled as many bags as they could into the pickup without breaking the chassis. He'd spied a generator in the shed at the pool complex so he grabbed a dozen thirty-foot-long power cords. He'd siphon fuel from the truck's tank to operate the generator and use the cords to operate the DVD players.

Next stop was the appliance store. It had been ransacked but they found a few portable DVD players and DVDs under the counter. On the way out, Reis glanced up at the CCTV camera. He was accustomed to being under the watch of security. Growing up, there were cameras on the front gate and around the house checking for intruders. In school, there were cameras in the corridors checking for weapons. Nobody would be monitoring these cameras. At least not store security. Perhaps the operators were watching on a monitor, but in the real world. It gave him a chill. Even if it was for his own safety, he didn't like the idea of being under surveillance.

The clock on the dash of the truck read three p.m. It took fifteen minutes for them to reach the road leading to the swimming pool. Evidence so far had proven the zombies in this game were more advanced than folklore suggested. They had used tools to build ladders up to dumpsters, fashioned tables into bridges to get over walls, and now they had formed a solid line of defense outside the garage.

Kelly couldn't ram through the door because they needed the door to remain intact while they prepared their trap.

"Drive as close as you can to the door," Reis told her. "Jack and I will hold them back and get it open. Then drive the truck to the far edge of the pool."

"Why are we doing this again?" she asked. "Why don't we just keep driving?"

"Remember when you said you felt as if you were being watched," Reis said. "Maybe we are. And maybe we need to play or we won't be let out."

"Like the vamp-mutts." Kelly nodded. "They appeared just when I'd decided to sit the game out."

"If we're going to be forced to play," said Jack, "then we should at least give them a show."

Kelly told them to get in the back of the truck and hold on, and then Reis felt her floor the pedal. She slammed on the brakes inches away from the door, pinning a handful of zombies under the wheels. Jack and Reis jumped out of the truck and immediately started swinging weapons. Reis could hear Kelly screaming as the truck was shaken by attacking zombies.

Jack managed to get the door open, Kelly drove the truck inside, and Reis got busy killing the undead. Within a few minutes, blood and brains stained the ground, and they'd made it inside the garage and had the door closed behind them.

***

Reis and Jack came out of the shed with the generator and a megaphone used by the life guards. The truck was parked near the deep end of the pool. Dumping everything beside the truck, they unloaded the cement bags off the back. The constant banging indicated the zombies would break through before their trap was set, so Reis told Kelly to move the truck into the shed as soon as they got the bags unloaded, and park it up against the door.

She drove off, and Reis and Jack moved everything that wasn't bolted down into a pile to create two walls that would act like a funnel. They plugged the DVD players into the power boards and hooked the cord up to the generator. The last item to be set up was the megaphone. Reis used duct tape to keep the button in the 'on' position.

"I hope this works," Kelly said. She was looking paler than usual.

The loud screech of metal meant they'd soon find out. Reis switched on the DVD players and placed the megaphone in front of the speaker. Music blasted across the pool. The zombies ran toward the sound.

Rather than tackle the obstacles Reis and Jack had created, the undead creatures ran along the make-shift funnel and fell straight into the pool, just as planned. Singing mermaids at the deep end urged on the zombies. They couldn't swim but their feet could reach the bottom. They waded through the water, too dumb to realize that the water was getting deeper the further they went. Their heads went under the surface, but the undead didn't need to breathe.

Reis, Jack, and Kelly were at the other end cheering on the zombies.

When it seemed like no more could fit into the pool, Reis gave the call to commence phase two of his plan. Kelly slit the bags of cement open, while Jack and Reis tossed the contents into the water. The thrashing zombies were agitating the cement, and slowly the water turned into gray mud. And slowly the gray mud turned into thickening cement which would eventually harden into a grave from which no zombie would ever escape without the aid of dynamite.

***

The three players emerged from the pool complex feeling less like heroes and more like survivors. At which, Reis finally understood the premise of the game. Okay, so it wasn't only 'kill or be killed'. It was about working together to defeat a common enemy under the watchful eye of a moral compass.

Reis drove this time, with Kelly seated beside him and Jack in the back. It felt good to have her by his side. Not wanting the trip to end, he drove around the streets. He came to a highway and decided to stay awake as long as he could to relish the moment.

On the highway, he saw evidence of the zombie invasion. Cars were overturned with their doors ripped open and windows smashed in. This time there were body parts in the middle of the highway like road kill. He avoided hitting anything on the road and once, when he swerved to miss a decapitated head, Kelly's sleeping body fell against him. He didn't hurry to prop her back up, though it became difficult to make the turns.

He drove past motels and burger joints, past suburbs and schools, past pastures and fields where he felt sorry for the mutilated cows. He still didn't want the game to end. The outside world didn't appeal to him anymore. He hated his parents and a bitch of a woman was trying to make his life even more of a living hell. At least in here, he could tell who the monsters were.

Darkness fell and he was finally forced to pull over. Kelly was still slumped against him and he fought the urge to wrap an arm around her. Jack was asleep in the back and it took Reis a second to realize that they'd both fallen asleep, which should have been the signal for the game to end and the pods to open. Twenty-four hours was almost up.

He pulled over the side of the road to wait for the end.

He didn't realize he'd fallen asleep too, until a ball of orange light exploded in front of him. When it cleared, he stood in a field with soldiers wearing anti-contagion suits.

A rifle was pointed at his head.

7

Reis

The soldier holding a gun to Reis's head wore protective gear – full-faced mask, body suit, gloves. He tried to stare at the eyes behind the mask but couldn't see a thing. This gesture might or might not have been perceived as hostile, but Reis wasn't about to beg for his life so what did it matter? As it was, the soldier was only interested in keeping his gun trained on Reis and not actually killing him. Which left Reis with the opportunity to study the situation better. Jewel had once hired Homeland Security to brief Reis on the dangers of abduction. He tried to recall the lessons but that vault of memories was best left tucked securely away in the deepest, darkest recess of his mind.

He snuck a quick look in both directions. On both sides were people, none of whom he recognized. About forty soldiers wearing full protective clothing kept the large crowd under control with rifles. A few people were flashing their player passes. The soldiers wore anti-contagion suits which suggested there had been some sort of biological or biochemical disaster. Behind the line of soldiers were five school buses with sheets of metal over the wheels and wire mesh over the windows. Obviously the players weren't about to die in the field. The soldiers would take Reis and the others somewhere else. Maybe to a treatment center. Maybe to quarantine. Without the welcome presentation, it was all speculation.

A voice came over a loudspeaker: "Hands behind your head! Get down on your knees! Hands behind you head! Get down on your knees!"

Reis slipped his hands behind his head but he refused to get on his knees.

"What's going on?" The guy beside him addressed the nearest soldier. It was never a good thing to engage the enemy in conversation. "The game is meant to be over."

The soldier didn't answer. Reis stared once more into the eyes of his captor, but the dark glass of the goggles was impenetrable. He couldn't even be sure his captor was human. A different soldier approached him and sprayed something on his chest. After a small coughing fit, Reis looked down to see yellow paint on his shirt. He'd been tagged. But for what?

Soldiers went around and tagged other players: yellow, blue, white.

The guy next to Reis started demanding to be let out of the pod, and then everyone started yelling. The soldiers took a step back, and players took this is a sign of retreat and advanced forward. But the soldiers only moved back so another team could take their place. This team sprayed the crowd with tear gas. Reis closed his eyes and held his breath. He'd have told the players around him to shut up, but his efforts would result in gas pouring into his lungs.

Maybe they *were* going to die in the field.

Something bumped into him, almost knocking him to the ground. Reis found his footing. Seconds later the loud boom of a gunshot put a halt to the shouts. He kept his eyes closed, and something leaked out of the deepest, darkest recess of his mind. His tutor from Homeland Security had taught him to slow his breathing so that the gas would have minimal effect. Smoke could sneak in through the tiniest of slits so he squeezed his eyes even tighter. He'd survived then. He'd survive now.

Something hit the back of his legs, buckling them beneath him. His mouth opened and he sucked up a lungful of the gas. Water streamed out of his eyes. It took every ounce of remaining strength not to lash out at his captors, but his inner voice told him to submit. For now.

How ironic that Homeland Security had prepared him for this. He hadn't thought so at the time.

Rule number one: abide by the rules set by the captors until you can figure out what the hell was going on. So he let the soldiers drag him onto a bus. At least the air was clear and he could breathe normally. Tears still blinded him though.

He was pushed down into a seat and metal chains fastened automatically around his ankles. A metal band restrained him to the seat. By the time his eyes had stopped watering and he could see clearly, the bus was moving. It was full of men tagged with yellow paint.

***

Reis wasn't in the mood for small talk, so he closed his eyes and ignored the man in the seat beside him. His mother had warned him from an early age that he was a target for ransom. The fact this was a game didn't lessen his panic. Abduction was abduction.

Now that the vault was opened, he let the memories loose, easily recalling the lessons as a child. The first few minutes of a hostage situation were the most dangerous. The danger increased the more a person resisted. Well, Reis was on the bus and not dead on the field so the odds were somewhat in his favor that his captors wanted him alive. His heart was racing and his adrenalin pumping; he took a few deep breaths to regain his composure. The training also called for him to be observant.

Kelly is wearing black jeans, a red shirt, and a cream jacket. It was a relief to recall the details. If he pictured her alive, he might be able to keep her that way.

He overlooked the players seated on the bus since they were as much a prisoner as he was; instead he focused his attention on the soldiers who walked up and down the aisle. They wore combat gear, full-faced masks and gloves, they held rifles at the ready, and above all they stayed quiet. No radio contact. No talking to the prisoners. Signs they weren't amateurs.

Since every hostage on the bus was male, Reis guessed they were going to be put to work in a camp. He'd find out soon enough. Until then, the captors held all the cards. He closed his eyes once more and used every ounce of willpower to steady his breathing. It would pay to be rested and composed and his mind kept clear so he could figure out a way to escape.

The bus lurched to a stop and the soldiers ordered everyone off. Reis quickly assessed the chance of escape, and since his group of men was met by ten more soldiers wearing combat gear and protective suits, he decided escaping would have to wait.

He and the other men were inside a large shed the size of an airplane hangar.

"Form a line here." The soldier's voice was muffled by the mask but the intent was clear when he pointed to a yellow handrail. "Hands on the rail. Both hands."

Resembling first-time skaters at an ice rink, the men shuffled along the handrail. At the end they were forced into prison-like cells the size of a small pantry. The cell had solid walls and a metal-grilled front door. A soldier moved down the line asking for their names. Reis listened out but didn't hear any names he recognized.

The soldier stopped in front of Reis's cell. "Name."

"Go screw yourself."

"Is that your first or last name? Or are you like Madonna?"

It surprised Reis that his captor would possess a sense of humor. There wasn't anything funny about this situation. But the remark had the effect of decreasing his temper. Almost.

"It's Reis Anderson."

The soldier wrote something onto a clipboard and moved on to the next cell.

"Name."

"Special Agent Ash Brogen."

"Is that your real rank or a made up one?"

"Does it matter?"

"Guess not."

The soldier moved on down the line and Reis crept up to the front of the cell.

"Ash?" he whispered. "You're the guy Kelly met the other day."

A hand appeared around the corner. Reis shook it, suddenly glad to find himself with an ally.

"I saw Kelly before they loaded her onto a bus," Ash said. "I tried to stop it happening." He groaned. "They conked me on the head. I hope she's okay."

"She'd better be."

"I'm sure she is. She seems nice."

"She is."

"But nice like she shouldn't be here."

"Good luck trying to convince her."

Ash chuckled. "So, how do you two know each other?"

"I've known Kelly and her brother since high school."

"That a fact? Is Kelly the reason you entered the game? I don't mean to pry. My wife is always telling me I pry."

Reis's parents were the opposite. They never asked questions. Never pried into his life. It went beyond not caring; they were almost alien to him. He pressed his forehead against the cool metal. He could have told Ash what he'd told everyone, that he was here to test a virtual game for his tour business. But that would have been a lie.

"I've come to escape reality," he said at last.

Even the threat of the unknown was preferable to the promise of the predictable. Stafford was calling and emailing to hound him into joining the political arena. Jewel was calling him almost every day to accuse Stafford of cheating, even though Reis knew that *she* knew that this was a lie. More recently, a woman from his past was forcing him to take a paternity test because she was broke and looking for an easy ride. Jewel had warned him to be extra careful around the ladies. Jewel had warned him about so many things and he'd ignored her. But maybe Jewel was right that the world was full of traps and hurdles designed to slot a person into a box they didn't want to be slot into. Maybe he should crawl home and live the life she wanted. In a way, things were simpler under their roof. Crazier, but simpler.

Footsteps sounded on the concrete floor. Somewhere down the end of the row of cells, a man was taken out and escorted away. Reis fought the urge to shout for help. It would do no good. As a child, during abduction training, he'd screamed for help. His trainers had shoved a sock in his mouth. He'd never shout for help here. No matter how dire the situation got.

"You seem to be taking this rather well," Ash said. "I've noticed the way you can zone out, like you're meditating or something."

"I'm just used to crazy, that's all."

"I wonder what's going on. Not just this game, I get that we're in some sort of biological disaster apocalypse. And I get that I went out of my way in Vampireland to earn credits to win a free game, which is how I met Kelly, by the way. But I didn't do anything to win two extra games."

Reis heard shuffling, as if Ash was moving around inside his cage. There was more banging and crashing from the next cell. Reis couldn't see what was going on, but Ash was making enough noise to attract the attention of the soldiers.

"Do you like mythology, Reis?" Ash asked.

"I guess."

"I love it, almost obsessed with it. Pandora opened a jar that contained all the evils to be bestowed upon humanity. By the time she closed the jar, all that was left inside was hope."

Hope was something Reis could use right now. Except he couldn't recall a time he'd done anything spiritual to earn himself any favors in that department. Yet, if anyone deserved a break, it had to be him. If only he could tell people why. But revealing the truth would mean being disloyal to his mother. No matter her faults, he wasn't the type to blab.

"We'll call this bitch of a computer Pandora," Ash said, "and pray there's still Hope inside for us, because I really hope I see my wife and kids again. I got three daughters, you know. My eldest went to college to follow a boy and came home with a law degree."

"Kelly works in law," Reis said absently. "As a paralegal."

"That a fact? When this is over, we should get the two of them together so they can sue these sons of bitches." Then Ash began shouting. "You hear me, Pandora. We're coming for you."

Ash's war cry spread like a grass fire and within minutes the shed was abuzz with raised voices all shouting at the computer. Maybe the operators assigned to their pods could hear, but Reis guessed maybe they didn't, because nobody came to let them out.

After a few minutes, a team of soldiers arrived. One approached the front of his cell and dragged him out. Then he was escorted at gunpoint to a room with dim lighting. A woman sat behind a desk. She wore a cardigan over a stiff white uniform, like an old-fashioned nurse. Her hair was pulled back into a pony tail. Her face was concealed by a cloth mask, the type worn by desert dwellers. There was a plastic chair in front of the desk.

"Take a seat, Reis Anderson," she said. "It's good to see you again. It's been a long time."

Reis remained standing. The soldier who'd escorted him into the room raced over and pushed him into the chair, while a second soldier fastened straps around his wrists. A million questions tore through his mind. Where was he? Why was he being held against his will? Why would this woman say it was good to see him *again*? And how did she know his name?

He stayed quiet, reflecting on his hostage lessons, but nothing more came to him.

"In answer to your unspoken questions," she said, "you're being held in a quarantine building at the Center for Disease Control. You went missing two days ago and we sent out a search party to rescue you. Lastly, we know each other well. I've missed you."

It was as if she'd read his mind, which sent shivers across his flesh. Now that Ash had given the cyber-game's computer a name, he could at least identify with his real captor. Pandora.

His skull began to itch as if she – it was cliché but cars and boats were given a female gender, so why not the computer? – was poking and prodding her circuits around in his mind.

"I don't know you," he said.

The woman tilted her head. "We were close once. Before the plague. I'm ashamed of my appearance now. I used to be quite the catch, though you didn't think so. You tossed me away."

It sounded like something he'd do. He was always accused of treating women poorly, but never intentionally. He just couldn't give them what they wanted.

"Pretend I just woke up from a coma," he said.

"Very well." She stood up and moved over to the window. "Ten months ago a virus swept across the planet destroying half of the world's population. This branch of the CDC is humanity's last hope. We search for those in the early stages of the virus and bring them here for safe keeping. We protect the carriers, such as you and the other men in the yellow sector, from the bad deadlies, those who are tagged as blue. Mostly we put the yellow sector men to work to help feed and clothe those in the outer regions who are in the advanced

stages and just wish to die with their loved ones. We try not to
involve ourselves with destroying the bad deadlies. We leave the
dirty end of the business to nature. But our crowning achievement
lies in the work we spend our dying breaths performing. We're
rebuilding the human race."

The hairs on the back of Reis's neck bristled. He searched for air
vents and realized it was the NADs bringing his surroundings alive.
He shouldn't feel dread. He shouldn't feel fear. This wasn't real. Yet
he felt everything as if it were actually happening.

"I don't know what you're talking about," he said at last.

She slammed her fist on the table. "Why do you fight me? Work
me with to rebuild this world, Reis. We used to work well together."

He pulled at the restraints but they were on tight. Kicking his
legs, he imagined he was smashing through the glass lid of the pod.
It was impossible to be in two places at once, which meant if he
wasn't *here*, then he was somewhere else. But this wasn't happening
somewhere else. It was happening here. He was trapped within a
paradox.

"It's Candice Velmont." The look in the woman's eyes was fierce.
"We dated for almost a year in college. But you dumped me when
things got too serious."

If Pandora had picked his brain for memories in order to create
characters, it had messed up this one. Candice and Reis hadn't dated
for *almost a year*. It had been more like a month. And things had
never been serious between them. Though Candice must have
thought so, considering she was the woman accusing Reis of
fathering her child. Reis suspected Candice was just trying to get on
easy street, but she was going about it the hard way. Even if he *was*
the kid's father – which he wasn't – he had enough money behind
him to make the problem go away. And the problem would *have* to
go away. Stafford didn't like scandals.

For a second, Reis couldn't move. He hadn't told anyone, not
even Jack, the name of the woman who was causing him his latest
hell. Pandora couldn't be snaking her circuitry through his brain. It
was impossible. But how else could he explain Candice's presence?
Unless he was dreaming.

"What went wrong, Reis?" Candice asked, though in his mind he
heard Kelly's voice asking the question, and his mind traveling back
in time to a few days after his twenty-second birthday. Daniel and
Kim Minnow insisted on celebrating with a family dinner. Kelly was
twenty and living at home. Reis had moved out of home first chance,
but since he'd grown up an only child in a big house, he'd asked Jack
to share the two bedroom apartment with him. They attended
different classes in college and had different social schedules, but

Reis found that he was struggling with 'sharing'. Relief had flooded through him the day Jack had met a girl and moved out. This particular night, the three of them went out for dinner. Afterwards, Reis and Jack made plans to head into town to continue partying. Kelly wanted to join in on the fun, but she couldn't drink legally, so they went to Reis's apartment instead. Perhaps he should have insisted she go home.

She was drunk, way too drunk, and there was no way he could send her home in her condition. He'd be skinned alive by her parents. Jack received a call from a woman around midnight and refused to let his sister stay at his place. The only option was to stay over at Reis's, and a quick phone call to her parents was made.

Reis would have offered Kelly his bed to sleep in while he took the sofa, but his room was a mess. Growing up with maids had not taught him the value of housework. He couldn't put her in the spare room because it was filled with his musical equipment. So he brought a blanket to the sofa.

"How you feeling?" he asked as he placed a blanket over her.

She moaned. "Crap. I blame you."

He blamed himself too. To the slow beat of music on the stereo, he reached for her hand and stroked it. His head was beginning to pound. His mouth was dry. His stomach was churning. Nothing to do with the effects of too much alcohol; she just disrupted his living fibers. And because he didn't think she'd appreciate him saying he knew how she felt, he said nothing.

She surprised him with her question. "Why have you never asked me out?"

"You're my best friend's sister."

"Jack isn't the boss of me."

"There's a code."

She closed her eyes. He thought she'd fallen into a drunken slumber. Good, this conversation was becoming dangerous.

"I'm glad you never asked me out," she said.

"What?"

"My friends think you're hot. Well, you are hot. But you're also cold. And distant like a cold moon. Like Pluto. So far away that there isn't any warmth inside you. Sometimes it's like you're a robot."

He didn't know what to say, but he didn't feel like a heartless robot. Every inch of him burned to hold her, to kiss her, to caress her. Within minutes, she'd fallen asleep clutching his blanket to her chin. While he watched her sleep, his insides began to simmer in anger. If she had lived his life she wouldn't say such things. But nobody would ever feel sorry for Reis Anderson. Jewel had said so and she had been right.

His insides had started to burn with something other than anger. He'd never realized how much he wanted Kelly until she'd rejected him. For the next few hours he lay in bed wondering if he wanted her *because* she had rejected him. Confusion coursed through him that night, causing him to toss and turn, wondering whether he should wake her and tell her how he felt. Surely there was a clinical explanation for his inability to express his feelings. But he knew it was psychological. Nobody could live the life he'd lived and *not* be afraid to show emotion.

The next morning, he woke to find Kelly gone from the sofa. The post-it note on the fridge stated that she'd called a taxi. He'd never spoken to her about that night, and she'd never brought it up. But that night the seed had been planted. He had strong feelings for her. Good ones. He wasn't sure what to do about them. And so he'd done nothing. A few months later, she'd met Matt.

***

Candice pulled Reis out of his daydream when she slapped her hand against the metal table. "What happened between us is all in the past. I'm interested in the present. You carry the virus inside you even though you display none of the symptoms. If I'm jealous of anything it's your ability to live a relatively normal life. Still, contact with you can advance a person from yellow to black in less than a day. These women are our best hope at survival. Now, tell me the name of the woman, or women, you've had intercourse with. It's the decent thing to do."

He laughed out loud. "Lady, you're off your tree."

"I know you had sex," Candice said. "I'm not jealous, if that's what's troubling you. It's just unfortunate because we had hopes all the women would be returned to us clean. I hope she's still at level yellow so we can impregnate her." She picked up a pen from the desk. "Tell me the name of the one you infected."

"Impregnate her. Are you out of your freakin' mind?" He had to keep reminding himself that this wasn't real. What sort of sick bastard programmed forced impregnation into a game?

His insides quivered; no longer sure this *was* a game.

Candice tapped the desk with her pen. "As a carrier you are compelled to disclose any intimacies. It's not only the decent thing to do, it's the law. Her name?"

"Go screw yourself."

Candice leaned back to grab a buff-colored envelope off a table behind her. She removed a series of large photographs, which she deliberately turned face-down on the table.

"We will all die from the virus, Reis. It is irreversible. Some will die more horribly than others and we are close to perfecting a vaccine to at least ease a person's suffering. If you care for the woman you infected, you will tell me her name. I will see to it she receives this vaccine when her time comes. We are not monsters here." Candice sighed, causing her mask to puff out and reveal a glimpse of green flesh. "Not yet anyway. Now tell me her name. I know you were travelling with a woman. The patrol team saw you together."

"Pandora," he said through clenched teeth, "Get out of my head and stop this crap."

Candice snapped her fingers. A soldier stepped out of the shadows. "Her name is Pandora. Find her."

The soldier left and Candice took great pleasure in turning the photographs over one by one. She held them up like flash cards. "Lesions on the face that burn the flesh away. Eyes that rupture and drip with blood. A compulsion to eat one's own flesh, even their own lips. This is the fate that awaits us all. You've done the right thing by giving me her name."

A lump formed in Reis's throat at the image of Kelly being subjected to this mad woman's wrath.

"What happens now?" he asked.

"That depends." She let a finger run along the edge of her cardigan. "It's against the rules for you to have sex, but I could overlook it just this once."

"I'm flattered. But rules are rules. What if someone found out? I don't care about me, but what would they do to you?"

She tilted her head to stare at him. "You're mocking me, aren't you?"

"Not at all."

"I think you are. Just for that, I'm going to impregnate them all. Let God sort out who's the fittest to survive. You'll rue the day you ever crossed me, Reis Anderson."

That was when he remembered why he'd broken up with Candice.

***

After Reis was released, everything transgressed like it happened to someone else and he watched from above. He saw his body ushered into a shower stall where he was given a set of clothes. Then he saw the soldier prod him with the tip of his rifle, pushing him along the corridor. His feet dragged along the floor as he returned to his cell. Why couldn't he have kept his mouth shut? Now Kelly was going to cop the full wrath of Candice, and even though this wasn't real, it was still the sort of thing that would stick in his mind forever. And it would stick in Kelly's mind too.

It was now apparent to Reis that something was wrong with the computer. Not just malfunctioned, but evolving somehow. Why would the game conjure up an ex-girlfriend, and not just any ex, but the one who'd turned up out of the blue with a ridiculous claim that Reis had fathered her child? As well, the players were supposed to elect which games they entered. They were supposed to receive a briefing presentation by the Command Leaders. And they were meant to be games of a quest or a hunt or kill mission. Certainly they weren't meant to take part in acts of atrocities. This scenario couldn't be on the general menu.

Panic was clouding his judgment. Stafford would know Reis was here because a surveillance team was always on his tail. He knew a few tricks to lose them, and he hoped this wasn't one of those instances. Someone would get him out of here. But why were they taking so long?

Reis felt the soldier's boot push him inside his cell. Terror clogged his throat, constricting his chest, sending a stabbing pain along his arm.

"Reis?" Ash called out. "Reis?"

He couldn't talk. His tongue felt thick.

"Reis, talk to me. What happened?"

He'd witnessed people having anxiety attacks and he was sure he was having one now.

"Talk to me Reis," Ash demanded.

"Kelly's in danger."

"Then we'll have to help her."

"How?"

There was a *creak* and a *clang,* and when Reis looked up, Ash stood in front of his cell wearing a grim expression. He slipped the bolt from the door and held out a hand for Reis to take.

"Special Agent Ash Brogen at your service," he said.

"Is that supposed to cheer me up?"

"Do I look like I'm trying to cheer you up?"

Reis clutched a hand to his chest. It felt tight and he couldn't breathe properly. He had to take tiny sips of oxygen to curb the pain in his head.

"You okay?" Ash asked.

"Just give me a second."

Ash nodded. Then his head swiveled left and right. "The soldiers have gone. Maybe they're on a coffee break. We won't have long."

The pain in Reis's chest started to subside. He now found it easier to breathe, but his legs had turned to jelly. Ash pulled the latch on his cell and stepped inside. Reis looked at the man who had saved Kelly. He could have been anyone, even one of the crazies. But he wanted to help Kelly so Reis took the offered hand and lifted himself up off the floor.

Just before the two of them ran outside the hanger, Ash trotted back to open a few cells doors, and he instructed these men to free the others. Then he rejoined Reis and they bolted through the large metal doors. Once outside, they stopped behind a water tank to stare out across the compound.

"I count five buildings," Ash said.

"Guess we search them one by one. Let's split up."

Ash pressed a hand against Reis's chest and pointed up at the towers where soldiers patrolled. "They're watching outside the fence so we might be able to move freely inside the compound. But I think we should stick together. Better odds when it comes to a fight."

They stayed close to the wall as they sprinted across the graveled ground toward the adjacent building. The door was locked. The windows were high in the walls, most likely for ventilation only. They'd have to get inside to search so they sprinted around the back.

A soldier sat on the ground by the door with his back leaning up against the wall. He wore a piece of cloth across his face similar to the one Candice had worn. At his side was a rifle, rested up against the wall. The soldier was scratching his face. Reis bent down and scooped up a handful of gravel. The soldier stopped scratching, turned and saw them, and Reis tossed the gravel in his face while Ash lunged at the rifle.

"You know the drill," Ash said, aiming the rifle at the soldier. "Hands on your head. Down on your knees."

The soldier flicked his gaze between Ash and Reis. The man was probably close to death anyway, what real threat was a gun? But he must have decided that even a few more hours of life was worth more than none, because he complied.

"Let's check inside," Reis told Ash. "See if we can hide him somewhere."

Ash ducked inside and returned seconds later wearing a huge grin. "Couldn't be more ideal."

They dragged the soldier inside. The room was filled with caged animals – monkeys, dogs, cats, birds, rats, foxes.

"Someone's starting a private zoo," Ash said.

"It's a lab."

Reis avoided looking at the animals. The new Kelly might be too mentally euthanized to care, but the old Kelly would have been in tears at the sight of this place. Reis had always known there was a sensitive soul living inside her. Masks, everyone wore them, the superheroes, the villains, ugly, pretty, rich or poor, everyone had one. She used to scold him for tormenting Angus the turtle by placing him on top of the remote controlled car, even though Angus used to find the means to climb on top. She used to yell at him to turn off the DVD if ever an animal was being injured in the movie they were watching; no matter how many times he'd told her it wasn't real, she would give him the lecture on how the thought would lead to the act.

What must she think of this place?

"He'll shout for help," Ash said as he pushed the soldier inside a large cage.

Reis handed the rifle to Ash so he could pick up a cage that held a spitting ginger cat. He placed this cage on top of one containing several large parrots. Then he pushed this tower opposite a cage holding a Doberman. The noise the animals made would be enough to drown out any shouts.

They were about to leave when Reis got an idea. Everyone wore masks, even those inside a virtual game. Reis shouted at the soldier to remove the cloth. The soldier shook his head and when Reis waved the rifle at him, the eyes that stared back were scared, yet still human. At last the soldier lifted his mask.

The soldier's face was green and scaly. His lower lip was chewed off. His teeth were missing, probably from being pulled out to stop him eating the rest of his face.

"And I thought zombies were ugly," said Ash.

The soldier's eyes turned from sorrow to hatred. They told Reis that this man knew he would never be cured, never be normal, and he hated Reis for being disease free.

Of all the fates awaiting mankind, this was the one Reis feared was closest to the mark. Billions of dollars were spent each year developing the makeup of the war of the future. World War III would look nothing like the previous two World Wars. There would not be thousands of ground troops and tanks and overhead planes dropping bombs to decimate and destroy. Weapons of mass destruction were relics. The chance of a projectile hitting what it targeted was startlingly low. Futuristic wars would use technology. WMDs would be lethal bacteria riding on the backs of nanotechnology – missiles as tiny as specks of dust. And while this type of precision-guided missile was accurate in its targeting, it was as indiscriminate as any other weapon. Death by bacterial warfare was also painfully slow.

Stafford was on the Board of Directors of a group designing such technology. And he was hounding Reis to give up his chosen career and begin his training as the replacement Stafford. Seeing this man only made Reis more determined to fight his destiny.

As they hurried out of the shed, Reis copped a glimpse of the headline on the TV on the wall: DAILY VIRUS UPDATE. He decided to ignore the update. It wouldn't help save Kelly; it was probably designed to lead him on a wild chase for a cure.

"You want to watch this?" Ash asked.

Reis shook his head. "I've lost my appetite for playing this game."

***

They didn't get far before they walked into a line of prisoners chained at the hands and feet, the prisoners Ash had earlier set free. The soldiers spotted Ash and Reis and raised their rifles. The prisoners fell to their knees to escape the bullets. Reis took careful aim at the soldiers but they were using the prisoners as a shield. Ash cried out and fell to the floor. Blood seeped out of his leg.

"Go," he yelled at Reis.

Reis tossed the rifle at him. "Cover me."

Ash started firing and Reis took off, running blindly, but he made it outside and ran straight into another troop of soldiers who had their rifles aimed at him.

"Drop to your knees and put your hands on your head," a soldier shouted.

It didn't take lessons in hostage situations to know he wouldn't come out the victor. This time, when they secured him to the convoy of soldiers, they used more force and doubled the bindings. He could see Ash on the ground, but at least the soldiers were tending to his wounds, which told Reis that maybe these NPCs weren't programmed to kill the players. Not wanting to test this theory, he shuffled along with the chain gang.

Moments later, the convoy was ushered through a large warehouse and taken to a room with shelving that reached to the ceiling. Rows of benches took up the floor space, with men standing at the benches putting items into boxes. Reis was taken to the rear of the factory, unshackled, and pushed into an empty slot. The start of a new career had begun.

On the bench were mounds of soap, toilet paper, soup, beans, tinned fruit, flour. Reis had resisted his family's legacy of affluence whenever possible, but he'd never done factory work. Stafford had once said that honest work was great, but why do it if you didn't have to. Jack's father, upon hearing Reis repeat this, had made Reis climb up the ladder to help clean the gutters. Daniel Minnow had been the father he'd always wanted. It wasn't lost on Reis that he wasn't the father he needed. Yet, as he stared down at the items, he missed Daniel and Stafford equally, so maybe getting what he wanted was no better than getting what he needed. It sucked that he was trying to justify his presence in the game and convert it into a lesson to be learned. This was supposed to be fun. It was turning into the root canal of mental therapy.

A voice to his left said, "You better start packing."

Reis turned to see an Asian boy of stocky build, wearing a T-shirt with a dragon on the front.

"They'll whack you with their whacking sticks if you stop work," the kid said.

"Aren't you a little young to be here?"

The kid smirked. "Child labor never went out of fashion."

"I meant a little young to be in the game."

"I know what you meant."

"What's your name, kid?"

"It's not Kid."

The teenager glared at Reis like he wanted to tussle with him. Reis immediately liked him. He reminded him of his teenage self.

"Sorry if I offended you. What's your name?"

"Douglas Smith."

"I'm Reis Anderson. How old are you?"

"Sixteen."

A guy in front leaned back and whispered, "We can overpower them you know. There are three of them and twenty of us."

"Don't listen to him," Douglas said. "He's not one of us."

Every step of this game was leading Reis further away from Kelly. Maybe the guy was another decoy. Maybe Douglas was one too. Pandora was obviously still tapping into his head, pushing wires around to manipulate Reis into venturing off onto another quest of her bidding. The trouble was that Reis had grown up with parents who'd screwed up his head gear. What could Pandora do that hadn't already been done?

"If they wanted us dead," the man in front said, "they'd have shot us in the field."

It was true that their captors wanted them alive. Still, it was no guarantee of their survival. The motivation to keep a hostage alive or dead could change as quickly as the weather in Texas. For now, the nature of the game was to keep the players alive, as evidenced by the soldiers shooting Ash in the leg and treating his wound. If this were a real situation they might have shot him dead as a lesson to the others. Reis was counting on the NPCs being programmed *not* to kill, giving him and this stranger a good chance of overpowering the them.

"Don't listen to him," Douglas hissed. "He's not one of us."

Douglas withdrew the laminated pass from around his neck and waved it for Reis to see. It didn't mean a thing; Zeus and Casey had been able to replicate the pass on a whim. Still, right from the beginning he'd had a feeling that something was odd about Zeus and Casey. He didn't sense anything odd about Douglas. He was just a nerdy kid caught in a place he shouldn't be.

Deciding to place his trust that Douglas was telling the truth wasn't an easy thing to do, since research showed that in a real apocalypse trust, would probably get more people killed than whatever had wiped out civilization. But a leap of faith had to start somewhere.

The guy beckoned him over. "We can take them."

"I'll pass," Reis said. "Someone has got to look out for the kid."

Douglas opened his mouth to object and Reis shook his head slightly and held up his hand, keeping his focus on the guy. Now that Reis looked closer, this stranger was bigger and stronger and looked mean enough to do whatever the hell he liked to Reis's body if he decided to go off the program. If he was an NPC, he'd probably shut down and resume normal programming if Reis and Douglas just left him alone. Not that Casey and Zeus had shut down when he'd activated their programming. Everything was all screwed up, but he could deal with it.

A minute passed while Reis and the stranger matched stare for stare. Finally, the guy turned around to pack boxes.

Douglas was smiling. "That was a neat trick. How did you do it?"

"I'm a Jedi."

"No, really."

Reis shrugged. "I suppose mind over matter works in this environment. We're supposed to be able to imagine outfits, right?"

"It would be cool if we could control the game." For a second, Douglas's eyes lit up then darkened. "But it's not like I haven't tried and failed."

Factory work still didn't have any appeal, but the roaming soldiers were starting to harass any player not keeping up with the task of packing boxes. Reis angrily threw soup tins into a box half filled with toilet paper. Then he leaned over to Douglas and lowered his voice. "You had better not be a decoy."

"I'm not a decoy."

"I'm just saying... Anyway, you were here before I arrived. How do we get out of this building?"

"I've no idea. But I reckon they'll let us have a break soon enough," Douglas said. "They can't starve us. And when they do give us a break, I'm planning on sneaking away and tracking down an office. I'll hack into a computer, though it will only be an exercise in confirming my suspicions."

"Which are?"

"We are in dangerous territory."

"*That's* your theory?" It felt alien but good to laugh. "Sorry, I shouldn't laugh."

"It's okay. I can be king of the obvious sometimes." Douglas flicked a nervous glance toward the soldiers. "I've got a lot of other theories. They all have the same ending though. We all die."

Douglas started packing items into boxes, glancing every few seconds at the clock on the wall.

"We're not going to die," said Reis.

Douglas ignored him and continued stuffing the boxes with canned goods.

"You *do* know they're not going to give us a break and let us stroll about wherever we like," Reis told him. "It goes against the basic principles of imprisonment. We'll have to create a diversion."

Douglas's face turned white. "No. I don't want to die."

"We *can't* die. We're not really here."

"That's not true," Douglas said. "I've seen players go down and not get back up. Like the mainframe is broken. Or it might be the pods that are broken. But they didn't get back up. I swear it's the truth."

Reis studied the boy; he was about the same age when Jack had befriended him. He couldn't be completely innocent because he was in a game that was for over eighteens, but he also didn't give Reis the impression that he was a badass on any level. When Reis saw the way the kid's hands shook, he decided Douglas could use a friend. Besides, it felt good to be able to perform this random act of kindness. He hadn't had the chance to do this for a while. Too many external pressures were eating at his generosity.

"You reckon you can hack into the mainframe?" Reis asked.

"If it's there." Douglas sighed. "My other theory is that everyone has packed up and left us to die, and now we're ghosts in the machine."

***

It turned out that Douglas was right about the soldiers giving them a break; a bell sounded and soldiers came in and told everyone to follow them to the cafeteria. While the workers were forming a huddle, Reis pushed Douglas underneath a bench. The kid was concealed behind a pile of boxes and Reis waited until the soldiers were preoccupied with shackling the workers, then he also slipped underneath his bench. He waited for about ten minutes before he peeled himself out of the crevice. The room was empty.

"It's clear," Reis whispered.

"I'm stuck."

Douglas had managed to get his T-shirt hooked on a nail. It took Reis a while to pry him loose, and when Douglas emerged he started sneezing.

"Quiet," Reis hissed.

"I can't help it. I have allergies."

Reis grabbed Douglas by the arm and led him across the floor to a section where shelves were stacked to the roof with cartons of supplies. Reis put his finger to his lips and scanned the area. He looked up for CCTV cameras and couldn't find any.

"I have another theory," whispered Douglas, rubbing his nose. "We're in the technological singularity apocalypse disguised as biological disaster apocalypse."

"I have a theory too. You're a decoy sent to annoy me."

"How do I know *you're* not a decoy?"

"I asked you first."

"So what? Are you ten?"

Jack's parents had done their best to push Reis into adulthood. They'd given him college brochures to read, an old Ducati bike to fix up, left him in jail overnight to sleep off a drunken spree. Growing up had come by default, yet it had taken a scared, courageous, sixteen-year-old kid to make him *want* to act his age.

"Let's go hack into the computer," Reis said. "And no offense, but I hope you're wrong."

Every factory had an office, usually on a higher level so the bosses could watch over the employees. Reis located an office at the far corner, and right now it appeared to be empty. The workers and soldiers hadn't yet returned, but it wouldn't be long before they did. The weakness in their plan was the metal stairs. If the stairs creaked they'd be discovered. This time they might do more than lock Reis in a cell. They might exile him to where the bad deadlies lived.

He and Douglas took off across the cement floor and they reached the office undetected. On the desk was a computer which Douglas headed straight for and Reis peered out the window to the floor below.

"Found anything yet?" Reis asked.

"This machine is old. It's still starting up."

"I'm really curious what you think you can do from inside here. We're virtual characters."

"There are over two hundred million users connected to the internet," said Douglas, typing madly away. "I have to be able to talk to one of them."

"How? I get the concept of avatars but anything we do can only be applied inside this virtual world."

"We're jacked into cyberspace. We *are* the internet. I just gotta find a signal that I can talk to. Hello, I think I've got something."

Reis moved away from the window to stand over Douglas's shoulder. On the screen was a series of numbers – ones and zeros. "What does it say?"

"Not much. It's pretty quiet out there. Still, CyberNexis is a high-security building. They could have built a dead zone around it. Or they might have used metal lining in the walls to jam signals. Businesses are getting metal walls installed in meeting rooms to stop cell reception. I'm thinking of doing the same thing at home, since I know how easy it is to hack into things."

"Can you talk to anybody, or just hear the signal?"

"Dunno."

Douglas opened up the internet browser and typed in the word HELLO.

No response.

Next, he typed in his name and clicked on his profile page. The kid in the photo wore a Spiderman t-shirt and looked exactly like the young man seated at the computer. The computer was maintaining their images, but Reis had to wonder what signs of damage might be on their real faces after this length of time in stasis.

The most recent post on Douglas's page was dated three days ago. There had been nothing new since.

"It's like we're stuck in time as well as in cyber-space," Douglas said.

"What could cause a shutdown of the global network?"

"Terrorists knocking out the satellites with nuclear weapons. A meteor hitting the satellites. Ash cloud blocking the signal."

Reis began pacing. All sounded like plausible explanations yet totally unhelpful. "What do we do?"

"How should I know? You're the adult. You're supposed to have all the answers."

"Sorry to disappoint."

Down on the floor, it was still devoid of workers but it wouldn't stay empty for long. He told Douglas to follow him and they made it down the stairs and out of the building undetected. As they prepared to run across the compound, someone wearing a lab coat and a surgical mask bolted past them. Reis could tell it was Kelly by the boots she had stalwartly refused to give to a teenage zombie.

"Kelly!"

She stopped and turned. Pulled off her mask. Her face was green but not from disease. She looked ready to puke.

"Are you all right?" Reis asked. "What happened? Did they hurt you?"

"Hurt me? I can't begin to describe what they were going to do." She tore off the coat and ripped off the laminated pass around her neck. She kicked them both across the compound. "This game can go to hell. I want out. And I want it now!"

"There is no way out," Douglas said.

Kelly whirled on him, her cheeks flaring in and out. Reis grabbed her and pulled her into his chest. "It's okay. Nobody is going to hurt you."

Instead of struggling, Kelly sagged against him. He could imagine what she'd endured; Candice had told him about forcibly impregnating the women. He still couldn't believe the game programmers had actually written this circumstance into the script.

"You're safe now," he said again.

She pulled out of his embrace. Then she turned to stare at the vast expanse of grassland on the other side of the fence. "I know a way to be safe permanently."

She sprung free of his hold and sprinted across the compound.

"Kelly!"

Reis ran after her. The soldiers in the towers finally noticed her and were firing at the ground. She stopped about twenty feet on the other side of the fence and held out her arms, as if willing them to kill her.

Reis sprinted faster, feeling a pain in his chest. He would put his body in the line of fire, but just as he reached her, an orange ball of light exploded in front of him.

"Attention players." The voice came from the sky. "This is an emergency broadcast. The game is experiencing technical difficulties."

Stepping through the sparking embers were three figures. They were taller than Reis, maybe seven or eight foot tall, all white from top to toe, with white outfits and white hair.

The voice in the sky rumbled. "Please accompany the operators into the awaiting transports while management fixes this problem."

Ahead was a limousine – also white. Reis picked Kelly up in his arms and ran towards the limo. She was still sagged against him as he fed her into the limousine where she curled up on the leather seat and began to cry. He sat next to her, holding her hand. The limousine took off and Reis looked out the window. Douglas was getting into another vehicle.

Pandora had opened the jar and let evil unto man. By the time the jar was closed all that was left inside was hope. Reis *hoped* this ordeal was over. He also realized that Ash shouldn't have called the computer Pandora. He should have called her Bitch.

8

Reis

The limo pulled up in front of a lavish hotel, and because Kelly had fallen asleep on the drive over, Reis carried her in his arms up the stairs. Tapestries hung on gold-gilded walls, zebra print rugs lined the marble floor, and mahogany tables held floral arrangements and ancient artifacts. None of this impressed Reis. He was ready for a hot shower, a hot meal, fresh clothes, but he would forsake all the niceties to take care of Kelly.

An operator greeted him at the elevator and waved him into one, then promptly followed. She pressed a button for the eighteenth floor. She didn't say a word, just stood beside Reis while they rode the elevator up. It stopped and she motioned for Reis to exit. She slipped past him and waved a hand over a panel at room number 13. Reis carried Kelly inside and placed her on the sofa.

"Follow me to your room," the operator said.

"I'm fine."

"It is not a request. You need to be in your own space when the system is rebooted."

Kelly had roused. "What's going on?"

"This way, Mr Anderson."

"I'm staying here," he told the operator. To Kelly he said, "You're safe now. It's over."

"It doesn't feel over."

"Give it time."

"Please, Mr Anderson." The CGI woman's unwavering tone belied the urgency in her words. "You must come with me."

He whirled on her. "I am not leaving her side."

"Go," Kelly said. Her voice was hoarse from crying. "I want to be alone."

"Kelly."

"Please. I want to be alone."

"Kelly, none of this is real. Nothing that happened to you was real." He pointed at the CGI woman. "*She's* not real."

"Real. Not real." Kelly's emotionless voice tugged at Reis. "It doesn't matter. I'm never going to be able to erase what almost happened from my mind."

She rolled over to press her face into the back of the sofa.

"Kelly –"

"Go away."

His heart fell to the floor, and as he followed the CGI woman out into the hall it felt as if the operator had actually stepped on it. Once outside Kelly's room, the all-white woman smiled at Reis and told him that Kelly needed time alone, as if she knew what emotions were. The truth of it was that more and more people needed shrinks than were physically available, so this pixilated version of a shrink would be the future of human counsel.

The all-white woman gently pushed Reis into a stylishly decorated apartment a few doors down the hallway. French doors led to a balcony that overlooked a city skyline. There was a large LCD TV on the wall, a competition-sized pool table near a bar, and electric guitars were set up in the corner – Stratocasters and Gibsons and the kind that sold for bucket loads of money at auctions. Angus the turtle was wandering around inside a terrarium.

"You like the room," she said, as if this was a fact. "Dinner will be here shortly, Mr Anderson. I have taken the liberty of ordering you a double bacon pizza."

He heard the soft click of the door closing and then guitar riffs pumped out of hidden speakers. He wanted to pick up a guitar and join in but he headed for the bedroom instead. He sat on the bed imagining Kelly was doing the same thing, except she was dying inside. From the haunted look on her face, today's game had been particularly cruel.

Falling back on the bed, he didn't realize he'd nodded off until a knock on the door woke him. Pizza had arrived. He wasn't hungry – couldn't be hungry due to the mists feeding into the pod. But room service was persistent. They knocked louder and quicker.

Reis opened the door but the hallway was empty.

A creaking sound from a door further down the hall drew him out of his room. Standing in the corridor was like looking through a portal into another world. Smoke rose from the ground, cars were overturned, streets were potholed. He saw two human-sized, upright step out of a building and turn their gelatinous heads from left to right to survey the streets. A small group of soldiers in full battle gear shouted to the aliens and tossed grenades at their feet. The explosion took out half the building. The aliens clambered onto the rubble and fired their weapons at the soldiers, vaporizing them.

The scene was loud with explosions, gun fire, and overhead choppers. To the left, Reis spied two familiar faces, Casey and Zeus Novak, wide-eyed with fear. He should have slammed the door in the decoys' faces, but he couldn't stay angry at two non-sentient beings doing what their programmers had intended.

A grenade landed close by, and Casey screamed. The look of fear on her face was genuine which told Reis that these two NPCs did *not* want to get blown to pieces. He called out to them and they ran in his direction but it was too late.

A grenade rolled towards Reis. Before he could close the door, the grenade exploded and he was propelled backwards.

9

Reis

The office window overlooked a city skyline. From behind, someone said, "Reis. Are you listening?"

Reis used the reflection in the window to peer at the man with dreadlocks, denim jacket, and tri-colored pants made from helm. The man sat in a beanbag with a green drink sat on the floor beside him. According to the plaque on his wall he was Dr Zeus Novak, Reis's shrink for most of his adult life – since a few weeks after his fifteenth birthday when his best friend's house had burned down. A nonconformist who was against commercialism, yet the shrink was fine with sending Reis the bill. He was also Reis's future brother-in-law.

"Sorry, Zeus," Reis said. "Can you repeat the question?"

"I asked why you thought Pandora had put you in a virtual world and was trying to kill you."

"At two hundred dollars a session I'd hoped you could tell me."

Thirty stories below, the lights at the intersection changed from amber to red. People the size of Reis's thumb crossed the street. Cars crept over the white line on the road like race horses at the start gate. An ordinary day in an ordinary city for ordinary people. Ordinary for everyone except him. Ordinary people didn't confront psychiatrists with crazy stories about monsters.

"I'm seeing them while I'm awake," Reis said, barely recognizing the subdued voice as his own. "On the way over here, I counted two, maybe three."

"Zombies or vampires?"

Nothing derisive in Zeus's tone or expression. Nothing that suggested he believed this story either. But theirs was not meant to be a relationship based on secrecy.

"Actually, it was more like twelve," said Reis.

It still brought a chill to picture the young zombies tearing at the limbs of an elderly zombie, and the elderly zombie had done nothing to fight back.

"Any headaches?" Zeus asked. "Many people who experience visions suffer headaches or a stabbing pain behind the eyes. Any sort of physical pain at all?"

"No headaches. No pain."

The shrink scribbled on his notepad.

"Okay, so maybe they're not visions," Reis said. "But they're not dreams either."

"I didn't say they were."

"And I haven't been abducted by aliens."

"You can't prove that. Dude, they have devices to wipe your mind."

Reis suspected Zeus of using humor to put his mind at ease. He'd have rather his shrink just gave him some of the dope he kept stashed in his desk drawer. Reis returned to gazing out the window, thinking on the day he'd first stepped into this room, almost thirteen years ago. Then, he'd felt as if he couldn't go on with life. He'd been fifteen and his two best friends had died in a house fire. Dr Novak Senior had taught Reis to accept what had happened and move on. Two years ago he'd finally said goodbye to Dr Novak Junior and this office, seeing Zeus socially since Reis was dating his shrink's younger sister, Casey. Reis hadn't found the will to live; he just hadn't let the fact he couldn't find it stop him from getting out of bed each morning.

"You're reminiscing," Zeus said. "What are you reflecting about?"

"Reflection? Is that what they call nightmares these days?"

Reis closed his eyes briefly and saw the flames that had engulfed the attic. He could still feel the hand on his back; someone had pushed him out the window and he'd rolled down the roof, falling two stories to the ground, breaking his ankle and wrist, but coming out of the ordeal with his life. Unlike his two best friends. To this day Reis couldn't tell if it was Jack or Kelly who'd saved him. In the nightmares that followed, he sometimes dreamed it was Jack, and other times he dreamed it was Kelly. It didn't matter who saved him; the guilt for each death weighed as equally on his conscience as if he'd grabbed his two best friends and tossed them aside on his way to escape.

"I haven't dreamed about the fire for a long time," Reis said.

"The zombies must be triggering the memory." Zeus's face remained impassive. "Tell me about them."

"There were five of these undead monsters reflected in a store window and when I turned around the street was empty. But their growls lingered like ghosts whispering in my ears. On the ride over, I saw four more at the bus stop. They attacked an old zombie, tearing it limb from limb. Nobody saw this, but I did. And then the zombies turned to look at me... with hunger in their eyes." The room was suddenly cold. "I know zombies aren't real, but I can't shake off the feeling that they exist."

"I meant tell me about your friends."

"Oh."

"But talking about the monsters works too. So the creatures you saw on the way over, are these the same creatures from your dreams? The dreams where you're in an apocalypse and you have to gather items to survive and then you have to kill things."

They'd never discussed monsters before – always guilt and self-loathing. Could Reis trust the counsel of a man wearing hippie clothing and living an alternative lifestyle? Reis was from a family mired by appearances, wealth, popularity, success. Zeus must have despised Reis, though he never let on.

"I didn't recognize any of them," Reis said at last. "Zombies are zombies, right? Reanimated corpses on the hunt for the living. What's a zombie apocalypse without a few thousand zombies? And what is an apocalypse but an unveiling of something hidden, such as guilt."

"Except, in your dreams Kelly and Jack aren't zombies," Zeus said. "They're your allies. And these are only games you're playing." Zeus consulted his notes. "You said, 'The Apocalypse Games is a virtual game where you survive end of the world scenarios'. You said they were created as recreational entertainment as well as for use in combat training."

"I guess."

"What I find odd is that your subconscious registers zombies aren't real yet it creates a fake world within a fake world."

"Who knew I had so many layers?"

Zeus rubbed his eyes. A sign Reis had learned that he was testing his shrink's patience.

"What techniques did you use to get rid of these images?" Zeus asked.

"The usual. I closed my eyes and told myself they weren't real."

"And this technique worked?"

The chill returned. Even with his eyes wide open, an image of the doorman at the shrink's building exploded across his vision. On the way up, the doorman had held his hand out to welcome Reis inside. His hat shadowed his face, yet Reis's breath caught in his throat when he saw the green flesh. He imagined him as a soldier from his dreams.

That had been thirty minutes ago.

"I know what you're thinking," Reis said.

"You're psychic as well? Okay. What am I thinking?"

"That I'm tired from overwork or stressed about the wedding."

"Let's go back to these dreams. Why did you step inside the —" Zeus consulted his notes once more "— what did you call them? Simulation pods."

"It wasn't a pod. It was a massage bed. Casey insisted I get a massage to relax."

"Massage beds don't have glass lids. So the pods from your dreams—"

"They're not dreams. They're visions." When he closed his eyes he saw his body hooked up to wires, bashing on a glass window. A symbolism of the feeling of being trapped. It didn't take a shrink to point this out to Reis. Yet he couldn't explain why he felt trapped.

"So the pods from your visions then," Zeus said. "Tell me about them. Why would you get inside one?"

"Because they were there."

"Did you and Kelly date as teenagers?"

The question, although not new, still shocked Reis. "I was fifteen when Jack and I became friends. Kelly was thirteen. Her father would never have allowed her to date at that age. I know I liked her, but I wasn't interested in a girlfriend. Not a boyfriend either before you go down that road. I was swathed in apathy and contempt, as you well know."

"How are the plans for the wedding coming along? Or should I not ask?" Zeus gave Reis a knowing smile.

"You should know. She's your sister."

"Now you know why I'm thinking stress is the cause. *Because* I know my sister."

"Casey is doing what any bride-to-be does. Making everyone on the planet crazy."

Zeus tapped his pen against his notebook. "Okay, so if it's not stress, I wonder about the significance of these dreams now. Why not years ago?"

The exact thought had consumed Reis for the past few days. If his shelved-away guilt was dragging its ass out of the dark recesses of his mind and coming home to roost, why create a metaphor of elaborate ways to destroy monsters? Why not just give him the answers?

"Did you know you can stop an invasion of zombies by luring them into a swimming pool and then throwing in bags of cement?" He didn't wait for Zeus to respond; it was a rhetorical question. "They don't have very good motor neuron skills so they thrash about which agitates the cement. Kelly and Jack helped me battle them."

"Kelly and Jack from your dreams or from your childhood?"

"From my dreams. They're both adults now."

Zeus wiggled his way out of the beanbag to get a fresh cup of juiced green goo. "I'm also curious why you're picturing Kelly and Jack as adults. They died when they were teenagers."

Zeus waved a cup at Reis. He shook his head. Ever since the dreams, visions, or whatever had started, he'd increased his intake of coffee, alcohol, diet cola, chocolate. Stimulants kept him awake. A healthy juice was likely to put him to sleep where the nightmares were worse. But the visions, which were now affecting his waking hours, were just as bad. He felt like he was fighting a battle he was not destined to win.

"Are you imagining them as they might be today because you want them at the wedding?" asked Zeus.

Reis hadn't thought of it like that. "I blame myself for their deaths," he said. "It's possible I feel bad they'll never get to have their happy ever after. It's possible I'm imagining monsters because that's how I think of myself."

"But in your dreams you destroy the monsters."

"Not all of them. I survive."

***

As Reis opened the door to his apartment, the scent of garlic and onion floated from the kitchen. Casey was home early. Probably Zeus had called her to say he was worried about him. He found her in the kitchen, where she poured beer into a glass and pushed the glass his way.

"How is my brother?" she asked. "Has he agreed to be your best man yet?"

"You know getting him into a suit is going to be impossible."

"I'm sorry if I'm causing you any stress."

He ruffled her pixie-blonde hair, then stopped suddenly, unsure why he'd done that. Shouldn't he have kissed her?

"What's for dinner?" he asked.

Casey returned to the pan on the stove and stared into it as if it were a deep well. "Garlic and onion... I think. That's the length of my culinary skills I'm afraid. I haven't had time to learn."

Reis feigned annoyance as he grabbed a store-bought jar of tomato and basil sauce from the pantry and an unopened packet of spaghetti. Casey was slim and attractive; he obviously wasn't marrying her for her cooking skills. But he wasn't a cook either, so it was either this or starve.

"I'm going to take a shower," he said. "Try not to burn down the apartment."

He let the hot water steam up the room while he stripped out of his jeans and shirt. He tossed them on the floor, but at the last second he tried to recall if Casey had complained about his leaving dirty clothes on the floor. It seemed like something a woman would nag him about, but his mind was blank. He left them on the floor out of habit.

He heard a noise and spun to see a shadowy figure standing inside the shower stall. In a flash, the figure disappeared. Zeus had said stress was usually the trigger for memories to resurface. Reis had argued that he wasn't stressed, but he must be to see things that weren't there. He got in the shower and forgot about the vision.

He couldn't say how long he'd been under the water, but Casey called out that dinner was ready so it must have been at least ten minutes. As he reached for the towel, he saw a dark shape, reflected in the foggy mirror. It was a soldier's face. It wore a gas mask. The soldier ripped the mask off and revealed a mouth wired shut. The soldier's bottom lip had been chewed off.

Casey came through the door at that moment. "Honey? Are you coming for dinner?"

"Don't you see it?"

"See what?"

"The soldier. His face is... scaly, green, half of it is missing."

"You're hallucinating."

She whipped out her cell phone and called Zeus who arrived at the apartment within minutes, as if he'd suspected something like this would happen and had been hovering outside the building. Casey wrapped a dressing gown around Reis and led him to the sofa. She ducked into the kitchen and returned with a glass of bourbon. No ice. Reis downed it in one gulp and asked for another.

"I think we should try hypnotherapy," Zeus said.

"You always want to test the latest fad in shrink warfare on him," Casey said hotly. "I won't allow it. What he needs is rest. The wedding's in two days. I'll call his boss and say he won't be returning until after the honeymoon."

"Hypnotherapy will help him. And it's not a new fad. It's a proven method of therapy."

"It's dangerous. What if it dredges up painful memories you can't suppress?"

Reis didn't mind that they argued as if he didn't exist. Right now, he wanted to slide down into the sofa and go to sleep for a long time. Lethargy pulled at him.

"He has concussion." This voice spoke inside his head. *"Don't let*

him sleep."

Reis opened his eyes. Zeus and Casey were still arguing. The voice from his head hadn't been either one of theirs.

A sense of déjà vu washed over him. For a second he wasn't sure that he knew the people in the room with him.

"All right. Let's give it a go," Casey said. "The wedding is two days away and Reis is a mess. And for what we're paying the photographer, I'm not having a single captured-moment ruined."

Moments later, Reis sat in the chair, now dressed in track pants and t-shirt, though he couldn't recall getting dressed. Zeus sat in the armchair opposite. Casey sat on the floor holding his hand. Reis's vision blurred and when he took a closer look, Casey was sitting beside Zeus on the arm of the chair. Someone else was holding his hand. He felt the pressure but couldn't see the cause of it. He suddenly felt light headed. Maybe he *did* have a concussion.

"Close your eyes and think of a quiet place," Zeus said. "It might be an open field."

"Not a field," he said quickly. Images jumped into his head. Soldiers in masks, buses filled with people, screams lashing through the air.

"Okay, not a field," said Zeus. "It might be a beach. Listen to the soothing sounds of waves lapping against the shoreline. Or picture yourself in front of a campfire. Picture it and tell me what you see and what you feel."

"I'm on a beach. Perfect weather. Not too hot, not too cold. The sun is warm. I hear seagulls, waves crashing."

"Good. What else do you hear?"

"Nothing, just the gulls, the wind, the waves."

"Focus on the soothing sounds. Open your arms to pull the sun down to you. It's bright so keep your eyes closed. But not so bright that it hurts. Even though your eyes are closed, you can still see because the past is in your mind, not in front of you. Do you understand?"

"Yes."

Behind his eyelids were bursts of orange. He saw a face. One he recognized from his visions. Jack Minnow.

"Reis! Are you all right? Are you hurt? Answer me. Did the grenade get you anywhere?"

"Why are you haunting me?" Reis asked the vision.

"He sounds concussed, Jack. We shouldn't move him."

Now there were two faces, Jack's and Kelly's. They were both grown up, not the teenagers who had died in the fire.

"Who do you see?" Zeus asked.

"My friends, Jack and Kelly."

"You mean the two people your mind is telling you are Jack and Kelly. They're dead. They died in a house when you were a boy."

"Yes, that's right. They're dead."

But the people in his vision didn't act dead. They continued to speak to him:

"Who's dead?"Kelly asked.

"Get up, Reis. They're coming. We don't have time to lick our wounds."

"Come on! We have to get out of here?"

"I didn't mean to start the fire," Reis said, relieved that he could finally admit the truth. He had kept this secret for so many years. A weight lifted off his chest. He felt as if he was floating on air.

Kelly's voice came from far away: *"Jack, what's he talking about? What fire, Reis? You're not making any sense. Hang on. I'm going to find a med-kit."*

"You told me Jack started the fire in the attic," Zeus said, though Reis struggled to tell which voice was real and which was not. "The flames engulfed the foldout ladder and the only way out was through a small window. You were pushed out through the window but nobody else made it out."

"I wanted revenge," Reis said. "I wanted to show everyone I wasn't a whiny rich kid. So I went up to the attic to make a bomb. The attic of the Minnow's house seemed the perfect place to build it, but then I heard footsteps and panicked. Jack's head popped through the opening first, then Kelly's. I tossed the cigarette into the corner and it lit the gunpowder."

The far away voices came again, this time a little louder. Reis was almost pulled into their dream world:

"He's delirious." This from Jack. *"Talking about a fire in the attic. We never lived in a house with an attic. And he's talking about cigarettes. He's never smoked."*

"He must have knocked his head on the wall. We can't let him fall asleep, Jack. God knows where he'll end up or in what state."

"Reis," Zeus said, so loud that Reis flinched. "I'm going to bring you out of hypnosis. When I count down from three you're going to wake up inside your apartment. However, before you wake up I want you to vanquish these monsters from your dreams. Do you hear me?"

"No more vampires or zombies."

"Exactly. And one more thing. I want you to say goodbye to Jack and Kelly. You won't be seeing them in your dreams again."

He watched his hand reaching out to touch the faces of the visions and he told them goodbye.

"Three," Zeus said.

"Stay with me, bro," said Jack.

"Two."

"I'm sorry," Reis whispered, letting the visions of Jack and Kelly fade into nothing.

"One."

Reis woke up in the apartment. A sense of loss tugged at him, like he was grieving his two best friends all over again. But he pushed this sensation down to the dark vaults of his mind. He wouldn't let them hold him back anymore.

***

Reis didn't bother to argue with Casey when she insisted he stay home from work. The desire to go was lost anyway. He was excited about their honeymoon, though the visions were causing amnesia because he had no idea about their travel plans.

The next morning, Casey buzzed around the kitchen making toast and coffee. She insisted Reis relax on the couch and read the newspaper. He didn't argue with that advice either. She brought him breakfast, flicked the TV onto the music channel, and he wondered why it had taken him so long to get involved in domestic bliss.

Of course, he realized this was a trap the moment she snuggled up against him.

"Honey," she said coyly. "I think we need to go shopping for a suit."

"But I have a suit." *Did he?*

"Yes, but now I want chocolate-brown for the men."

She smiled and somehow he forgot to be angry that she'd tried to manipulate him. But the toast was dry and the coffee was warm so if he went with her to the mall he might be able to grab a decent breakfast.

On the way out, a photo of his parents on the wall captured his attention. He stared at the smiling couple in the photo, trying to figure out what was wrong with the picture.

"You okay?" Casey asked.

"My parents aren't happy."

She laughed and her hand reached up to her throat. "Of course they are. And they're super excited about the wedding." She ran a finger along Reis's chin, stroking his stubble. Her voice lowered and she winked at him. "I know a way to help you relax."

Reis's body stiffened. He was suddenly afraid of being close to her. He hurried to the front door.

THE APOCALYPSE GAMES - PANDORA

"Zeus will meet us at the mall," she said. "We'd better get there before he realizes I've dragged him under false pretences. I told him you'd had a relapse."

The mall was a fifteen minute drive, though the clock on the dash must have been broken because it indicated that no time at all had passed. Reis was keen to grab a coffee and bagel, but like a man who'd been bludgeoned over the head, he followed Casey to a place where she could make him buy yet another suit he'd never wear again. She ushered him into the change room. He had his doubts about chocolate-brown.

"Thanks so much for doing this for me," Casey said, slipping into the change room with him.

"Whatever makes you happy," he said.

Her eyes widened and a smile broke out on her face.

"*You* make me happy, Reis," she said. "You've no idea how much. I don't know how long we'll have together, but I'm going to cherish every minute."

It was an odd thing to put a limit on their time together, yet Reis also felt as if time was running out.

"I do love you," she said.

She gazed up at him with expectant eyes, but the reply was trapped in his throat. He wanted to reply that he loved her too; he must have loved her if he was marrying her. But something prevented him from saying the words. He put his shyness down to being in a public place with a bald man running a hand up the inside of his leg to ensure the size was accurate.

"Your mom rang me earlier," Casey said. "She tells me she's inundated with calls about the wedding. Mothers of the bride are often the talk of their neighborhood."

"Jewel is already the talk of the neighborhood. She drives down the street and women hurry to lock up their husbands."

"You shouldn't say mean things about your mother. At least you know your parents. Zeus and I don't have any."

"Sure you do. Their names are —"

His mind struck a blank. Of course he knew their names.

"Reis, are you all right? You've been vague all morning. Every since... Did Zeus zap your brain with his mumbo jumbo? I swear I'll kill him if he's done any damage to your mind."

"I'm fine. I just haven't eaten, that's all."

"Oh, look at me being selfish again. I'm a horrible cook and you'll starve if you don't eat."

She told the bald man at his crotch they'd take the suit and then she dragged him to the café. Being midweek, the place was quiet. Just Reis and Casey, and one other patron; a large, black guy wearing a beige trench coat, which Reis found odd since it was a warm day. The guy was as tall as Reis, but built like a footballer. Reis kept his eye on him the whole time. When the guy tipped up his coffee mug, Reis saw it was empty. His chest gave a squeeze. The guy was casing the mall.

"Let's walk this off," he told Casey.

He pulled Casey in behind him and kept an eye on the guy in case he jumped up and produced a gun. If he wanted hostages, the guy should have gone somewhere with customers. It hit Reis that maybe this guy needed only *one* hostage. The kind of hostage guaranteed to bring him a retirement fund. A kind of hostage like Reis Anderson, son of Jewel and Stafford Anderson.

Reis stormed out of the café, but when the guy didn't follow, he immediately felt ridiculous, as if this guy was just another of his imaginary friends. He was imagining a lot of things lately. Something was wrong with him, possibly a tumor. It was the only explanation for the hallucinations and the ache that throbbed at his neck and back of his head.

"I've got to take a leak," he told Casey.

"Must you say it like that?"

"It's how I always say it."

Except he wasn't so sure of any of his habits or common phrases.

The guy in the trench coat followed him into the bathroom. His mother had warned him that rich kids were kidnapped for ransom money. She'd also warned him about perverts. This guy could be both. He could also be selling religion. Reis wanted none of whatever this guy was peddling so he reached for his cell phone.

"Go ahead. Call the police," Trench Coat Man said. "You won't get through."

He punched in the numbers anyway.

"I'm telling you. This is a fantasy world and you're cut off from outside communication."

Reis got a busy signal from 911, which was impossible. Even if he had no cell service in the mall, emergency numbers still worked, as long as the phone had battery charge. He knew this because twice a year he held a charity event and badgered the guests into donating their old phones, which he then delivered to local women's shelters, homeless shelters, youth hostels, low income families, and senior citizen's home. It was the single most important thing he did all year. And yet it meant nothing because he still went home the same person.

"Reis!" Trench Coat Man was practically shouting. "I've come to tell you to wake up."

Recognition triggered in Reis. He copped a whiff of familiarity, but where he knew this guy from escaped him.

"Did you fix my car recently?" Reis asked.

"It's me. Ash Brogen. You're dreaming and you need to wake up."

Reis washed his hand under the faucet, all the while scanning the room for a way to escape. There were no windows. The basins were fixed to the floor and wall.

"You're dreaming, Reis. Those two people you're with, they're not who you think they are."

"Who? Zeus and Casey?"

"They're decoys. You've already been played by them in the zombie apocalypse. And now they're playing you to keep you trapped in this... this dream state."

"I'm not dreaming. I'm having visions. Big difference." Two hundred bucks an hour had confirmed this. But why was he arguing with his would-be captor? It would only make the guy angry.

Ash sighed, his head dropping to his chest. "I didn't want to say this, but I figured out it might be possible to talk to you through a meditative state. I have three daughters and a wife and they make me do all kinds of crazy chick stuff."

Ash did have three daughters and a wife, but it was odd that Reis knew this when he'd never met the guy before.

"You should get help," Reis said. "I know a good therapist."

"This is a dream. Don't believe me? Your name is Reis Anderson. You're in a virtual game. You and me were in a cage and we were tagged with yellow paint."

Reis shook his head and backed up a few steps. This man was crazy.

"You've got to trust me," Ash said. "Those two are dangerous."

"And you're not?"

It was going to be difficult to get past the giant man, but luck was on Reis's side when another patron entered the men's room. Reis used this moment to dash through the gap in the door, but the big guy followed him out, calmly at first. When Reis started jogging, the big guy chased him down like he wanted to bring Jesus into his life.

"This is the dream?" Ash shouted. "Take a good look at your perfect world. You'll see the cracks. You'll discover what's wrong. Those two make you feel happy and complete, but I'm telling you, they're designed to keep you away from Jack and Kelly."

The mention of two dead friends brought Reis to a halt. Maybe this guy could get information about him off the internet, but what had happened to Jack and Kelly was part of a sealed record.

"Jack and Kelly are dead," said Reis.

"Wrong. If you think they're dead it's because those two planted that suggestion in your mind. They want to keep you trapped here.

It's a death dream. You've got to wake up."

Someone called out to him and he saw Zeus and Casey running towards him.

"You have to cut the link," Ash said in a hurry. "And you have to do it soon."

"How?"

This one simple question opened up more. Why would he believe this stranger over his fiancé? If this was a death dream did that mean he was dead?

"Take control of the dream," Ash said. "Tell yourself this isn't real. Tell *them* they're not real."

Ash took off running before Reis could tell him that if Casey and Zeus weren't real, then neither was Ash. And why would Ash run off scared? But Ash hadn't 'run off'. He'd disappeared.

Casey and Zeus were now only a few stores away. Reis checked his phone again for service. Still nothing. He scrolled through the history in the phone. It was empty. No registered calls. No text messages. No list of people in his contacts. The phone had been erased. But why?

***

Later that night, lying in bed, Reis's head hurting from trying to remember things like Casey's birthday, his home address, how he'd gotten from the mall to bed. He'd also become fixated on the plastic tiara propped on the dresser. The words 'blushing bride' were aglow from the light coming from the bathroom. It was a trinket from Casey's bachelorette party. He let the bright lights seep into his consciousness, yet he struggled to recall *his* bachelor party. Was it a week ago? Two weeks? A month? What did he do? Did he go to his parent's holiday house and have a huge party? Did he go to Vegas with the boys? *Who were the boys?*

An arm trailed along his back and weaved onto his torso. The gesture should have warmed his insides, instead it chilled him. Every effort to remember details of their life together ended in a thick fog.

He lay on the bed, stiff like rigor mortis was settling in, adding to the theory that he was dead. He listened to the sounds of domestic bliss – a clock ticking, the gentle breathing of a sleeping beauty, trucks in the distance. The sheets were scented in a fragrance he couldn't detect. The digital display on the clock read 3:21 a.m. It never wavered. Minutes passed. Then an hour. Still 3:21 a.m.

Everything seemed to be happening in real time, yet what had occurred was a load of blank pages, as if his mind was slowly being erased.

When he couldn't stand staring at the clock anymore, he found himself sitting in the darkened living room on the couch. Casey wandered out of the bedroom and switched on the lamp.

"What are you doing?" she asked him.

"I don't remember buying that TV," he said.

"That's because we didn't. It was an engagement present."

"From who?"

"Zeus."

"I don't believe you."

She scowled. "What's wrong? You're scaring me."

The antique dining table captured his attention. As an antique, it should have had a story behind it, but he didn't know it. The cushions on the sofa were black velvet; not his choice, but surely he'd recall Casey bringing them home. There were curtains on the windows when he knew he preferred blinds. And where was his collection of Batman figurines?

Other items of décor confused him. The glass bowl on the coffee table was filled with shells, yet he had no idea who'd collected them or the last time he'd gone to the beach. Angus the turtle was also missing. Everything in this room was alien to him. Including Casey.

"Come back to bed," she said, her hands twisting around the engagement ring on her finger.

"I don't remember buying you that ring. I don't remember anything."

Suddenly this lifestyle suffocated him. He got up and charged toward the front door.

Casey chased after him. "Honey. Where are you going?"

"To find a bar and drink till I remember."

"Okay, but I have to warn you, it won't work."

Reis pulled open the door and crossed the threshold...

And entered the living room. Casey stood by the sofa, illuminated by lamplight.

"What's going on?" he demanded. "What sort of trick are you playing? Have you and Zeus drugged me?"

"I told you it wouldn't work." She fell into the sofa. "You can't leave."

"Of course I can leave."

Reis turned and ran through the front door...

And he ended up in the living room, only this time both Casey and Zeus were sitting on the sofa.

Zeus lifted his hands in a sign of defeat. "It's like Casey said, dude. You can't leave."

"But it's okay," Casey said. "We like this world. We like you."

It was ironic that the man he'd thought was coming to kidnap him had instead been coming to warn him. These two were dangerous all right. They'd drugged him and were holding him captive until Jewel and Stafford forked over the ransom money. They resembled none of his previous captors, which only meant that Jewel was right to warn him that the evil people who wanted to hurt him looked just like regular people.

At least now he'd find out if he had any value at all to his parents.

***

"Please don't be mad," Casey said. "This isn't our fault. Pandora did it."

At the mention of Pandora, the fog in Reis's brain began to clear. Like a setting sun, the moment was ending and with it would come a new time. One that wouldn't stand still and he felt as if the clock had started to tick again.

But this time was a crazy time. The land of crazy decisions that led him to be trapped inside a virtual game. His last recollection of the game was of a limousine ride to a fancy hotel, someone had knocked on the door, he'd gone out into the hall and found himself in another world.

"How do you know about Pandora?" he asked, rubbing at his head.

Casey bit her lip. "We can kind of read your mind. Just a little bit. Snippets here and there. Who's Kelly?"

Reis burst out laughing. It made sense now. At least as much sense as this fantastical situation could make. He was hard-wired into the computer and it had conjured up an image of Candice. And now it was conjuring up a world where he was getting married. If the computer was born at the time of the malfunction, then a few days might give her the intelligence of a young girl who might like to play dress-ups with her toys.

Reis stopped laughing. It didn't sit well with him to be considered a toy for the computer to mess with. "So if you're connected to Pandora, why has she got me dreaming of this world?"

Casey sighed. "We really have no idea. I believe this is what's called a death dream, which means you died in the game and your consciousness has been put into limbo until you can be slotted into a new game. Don't ask me how she does this. And don't ask us how to get out because we don't know that either."

"What *do* you know?" Reis asked.

"We know we're safe here," Zeus said. "Nobody wants to kill us."

Reis could understand why they'd want to keep him here. If he woke up, they'd be thrust back into the world of senseless violence. The problem would be what happened if he didn't wake up.

He stepped though the front door, and once again found himself in the living room, only this time he was sitting in a dining chair and ropes were restraining him around his chest and feet. Zeus and Casey stood before him, their eyes wide. They huddled together like a pair of frightened children. What had they to be frightened of? They were his captors.

"Let me go," he said through clenched teeth.

Casey's voice shook. "We're not doing this."

"Pandora," Reis shouted. "Let me go."

He heard a far off giggle, like that of a child playing hide and seek. "When I find you, I'm going to cut every single one of your wires."

"Stay calm," Zeus said. "You'll only hurt yourself. Or us."

"Untie me. Please."

Zeus's eyes flicked left then right. In a quiet voice he said, "What if she punishes me for helping you?"

"Who? Pandora?"

The NPCs were acting like frightened children. The mainframe computer was acting like a spoiled child. Nothing in Reis's kidnapping training had prepared him for abduction by children. He could possibly help his situation by *not* treating them like adults.

"If you untie me, we'll get ice cream."

The promise of a treat worked on Casey; she hurried to untie him. Zeus hung back, his unwavering scrutiny of the apartment indicating his reluctance to summon Pandora's wrath.

"Nothing bad will happen," Reis told Zeus. "You can't actually die. In fact, you're far less likely to suffer real damage than the players."

"Getting killed feels real enough," Zeus said.

The moment Reis was untied, he stretched his arms and legs, but he didn't get up out of the chair. The urgency to get back into the game had fled, to be replaced by curiosity. If he was having a death dream, then he must have died. Yet there were no wounds nor was he experiencing any pain. Perhaps he was no longer in the game at all.

***

Casey leapt up from the sofa and said, "Before this ends there's something I want to do."

She ducked into the bedroom and returned wearing her wedding dress. It was a typical wedding dress – white, floor length, lacy. There were tears in her eyes. What harm could be done by indulging in her fantasy?

"Go get the suit," Reis said.

"Might as well get mine too," Zeus said with a resigned sigh.

Casey squealed and ran back into the bedroom, returning with their suits. The two men slipped out of their clothes while Casey had her back turned. When they'd finished, she was crying so hard, Reis wondered if he would ever figure women out.

"I didn't mean to make you cry," he said.

She shook her head. "They're tears of joy. I've never experienced them till now. I'm just a little overwhelmed, that's all."

"Well, you look beautiful."

While Zeus took photos of Casey using Reis's cell phone, Reis found a bottle of wine in the fridge and poured three glasses. They'd raised their glasses together and had taken their first sip when there was a knock at the door.

"Did I lock the door?" Reis asked.

Casey shrugged. "I didn't know you needed to."

The second series of knocks were louder and angrier.

"Don't open it," whispered Zeus.

The knocking turned to loud thumping. The door shook with the impact. After a loud *crack*, the door flew open and Ash stood in the doorway holding a shotgun in his hands. He aimed the gun at Zeus.

"Reis, get away from them," Ash shouted.

"Wait. Ash. It's not what you think."

"Not what I think?" Astonishment washed across the big guy's features. "You're dressed up for a wedding."

"You've got it all wrong. Casey and Zeus are innocent. It was Pandora who trapped me here."

Ash lowered the gun, but only a little. "I believe Pandora trapped you. But these two did nothing about setting you free."

"What would *you* do?" Casey asked hotly. "It's a warzone out there. But in here, why it's heaven."

"You kept him against his will. That makes him a prisoner. And it's wrong."

"I'm free to go," Reis said. "I'm just not sure I want to."

Ash lifted a hand off the rifle long enough to rub his chin. "I can understand why these two want to hide inside your mind, but it's dangerous for you. We're already in trouble from the length of time we've spent inside the pods. You've got to come back to the world you belong to or you'll get cyber madness."

"Have you found a way to end the game?" Reis asked.

Ash shook his head.

Reis nodded. "Well, there you go. Either way I'm screwed. Might as well get drunk."

Ash stepped into the room and lifted the gun an inch higher. "You have to come back. Jack and Kelly need you."

"They don't need me. They never have."

"Okay, you need them."

Reis laughed. "I wish that were true. You don't get to be me without developing a sense of segregation and superiority. I don't mean to be smug. My father drilled into my head that everyone was beneath me. It took a while to get that train of thought out of my head. But what's left is a well of emptiness that I can't fill and neither can anybody else. Alcohol's the only thing that does a half-decent job."

A loud *boom* made him jump. Zeus dropped to the floor. Blood spurted out of his chest.

"You shot him," said Reis, shock and revulsion washing over him. "What the hell did you do that for?"

Ash glared at him. "We're running out of time."

Casey ran to Zeus, calling Ash every name under the sun. She picked Zeus up to her chest. A second *boom* caused her to fall in a heap over Zeus's body. Blood covered the carpet.

"You asshole," Reis shouted. Nothing in his training had prepared him for this. "Stop shooting them. They didn't do anything."

Ash aimed the gun at Reis. The third shot deafened him. Something hit his chest. Then it was dark.

10

Reis

Reis woke with a jolt.

Kelly was leaning over him. Her face lit up with relief. "Thank god you're okay."

God had nothing to do with it; Reis was alive because he couldn't die, though he wished he could. The gun shots still echoed inside his head. The image of Casey falling on Zeus played over and over in his mind. Puddles of blood. Pools of sorrow. Nothing would ever be the same now that he'd witnessed firsthand their senseless deaths.

His eyes adjusted and the setting turned from carpet to concrete, from furniture to shelves, from coffee to gasoline. For the first time, Reis knew the pain that others spoke about. His ribs and back ached. He could barely breathe. He'd twisted his ankle and pain shot up his leg. But it was his chest that hurt the most. He'd taken a liking to Casey and Zeus and they'd been shot for no reason, because Reis had wanted to stay.

"You were thrown against a wall when the blast wave hit," Kelly told him. "It knocked you unconscious so we dragged you into a basement."

Jack was standing up on a crate to stare out the window. Ash was in the corner, leaning up against the wall with his eyes closed. Kelly gave Reis a reassuring hug then moved off to shake Ash awake. If Reis could have gotten up off the floor he'd have gone over and beaten the big guy over the head. First chance he got, he'd get back at Ash. Revenge was the last of the free things in life. Reis had not come here seeking purpose, but he'd found it. He'd play this game the way it was intended. Kill or be killed.

"Wake up, Ash," Kelly said. "We've got him. He's back. It worked." Over her shoulder, Kelly said to Reis, "You were unconscious. Ash found us and he suggested we try astral projection. It's not something that usually works for him, but in this world where anything goes, I guess anything went."

"How long was I out?" He ran his hand over his body, searching for gunshot wounds. Nothing. Just the ache from being thrown against the wall. He should have been elated at his immortality, yet it was another reminder that the longer he stayed in the game, the harder it was going to be to return to reality. For all of them.

"You were gone for a couple of minutes," said Kelly. Reis tried to sit up but she gently pushed him back down. "Rest. You took quite a hit."

"Do I want to know where I am?"

"*You* probably do. I, on the other hand, wish I could be unconscious and escape this nightmare."

"You don't want to go there."

Yet she did, he could see it on her face.

Ash awoke and Reis began to crawl his way over. His fingers dug into the concrete, tearing at his fingernails. Good. The sharper they were the better they'd be at tearing out Ash's eyes for what he'd done.

"You're a jerk," Reis said.

"I had no other choice," Ash said quietly.

Kelly flicker her gaze between the two men. "Whoa. What the hell happened between you two?"

Reis fumbled around for a weapon. He found a chunk of cement with rebar and threw it at Ash. "Get him out of my sight."

"You would have done the same thing," Ash said. "You're worth more to us than they are.

"Stop it." Kelly was shouting, her face turning red. "We have more important matters to attend to."

Reis kept his eyes locked on Ash. "They didn't do anything wrong."

"That's enough," Jack said. He jumped down off the crate and threw a backpack over his shoulder. He took a map out of his jacket and fiddled with a radio which was clipped onto the outside of his jacket and linked to his ear. He acted like he knew what he was doing. Reis had never seen him so serious. "We've got to move. Another group of infantry aliens just landed in Sector B. We have to get to the armory before those things find it."

"Which idiot died and made you the boss?" Reis said with a scowl.

Jack stormed towards the door. "All of them."

And then the wall exploded.

INSIDE THE SIMULATION POD

PRESENTATION BY
COMMAND LEADERS JONAS BARRETT AND STEPHANIE GEY

Command Leader Jonas Barrett:
Greetings players.

If you are watching this presentation, humanity has undergone a major catastrophe, though it is yet unclear why sixty years ago humans began dying before reaching sexual maturity. Suffice to say the numbers of human survivors have dwindled due to the inability to create new life. As well, there are no more adults so lives are lost daily due to disease, malnutrition, lack of hygiene, and lack of education. Children inhabit and rule the new world while their numbers continue to decline. At last count there were less than a million children left on the planet. Most are aged between five and twelve.

Command Leader Stephanie Gey:
If you find yourself in the midst of an age apocalypse you will need to prepare a panic bag before making your way to the nearest safe zone.

Your panic bag should contain the following items:

Medical kit, face masks, gloves, disinfectant wipes. Disease and bacteria will be rampant.

Junk food and candy may be considered as valuable sources of bribery. Research shows that in a world without adults, children will eat what they like. And let's face it they like junk food.

Weapons for self defense. Don't underestimate their barbarism. Scientists predict their brains will begin de-evolving to those similar to Neanderthal man.

Bottles of drinking water to sustain you on your journey to the safe zone. Crackers, nuts, dried fruit, energy bars.

Rope, batteries, torches, whatever you can use to travel at night.

Rope and tin cans can be an effective perimeter warning.

Pantry foods such as tinned food, pasta, flour, sugar, and rice.

Fire lighting tools for cooking and heating.

Seeds to grow crops for future communities and to improve overall health.

We at Simulated Military And Recreational Training have designed this program because we are committed to the survival of the human race. As a result, we have put together the following tips for players encountering an age apocalypse.

Command Leader Jonas Barrett:
Quite right, Stephanie. Adult humans are nonexistent. It's possible the children are neither curious nor rational. They will selfishly defend their turf. Without adult supervision it's predicted they will have gone wild, almost to the point of being de-humanized. Only once you have established a secure community and commenced repopulating the planet can you venture out to make contact with the intent to re-humanize them, though scientists also suggest you'd have better chance at taming a pack of wild wolves.

Without schools, they will develop a minimalistic language. Without forms of authority they will regularly ignore leaders so don't go in there with the attitude that you can whip them into gear.

Command Leader Stephanie Gey:
The tips don't stop there, Jonas. I have a few more to help the players:

The children will live in small groups of about five or ten, never more than twenty as this will be too unmanageable.

The smaller children may never have overcome their fear of the dark so traveling at night is recommended. You might also make noises to deter them from venturing out into the dark.

There is no electricity or clean water or food. The same places you source food and bottled water are the same as the children. And since they have no cooking skills they will head for the same aisles in the supermarkets for packaged items as you. They will often be nomadic, moving from one area to another once the source of food runs out. What food items they find will be guarded by the elder children who won't hesitate about killing to protect stores. They have not developed their reasoning skills and at this stage it isn't considered they will ever.

Your presence will be viewed as a threat and you must avoid interaction with the children of the apocalypse at all costs until your numbers outweigh theirs and even then you may need to use force to bring order and regulation.

Command Leader Jonas Barrett:
Good luck players. And stay alive!

Command Leader Stephanie Gey:
It breaks my heart to hear you say what needs to be said.

Command Leader Jonas Barrett:
They might be kids but this isn't playtime. Welcome to the apocalypse. Let's hope you survive.

11

Kelly

Kelly Lawrence was picked up by a figurative tornado and dumped into the nightmare version of Oz. Ten feet away sat a rusted swing set with broken seats, a sand pit filled with rubble and junk, and a teeter-totter broken in half. Litter might have danced on the breeze except that there were layers of dirt and weeds bogging it down.

The playground was situated in a park half the size of a football field. The grass was overgrown and weeds sprouted out of every crack or bare patch. A maintenance crew hadn't been here for a long time, and with no adults around to coax, cajole, bribe, or nag, no maintenance was likely to ever occur again. Three sides of the park were surrounded by woodlands. Lantana vines crawled over the trees, turning the woods into forest glaciers. On the fourth edge was a row of houses. Broken windows. Overgrown garden beds. Lawn that reached the windows. Junk and rubbish were strewn across the driveways.

This end of the world didn't have any trace of Matt's imprint. It was cold and unfriendly. And judging by the presentation she'd watched as her figurative tornado had whirled her around inside its maelstrom, it was also designed to test her morality like no other game had so far. She was glad this setting didn't remind her of Matt; what sort of sicko would program a game where the premise was to kill children?

Kelly's skin crawled with the sense that she was being watched. When something flashed in the corner of her eye, she spun to find Ash Brogen standing a few feet away.

"We've got to stop meeting like this," he said. "People might start talking."

"What, no Special Agent Ash Brogen to the rescue?" she asked.

Kelly hadn't come into the game expecting to make friends, but she'd found one in Ash.

He shrugged. "I gave up the badge. Nobody cares."

"I do. What happened between you and Reis?"

Ash winked at her. "What happens in a death dream stays in a death dream."

His happy features crumpled fast. She'd noticed that it was getting harder for the players to maintain good spirits. There were moments when Kelly was the cheerful one in the group, and that was saying something.

A loud *crack* rang out, followed immediately by a *ping*. Something had hit the frame of the swing set. Kelly looked back towards the houses and saw a child standing in a driveway; he wore a brown jumper and brown pants, but this could have been the product of years of accumulated dirt. He couldn't have been older than eight or nine. He held a pistol in both hands like he'd been trained to shoot from inside his mother's womb.

A second *crack* then a *ping* as the bullet hit the teeter totter. Closer than the first bullet. The kid was adjusting his aim. He wouldn't miss a third time.

"Run," Ash shouted.

Kelly and Ash took off across the park to seek cover in the woods, but as they neared the tree line, a handful of grubby faces poked out from within the dense thicket of trees. The sun reflected the glint of steel. A bunch of kids stepped out from the trees and swung knives and swords through the air. Ash and Kelly veered right and ran for a copse of trees at the darkest corner of the woods. Here, the lantana was thickest, and it offered a hiding spot to watch the park and the houses. But it also meant something could be in the woods surrounding them and they'd never know.

"Kids with weapons." Ash shuddered. "What sort of sick world is this?"

"I guess it's because they don't have adults to protect them," she said. "They have to do it themselves."

"So if one kid decides to steal another kid's toy he's going to lose an arm." Ash shook his head. "I'm sure glad they're not in my house. My girls are always fighting over makeup."

Kelly peered across the field, searching for the kid with the gun. He was no longer standing on the driveway. Didn't mean he wasn't watching her. She still couldn't believe he'd shot at her. But she knew that not all kids were interested in candy and toys. Some were as evil as their grown up counterparts. On the days these cases came to court she made it a mission to be assigned somewhere else.

"There's something like fourteen million people with hunting licenses in America," said Ash. "These kids might never run out of ammunition."

"While we enter the game empty-handed."

For this particular game, entering empty-handed was a good idea. She didn't need a career in law to know that killing children was wrong. Although there were players that might not agree with her. And she'd thought the previous game was brutal.

"We should go," Ash said. "Do as the presentation says and make our way to the safe zone."

This was a different Ash to the one she'd met that first day. Then, he'd been eager to run headlong to adventure, and she had to admit she was relieved that he had restrictions on who or what he'd kill for the thrill. But that line was getting close to their toes. Would he still have that same conviction when he was faced with choosing who died?

"Where do you think is the safest place for us to hide?" she asked.

"Old folk's home. Vegetable garden. Dentist's."

He was joking, but he had a point. Since these kids were armed, Kelly stood a better chance of not having to act in self defense by finding somewhere that kids didn't want to go.

"I always hated anywhere in the dark," she said, looking up to the sky. The sun was directly above which meant there was another six to eight hours at least before nightfall. She might not have to play this game at all. Reis had proven that dying inside the game took you to another place, and she was convinced she'd find Matt. But the idea of being killed still struck a chord in her. And the idea of killing herself even more so. The human will to live was simply too strong.

"We'll survive *not* killing them by staying out of their way," Ash said.

He headed into the forest and Kelly followed. The Lantana vine was thick, and Kelly wished they had a machete or a sword. But that could indicate that she might need it to protect herself. She didn't want to give herself any reason to cross the line Pandora was drawing. What made the notion of self defense almost impossible to bear was how easy it was to forget that this wasn't a real world. Overhead, birds cried out. Underneath, twigs snapped. In the distance, insects chirped. She brushed her hand along a vine and felt the different textures. Cool, wet, even sharp as her finger traced the edge of a leaf. The ground stank of rotted vegetation baked by the sun. Flies buzzed around her face.

It all seemed *real*. Considering she'd lost her sense of bearing days ago, perhaps this was the real world and the life she knew before this was the fake one. As if she'd woken up from a coma. In which case Matt wasn't dead. But if this was real and the old world was fake, then Matt would never have existed.

"I don't know what real and what's not anymore," she said,

surprising herself with her out-of-the-blue statement.

Ash stopped and looked her straight in the eye. "It's possible the end of the real world *could* see children survive and live separately to adults, and these children *could* become experts in warfare. In which case, there is the real possibility that adults would have to defend themselves against children. But not here. Not now."

"So why are we running? Why don't we try to communicate with them?"

His eyes hardened. "We're supposed to die in the game and get rebooted back in. But it's not the case anymore. We die and experience death dreams. And I don't want to go through that again. I'm gonna sit this game out, avoid the kids altogether, avoid having them kill me, avoid having to consider killing them."

Kelly bit down on her lip. In contrast, she wanted to experience the death dream because she was convinced she'd find Matt in this limbo land. It shamed her that every opportunity that came by to get killed, she was too weak to let it happen. Her fight for survival kicked in and overrode her intentions and there never seemed to be a scenario that felt right to die. She didn't want to get mauled to death or eaten to death or die of a horrible biochemical disease.

Perhaps she hadn't really thought her decision through. But there was a point to *this* game, it was staring her in the face. The point was to survive. Get out. Go home. Survive this world. Survive the real world. How did you eat an elephant? One bite at a time. Her dad had taught her that.

"They must miss their parents," Kelly said, once more surprising herself that she was admitting her fears out loud. She had maintained a level of concealment for most of her adult life, and this mask was slipping away. But she couldn't help it. Her chest ached with longing for her parents. Her chest also ached with the pain they must be feeling. She hadn't exactly told them she was going to hook herself up to a giant computer. Her parents would be frantic by now; they'd have called the police, the hospitals, they'd have called Jack and discovered that he was also missing.

This last thought almost caused her to double over. Her parents had barely coped with a grieving daughter. How were they meant to cope with the news that both their children were missing?

Ash sighed. "My family doesn't care where I am."

Kelly waited for Ash to elaborate. He didn't so she prodded. "Why do you say that?"

"My wife wants to leave me. It's the reason I'm here. I've got nothing left for me outside. Let's keep walking. Get as far away from trouble as we can."

It seemed his efforts to evade trouble had only landed him in more. She wanted to ask him how that was doing for him so far, but she knew how it felt when people wanted to dig around inside your mind and you didn't want them to. She stayed quiet; she could wait until he was ready to talk. Overcoming grief always took longer than anyone wanted.

It felt as if she'd walked for hours, but the sun only traveled a few inches across the sky. Finally, Ash held up a hand. "Wait. Do you see that?"

He pushed aside a branch. Ahead was a clearing about an acre in size and a wooden hut sat in the middle. Dotted around the property were the rusted shells of cars and farm machinery.

"It might be a trap," Kelly said.

"It's most definitely a trap."

When Kelly thought she'd had enough of sweat dripping down her neck and insects nipping at her face, a man appeared in the doorway of the hut. He carried a rifle and it was aimed at ground level. He stopped at the edge of the patio, twisted his head left then right then left again, and with a determined look he charged down the steps and around the back of the hut.

"That's Zeus," Ash said. "He's a non-player character, though not like the usual NPCs. He has a sister, Casey. She must be close by."

"I thought all the NPCs were children."

"They are children."

The voice had come from behind. *How is everyone sneaking up on me?* thought Kelly. The players didn't stand a chance if they couldn't move around the game unpatrolled.

Kelly turned to find a short, slim woman with pixie-blonde hair aiming a gun at Ash.

"I ought to shoot you," Casey said, her blue eyes boring into Ash's.

"I know I deserve payback," Ash said. "But please don't shoot me."

"Give me one good reason why."

"I'll give you loads of reasons. I did it to save a friend. It's meant to be *players* who rule this game. Plus, I don't want another death dream."

Casey lowered the gun. "I do wish you players would stop dying. Zeus and I keep flitting in and out of your dreams. Some are mean. Some are nice, like the dream *your* boyfriend had." She winked at Kelly. "You are one lucky girl."

"I don't have a boyfriend," Kelly said. "And how do you know who I am?"

"Aw, unrequited love." Casey stifled a laugh. "Poor Reis. I know who you are because I know all the players. The data came with the upgrade."

"What upgrade? What are you talking about? Why are you holding us hostage? You've got to let us out. I have to get home."

Casey shook her head. "I don't have time to explain but I can assure you that I'm not the one keeping you here." She stared levelly at Ash. "It's Pandora's will."

"You know about Pandora?" Kelly asked. She shouldn't have been surprised. The parts on a car all operated in collaboration with the other parts.

"The little shits who chased you here will come looking for you," Casey said. "I suggest you come inside the cabin where you'll be safe." She brushed past them and over her shoulder said, "I don't know who dreamed up this setting, but shame on them."

Ash moved as if to follow Casey but Kelly grabbed his arm. "What's going on? What does she mean about Reis and unrequited love? Is she talking about me?"

Ash looked away. "I don't know if I should say anything."

"Ash, please. What does she mean about unrequited love?"

He shrugged his shoulders. "I have no idea. All I know is when I found Reis, he and Casey were getting married."

"And you shot her for that?" Kelly let out a singular laugh. "She should get a medal. Do you know how many women's hearts he's broken because he can't commit to a relationship?"

"Casey seems to think he cares about you."

"Don't be absurd. Reis only cares about himself. Besides, my husband is dead. I have no room in my life for love."

Kelly didn't have feelings for Reis. But she once had. A teenage girl's crush on the gorgeous boy her brother had brought home. But Reis was a royal cad. Meaner than Jack had ever been to her. He'd once sweet-talked her into watch the movie "It" by Stephen King. Afterwards, he'd donned a clown mask and terrified the life out of her. She'd steered clear of him after that, even if she'd still secretly adored him. As she grew older, she never quite trusted that he wouldn't do something like sweet talk her into going out with him only to turn around and break her heart.

It didn't make sense that Reis should experience unrequited love since he barely tolerated Kelly. She saw the way he looked at her. She'd never done anything to earn his wrath.

Halfway down the track, Casey turned around. "Are you coming? Unless you want to stay out here and face the kids. In which case you'll need this."

Casey tossed her gun into the air and Ash caught it one handed. Kelly decided she'd rather be inside the hut. She followed Casey down the track and into the house. The cabin had wooden floors, wooden walls, wooden roof; aged to gray with disuse and dotted with wood rot. Half of at least two walls were nailed together by planks or pieces of tin sheeting. The windows had been boarded up with whatever materials the occupants had found lying around. The furniture was made of plastic and rusted metal. Years of dirt covered every surface. The place stank of decay. It was still better than being outside where kids with knives and guns wanted to kill her. Just as Kelly picked up a dust-filled ornament from the table, Zeus walked inside the hut. He immediately raised his rifle at Ash.

"Put down the rifle," Casey told him. "I've forgiven him. You can do the same."

"You shot my sister," Zeus said to Ash. "I'll never forgive you."

Casey moved to stand in between Zeus and Ash. "This is Kelly," she told her brother.

Zeus took one look at Kelly, dropped the gun, and in two strides he was standing in front of her. He wrapped his arms around her and almost crushed her.

"It's a pleasure to meet you," Zeus said.

"Settle down," Casey said. "She doesn't know Reis fancies her."

Zeus released his hold on Kelly and when her feet touched the ground her stomach tightened into a ball. Things had gone from frightening to weird. She'd gotten used to people talking about her situation behind her back, but discussing them in the open was something new.

Any discussions on this topic were put on hold when something banged against the outside wall.

"Little shits," Zeus said, ripping open the door. "That's the last time they'll throw rocks at my cabin."

***

"Zeus. Get back in here," Casey shouted. "Aw, to hell with it. This is my home, too."

She muttered a few curses, swiped a pistol off the table, and ran out the door after her brother. The door slammed shut behind her. Shots were fired. Kelly ran to the window to peer through a crack in the boards. Less than fifty feet away were hundreds of children; double the pack size the presentation had alluded to. Kelly wanted to picture them as cherub-faced angels, sweeping model planes through the air and pushing dolls in prams along the sidewalk. But these kids carried sharpened rocks and shields. They grunted and chanted, and some shouted war cries designed to inflict terror. It worked. Kelly was gripped with fear.

Zeus stood on the porch with his rifle aimed at the crowd. At least he shot over their heads.

This only enraged the kids because they charged towards the cabin.

Zeus lowered the rifle and shot directly into the crowd. Kids fell to the ground. Other kids threw rocks at the cabin. One hit Zeus in the head.

Zeus fell and Casey jumped off the porch and ran onto the field. She fired shots repeatedly into the crowd of children. As each one fell, bile rose up in Kelly's throat until her head swooned.

Ash picked up a rifle and poked it through the window.

"What the hell are you doing?" Kelly shouted.

"Shooting those two crazy idiots."

For a second she'd thought he might be shooting at the kids. Players weren't supposed to kill other players, yet she'd almost reached for a gun to shoot Ash to stop him committing such a heinous crime.

Objects hit the outside of the cabin and Kelly didn't know who'd fired or what was hitting the outside, bullets or rocks, but she knew she couldn't stand another minute of this fight. She covered her ears with her hands to block out the gunfire and the screams.

"The kids have overpowered Casey," Ash shouted. "I'm not going to shoot a kid just to save her."

But what would he do if the kids made it into the cabin?

More gun fire. More shouts.

"They've got Zeus. Shit, they're coming this way."

Kelly leapt up to pace the cabin. The dilemma of this game was hitting home. Shoot to defend, or die horribly at the hands of killer kids. She found herself doubled over in the corner dry retching because she hadn't eaten real food for days. This isn't real, she told herself. Whatever she did would have no consequence.

Rocks were pelted at the hut, splintering the wood. A large rock smashed into the window, almost shattering the flimsy board. No matter how hard she internally debated the ethics of killing virtual children, she always came back to the same conclusion. What if this was real? Wanting to die in order to experience a death dream had been her goal, yet her sense of self preservation had refused to let her walk into the line of a bullet. She'd defended herself because those who'd wanted her dead were the true monsters.

But these monsters were children.

"What do we do?" she asked Ash.

He looked as miserable as she felt. "I can't have another death dream. And I can't kill children."

She wondered why he was so afraid of the death dreams. Ever since Matt had told Kelly that players who died in the game could enter a limbo land where their dreams came true, she'd had her heart set on being with Matt. The way Ash talked, his dreams were nightmares.

He guided her to the far side of the cabin.

"When my wife told me she was gonna leave," Ash said, "I kind of went crazy and told her that if she left she'd be dead to me. It was the last thing I said to her. It was a stupid thing to say. Totally not true." He took a deep breath. "I died in the zombie game, and when I woke up Leanna and me were at home and arguing. She told me she's gonna leave. This happened in real life, but this time, I think I have a chance to make amends, so I don't tell her she'll be dead to me. Instead, I tell her that I'm going out to cool my head. So I drive around for a bit. Then I decide to head home to apologize. I'll beg her to stay if I have to. But when I get home she's dead on the floor. Not just dead, she..." his voice broke and he closed his eyes.

"It's okay. You don't have to tell me," Kelly said. She knew how hard it must be for him to talk about it.

He kept his eyes squeezed shut. His voice was hoarse as he said, "She had killed the girls first."

"Ash. That's awful. No wonder you don't want to relive that nightmare."

"*Again*," he said, opening his eyes. "I've had the same nightmare twice now. I can't do it *again*."

"But it isn't real." Which hurt in a way, because Kelly had been counting on the death dream feeling real. She didn't want to just *see* Matt, there were photos for that. She wanted to hold him, kiss him, hear his voice rumble against her shoulder as he held her in his arms.

Another rock smashed into the window. The back door, which had been temporarily braced before the fighting outside had started, now opened an inch. She could see children on the other side pushing at it.

Just when Kelly made the sign of the cross to beg forgiveness for what she was about to do, there was a loud crash. A large 4WD burst through the back wall.

Three soldiers jumped out of the vehicle. They did a quick visual survey of the hut, then one soldier hurried over to the window where he ripped off the board and fired into the crowd. The *rat-a-tat-tat* of repetitive gunfire should have drowned out their screams, but Kelly could hear them inside her head. The sound would live there forever.

Numbed by the horror, she didn't realize she was being shuffled into the vehicle until it backed out of the cabin and drove off into the woods. The 4WD had five seats in the rear and two up front. She sat on the back seat with two soldiers in the front and two more in the back, facing her. Ash sat beside her. She reached for his hand and gripped it tight.

Finally, she studied the faces of her rescuers. They were teenagers. But were they friend or foe?

"You is safe now," the soldier seated opposite her said. His name tag on his shirt said STEPHENS.

The truck bounded through the bush, bouncing over logs, knocking down saplings, smacking into branches. When she reached for the seat belt, Stephens laughed. He and the kid next to him – his name badge read DRAKE – seemed to get a thrill from being thrown about like loose luggage.

"They were children," Kelly said to Stephens.

He shook his head. "Not children."

"So what are they?"

It was Drake who answered. "They not growed up."

A world without adults meant no need to learn proper English. She'd have to force herself not to correct them, and since they weren't real what was the point of investing her time on educating them? It would also be easy to justify her actions if she could convince herself of their un-realness.

What a cop out. What an unbelievable line of defense. Dear Judge, I killed them but it's okay, they weren't real.

Drake reached into his shirt pocket and she flinched. He paused with his hand in his pocket, studying her with a hint of a smile on his face. Then he produced a stick of gum and waved it in her face.

"Take."

"No thanks," she said.

Drake shrugged, and popped a piece into his mouth. While he chewed, Kelly scrutinized him. As a teenager, Jack had never done anything without there being an ulterior motive. He'd offer to clean her room, but only if she gave him money for the movies. He'd steal her DVDs and offer to return them if she did his homework. These kids had saved Kelly, and since they were teenage boys they'd have an ulterior motive. But what?

Strapped in by the harness, Kelly was saved from hitting her head on the roof of the car interior each time the driver launched the 4WD over a fallen log. Yet the boys cheered and laughed, and one of them started a tally. When she hit her head against the window, they burst out laughing and added her to the count. She found she couldn't get angry at them. Something as simple as this childish play was the most normal she'd felt in a year.

The vehicle continued to plow down trees and the boys continued to whoop and cheer at each knock to the head. Kelly had earned four points by the time the truck stopped.

"Home," Drake said.

It occurred to her that maybe they'd abducted her to do the housework. She would be their Snow White. Her body may have been lying in a glass coffin, but this was not a fairy tale. Nothing in this virtual world was as innocent as a childish story.

Everyone got out. Drake beckoned to Kelly and Ash to follow. Perhaps they'd only saved them to kill them. But she didn't get the impression these kids were anything like the ones back at the cabin. Drake pointed up into the trees. The canopy blocked out the sun but Kelly could see a wooden structure halfway up. Drake whistled and a large pile of rope landed at his feet.

"Up," Drake said.

"I'm not climbing up there," Kelly said. It was too high, too risky, and just looking up was spinning her head. She'd never seen the fascination in tree houses, not while her room was beautifully decorated with pictures of horses and dogs, and not while it was indoors with plumbing and kitchen nearby.

Ash picked up the rope. It was fashioned into a ladder.

"It seems a hideout is exactly what we were looking for," he said.

Or it could be where they took all the people they saved only to kill them slowly and painfully, though it made more sense to build their torture chamber on the ground.

Kelly took hold of the rope ladder, but her feet wouldn't budge. Once more she looked up. Heights had never interested her. Nor had adventurous activities, but Matt had often told her she should try new things at least once. Even if she never did it again, she could at least say she'd done it. A wave of sorrow washed over her and she fought to keep it at bay. Now was not the time to dwell on the list of things Matt would never do.

She took hold of the ladder but paused with one foot on the bottom rung.

"Safe," Drake said, giving a tug on the ladder.

"No such thing as safe," she said.

Stephens whispered into Drake's ear. Drake nodded then handed Kelly his gun.

"I think he wants to guarantee your safety," Ash said. "Besides, if they so much as look at you the wrong way, I'll toss them out of the tree house."

Kelly closed her eyes. They'd misunderstood. Safe wasn't a gun in a pocket to protect against assault. Safe was a world without evil people. And that world didn't exist. It still made her stomach churn as she recalled how she'd had to walk out of a court session when a perfectly normal looking person had been brought in for sentencing, charged with stealing dogs to use as bait in dog fights. Cruelty and death for the sake of money. What a horrible world to raise children in.

And this was the product of a horrible world. Horrible children.

Kelly pushed the offered gun away. Safety was a sham.

It took a few steps to get used to the swing and pull. Halfway up, she looked down and realized she could let go and she'd be free to slip into her death dream, but she found that she was curious to know what the boys had intended by rescuing her. This was the first time in a year she hadn't dwelled on her grief. A surge of guilt hit her that she could forget about the grief in exchange for a few minutes of curiosity. And since none of this was real, and her grief *was*, she felt as if she'd insulted Matt. But she was halfway up the ladder and it was too late to go back.

The climb wasn't as hard as she'd expected. Up top, it was dark and the fresh pine air was delightful in its effect to counteract the filth the teenage boys had generated. Tattered sleeping bags were piled atop one another in one corner, empty food packets were piled in another corner, inches of dust covered the floor, and cities of cobwebs covered the cornices. Kelly went on high alert for sights of rats, mice, raccoons, but not a single whisker appeared. Perhaps the boys ate whatever poor critter accidentally passed through their home.

Whoever had built this elevated fort had done a good job; the tree house was well built and secure. The walls were thick and there were small openings in three walls that overlooked the landscape below in all directions. From the doorway, Kelly noticed the swings of the playground. From a crack in the side boards, the cabin was easily visible. No wonder these lost boys had known where to find Kelly and Ash.

Again, she had to wonder why.

***

Ash sat on the floor while Kelly trod lightly to check out the fort. There were family photos on the walls, possibly not these boy's families, but it was a reminder that real or not, the fight for survival was not a solo sport. There were families and friends who relied on loved ones making it through the day and returning home. Kelly had been like a ghost this past year. Nothing could stop her missing

Matt, nothing could stop her loving him, but she had to let him go or she'd eventually lose herself. She finally realized the purpose of the game, and it was to prove who could hold onto their identity as a human being, and who would let it all go for the sake of a thrill kill. She couldn't be the latter. Real or not, what she did inside this game determined the sort of person she was under any circumstance.

In the distance, a swarm of angry kids marched across the playground, heading for the forest. They would be coming to test her humanity. Once again she would do everything she could to keep it, even if it meant her death.

Kelly turned her attention away from the window and back to the boys. "Why are you different to the children down there?"

"They not children," Drake said.

"What are they?"

"Not growed up."

"Yes, you said that. But what does it mean?"

Drake sat down on the floor and Kelly followed suit.

"It weren't adults dying made this world the way it is," Drake said, slowly as if struggling with the words. "It was children *not* dying, not growing up, always wanting to be fed. They eats and they eats. You understand?"

Kelly shook her head.

From the doorway, Ash said, "He means they're cannibals."

She wanted to hug Drake for sparing her the horror of being eaten alive, until it dawned on her that he might have plans of doing it himself.

"But you lot grew up," she said.

Drake nodded. "We're only ones." His eyes landed on Kelly's and remain there. "We ain't ever known a female to grow up though."

Despite the discomfort of the intense scrutiny, Kelly refused to look away. If this was a challenge, she met it face on. But Drake didn't remind her of a homicidal killer. He resembled the kid who washed her car at the car wash.

"That doesn't explain why you saved us," she said, regretting her decision to refuse a weapon. But he was still a kid. Besides, Ash was her best defense right now. And he was circling the small room as if preparing for a fight.

Drake withdrew another stick of gum from his pocket. Once again, he offered it to Kelly and once again she shook her head.

"I don't eat gum. I don't want to rip out a filling."

Drake's intense gaze turned to one of confusion. These kids had never visited a dentist. Nor had they visited a doctor. They had survived in a world without adults to vaccinate them against disease or educate them on hygiene. But merely surviving wasn't enough.

She was learning that. She'd been surviving for twelve months and it wasn't enough. She had to face up to the truth that life was meant to be *lived*, that it was more than just a series of breaths. She needed to move on, and this was the first time she felt ready to admit it.

"Drake. Why did you save us?"

He stared down at his fingers. His nails were chewed and dirty. He wiped at his nose. His teeth had probably never seen a toothbrush or toothpaste. There was a cut on his wrist that hadn't healed properly. With no adults around, nobody was there to fix their injuries, force them to bathe, or teach them. Yet these kids had learned to drive a truck, build a fort in the sky, and defend themselves.

Kelly noticed that the clothes they wore were slightly too big. The cuffs on the pants and jacket were rolled up. And they were different types of uniform. Drake wore the camouflaged colors of the army, Stephens wore dark blue and only now did she notice that the patch on his uniform was of a police unit. One boy was dressed in black, the other in a dark gray uniform.

She decided to start with a question he could answer.

"Is Drake your name?" she asked.

He shook his head.

"What is it?"

"Can't remember."

"Can't or won't?"

He looked away. "That life gone now." He pointed to the name stitched onto the chest of the army uniform. "This who I am now. I a survivor. We all survivors."

The other boys grunted.

All sentimentality Kelly felt for the group died when Drake pointed at her and said, "Take off shirt."

Ash charged over and held his clenched fist inches away from Drake's head. "I'll kill you before you touch her."

Drake skated back a few feet on his backside. His eyes widened. "No. We want blood. For cure. Here. I show."

He stood up and snapped his fingers. Kelly had jumped up and raced over to the open door, ready to flee. The boy in black hurried over to a dark corner and returned with a large bound book. He held it out in front of him. It was a medical journal on curing diseases.

"Blood for cure," Drake said.

"But you don't know what's wrong with you," Kelly said.

"No. But you not have disease. Please."

Ash rolled up his shirt. "You want blood. Then take mine."

"No good. You..." Drake's features twisted. Stephens wandered over and whispered into his ear. They continued whispering to each other, occasionally glancing over at Kelly. Stephens had a gun in his hand, and when he used it to scratch his head Kelly realized that they could shoot her and get her blood or put the gun to her head and force blood out of her veins. But they were *asking for it*. Somehow, in the dreadfulness that was their world, they'd held firmly onto the civility that had most likely destroyed them.

"You think my blood isn't contaminated with the virus," Kelly said.

Stephens snapped his fingers as if magic had just occurred. "Yes. Not contaminated."

"Why do you need her blood?" Ash asked.

"Men are carriers."

Stephens hurried off to the dark corner and returned with a medical bag. He dropped it on the floor and it fell open. Inside were typical medical items – bandages, swabs, band aids. Kelly bent down to pick up a package with a syringe and a needle. The packaging was intact, which meant the equipment could still be sterilized. The problem was she had no idea how to draw blood and she had no intentions of letting anyone without the proper medical qualifications near her veins.

She dropped the syringe. It was ludicrous to even consider the suggestion of a blood transfusion. If this were real, she'd be faced with this situation. But this wasn't real. It was a game, and not one about killing, but about survival. This game was getting the players to think about what they would do if this *were* real.

She had no time for such tests.

"This still doesn't explain why you're different to the others," she said.

"Has to do with adrenal glands," said Drake. "Women reach one age and stay there. Men reach another age and stay there."

"You mean all those children are girls?"

Kelly glanced out the window. She couldn't see the kids anymore but she sensed they were in the forest.

Drake nodded. "Some eighty years old."

"So no more babies," Ash said.

Kelly's skin began to crawl. An outcome of an actual apocalypse would be the need to repopulate the planet. She'd had enough troubles convincing herself that the old world wasn't a horrible place to bring children into, how could she bear thinking about babies in an apocalyptic world?

"No more babies," Drake replied. "We read books to search for cure. But if this no work, backup plan. That's why we taked both of you. One man. One woman."

Kelly let out a high pitched laugh. "I'm not—" She was at a loss for words. "It's not going to happen. No offense to Ash, but I'm never having kids."

Drake shook his head. "How else save the human race?"

Kelly tugged at the hem of her jacket, checked to make certain the buttons of her shirt were done up, desperate to conceal her femininity. Her eyes searched for an escape route, but the only way out was climbing down a rope ladder or plummeting fifty feet.

"I don't care how you save it." She leaned out over the edge. "Nobody is forcing me to have children. You hear me? Not in this world. Not in the real world."

Growing up, she'd watched the news channels with her father, and one day she'd watched a report on rhinos in Africa that were slaughtered by poachers for their horns and left to die. She'd bawled her eyes out and had begged her father to take her to Africa so she could cut the noses off the poachers. Once her radar for bad news had been activated, senseless death was all she saw. She'd begun to despise people and nothing could soothe her soul. Except the sweet, gentle giant she'd met in a coffee shop. Matt had come into her life at a time when she couldn't see any purpose to life, not just hers but everyone's. Matt had been her handsome prince and now her savior was nowhere to be found.

Not in a tree house at least. She leaned further out over the edge.

"Honey," Ash said with a nervous tone. "Come away from the door."

"Why?"

"Because you'll fall."

She smiled. "I've been falling all my life. It's about time I landed."

Kelly let go of the door.

***

Falling through the air was like falling asleep. She closed her eyes and felt a smile on her face, though it could have been the impact of landing on the ground. She should've felt pain as bones broke, muscles snapped, and pulverization crippled her. Instead, dandelions tickled her face. She lifted her hand and plucked at a flower. She shouldn't have been able to move any part of her body. But this wasn't reality. She wasn't dead. She couldn't die. This was immortality, and it came with a clear blue sky, flocks of birds, fluffy white clouds, dandelions and tall grass, and no hint of danger.

The tree house and forest were gone. She leaned up on her elbows and her heart skipped when she spied a figure coming her way. She recognized the swagger, and jumped up to greet him.

"Matt. I found you."

Except this wasn't Matt, just a computer generated version, opaque, not quite in focus, like looking at old video footage.

"I've missed you." Kelly burst into tears. "I need you. I can't live another day without you."

"Of course you can."

She shook her head. "How? I'm dead inside. Let me stay here with you."

Her body was in stasis inside the simulation pod with oxygen, water, and food pumped inside to keep her alive. She could stay healthy inside the pod for three days. After that her muscles would start to atrophy, she'd suffer cyber sickness, and the longer she stayed in a virtual world, the harder it would be to cope with reality. If these were the risks, she was willing to pay them. She could become a blip in the machine. She and Matt would spend eternity together. Immortality in cyberspace. The potential was momentous.

"This is a dream," Matt said. "But you don't have to wake up yet. I've got so much to show you."

Matt beckoned her to follow. The wild flowers were beautiful, swaying, fully in bloom, deep reds and vibrant pinks, but Kelly couldn't take her eyes off her husband. It was so hard to believe her sweet-natured, gentle giant was alive and almost exactly as she remembered. He even wore the forest-green shirt that went well with his jeans. Her favorite outfit. The one he'd died in.

Her smile faltered.

"What's wrong?" he asked.

"Nothing." She shook her head and put on her biggest smile. Always with the mask, but this was what she'd come here for; the least she could do was be happy about it. And she *was* happy. Blissfully so. Albeit a bit like staring at a fake diamond, pretending it was real, but sometimes kidding herself was the only solution.

"Show me this world you built," she said.

He took her to the edge of the meadow. Ahead was a field of poppies with an emerald-green castle in the distance. It was a scene from The Wizard Of Oz. The first time she'd watched it, her father had pretended to have magical powers that would turn the movie from black and white to color at the click of his fingers. On the edge of her seat with excitement, she'd sat waiting for the moment. When Dorothy reached a hand to open to door to Oz, Dad had gone over to the TV and said, "Watch this sweetheart." Then he'd clicked his fingers and like magic, the movie was vibrant with color. For years afterward Kelly had truly believed that her father possessed magic.

Except she'd never told anybody this, so how could Matt know.

He put a finger to his lips. "This is my secret place. I built it for you, but it's my home in here. I'm glad you found me."

"Me too."

She'd always known that seeing him would hurt, and it did. But only a little.

"Kelly, is it true what you said in the tree house?" Matt asked.

"What did I say?"

"That you didn't want children."

Had he heard? Or was he able to read her thoughts inside this strange world?

"I thought we were trying to get pregnant," he said.

She had to look away. This was the only lie she'd ever told him and the disappointment she saw in his eyes crushed her happiness like a meteor landing on a bug.

"Let's not talk about this now," she said. "Let's enjoy being together. I've missed you so much."

They walked along the yellow road, heading for the poppy fields. Perhaps this was a fitting end; to go to sleep forever. She could be the princess in the fairy tale now that she was with her handsome prince.

But even Oz had its bad side, and the blue sky overhead flickered with lightning.

"You still didn't answer my question," Matt said.

They came upon the field of flowers. The heads bobbed and tickled her shins. She bent down to pluck a blood-red poppy, lifted it to her nostrils and breathed in the perfume. She could touch it and smell it, but it was a trick. Her father had used magic to make a young girl smile. Matt was using magic to make a grown woman smile. None of them understood that if she wanted to smile, she'd do so.

"I don't like people," she said. "You know that."

He bent down to pick a flower. He handed it to her, yet touching his fingers was like trying to hold air in her hands. That was when she knew the limits of their eternity. He inhabited one plane of a virtual existence, she inhabited another. Trapped on opposite sides of the mirror.

He let the flower fall and stroked her cheek. But she felt nothing.

"Which people don't you like?" he asked.

"All of them. People are evil, corrupt, greedy, cruel. Particularly cruel. I hate that about humanity. It's ironic, isn't it? We call ourselves humanity yet there's very little about us that's humane. What must the gods think of us?"

He lifted a finger as if to run it along her cheek. "They think you are sad and wonder if something happened to make you so."

"No. I was born this way. I wish I could be blissfully ignorant and just enjoy life. But I can't. I see what's happening and it hurts so much. I thought I could do something good by working in law, but it's just making me worse."

"So get another job."

She laughed. "It's not that easy."

"It's not that hard either. Kelly, the day we told your parents that we were getting married, your father pulled me aside and warned me that I was never to hurt you. He said you were a sensitive soul. I thought he meant that you cried if you burned toast."

Kelly laughed. "How are you even saying this? You're not real."

More importantly, how had her father known this about her? Her parents didn't know her, or if they did, they certainly never acted like it. They'd kept buying her horse figurines because she'd once had a fancy to collect them. She'd been eight at the time, yet they'd continued to treat her as if she'd never grown up.

Was this game sending her a message? Was it time for her to grow up, remove the shackles of grief, and return to the land of the living?

Matt was smiling. "Your mother pulled me aside and said the same thing. Then Jack. I wondered what sort of delicate flower I was marrying."

This couldn't be true. Nobody *knew* her. Not her deep down self. She'd walked around with a mask for so long it had become second nature to smile and laugh.

The biggest trouble about returning from this well of despair was this: she didn't know who she was anymore. She'd worn the mask for so long she'd managed to conceal her identity from herself.

"It's true there is evil in the world," Matt said. "But there's also good."

"Good deeds are merely measures to counteract the badness." It felt good to be arguing with Matt they way she used to. Sometimes they would stay up late to discuss politics, religion, culture, the state of the current health system. Why had she never been able to tell him the truth?

That she didn't belong in the world of consumables and profit and selfishness.

That she felt as if she had no identity so she'd let her grief become who she was.

That without this grief she might be nobody.

"You can't give up on living," Matt said. "I'll be here whenever you need me. But it's time to wake up."

"No. I want to stay here."

Matt started to walk down the path towards the emerald castle in the distance. As Kelly chased after him, he grew smaller and further away. She felt herself grow tired. She fell down, tried to get up, but her body wouldn't move. The ground beneath her began to get cold and hard. Sparkling atoms tore across her vision.

A new game was starting up. But it didn't matter that she was trapped in this game. She could see Matt again. All she had to do was die and there was no shortage or situations to accomplish the task.

The blue sky faded to white, and she felt something sharp and hard pressing into her back. Her neck ached. She opened her eyes and she was in a basement of sorts. She glanced around to see Reis standing over by the window. Jack was loading gear into a backpack. Reis caught her gaze and held it.

She looked away. Seeing Matt again had proven how much she still loved him. She would not betray his memory by acting on a childhood crush.

She pushed herself up from the ground and helped Jack load gear into the backpack.

The other players might feel trapped, worried about waking up in a new game, but she felt alive. Forget welcome to the apocalypse, she thought, this is welcome back to the land of the living.

PRESENTATION BY
COMMAND LEADERS JONAS BARRETT AND STEPHANIE GEY

Command Leader Jonas Barrett:
Greetings players.

If you are watching this presentation, humanity is under attack by alien invasion. Eight hours before contact, astronomers detected an object approximately eight thousand kilometers from Earth. Having crept into our orbit without warning, Global Space Control used satellites, telescopes, and radar to determine that the object was not natural. Three hours before contact, the Unified Bureau Of Outer Space sent a transmission in one hundred different languages to the object. There was no reply.

The craft crept closer to Earth.

Command Leader Stephanie Gey:
At contact, the alien spaceship knocked out satellite communication. Cell phones, TV images, internet, and most other forms of communications around the world failed. We don't know why they're invading Earth. We can only assume we have resources and they want them. Whatever their reasons for venturing far across the galaxies, we don't believe these invaders are friendly.

Command Leader Jonas Barrett:
Three hours after contact, our government sent a squadron of fighter planes to intercept. On the ground, experimental weapons

were deployed to no effect. Five hours after contact, a submarine in the Indian Ocean released a Trident II ballistic missile, carrying almost three point five tons of destructive power. The missile broke apart into eight self-guided warheads and fired upon the ship. Our mightiest weapon had no impact.

It is now twenty-four hours after contact. Humanity is ordered to evacuate into the safe zones and regroup to unite against this common threat. There is no such thing as a civilian anymore. We are all soldiers in this fight for Earth.

As with all apocalypses, proceed with caution.

Command Leader Stephanie Gey:
If you find yourself in the midst of an alien invasion apocalypse your first priority is to flee and seek shelter in caves, tunnels, sewers, deserts, forests…anywhere away from major infrastructures where aliens are most likely to first attack. You will need to prepare a panic bag before making your way to the nearest safe zone.

Your panic bag should contain the following items:

Handheld radios or walkie-talkies.

Flashlights. Batteries. Knives and other easily transportable weapons.

Medicines, bandages, cough syrups, antiseptic lotions, masks, disinfectant, and pain killers. On a side note, astro-biologists believe humans are in danger from alien bacteria, and the opposite is also true. Aliens may be in danger from human disease so germ warfare may be a possible solution.

Command Leader Jonas Barrett:
Doesn't Stephanie find the most far-fetched and fantastic facts. Here are some more items for your panic bag:

Detailed maps of the cities and countryside, especially maps that contain locations of tunnels and underground systems.

Thermal clothing and wet weather gear to endure the damp or cold conditions found underground and in remote areas.

Bottles of drinking water. Crackers, nuts, dried fruit, energy bars. Pantry items such as tinned food, pasta, flour, sugar, and rice.

We at Simulated Military And Recreational Training have designed this program because we are committed to the survival of the human race. And because we are serious, we have put together the following tips for players encountering an alien invasion apocalypse.

Command Leader Stephanie Gey:
We're dead serious, Jonas. Yes, that was a play on words in case you didn't recognize it from this and earlier attempts. The tips for survival are as follows:

Immediately distance yourself from the spaceship and nearby major infrastructures which aliens will target, and head to remote areas, preferably by underground tunnels and sewers.

Human numbers have dangerously dwindled. Gathering survivors to form an army is your next priority.

Lure aliens that have landed on the ground away from the ship and capture if possible. Capturing their technology could be the key to winning this war.

Your supplies will need to be replenished often. Search houses, stores, and factories for whatever supplies you can find. Looting abandoned sites is no longer considered a crime, however looting of other human base camps is.

Attack from aliens will come from the sky, as this is where their technological advantage lies. Underground basements and tunnels serve as ideal safe zones. Fortify these safe zones from invading troops.

Command Leader Jonas Barrett:

I've got an interesting fact coming up, too. But first, more tips for survival:

Regular combat training in the use of knife and stake wielding will increase the survival rate of those inside the safe zones as well as stave off lunacy that is derived from many humans coming to terms with the fact that we are not the superior species after all.

According to experts, the destruction of civilization is inevitable and predictable. Yet, at the same time, the key to long-term survival is other people. Not everyone will be stable enough to deal with an alien invasion. This needs to be taken into account when preparing battle plans and assigning duties.

Here's the interesting fact I was telling you about. Often in a major crisis people try to think up major solutions. Sometimes simpler is better. Don't discount any idea how big or small. And don't always rely on those in high places to save the planet. History has shown that low tech assaults often succeed against superior technology. A human triumph over alien technology may have less to do with strategy, and more to do with human courage.

These aliens have travelled far from their homes. One advantage is that they can't rely on reinforcements. Every alien being or ship lost is not going to be replaced – a critical weakness. Therefore we must never give up the fight.

Most importantly, let no alien live.

Good luck players and stay alive!

Command Leader Stephanie Gey:
Surely you can do better than that. My aging dog has more enthusiasm.

Command Leader Jonas Barrett:
Of course I can. I'm a professional. Players. Welcome to the apocalypse!

12

Jack

"Command Leader Jack Minnow," a voice over the radio said.

Jack pressed the button. "Yow."

"You're supposed to reply with your name and rank. Anyway, you're clear to proceed."

Being granted clearance to rush out into the sweeping beams of a spaceship wasn't providing the necessary motivation to do so. Yet it wasn't the spaceship in orbit that Jack objected to. The way it hovered against an azure-blue sky, cloudless, perfect, not a hint of smog, was an affront to everything he'd lived for. The end of the world should have come with a sky streaked with shitty browns and puke greens. He could picture the aliens laughing in the cockpit and saying, send us your missiles, send us your planes, don't mind us, we'll just be hanging here eating all the world's pizza while you blow yourselves up.

The human strike force team hadn't made a dent *at all* on the outer shell of the ship. They'd lost thousands of good men trying. And the crazy thing was that Jack Minnow was so immersed in this game he overlooked the fact that none of the dead men had ever been alive to begin with.

Everything seemed so real. And he loved it.

He led the way up the stairs from the basement of the discount furniture store. Reis and Kelly followed close behind. Ash had departed quickly, on account of something that'd happened between him and Reis while Reis was out of it. But splitting up was essential if they were to beat the aliens.

Jack had entered this game the preferred way – with a presentation from his favorite TV host CL Stephanie Gey, and a CGI combat suit. They all wore combat gear, though Jack's digital crest on his badge identified him as a command leader, while Reis and Kelly wore digital badges that identified them as ground troopers. Had Jack landed here in his civilian clothes, he might not have taken up the role of leader so easily. He smiled. Who was he kidding? This was a dream come true.

They used the furniture in the showroom as cover to sneak toward the front door. Once there, crouching down out of sight of patrolling aliens, Jack spoke into the radio.

"Come in Eyeballs. Anyone getting signs of activity on Hassler Street?"

Lifting himself up a few inches, he peered through the glass panel in the door, but his vision was limited. Didn't mean the frogspawns weren't out there waiting to vaporize them. Ugly looking things these aliens, like tadpoles if they walked on their hind legs, and opaque-red, like jelly. Someone over the radio started calling them frogspawns and the name stuck. The frogspawn weapons were far superior to anything on earth. And they'd put Jack in charge. If he wasn't having such a ball, he'd have been concerned for the safety of humanity. He was a natural born klutz. In the real world he was in charge of operations for *Quest*, which equated to looking after the website, the accounts, the promotions, and organizing beer and food for Friday afternoon Ping Pong Olympics in the parking lot. Nobody's life depended on him.

A static voice came over the radio. "Hassler Street is clear. Proceed."

No sign of aliens, but their ship floated in the sky sending an array of sensors down to the ground, seeking out humans. They reminded Jack of disco lights, except with the ability to dissipate a person. Add vodka shots and it could be a normal night out in a San Diego nightclub.

"Across the road is an entrance to a subway system," Jack said. "It's guarded by my men. If the sensors stay on the other side of town we'll make it with minimal fuss."

"Your men?" Reis eyed him with suspicion. "You're seriously a leader?"

"Yep. I woke up with a troop to command. Actually, I command all of the ground troops. Word of advice, it doesn't pay to rise through the ranks of this military. There's no glory. Anyway, we were on our way to the armory when the ship fired missiles at the ground. You got knocked against a wall and were out of it for a while. The second assault got Kelly."

"I can barely remember the presentation."

"Me either," Kelly said.

Jack quickly briefed them. He finished by saying, "Our mission is to keep the frogspawn's attention off the armory where we're building the weapons to take out the ship."

"I don't like the sound of being a ground trooper," said Kelly.

"Can't I just go to the armory and do filing or something?"

"That is a very sexist thing to say. I should make you drop and give me twenty."

"Fine, then give me a weapon and I'll draw them out so you can finish the mission."

"Be serious, Kell. I never get to be boss. We're doing this my way. And as a team."

Jack shifted on the balls of his feet. It'd be just like his sister to ruin his chance of being in the spotlight, even though there was no glory at being a command leader. The orders came in thick and fast; he barely had time to accomplish anything. More importantly, they'd signed on as team so they should play as a team. A team where he was the boss.

"Fine," Kelly said. "Let's all get ourselves killed."

Reis shook his head. "I can take her to the armory."

Jack reconsidered keeping her on his team. Her absence meant she couldn't spoil his fun. But he'd made a vow to shadow her. Her absence also meant she'd be in the company of Reis which worked in Jack's favor. Except that without them he'd have nobody to be in charge of. This dream job had put him smack bang in the middle of the action and privy to top secret information. Plus he got to act the superhero. Who wouldn't like that? But pride swelled faster with an audience.

Besides, if these two ran off and left him to play this game by himself what did that say of his leadership qualities?

Then again, maybe he was too indecisive to be in command.

A static voice came over the radio, different to the first voice. This one sounded frightened.

"...anyone out there? Hello. Come in..."

The blood drained from Jack's head as he recognized the voice.

"...if you can hear me, my name is Douglas Smith and I'm under attack."

"Douglas. This is Jack Minnow. Where are you?"

Static. Silence. More static.

At last, the voice said, "I'm inside the cinema. Jack, they're outside. What do I do?"

"Hang on." He pulled off the backpack and took out his map, searching for the cinema. Attractions were usually featured on maps and he located the cinema on Roper Road. "Douglas, stay where you are. I'm on my way."

Kelly gripped his arm. "You just said we should stick together."

Save the kid or save the woman. How did superheroes deal with these tough choices?

Jack had met Douglas at the hotel the operators had taken him to during the biochemical disaster apocalypse. They'd ended up sharing a limousine and Jack had immediately taken Douglas under his wing. They'd sat in the hotel room eating pizzas and playing cards. Douglas had told Jack his theories – broken computer, broken pods, training exercise, military game, terrorist attack. The kid had an active imagination, which was in stark contrast to everything the older generation kept predicting about kids who played video games.

"I have to go get him," Jack said. "You two got the armory and take charge of the small-scale explosive attack."

"What small-scale attack?" Reis asked.

Jack suspected Reis might have been pulling his leg, but his friend was usually too literal to involve himself in pranks, so he suspected he was suffering from shell shock, even though he told himself it was more likely cyber sickness. Gamers got it from playing in 3D for too long. He must have it, too, he realized, because he couldn't keep his thoughts under control. They were flying all over the place.

"General Yulrich will fill you in when you get to the armory," Jack said. "I'm going to help Douglas. He of all people shouldn't be suffering this never-ending horror."

Then he took off out the door and down the street before anyone could remind him that none of them should.

***

Moving vehicles made easy targets for the spaceship, like a bird on a fence watching a grub, so Jack scurried down Roper Road using the shop awnings as cover. The military used the traffic lights to communicate. The set of lights on Roper Road were green, which meant the Eyeballs – people with eyes on the streets via telescopes and non-satellite-reliant CCTV cameras – had communicated to the Office Boys – those in front of the computers that controlled anything relying on cables instead of satellite to operate, such as the traffic system – that the area was free of frogspawns. When Jack turned down Redbar Street, the lights were red. Not a good sign.

He unclipped his radio. "Douglas. It's me, Jack. You still there, buddy?"

The silence over the radio filled him with dread.

"Douglas, come in."

Static.

Then a quiet voice said, "Jack. They're outside. Don't talk. Just come."

The absolute silence that followed could only mean one thing: Douglas had switched off his radio because the aliens were close. So Jack bolted down the street waving a pistol in his hand, even though guns were useless against the aliens. But it felt good to be taking control of the situation.

A multitude of good men had already discovered guns were useless against the aliens. The creatures were able to absorb the bullets and spit them back out. Another multitude of good men were working night and day on finding or creating weapons that could kill the aliens. So far, nothing permanent had been discovered. Capturing the frogspawns alive was paramount in determining what could kill them. The trouble was capturing them. The same bracelets that vaporized a person seemed to be linked to the ship. An alien only had to sense a threat and it disappeared in a flash. Not that humanity offered any threat. Did salmon offer any threat to the grizzly?

As Jack ran, the thrill of the game coursed through him. Inside the virtual world he was invincible. Nothing could defeat him. No longer the klutz who staggered into furniture or spilled drinks on himself. He was The Man. And The Man could get used to The Power.

Rounding the corner, he saw half a dozen frogspawns. Douglas should be safe as long as he stayed concealed behind a layer of concrete, which the command leaders had discovered offered the safest hiding place for humans. The frogspawns used a series of clicks and chirps to detect signs of life, sort of like sonar, and they had trouble penetrating through solid concrete. Which explained why everyone had fled underground when the invasion occurred. It would have been erroneous to assume that because the aliens appeared stupid that they were. The frogspawns possessed intelligence. They watched the human survivors fleeing underground and they understood that to follow was foolhardy, so they sent electric charges into sewers and tunnels in an effort to thwart the booby traps.

Where their intelligence failed was underestimating the human desire to live. There were teams known as the Brassieres who baited aliens just to get them to enter carefully chosen spots. Where the frogspawn intelligence won was realizing that humans couldn't stay underground forever. They'd also realized that many of the tunnels didn't connect up to places the survivors needed to be. For example, the armory where preparations for a full-scale attack were underway could only be reached across open ground. Many lives had been lost coming in and out.

Jack shook his head. It was as if years of information had been directly implanted into his brain, because he couldn't possibly know the backstory of the world he was in charge of saving.

Saving the planet was suddenly immaterial to Jack. Right now he only wanted to save one boy.

Stealth like, he crept up to the side wall of the cinema and unhooked the radio.

"Can you read me Eyeballs? I'm on Roper Road at the cinema. There's a trapped civilian inside. Can you tell the Brassieres I need a diversion to clear the area of frogspawn?"

He slipped the radio onto the clip on his jacket, crouched down low, and kept his gaze on the sky. He waited a few minutes, then a pair of flying drones appeared. The drones buzzed the aliens. Posing no threat, the aliens paid them no mind. Then the drones dive-bombed the aliens. This captured their attention, yet one of the aliens made a screeching sound as if to order the others to ignore the nuisance. When a drone exploded and acid splattered onto their gelatinous faces, they took action and chased after the tiny weapon, giving Jack clearance to slip inside the cinema.

He checked behind the candy bar and the ticket booth, calling out for Douglas in a low voice, until he found the kid hiding in the projection room.

"Am I glad to see you," Douglas said as he untangled himself from reels of film. "Any new theories?"

While gorging on pizzas after the limousines had taken them back to the hotel, Jack and Douglas had decided to hold a competition. Douglas lived in Pasadena, California, which meant he and Jack were practically neighbors. Their wager was simple – the one with the correct theory had to buy the other tickets to the next Star Wars movie.

"Your theory that the pods are broken is still the winning bet," Jack said. The two of them exited the cinema and found a car to crouch behind. "Where did you get the radio?"

"There's a museum attached to the cinema full of old gadgets. I swiped the batteries from an usher's torch."

"Good work."

They'd also decided that since they were trapped, they might as well learn as many practical skills as they could. Though Jack had only suggested this as a way to keep the kid's spirits high and his mind off their predicament. If Douglas suspected the ruse, he never let on.

"There's a bunker I can take you to where you'll be safe till this is over," Jack said.

Douglas shook his head. "I don't want to hide. Well, obviously I had to hide out in here because I didn't have any weapons. But shooting aliens is what I came here to do."

"What about your theory that people are dying for real? Or have you dismissed that already? These frogspawns have weapons that have vaporized millions of people. I'm sorry, Douglas. I can't take the chance of them vaporizing you."

"I didn't work all summer to be babysat. I'm the highest scorer in *Warcraft*, *Alien Hive*, and *Zombie Battlefield*. I paid my money to play just like you."

Jack raised an eyebrow. "Yeah, about that. I worked all summer at your age and no way did I earn five grand."

Douglas's lips began to quiver and Jack regretted belittling him. His first job had been serving frozen yoghurt. He'd hated every minute but he'd wanted to spend the money any way he pleased without having to justify his whims to an adult. Ignoring his dad's suggestion to bank the money, Jack had gone directly to *Clarence's Props and Costumes* and blown the lot on cosplay outfits for Comic-Con.

"What do I care how you got the money?" Jack said. "You're here and I'm happy to have you on my team. But seriously, even if you got the money, how did you get into the game?"

"Fake ID."

"And nobody even questioned you?"

Douglas shook his head.

Jack got the sense there was more to the story, but for now they had to press on. The two of them ducked and weaved their way down the street. At the end, they stopped. Jack used a mirror on a stick to peer around the corner. "Shit. Two frogspawns."

"Let me see." Douglas grabbed the mirror and pushed Jack out of the way. "They're ugly."

"They probably think we're ugly."

Douglas snorted. "Speak for yourself."

Jack slipped the mirror back into his jacket. He got out the map and checked for a route. "Okay, when I say go, we head around the back and run like hell across the parking lot. Got it? There's a subway entrance about ten blocks away."

Douglas ogled the pistol. Then his gaze swept up and down Jack.

"What I don't get," Douglas said, "is how come you entered the game in combat gear and I didn't."

Jack didn't get it either. He hadn't wanted Kelly ruining his mood, and now Douglas was ruining it by opening the door to doubt.

***

Constantly scanning up and down the street had given Jack a sore neck.

"You wanna fill me in on what happened while I was stuck in the cinema?" Douglas said.

"It's been twenty-four hours since aliens invaded, though everything was established before the players arrived. We have no satellite communication. It's all old-school technology. The story goes that survivors tracked down analogue phones and converted them into long range radios. There are humans posted in well-secured bunkers who use telescopes to check the ground for the aliens, they're called Eyeballs. Then we got the Brassieres."

Douglas snickered and Jack scowled at him.

"They're the team who set booby traps all over the place. They're good at creating small diversions whenever we need to make a break across open ground. Then we got the Chem boys who make bug bombs—"

Douglas's eyes widened. "This game is *all right*. Are we losing or winning?"

"What do you think?"

"Can I have your gun?"

"No. Anyway, we can't get near the ship. Planes get shot down before they reach it. Missiles get blown up, or if they make it they don't have any impact. But there is a plan to destroy the ship with a series of small-scale explosives to divert the attention of the frogspawns so we can launch the big scale attack. We're filling balloons with a compound that should eat through the hull of the ship. Once there's a breach we can aim explosives inside. We're releasing the balloons tonight when they won't be detected by radar or seen by the naked eye. We have one chance, and because its low tech, we think it'll work."

Douglas scanned the alleyway. "You keep saying 'we'. Does this mean I'll eventually get a gun?"

Jack relented and shoved the pistol in Douglas's hand. "Fine. Take it. But I have to warn you that it doesn't work on frogspawns."

"Cool." Douglas stroked the butt of the gun. "Wait. It doesn't work on them?"

Jack shook his head. "Having it's more of an ego thing."

A *bang* echoed along the street and Jack pushed Douglas against the wall. The noise turned out to be a trash can getting knocked over by the wind.

"Do we know why the aliens are here?" Douglas asked. "It might help figure out how to beat them."

Jack suppressed a smile. The kid was acting more grown up than half the adults in the game.

"Resources are the best guess," Jack said. "The ship sends down a bunch of frogspawns. They run around shooting anyone they find. You don't want to get shot at. Their weapons vaporize a person. Let's go."

They jogged a few more streets and then stopped at a street corner. Jack pressed his ear against the wall listening out for the series of *clicks* and *chirps* the aliens used to communicate. But he wouldn't have heard anything over the loud beating of his heart. Each new game required a different skill level, and it added to the excitement. He couldn't understand why everyone was complaining about being stuck inside the game. It was as much fun as the brochure claimed.

"I sold my parent's stuff to get the money," said Douglas. "Stuff they didn't want like old lawn mowers and old laptops. I didn't steal it. They knew I was doing it. They just think I'm saving up for a car."

"You don't have to explain it to me. I understand."

"I'm just saying, I *want* to be here. I can handle it."

Jack suspected the kid could handle himself. Just like Kelly was handling herself. And Reis was doing fine. It gave him a tinge of sadness to realize that his team mates didn't need his help. Maybe he was better off playing the next game on his own.

The map in his hands shook as his words sank in. *The next game.* Why did he have the feeling he was never getting out of here?

Jack opened up the map and pointed to a spot. "Here's Sector G where we need to be." His fingers moved three inches to the left. "We're here."

Douglas groaned. "That's all the way across town."

"And dangerous to get to. But if you say you can handle it, we'll head there."

Just don't die on me, Jack thought. He couldn't live with himself if that happened.

A truck pulled into the street.

"Shit."

Jack dragged Douglas to a spot behind a dumpster, though this was usually the first place the frogspawn foot patrols checked for humans. The truck drove by doing maybe four miles an hour, and an idea formed in Jack's mind for a way to reach Sector G. He pulled out a device that resembled a radio and switched it on.

"What's that?" Douglas asked.

"An electric field sensor. The aliens communicate by using a range of pops and chirps, similar to some fish. This tunes into the electric frequency of their language. Sharks have the same ability to perceive electrical stimuli. And like sharks, these buggers can freeze the signals they emit if they sense danger. I'll check inside this building for signs of activity."

"Why? Is there a tunnel under the building?"

"No. I have a plan. Just wait here for a second."

He hurried inside and checked through the settings on the EF sensor just to be sure the building was clear. Then he poked his head outside and told Douglas to follow. They went up two flights of stairs. Up on the roof, Jack removed two masks from his backpack. They were the type used in early wars against gas attacks. They had two bug eyes and an apparatus like a tuna can which was filled with oxygen.

He handed a mask to Douglas. "Put this on, then no talking. Okay?"

"Why?"

"Talking uses up oxygen."

Besides, the kid's constant barrage of questions was starting to get on his nerves. He had to remind himself that he was perfectly safe inside his pod. There was nothing to worry about. This was just a game.

Jack slipped a mask over his face as well, and then he leaned over the edge of the building. The slow moving truck was directly below. He tossed a grenade down at it. It didn't explode the way a normal grenade did. It landed on the canvas roof.

"That grenade is a dud," Douglas said.

"No talking."

"But it's a dud."

Jack sighed. "Aliens aren't used to our biosphere. Eyeballs tell us they beam down the surface, blast people, and beam back up. We think it's to realign their senses." He paused to let his lungs fill up with oxygen from the small canister. "The grenade is filled with human germs undetectable to the naked eye."

"Cool. And you said naked."

Jack shook his head. At least having this kid around was a soothing salve to the worrisome mind.

They didn't have to wait long to find out that the theory had merit. The truck crawled to a stop. They hurried back down and ran down the street. The truck sat motionless in the middle of the road.

"What if it's a trap?" Douglas asked.

"Only one way to find out."

They used store awnings as cover from the sweeping beams overhead as they crept up on the truck. Jack opened the door and a frogspawn spilled out onto the ground. It moaned, so Jack knew the bacteria bomb had slowed it down, but he didn't know for how long.

This was the closest anyone had come to a living frogspawn. Capturing an alien dead or alive wasn't Jack's mission. The Eyeballs had already confirmed that the bracelets the aliens wore around their wrists were the weapons used to vaporize people. It also teleported them to and from their ship. Part of humanity's mission was to steal whatever alien technology they could get their hands on. Jack took the bracelet and stepped over the jelly-like body to get out of the way as more frogspawns fell out of the truck.

He and Douglas dragged the aliens off to the side. Then Jack put a call in to the Office Boys to tell them aliens were on the sidewalk if anyone with wheels wanted to slice or dice them or do whatever the hell they wanted. He had other plans. He and Douglas ripped off their masks and got into the truck. Jack drove at ten miles an hour, a slightly faster speed the aliens had driven during their patrols but time was ticking away.

Up ahead a set of traffic lights turned amber. Jack pulled the truck into a side road and told Douglas to get down out of sight.

"The traffic lights still work," he told Douglas, "because they run on solar and underground cables. We still have control of them. Green means the way ahead is clear, red means the way ahead is full of frogspawns."

"And amber means caution," said Douglas. "I'm not an idiot."

His actions said otherwise. Douglas continued to stared out the window as if challenging the aliens to come and get him. Jack realized he was doing the same. Maybe the bracelets in the truck made them invisible to other aliens, because this group didn't even look their way.

The aliens disappeared from view and Jack pulled the truck out onto the street.

"That was awesome," Douglas squealed. "We were so close and we escaped unharmed."

Jack had to agree. The sense of invincibility once more filled his lungs and it was as if nothing could harm him. Yet why did he get the sense the game was lulling them into a false sense of bravado?

"You got brothers and sisters?" Jack asked Douglas to make small talk.

"I have two sisters. One younger, one older. I'm the middle child."

"I've got a sister, Kelly. And Reis... I suppose he's like a brother. I've known him since I was fifteen."

"My parents will be worried about me."

Jack let out a sigh. "Now why did you have to say that? I've been trying not to think about everything back home."

"Sorry." Douglas looked it. "My parents don't know I'm here."

"Same here."

One of Jack's saving graces was the ability to push thoughts such as this to the far reaches of his mind. Douglas had taken a knife to the fabric of concealed thoughts and butchered them, leaving them exposed, bleeding, naked for everyone to point at. At least this explained the sudden drop in chatter. Now Jack wished the kid would talk if only to avoid facing the truth. He was trapped in a computer and nobody knew he was here.

It wasn't long before Jack turned off down a stretch of old highway that was now occupied by the Human Resistance Movement. The road led to an irrigational tunnel that formed part of an underground military planning station. It also led to a few farmhouses whose basements served as weaponry stores. Each time the frogspawns seized weapons and resources, more were delivered to take their place. Hijacking this truck had solved his issue of how to transport the weapons from Sector G to Ground Zero.

He almost planted his foot on the gas pedal in his excitement to get to the site, but the overhead sweeping beams zoned in on fast-moving vehicles. He drove slowly until he came to an intersection. Perhaps he should leave this to the professionals, he thought. It certainly seemed as if there were players in the game better prepared for warfare than he. Acting the hero could get Douglas killed and he'd have to contend with another set of parents grieving the loss of their child.

It was this last thought that hung around, causing Jack's shoulder to sag. "I can't let you come with me," he said. "It's too dangerous."

"Oh, come on. Nobody lets me play along with them. I'm good in a crisis. Once, my cousin fell off his skateboard and broke his collar bone and I called triple zero—"

"What if you get shot?"

"What if *you* get shot? Have you stopped to consider the trauma *I'd* be exposed to? Seeing something like that, it could haunt me forever. I'd seek retribution, possibly do something stupid like take a posse to Russia and get myself killed—"

"*All right*. You can come with me. But stay low and do exactly as I say."

The smile that lit up the kid's face was almost worth going against his better judgment.

To the left lay a series of farmhouses. Jack turned left. "And for the record," Jack said, "someone will notice we're missing and come searching for us."

"If my parents find me they'll ship me off to live with my cousin in Florida. They don't exactly get my preoccupation with video games."

"I wish I could say that I'm starting to lose my fascination. But it's not true. I know we're stuck and it can't be a good sign—" Jack stopped. "I shouldn't be telling you any of this."

"Stop treating me like a kid."

"It's hard not to since you *are* a kid."

"Fine, I'll treat you like a jerk since it'd be hard not to."

Jack gripped the steering wheel and took three deep breaths. Douglas was being unreasonable, argumentative, and reproachful. Damned kid, but Jack knew that if something happened to the boy, it would be his fault and he'd have to live with the guilt. But something had already happened to Douglas, to all of them – they were trapped in an apocalyptic merry-go-round. Sure, they could survive a few days in the pods, but not forever. The operator had made a point of explaining the limitations during hook-up. And it was this final thought that slapped at Jack like an angry wind. How had Douglas, clearly under-age, been allowed to be strapped into the pod and hooked up to the machine?

"Are you sure you're not a decoy?" Jack asked.

"Would I be worried about my imminent death if I was?"

"Nobody is dying inside the game. The pods are built to last for longer than they've led us to believe. Like expiration dates on packaged food. Manufacturers only list dates so consumers will buy more products. I'll bet the operator saying we can only last three days is how CyberNexis intends to sell more tickets."

Douglas nodded. "I guess. But our muscles will weaken from disuse. Our lungs will no longer function on their own. We'll have developed bed sores. If we ever get out of here, we'll be vegetables."

Jack still had to worry about a facility that would let a boy inside. Because if they let a boy inside, who else had they let in?

13

Jack

Jack had made it his mission to remain positive, but the kid had made a good point. When they emerged out of the pods, they wouldn't be healthy. And just as quickly as Douglas's mood had dipped into the danger zone, he must have found the lever to pull up because his eyes were suddenly bright with excitement.

"So, if the germ bombs work to slow the frogspawn," Douglas asked, "why don't we attack them with a massive dose of the bacteria?"

"Because it's also toxic to humans. We're talking a concoction of small pox, anthrax, malaria. Like the nasty stuff we saw in the biological disaster apocalypse. The Chem Boys are trying to refine the bug bombs so it affects only frogspawn DNA, but that could be weeks, months, even years. At the rate people are being annihilated, we don't have long."

"About another fifteen hours," Douglas said earnestly.

As long as the game lasted.

Douglas pointed at something flying in the sky about a hundred feet away. "Are they drones?"

"Yep. We use them for all sorts of things – to carry messages, to create diversions. The Chem Boys could be testing ways to release the bug bombs."

"I didn't think I was in the cinema that long. It's like the game has been playing for weeks."

"Probably has. We landed in the middle of the apocalypse and I entered the game with a back story. It's like..."

He could sense Douglas watching him.

"Like Pandora's in your head," said Douglas.

Jack focused on his driving.

Douglas spoke in a low voice. "I had a death dream before this game."

Jack's blood chilled. The tone of the kid's voice didn't imply the death dream had been pleasant. He waited for the kid to elaborate. He didn't, and he wasn't sure if he should push him.

"You want to talk about it?" Jack asked.

"I saw the pods. Everyone was dead."

"You must have been mistaken. We can't die."

Douglas scowled at him. He said nothing more for the rest of the trip. Jack's mood sank as the appeal of the game started to fade.

Just then, a farmhouse came into view and Jack drove until he pulled up out front and parked as close to the house as he could. He could only hope that as he and Douglas moved around the truck that the spaceship's scanners were fixed on another location, or that if they saw movement they'd assume the presence of a truck meant that aliens were searching for weapons.

"You want to help load supplies or you want to stay here?" he asked Douglas. "You might be able to find a uniform."

"Whatever."

To deter the frogspawns from checking basements, the Human Resistance Movement had traveled all over the countryside leaving a lot of stuff in plain sight and concealing the golden eggs, as they called them, in the basements of farmhouses. But you could never tell if a house had been raided already or if the frogspawns had found the supplies. This house looked like it hadn't been visited by either side. Jack grabbed flashlights, batteries, and a small first aid kit while Douglas changed into a uniform. As they headed for the front door, muffled voices came from the basement.

"Can't be frogspawns," Jack said. "They use clicks to talk to each other."

The electric field sensor in his pocket was beeping like crazy. He tiptoed to the basement door. Sounds came from below. The door was secured by a punch code. The series of numbers sprang to mind automatically, and he punched them in.

The door opened.

Shouts came from below. "Help. Is anyone there? Help."

How had survivors become trapped in the basement?

Jack bolted down the stairs and pulled up short when he saw a mahogany desk in the center of the room. Behind that was a leather chair, and in front were two cowhide visitor chairs. Along one wall were a couple of filing cabinets, a liquor cabinet, and a coffee station.

Standing behind the desk were two people he recognized from the presentations: Command Leaders Jonas Barrett and Stephanie Gey.

"It's about time you found us," CL Gey shouted. "We've been stuck in this room for days. You people are paying double the rate you paid for the filming."

Douglas took a step toward the presenters. "You're Stephanie Gey and Jonas Barrett."

The woman gave him a twisted, yet sad smile. "We're actors, honey. I'm Paige Swanson and this is William Rush."

Douglas held out his hand, but only William stepped around the desk to shake it.

"It's so nice to meet you," Douglas gushed.

"I don't mean to be rude," Jack said, "but what are you doing here?" This was supposed to be a basement stocked with guns and ammunition. Hardly the kind of place for celebrities to inhabit.

"We've been waiting to be let out," Paige said.

"We're waiting to be rescued too," Douglas said. "The game malfunctioned but someone will be letting us out of our pods soon."

Paige waved her hands in the air. "I'm too tired for improvisation. I want a hot shower and a cold drink. Excuse me."

"Wait," Jack said. "You can't just walk out of here. It's a war zone out there"

Paige looked at him as if he were crazy.

"We're trapped in the game," he explained. "Hooked up to the computer playing a never-ending cycle of apocalypses. You ought to know. You're part of the crew that put us here."

"Like I told you, I'm an actor. I have no intention of playing any of these games."

William wore a concerned expression on his face. "Paige and I finished recording the presentations. Then we were given a tour of the facility. Not long after that all the lights went out and we've been stuck in Max Winterdom's office ever since."

"Who's Max Winterdom?"

"The creator of The Apocalypse Games."

Jack started to laugh. He turned to Douglas. "What do you reckon? Decoys?"

"Yep. Decoys."

William shook his head. "I don't follow you. What did mean when you said the game had malfunctioned?"

"Come on, William," said Paige. "We need to get out of here and call our agents."

"Hold on, Paige. If something's wrong, we need to know."

Jack flicked his gaze between the two actors. It was hard to tell if they were genuinely confused or acting. He was all for a bit of leg pulling, to a point.

"Why don't you tell me your version of events," said Jack. "Then I'll tell you mine."

William nodded. "Paige and I finished the recordings, and then

Max arrived and said he'd give us the grand tour."

"And?"

"And that's it. We must have fallen asleep, though I don't recall doing so, and we woke up in here. I've lost track of time. It's been a couple of days I imagine. We've survived on the panic bags they gave us during the tour." He pointed to the corner. "They're filled with water and food, but they also contain torches, medicine—"

"There was a liquor cabinet but we cleaned it out on day one," Paige said.

"Not *we*, dear," William said dryly.

"So why hasn't your agent or camera crew or whoever rescued you?" Douglas asked.

The two actors shared a glance.

"This is pretty embarrassing," William said, "but Max demanded we sign a confidentiality agreement and say nothing about the games until after the launch. It's not unusual to sign such agreements. The movie industry is extremely competitive. I take it from your presence that the launch has occurred."

"Launched and failed," Jack said.

He explained the problems with the game and how over one hundred player's minds were trapped inside the mainframe computer. Each day the ability to tell the difference between reality and fantasy was getting more difficult.

"You say the pods are broken," Paige said. "Well, I know where they are. I'm sure two smart boys like you can fix them."

William nodded. "We were filming in a room off the main foyer. We were shown the pods. They're just down the hallway."

"You saw the pods." A sinking feeling settled in Jack's stomach. "Did you by any chance get inside one?"

"Of course we did," Paige said. "We wanted to watch one of the presentations."

Jack began laughing, hysterically, like he couldn't stop himself, even when everyone was looking at him like he was crazy which he probably was.

"You got inside a pod," he said. "Which means you're in the game. And nobody knows you're here because you signed a confidentially agreement. I didn't tell anyone because I'm here with the only people I'd tell. Douglas didn't tell anyone because he's here illegally." Jack raised his voice. "Does anybody know we're here?"

"What you're saying doesn't make sense," William said. "We'd know if we were in the game. We'd wake up in the middle of an apocalypse. We haven't left this room."

"And I'm not about to spend a second longer here. Excuse me." Paige grabbed her handbag off the filing cabinet and slung it over her shoulder. "If you want to find the pods, they're down the hall to the right. I'd show you but I've got a life to get back to."

"Wait, Paige, you might want to prepare yourself—"

"For what? Leaving this awful room which smells like a gym. Having a real shower instead of licking myself like I'm a cat. Going home to a real bed and not a stack of files on the floor. Believe me, I'm prepared."

Douglas hurried after her, turning on his flashlight. "Here, let me help you."

"I don't remember there being stairs," Paige said as she disappeared from view.

William hung back and now turned to Jack. "If what you're saying is true, we're in serious trouble. I know what's coming."

Paige started shouting for help and Jack hurried up the stairs. He got to the top just as Paige ran out the front door.

"Be quiet," Jack hissed. "Or they'll hear."

Paige was on the front porch, her eyes wide and her hands twisting around her handbag. "This can't be happening. We have to get out of here."

"Tell us how and we will," Douglas said.

She whirled on him. "You don't know what's coming."

William moved to stand beside Jack. A wry smile pulled at Jack's lips as he placed a hand on William's.

"You know I'm gonna say it," Jack said.

William shook his head. "Please don't."

"It has to be said."

"Fine. Get it over with."

"Welcome to the apocalypse."

***

Jack checked the sky. There were no rays of light indicating that landing parties were arriving on Earth. They'd have to make a quick exit. "It's clear. Let's go."

"Are you crazy?" Paige said. "I know what we're up against. Everything will try to kill us. I'm not setting one foot out there."

"Pandora is keeping us prisoner," Jack said. "We've got to stick together and find a way out. I'll get you safely back to the armory."

"Pandora?" Paige had a confused look on her face.

Jack explained how it helped the players to put a name to their faceless captor. He finished by saying, "This farmhouse isn't safe but if you'd prefer to stay here... Douglas and I will be on our way."

"You're leaving us," Paige said.

Douglas grinned. "We came here to battle aliens and it's what we're gonna do."

"I'd like to play a game," William said. "Seems only fair to know exactly what I'm promoting."

It wouldn't hurt to have an extra pair of hands, thought Jack.

"I don't want to play." Paige hugged her arms around her body. "And I don't want to stay here. Just to be clear, if we see any trouble I'd like to avoid it. I have a low threshold for pain."

Since there were no weapons in the basement, Jack agreed that heading to the armory was the best course for all of them. There wasn't much activity on the ground anyway. Plus, time was running out. A call had come in for the troops to gather in readiness for the big-scaled attack.

The truck had two seats up front and two rows of seats in the back. Paige sat up the front with Jack. The conversation was polite, small talk that seemed out of place but also was the most important sort of conversation because it felt normal. It meant Jack didn't have to dwell on what might happen if he got everyone killed. He tried to radio Reis and Kelly and hadn't been able to reach them. After a few miles Paige started to relax. She told Jack about her acting career and how this was just a gig to play the bills.

"Acting's a tough gig," she said. "Harder than I realized. And now I'll be forever known as the face of the malfunctioning apocalypse."

After another half mile Jack decided he couldn't afford to travel at ten miles an hour. At this rate the game would be over, so he drove at top speed, almost one hundred miles an hour. By chance, or because the game was skewed in the player's favor, they reached the armory undetected. The large metal gates to the bunker were guarded. Everyone had to step out to prove they weren't aliens wearing human skins. Then the gates slowly opened and Jack drove inside the tunnel. This was when they were at their most vulnerable. The frogspawn were highly adaptable in these dark conditions. But their group made it inside the underground bunker and piled out of the truck. Paige was instantly recognized. Every male in the room hurried to attend to her. Her gloomy mood disappeared and she requested a room and a hot shower like this was a hotel. Everyone was happy to oblige.

"I guess we grab some weapons and head out to Ground Zero," said Jack.

"Not so fast," a voice from above called out.

Jack looked up to see a soldier standing on platform. "The General wants to meet with you, Minnow." Then he pointed to William. "You, too, Barrett."

William shrugged his shoulders. "We might find out what's going on."

They climbed the stairs, and as a Command Leader, albeit of lesser notoriety than Paige and William, Jack was ushered into the command room but Douglas was told to wait outside.

"General Yulrich," the soldier said. "May I present CLs Jonas Barrett and Jack Minnow."

The General, a tall man without hair or eyebrows, indicated for them to take a seat. On the rear wall was a large picture of the White House and a flag. Yulrich took the seat at the head of the table.

"What's the news out in the field?" Yulrich asked Jack.

"I've had a chance to test the bug bombs. It worked."

"Good. The balloons are being filled now. We'll wait for night to fall. Only three hours to go. The Chem Boys have loaded arrow tips with bug liquid which we'll need men to arm themselves with. I'm leaving you in charge of that operation, Minnow. Now... Barrett."

Jack noticed that it took William a second to realize that Yulrich was talking to him.

"Ah, yes, that's me," William said. "What can I do for you, sir?"

"I'll need you to head up the main operation at Ground Zero."

William's face began to pale. "The main operation?"

"Yes. I need someone with your skills and experience to make sure the troops heavily defend Ground Zero. You've got the air of command. Keep their morale high."

Jack caught William's worried look. "General, maybe CL Barrett would be best served keeping the morale of the troops high at the pre-victory party."

"What pre-victory party?" Yulrich glanced at the soldier whose face remained impassive. "There's no pre-victory party organized. Who authorized this?"

The soldier at the door coughed. "Sir, CL Stephanie Gey is also in the compound. She might have mentioned something about wanting a glass of wine."

Yulrich's face softened. "Well, of course we'll have a pre-victory party. And a post-victory party. The faces of the Human Defense Movement must stay here at Base." He indicated to the soldier by the door. "Commence plans for the party."

Next, Yulrich ran through the plans of attack for the afternoon.

"I owe you one," William whispered in Jack's ear.

At last Yulrich stood up. "It's settled. CLs Barrett and Gey will be the guests of honor. CL Minnow will lead the ground troops and hold them at Ground Zero. Succeed Minnow, and you'll be the hero of the day."

***

Douglas was waiting for Jack in the corridor. "What's the plan?"

"We're going into the city to organize the assault on the alien ship."

"Great."

Down at the weapons station, a truck had been loaded with archers and weapons. This time Jack didn't bother driving at ten miles an hour. The war would be over if he stuck to the limit set by the invaders, what's more the space ship was sweeping the area off its starboard side.

Douglas was unusually quiet on the ride back to the city, sneezing every now and then. Jack glanced at the boy.

"Allergies," Douglas said as explanation.

There was enough dust circulating through the air to cause allergies. In springtime, Jack sometimes got hay fever.

"Can you turn off the air conditioning," Douglas said. "I'm cold."

Jack felt neither hot nor cold. When Douglas yawned, he realized he also felt neither awake nor sleepy. Why would the NADs connecting Douglas to the mainframe be giving him typical human conditions?

New theory, Jack thought. Douglas really is a decoy because players don't suffer from their usual physical ailments. He didn't mind if Douglas was a decoy. He liked the kid. And he wasn't going to let a decoy stop him becoming hero of the day.

But what if he wasn't a decoy?

"You do realize this could be a suicide mission," Jack said. "Maybe you should have stayed behind."

"Maybe *you* should have stayed behind."

If he was a decoy, they'd designed the personality of a teenage boy perfectly.

Jack sped along the open road, crossed an intersection without looking, and was on the highway heading to Main Street. He kept glancing up at the giant ship, no longer frightened by it. Saddened almost, that he was about to destroy such a wonderful piece of technology.

The mission was simple. Balloons would be delivered to the town centre by the Hallmark Crew. Jack's crew, archers called the Merry Men, would fire arrows containing anti-bug spray – the concoction Jack had earlier let off with his grenade – at any frogspawn who tried to stop the balloons lifting off.

At the town centre, Jack pulled up in front of a pizza place. Men appeared from out of nowhere and opened the doors to a converted garage. He drove the truck inside and everyone got out and unloaded the weapons. The Merry Men disappeared inside the pizza parlor.

"Is that it?" Douglas whined. "We just hide in here."

"No. We need to get into position around the space ship, but we have to wait until the Hallmark Crew arrives with the balloons. Yulrich said three hours until they were ready. Nightfall until they are released. Nightfall is still two hours away. "

"I wanna check out the ship," Douglas said.

"No. Our orders are to stay here and defend this post."

Douglas scoffed. "Pl-ease. What orders? We're not really in the army. Don't you want to find out why the aliens are here?"

Of course Jack wanted to find out. But Reis had warned him that decoys steered the players off course. And Jack's course right now was to be hero of the day.

"You said these bracelets are teleportation devices," Douglas said. "So why don't we beam up and check out the ship? It'll only take a second."

Jack was dubious and also envious. To be sixteen and reckless.

"Nobody has used the bracelets before," Jack said. "What if we can't breathe on their ship? What if that device beams you to their home planet? Too many variables."

Douglas grinned. "Only one way to find out."

The kid rushed for the door and was outside before Jack could catch him. Two frogspawns appeared across the road in the park. The frogspawn hadn't yet noticed Jack and Douglas.

Jack struggled to keep his voice quiet. "Douglas. Come back inside."

Douglas fiddled with the bracelet. Jack tried to take it off him. Douglas pulled away and pressed at the buttons, but it was like it was programmed for alien DNA. It did nothing. Didn't even beep. At last the frogspawns across the road noticed them. They stopped mid-stride and lifted their arms up to chest height. Jack grabbed Douglas by the arm and spun him around to run back into the pizza place, only to see three more walking tadpoles heading their way. These aliens stopped mid-stride and their fishy faces quivered like they were gasping for air.

"Get inside," Jack hissed. Although he'd cop it for messing up this operation, he couldn't let Douglas get zapped.

Douglas was wide-eyed when he saw that the aliens had their bracelets trained on them.

"No!" Jack shouted, running in their line of fire. "Shoot me!"

His diversion didn't work. They shot Douglas, who vanished

before Jack's eyes and took a large part of his breath away. Then the aliens aimed their bracelets at Jack. He imagined he heard them laughing.

Shit. He'd messed up.

He was engulfed in the spray of something shimmering and cold.

***

Jack had expected getting shot to mean 'game over'. He hadn't expected to materialize inside the spaceship. He stood in the middle of a large, dome-roofed room with Douglas standing next to him.

"You reckless fool," Jack said.

"I'm okay."

"If you think disobeying orders is acceptable, then you're not okay."

Douglas grinned like it was a compliment. Jack wasn't sure if he should hit him or hug him. Around the walls were cages the size of houses. Each cage was crammed full with humans, perhaps a hundred per cage. A quick count and Jack reckoned there were almost a hundred cages. Which meant thousands of captives.

In a separate cage, off to the side was a lone German Shepherd. Oddly, the sight of captured humans was something Jack could handle. But a dog... he turned into a blubbering mess as he hurried to undo the pen door. The dog wandered out, shook its coat, and wagged its tail.

"Where are the aliens, buddy?" he asked the dog.

A frogspawn wandered around the corner at that moment, and the dog took one look at it and bared it teeth. The frogspawn squealed and backed up. Its high pitched screams echoed across the cavernous spaceship as it ran from the animal. The dog bounded across the shiny surface and a short while later, when it returned, it carried an alien arm in its mouth, which it dropped at Jack's feet. This arm contained an alien bracelet.

Jack bent down to scratch behind the dog's ears. It rolled on its back to beg for a scratch on the stomach.

"Good boy," he said.

"It's a girl," Douglas said with a shake of his head.

"Huh?"

"The dog is a girl. Look. No bits."

"You remind me of my sister. She always has to be right."

At least that was how he remembered the old Kelly, the one before Matt's death. Bossy, opinionated, and stubborn, she could argue for hours of the uselessness or practicality of the color red, depending on her mood. She was often impulsive, a trait he'd envied. She'd once driven two hours for a pineapple cheesecake. This act had displayed two of her typical personality traits – impulsiveness to abandon all plans and drive to the shop, and obstinacy because Jack had said it wouldn't taste any good. Turned out it was delicious but he'd refused to admit it. He guessed he could be stubborn too, and he possessed similar traits and a sibling sixth-sense, which was one way he'd known that she was aching inside unlike any ache she'd ever felt. The other way was from personal experience, but at the time he hadn't told anyone about a college girlfriend's death, preferring to grieve alone.

He hoped his real sister would return to him someday. He missed her. And he needed her.

Jack slipped his mind back into the present when he yanked the bracelet off the alien's arm and strapped it onto Douglas's. "We know this one works. Take it and beam down to the surface."

"No way. I'm not leaving your side."

"I'm not kidding." Jack checked his watch. Five p.m. "This ship is going to be blown apart in two hours. I want you out of here and long gone."

"Two hours is enough to check this spaceship out and leave. I mean, have a look around. We're on a friggin' space ship."

Jack did a slow circle. The walls, ceiling, and floor were composed of a dark, dull metal, and the sound of clanging and humming reverberated around the cavernous room like a million washing machines on spin cycle. Hundreds of lights were fitted to the ceiling so it was like gazing up at the stars. For a moment he forgot that only a handful of these captives were players, if any at all. Whether players or non-players, most were crying and groaning. Somehow, knowing they were NPCs didn't lesson the horror of witnessing their capture.

"I know what's going on," Douglas said excitedly. "We're not being destroyed. We're being caught."

Jack now saw the pattern of the cages. Old women huddled together in one cage. Another cage filled with old men. Next, a cage filled with young men about Douglas's age. Two or more cages filled with men around Jack's age.

"We're being caught and separated like fish," Douglas said.

"You mean to say these aliens travelled across the galaxy to go fishing?"

"Not fishing. Humaning."

"It's a long way to come for food."

Douglas shook his head. "Not really. My dad once drove fifteen hours to catch cod."

"We have to get everyone off this ship," Jack said. "A full-scale attack is set to launch. Everyone on board will be blown to smithereens."

"They're not real." Douglas was gazing up at the high ceiling. "None of this is real."

"Do you want them to die?" Jack asked, dreading that the answer might be yes.

"Course not," Douglas said. "I was just saying, if we didn't save everyone, it wouldn't be real. So it won't matter."

"It does matter." Jack had finally understood what this game was about. "What if this *was* a real situation? Pandora keeps asking us to draw the line and choose a side. I will not become the anti-hero."

Although he was fast losing hope that he'd even get to be *the* hero.

"I suppose you're right." Douglas reached into his jacket and pulled out his radio. "Anybody out there. Come in. This is Douglas Smith."

There was a bunch of static. Jack beckoned for the radio and fiddled with the dials.

"Anyone got ears on this channel," he said. "Listen carefully. This is Command Leader Jack Minnow. The aliens aren't vaporizing humans, they're teleporting them to the ship to use as food. I am on board the ship. Everyone is alive. I repeat. Everyone is alive. Call off the attack and launch a rescue mission instead."

He waited a few minutes to be sure someone had received his message. He got a reply, just not the one he expected.

"Negative." The voice belonged to Yulrich. "The attack is to proceed as planned. You are further ordered not to reveal plans of the attack to any survivors on the ship. This mission must not fail. We'll send another Command Leader in to lead the Merry Men."

Radio contact was cut.

"That jerk. He's leaving us to die." Not just the PCs and NPCs caught in the pens, Yulrich had signed the death warrants for him and Douglas as well. Jack changed frequency on the radio and put out another mayday call.

"Can anyone hear me? This is Jack Minnow. I'm on board the ship. Cancel the bomb attack. I repeat. Cancel the bomb—"

A voice came through. "Jack, this is Reis. Are you all right?"

"Reis. Am I glad to hear your voice? I'm alive and so is Douglas. Listen to me. The frogspawns are harvesting humans, not vaporizing them. I've got the means to teleport everyone off the ship but it will take time. It also might be safest done at night. You've got to get General Yulrich to delay the bombing until I can get everyone off board."

"I'm not sure he'll like that idea. Word is he's got a street parade organized. If you can get people off board, I'd do it sooner rather than later."

"Okay, but before I start transporting survivors down, I need eyes on the ground. I have no idea where I'm sending them to."

"Got it. I'll find the Eyeballs."

"Reis, one last thing. The frogspawns are afraid of dogs. Do we have German Shepherds guarding the armory?"

"Let me check."

It felt like hours ticked by until Reis responded.

"We have dogs. I'll call you when I've got visual. Reis out."

Douglas stood with his legs apart and his arms folded across his chest. He glared at Jack. "You go down if you're so afraid to be here."

A burst of static came over the radio and Reis said, "Jack, can you hear me?"

"Yow."

"I've got visuals for a five mile radius below the ship."

"All right. I'm sending someone down."

"Jack." Douglas stood there clenching his fists. "You can't do this to me."

True, Jack did want to zap him down to the ground, protect him, keep him safe, and it's what he should have done. If this was a real situation it would have been criminal to do anything else. But Jack knew how it felt to be sixteen and stuck in the horrible middle ground where you weren't a child and you weren't an adult. Where you resented being treated as either as you struggled to find your identity. Where nobody believed you or trusted you and everyone thought you were a useless idiot. At least that was how he recalled his youth. He'd been a clumsy, gangly teenager who'd often got injured playing sports. His parents had wanted to him to be a grown up without undertaking any of life's valuable lessons such as underage drinking and cheating on exams. Too old to play with adult games, too young to play kid's games. Sixteen sucked. The kid deserved a break.

"Give me some credit," Jack said.

He aimed the bracelet at the dog. She disappeared without a sound or a flash of light.

Reis's voice came over the radio. "I see a dog. Sector B. Warehouse district. Wait, it's spied an alien. And it's off. Yep, you're right. They do *not* like dogs."

"Reis, it's important you get the Merry Men to Sector B to secure the area, and get the General to hold off on the attack," said Jack. "Douglas and I will transport everyone off the ship."

"I'll see what I can do. Reis out."

Suddenly Jack felt light headed, couldn't breathe. Maybe it was the alien air. He suspected the frogspawns had large lungs to hold their extraterrestrial air and when it was expended they returned to the ship to realign their sensors. Maybe Jack's lack of oxygen was nothing to do with *this* environment but the one in the simulation pod. Was an operator trying to pry open the glass lid? He'd been too quick to accuse Douglas of being a decoy simply because Jack had believed this virtual environment to be flawless to human ailments.

His vision flickered as if lightning was striking the chamber. An image of a dark haired woman flashed across his eyes; his college girlfriend, Mary-Ellen. The college girlfriend who'd died and become the reason Jack could empathize with his sister. Jack hadn't thought about Mary-Ellen in years.

"You okay?" Douglas asked.

Jack blinked, as if the problem was organic. Most likely the heads-up display unit was on the fritz. Everything else seemed to be. Damn this malfunction. Without communication to the outside world, he had no idea what was going on.

"Let's get everyone off the ship." Jack refused to let any of the worrying thoughts rob him of his glory. He and Douglas began teleporting the captives down to the ground. Women and children first. Then the young men. Then the old men, though somewhere in the back of his mind he wondered about the wisdom of leaving the healthiest and fittest to last. In a real battle, saving the vulnerable was top priority. But wasn't having the healthiest and fittest troops to defeat the enemy also a priority? The lesson of the day was compassion versus strategy. Risk killing the troops, humanity might not win. Risk killing vulnerable civilians, humanity definitely lost.

With each passing minute Jack found his attention wandering to the main door where he expected to be overrun with red tadpoles. But twenty minutes later they'd managed to teleport one quarter of the captives. After thirty minutes, Jack's nerves began to make his hands shake. If Reis hadn't managed to stop the attack, the balloons would be launched. He wasn't worried about his death, but if anything were to happen to Douglas, the way something had happened to Mary-Ellen, he wouldn't be able to live with himself, the way he barely lived with himself now.

Images flickered once more across his vision like silent movies. A funeral. A coffin. A young boy. The back of his neck started to ache.

"Get out of my head, Pandora," he said.

"Jack." Douglas sounded far away. "Jack. You all right?"

Just like that, the visions cleared and a sense of determination to save those he cared about charged through his body. Douglas would hate him for what he was about to do, but so be it. At least the kid would be alive to hate him.

"Keep an eye out, will you?" he said to Douglas. "Just stand at the door and tell me if anything comes."

Douglas pouted but he did as he was told. And when he got near the door, Jack aimed the bracelet at the kid and teleported him down to Earth. He heard the kid's cursing long after he'd vanished.

It took another fifteen minutes to get another quarter off the ship, and another hour to complete the task. Each time a frogspawn wandered into the containment area, Jack zapped the alien down to the ground where he hoped the Merry Men waited to take them out.

By the end he was exhausted, yet satisfied. A job well done. Worthy of the title 'hero of the day'. The only problem now was the ship hovered a mile above the earth and he had no idea how to save himself.

The bracelet had three buttons. Blind luck had caused Jack to press the top button which had transported the captives from the ship down to the surface. Would it work if he pointed it at himself? He tried it, and found himself teleported to the ground. The Merry Men were armed and ready, and the rescued captives were running from the area. Just as well, because a large troop of frogspawn appeared seconds later.

"Fire." The Merry Men shot arrows into the aliens.

"Jesus, let me get out of the way first," Jack shouted.

The aliens must have raided one of the military's weapons stores because they were heavily armed with human weapons, which they fired at the Merry Men and at the fleeing captives. Humans and aliens fell. Jack ducked and weaved between the fighting until he found cover behind a car. He still wore the alien bracelet and he zapped a few aliens back up to the ship.

A frogspawn carrying a rocket launcher on his shoulder spied Jack and turned to face him.

"Shit."

Jack ran for cover. But the blast never came. One of the Merry Man had taken down the frogspawn before he could squeeze the trigger.

The fight lasted twenty minutes, but it felt longer. When it was over, Jack's heart was racing. He thought he'd drop dead from exhaustion and adrenalin overload.

An explosion in the sky startled him. He looked up to see the space ship making its rapid descent to Earth. Flames engulfed the hull and the ship vanished from sight behind a row of buildings. Seconds later, it landed with a thud that could be felt in Jack's chest. It sent an ash cloud up into the sky. Nobody – alien or human –

could survive a fall from the sky.

The players had defeated the enemy. The game was over.

In that moment it was easy to tell the players from the non-players. The players were the ones with doubtful expressions on their faces, wondering if the game was really over.

14

Jack

Minutes later, the game had not ended and the players were stood around waiting for something to happen. A new game? Release from the pods? Something. Anything.

But nothing happened.

As if Jack's thinking about 'what next?' was a trigger, he found himself shifted in time and sitting beside Douglas in the back of an open-topped Cadillac with the German Shepherd acting as a buffer between them. Douglas was livid that Jack had betrayed him, Jack was adamant he'd done the right thing in keeping the kid alive. They were joined by the two celebrity command leaders, William Rush and Paige Swanson, who sat up front in their CL uniforms.

General Yulrich was a few feet away from the Cadillac talking to his soldiers.

William leaned over the back. "Is this a typical finale to a game?"

"No," Jack whispered. "But I'm not complaining. I reckon we could all use a break from the violence."

General Yulrich broke from the group and wandered over to the Cadillac. "Command Leader Jack Minnow. I said you'd be hero of the day and you didn't let me down."

Now wasn't the time to remind the general that if his orders had been followed, everyone on board the ship would be charcoal and ashes.

Apart from having no hair, the general reminded Jack of his father, providing encouraging words, sometimes over a beer, even after Jack had done the opposite of what his father had told him to do. And his mom would always celebrate an achievement, usually with a home baked pie. Jack sighed thinking about how worried his parents would be. Four or five days would have passed since he'd contacted them.

"The full count came in," Yulrich said interrupting his thoughts. "You rescued one thousand and eighteen people from the space ship."

Jack's mood began to lift.

"He had help," Douglas said with a sneer.

Despite Douglas's aversion to being teleported to the ground, it'd turned out to be a strategic marvel because Douglas had used his radio to pester Yulrich into holding off the attack until Jack had transported everyone off the ship.

"How does it feel to be the youngest Command Leader?" Yulrich asked Douglas. "You'll also be the youngest recipient of a medal for bravery."

Before Douglas could reply, the general slapped a hand against the car door. The engine burst into life and the car pulled out the garage and headed for the street parade.

"I can tell you a million times that I'm sorry," Jack told Douglas. "Except I'm not."

"You did it so you could take all the glory."

"I did it to save your life."

Paige turned around. "Douglas, sweetie, I'd have done the same thing. You're too precious." She turned to face Jack. "What happens now?"

"I'm not sure. We've defeated the enemy so it should be game over. This is new."

"This is Pandora wanting *her* glory," Douglas said.

It made sense. If Pandora was tapping into their minds, she might discover that Jack yearned for the accolades. And the NADs worked both ways. If she was evolving, as Jack reckoned she was, maybe she yearned for recognition of her genius.

Pandora's evolution begged the question: what was she evolving into?

The car arrived in town and people were lined up along the street. Jack had seen plenty of street parades, but he'd never sat in the lead car.

"Smile and wave," Paige said. "I might as well embrace being the face of the malfunctioning apocalypse."

They drove down Main Street, and when the car did a victory lap around the burning remains of the space ship, Jack wondered how Reis could think this type of fanfare was crap. Jack *loved* the attention. By the time he was asked to deliver a speech he'd built up enough courage to get over his fear of public speaking. It helped that Dixiebell – Jack had named the dog after a stray he'd grown particularly fond of – wandered up on the stage the same time as him and sat beside him like his new best friend.

"May I introduce Command Leader Dixiebell," Jack said. The audience cheered and whistled, calling the dog a hero. "I rescued her from the alien spaceship," he added quickly. "She wouldn't be here today if it wasn't for me. None of us would be here."

While the audience applauded, Jack's words sank in. *None of us would be here.* He'd done it. He'd saved the world. Sweat broke out on his brow at how exhilarating and terrifying the ordeal had been.

Then his throat dried up because if his plan had backfired, same result, none of them would be here.

He cleared his throat and read from a speech one of the General's staff had typed up. He didn't really take notice of the words or the audience's reaction to them. In the back of his mind it became clear that his intentions to save Douglas were not for the boy's benefit but for his own. He had sought redemption by sending Douglas down to the ground. It could have gone horribly wrong. And one life saved didn't make up for one life lost.

Jack ended his speech and moved off to the side while the other CLs spoke of their part in the victory. He hardly heard a word.

It felt like the speeches lasted longer than the war. When at last the CLs were relieved of duty, Jack shook the hands of people who waited at the bottom of the stage stairs, then he pushed through the crowd to find Kelly.

He found her with a bottle of wine in her hands.

She stumbled towards him and gave him a big hug. "Mom and Dad would be proud. Sorry, I'm drinking to forget. I don't like it here. Can we go home now?"

"If it were up to me, we'd have gone home days ago."

"Really? I thought you'd be enjoying all this. My brother, the hero. Savior of Earth."

She staggered back a few steps and Reis caught her. Jack noticed the way Reis looked at his sister. As if she was a delicate flower. She was far from delicate, but he was pleased they were spending time together. They'd been good friends once. Jack now hoped for more, and he hated that his motives were purely selfish. With Reis busy, it would mean fewer disasters in the relationship department for Jack. He knew he should get over his jealousy, after all Reis had never displayed any interest in Jack's date, but it still hurt whenever he got dumped and a week later his ex-date asked to be introduced to Reis Anderson.

"The party is premature," Kelly said. "This war ain't over."

Reis nodded. "While you were giving your speech, we spied a couple of the frogspawns materializing in the parking lot. They ran off into the night."

"That's not possible," Jack said. "The ship is on fire."

Reis shrugged. "Then why are we still here?"

"Yeah, Jack," said Kelly. "Why are we still here? We beat the aliens. Isn't the game supposed to end? Yet, we're still here."

"And we're burning the enemy's home," Reis added.

The implications of his friend's remark sank in. "We're burning the ship and if the frogspawns have their teleporting bracelets, they might be sending humans into the fire. Jesus."

"Bingo," Kelly said. "Though I'm not sure I care. We *should* all burn in hell for what we're doing to this planet, to the animals, to ourselves."

"Okay, that's enough wine." Jack grabbed the bottle out of Kelly's hand. His sister's rant about the world burning was nothing new. He just hadn't heard it for a few years, not since she'd started dating Matt. While he wished for her return to normal, he hoped this trait would stay in the shadows.

"How are you even getting drunk?" he asked. "We're not flesh and blood."

She shrugged. "Don't ask me. I'm just here to meet a dead guy."

"What?"

She looked away. "Nothing."

"Kelly. What's going on?"

She sighed. "I might as well tell you. Matt's voice and image are built into the game. He told me about it before he died. I came here to find him."

Anger burst inside Jack at his sister's selfishness. He'd entered the game to keep an eye on her, thinking *she* was doing something noble, but she was going to ruin everything by undermining his actions.

"Come on, Jack," she said. "Don't act surprised. What other reason would I have to come here? This is the most stupid thing I've ever done and you know it. When have I ever played video games?"

"You're unbelievable. I came here to protect you."

She shook her head and began to sob. "I'm sorry. Why am I being so horrible to you? I'm just so sick of being here. I need to go home. It'll be... in a few days it'll be one year since Matt died."

His anger disappeared and he hugged his sister. Reis slipped into the darkness. Jack let him go. Console his sister or console his best friend. Why did he never think of consoling himself?

***

While Kelly cried on his shoulder, Jack glanced over at the stage. Yulrich was talking to a bunch of official looking people. The will to march over there and tell the general to stop turning the ship into his personal fireworks display had left. His sister needed him more than the PCs and NPCs.

Kelly dried her eyes. "Where did Reis go?"

"You know him. He likes to be alone sometimes."

"Was I horrible to him?"

"He's a big boy."

She rubbed at her eyes. "Jack, I want this nightmare to be over, which is why we need to tell the general that we didn't kill all the frogspawns."

"What then? Another apocalypse? Kell, we're advancing through levels of a video game and it's getting harder and harder to win. Paige was scared when I found her, naturally, but she was scared because she knows what's coming. I don't know that we're getting out of here, and frankly I'm a little worried."

She nodded. "Me too."

He winked at her. "You're supposed to tell me I'm being ridiculous."

"What's the alternative? Give up." A bubble of laughter escaped. "It's not that easy to do."

Kelly puffed out her chest and marched up to the General. Jack hurried to join her, but the General's men wouldn't let either of them anywhere near him.

"Fine," Jack said. "You tell him the aliens are still out there. They ran off toward Sector H. I'm taking a truck and going after them, alone if I have to."

And alone it was. Kelly had changed her mind and wanted to crawl under a rock. So Jack charged toward the parking lot. People began following him, maybe players or non-players, it didn't matter. They got into their trucks, and just as Jack started the engine of his stolen military truck, something exploded inside the spaceship.

***

Jack drove for a spell, then he stopped the car and killed the headlights. As he stared out through the windshield, the frogspawns' red flesh glistened under the moonlight. Impossible to count but Jack guessed there were fifty or more aliens congregated in the middle of an open field. Impossible to think they'd reproduced, yet if they had, humanity might be screwed after all.

He decided against radioing for help. There were plenty of civilians on hand, but since they hovered in his peripheral vision, he guessed they were all NPCs.

Just then a truck pulled up beside him. A man wearing a player-designated combat uniform hopped out and headed over to greet Jack.

"Neil Cooney," the man said extending his hand in greeting.

"Jack Minnow."

Neil was a lot shorter than Jack, only reaching shoulder height, but the man had a fierce look in his eyes.

"I was up at the farmhouse when I ran into one of these jelly freaks," Neil said. "Saw your headlights and thought I'd check it out. Looks like you found a pod of frogspawn. Good one."

"Except there are too many of them," Jack said. "And not enough of us."

Neil surveyed the area. "NPCs just get in the way." He shrugged and went round to the back of his truck, returning with two samurai swords. "Chopping off their heads guarantees they don't get back up."

Jack laughed, even though this guy terrified him. He looked the type to give his five-year-old child a gun for Christmas. He grabbed a sword, and became mesmerized by the moonlight glistening off the blade. Familiarity coursed through him. This sword was similar to a sword he'd worked one summer for as a kid to buy. But when his dad had intercepted the package and made Jack return it, stating he didn't want weapons in the house. Jack hadn't even had a chance to hold the weapon up into the air.

Jack traced a finger along the blade. "Typical that the military spent time and resources finding ways to destroy these things and all we need to do is cut of their head."

"She's pretty," Neil said. "Keep her. She'll be gone by tomorrow anyway because we'll enter the next game weaponless as usual."

The darkness was broken by the sound of engines. The same moonlight that lit up the sword guided a small convoy of cars to their location. People got out, although Jack didn't recognize any of them. He kept an eye out for Reis, but his friend never appeared.

At least the numbers were now more evenly matched.

"We can handle this." Neil scowled. "We don't need back up."

"Speak for yourself," Jack said.

Still wearing a CL uniform, Jack decided he might as well take charge of the operation and direct the teams into position. He should have called for the military, but this wasn't Yulrich's game to play. It was up to the one hundred people lying inside simulation pods with the notion that they might die to fight for the right to live. Jack withdrew the map that showed a road running alongside the field. He instructed two cars to drive up and position themselves at the furthest edge. One team of cars would remain on the road. A third team, consisting of the fittest men, would run on foot to flank the right side, and the final team would attack from their current position. Using radio contact, all four sides would then attack the aliens at once, leaving the enemy nowhere to run or hide.

Neil waited until the cars had left before he said, "Nice plan, but you do realize the uniform you're wearing is part of a fantasy world. In a real situation, we'd take a vote on who was in charge."

"So take a vote," Jack said.

Neil grinned. "I'm just messing with you. If this was a real situation I'd be in the hills by now. I'd have taken my bug-out bus with my family and enough food to last the rest of our lives. That's our doomsday evacuation plan. Don't get me wrong, I'm loving the chance to shoot giant bugs, but if this were real, survival would be the key. I have a family to take care of."

Jack understood family. He'd followed his sister into the game to keep her safe. Instead of trying to be the hero, he should have been searching for way to get her out.

"So what do you think is going on?" Jack asked Neil. "Not right now, but..."

Neil raised an eyebrow. "You mean the game? Difficult to say. We've had no contact from outside. That orb in the sky and the limousine rides was just a BS distraction. We weren't being rescued." Neil cast a glance around. "CyberNexis is funded by the military and built inside an old military base. I reckon the malfunction is the result of a terrorist attack."

"An attack like that means people will be looking for us."

"I'm counting on it."

The first team radioed that they were in position. Jack had expected the rumbling of the car's engines to alert the frogspawns, in which case the giant bugs would flee, and Jack's conscience would be clear because he was starting to have doubts about ambushing the frogspawn. So far, they appeared to be setting up a camp in the field, as if they knew their ship was struck down and they were stranded on Earth. Or maybe the fact they were hiding in plain sight meant this was a trap in which case everyone would die.

Just as the second team radioed in, a full-sized military vehicle pulled up. Out jumped thirty or more soldiers in full battle gear. Leading the troop was General Yulrich.

"You're not taking any more credit for defeating these vermin," he said to Jack. "From now on, any credit will be going to me. What's the situation?"

Neil stood behind Yulrich, slowly shaking his head. Even Jack had to admit that the NPCs were acting an awful lot like players. He guessed it was a result of the evolving program.

"It's okay, General," said Jack. "We've got it covered."

Yulrich disagreed. "Stand down, CL Minnow. *I've* got it covered." He began talking to his men is hushed tones and secret code, and then Yulrich and the soldiers jogged into the woods and were swallowed up by the darkness.

Neil stared after them. "They're getting smarter, thinking on their own. That's dangerous. For us."

General Yulrich radioed that his team were ready to begin the attack. He began a thirty second countdown.

"Maybe we should have told him about the swords," Jack said. "Maybe we should have told the other players too. Hardly seems a fair fight."

"No such thing as a fair fight anymore," Neil said, and then he took off across the field with his sword high over his head.

***

All four groups appeared out of the woods at different intervals, but they all met in the middle, converging on the group of frogspawns at the same time. Screams erupted from both attackers and the enemy. The aliens didn't know what hit them. Bullets, knives, taser guns, machetes... multiple forms of weapons came at them, and at such ferocious speeds that they'd no chance to surrender.

This wasn't survival. It was a simulated game and it was a fight for planet Earth. Even if the aliens had waved white flags, their surrender wouldn't have been accepted.

Jack allowed his primal instinct to take over as he sliced the heads off the aliens. Frogspawns aimed bracelets at their attackers, sending humans into the burning remains of the space ship. As soon as Jack or Neil were near enough to detach an alien arm, they did so. The alien flesh might have been red but their blood was green. By the light of the moon, Jack noticed that only green blood had spilled. The aliens had had no weapons other than their teleporting bracelets.

As the last frogspawn lay dying on the ground, it hit Jack with a thud. The enemy had been defenseless.

***

The massacre of frogspawns took less than half an hour, and the ground was thick with green sludge that glowed beneath the moonlight.

Bile rose up in Jack's throat. *Their only defense was the bracelets that teleported them to the ship.* He had just taken part in the mass slaughter of unarmed beings.

"That was too easy," Neil said, wiping the blood off his sword. "Hey, you okay? You look like you're gonna throw up. Did you eat their blood or something?"

Jack tried to shake off the sickening feeling, but it ground at his insides like he'd swallowed broken glass.

"The game should have ended," Jack said. "We brought down their ship. We won. But Pandora forced us to play just one more hand."

"So?"

All around was evidence of how savage humanity could be when it wanted to. Jack had to turn away from the sight. This was just a game. It wasn't real. He couldn't be held accountable for the deaths of innocent creatures while he was in a virtual game. Senseless violence was the *whole point*!

He stumbled his way back towards the car. He couldn't even throw up because he had no food in his stomach.

He heard footsteps behind him.

"We shouldn't have done that," he said, thinking it was Neil. But when he turned, he was facing a wounded frogspawn. It clutched a severed, jelly-red arm that still had its bracelet intact.

"Wait," said Jack. "It wasn't my fault. I didn't know you were unarmed."

The frogspawn made a series of *clicks* and *chirps*. As the ball of white light emerged in front of Jack, he realized that the humans hadn't made any attempts to communicate with the aliens. They'd just killed on sight.

And worse, it'd been Jack who'd led the army that had slaughtered them.

INSIDE THE SIMULATION POD

PRESENTATION BY
GAME CREATOR, MAX WINTERDOM, AT THE LAUNCH PAD

Greetings players.

Ever since dinosaurs walked the earth, mankind has been under threat of extinction.

As mankind's numbers continue to grow exponentially the threat of extinction is only increasing, so when every nation's leader got together at the global summit that October day of 2020 and decided something had to be done to ensure mankind's survival, I commissioned the team at Simulated Military And Recreational Training (SMART) to create dozens of apocalyptic survival training programs and take home kits to ensure that every man, woman, and child was adequately prepared to survive any threat of total annihilation from any source, natural or manmade, and even any source of threat from out of this earth.

SMART is a blend of military muscle, corporate know-how, passionate professionals, and strategic sagacity. They are a team of experts in survival who are committed to helping humans survive the end of the world.

But firstly, what is an apocalypse?

In religious contexts the word 'apocalypse' usually means the unveiling of something hidden. Today, it is commonly used in reference to the end of the world in general.

What the end of the world will really look like is something we can only speculate on. And SMART have indeed speculated on what they think any number of apocalypses will resemble. By creating scenarios based on science and mythology, players from all walks of life will be able to participate in and enjoy these simulations.

For many, The Apocalypse Games is more than a game. It's a chance to unveil something hidden.

Who are you really? You'll soon find out.

15

Jack

An alarm clock buzzed. As Jack Minnow stirred awake, the memories of the day he'd entered the virtual game scattered like birds at the crack of gunfire. He woke up to the pleasant sight of a beautiful woman in bed beside him. It had to be a dream. Or a cruel trick.

The woman had black hair; it fell in big waves around her face. A lazy smile danced on her lips. The moss-green eyes that stared through messy hair mesmerized him. He'd only known one woman to possess eyes this color.

"Mary-Ellen?"

She groaned and swept the hair off her face. "Who else were you expecting?"

A sense of displacement separated his mind from his body; as if he existed on two planes, one supernatural and one ridiculous. Neither plane was real, yet when Mary-Ellen's icy-cold toes brushed against his shin, he yelped.

She giggled and swiped at her hair once more. A habit Jack used to find mildly annoying, since he often got his fingers tangled in her hair and once a zipper, yet it was suddenly the best gesture in the world. It meant she was alive. It also meant Jack was dead, at least virtually dead. This death dream wouldn't be so bad if he got to spend it with Mary-Ellen.

A flash of gold on her finger meant she was married. Instinctively, Jack rubbed his thumb along his finger and discovered a wedding ring. She was married. So was he. Didn't mean they were married to each other.

He reached out to stroke the hip of the girl he'd dated in college. Just as his fingers found her soft flesh, the bedroom door burst open. A young boy ran into the room. He bashed into the base of the bed, bouncing bounced up and down like he either needed to go to the bathroom or evil clowns were chasing him.

"Mommy. Daddy. It's my birthday. Guess what? I'm five."

Mary-Ellen propped herself on her elbows. The loving smile she showered on the boy could've lit up a city and made grown men jealous. "Wow, you're five? I never would have guessed."

"Can I open my present now?" the boy asked, still bobbing up and down.

Jack could relate to his excitement. Birthdays were the happiest moments of his childhood.

Mary-Ellen lightly punched Jack in the leg and pointed to the door. "Caleb wants to open his present."

Caleb's eyes latched onto Jack's faster than a greyhound's latched onto its rabbit-shaped lure. At least the kid had stopped his frantic pogo dance.

"Can I, Daddy? Can I?"

He stared at Jack expectantly, but Jack's brain was still suffering from the shock of Mary-Ellen and a kid in the same room as him.

"It's in the garage," Mary-Ellen said.

Caleb bolted out of the room.

"Don't open it until we get there," Mary-Ellen shouted. She turned to Jack. "You know he's gonna wanna ride that thing all day." With a groan, she pushed herself out of bed and slipped into the dressing gown she'd lifted off the floor. She walked toward the door, but at the end of the bed she yelped out in pain. "Ah, Christ, I've stubbed my toe. Jeez, that hurts. I swear I need to walk around the house in combat boots. Haven't you moved this bed yet like I asked you to?"

Jack wasn't really listening. His mind had drifted off. How could he have a wife and kid?

"Thanks for caring," Mary-Ellen said, picking a cushion up off the floor and throwing it at his head.

This snapped Jack out of his reverie. "Sorry, Mare. I zoned out for a second. You want ice for your toe?"

"No. I want coffee and to never invite the Kennedys over for dinner again. They can drink as much as they like, they don't have a five-year-old who thinks dawn is 'up time'."

Once more, Jack only half listened. His head was fuzzy and he had trouble tussling with the fact he had a son to a woman he'd dated in college. It wasn't right. Pandora was messing with him. Although the math *did* add up somewhat. He was twenty-eight. Caleb was five. Mary-Ellen must have been pregnant at twenty-two, twenty-three. Around the time they'd dated.

Mary-Ellen's green-eyed-glare locked onto Jack's like a tractor beam, pulling him out of bed. He followed her down the hallway and towards the garage. There, in the middle of the room sat a large object wrapped in colorful paper. The shape gave its identity away in a nanosecond – a bicycle. Caleb hopped up and down. The boy's excitement was contagious. A first bike was a special moment for a boy. Jack had ridden his bike up and down the street all day, driving his mom and dad nuts with worry that something would happen to him. Something had; he'd fallen off and broken his arm.

Caleb tore into the wrapping. It took him about three seconds to uncover the red bicycle. "Daddy, can I ride it?"

"That's what it was built for."

"Breakfast first," said Mary-Ellen.

Around a yawn, she told Jack to make sure Caleb didn't go outside while she made coffee and toast. Jack stared at the boy, not having a clue how to speak to him. The kid was chatting away nonstop about all the adventures he'd take on his bike. Jack was relieved when minutes later, Mary-Ellen called out from the kitchen. Jack sipped his coffee. Cream with two sugars. Her remembering how he liked his coffee warmed him more than the beverage. Until it sank in that this was a delusion created by Pandora tapping into his gray matter, so a CGI woman *would* know how he liked his coffee.

Real or not, caffeine did the trick of kick-starting his brain into gear. He decided to investigate his surroundings for clues. In the garage were boxes marked CHRISTMAS DECORATIONS. A clothes dryer sat on the floor as did a rusted-up exercise bike, tools, and broken furniture. He guessed that the car – if they had one – sat out in the driveway. In the house, some of the walls were wallpapered and the rest were in need of a fresh coat of paint. The kitchen floors were linoleum and the carpet in the rest of the house was worn, yet clean. Cheap furniture filled the house and framed photos adorned the walls. The house had none of the style of his city apartment, yet it was neat and tidy and made him incredibly homesick. His tour ended back in the kitchen where Mary-Ellen's look of disapproval had settled on Caleb. The kid had only eaten two mouthfuls of toast. No wonder he's so small, Jack thought.

Mary-Ellen's eyes implored Jack to do something.

"Eat up, buddy," Jack said. "You need muscles to push those pedals."

Caleb nodded and wolfed down the rest of his toast. Then the kid got up, dropped his plate in the sink and wrapped his arms around Jack's legs.

"I love you, Daddy."

Caleb raced into the garage before Jack could reply. He doubted he could've said anything anyway; his throat had choked up.

"You sure have the knack," said Mary-Ellen. "I can't get him to eat a thing."

The coffee was suddenly hard to swallow. Jack set the mug in the sink and carried Caleb's bike out into the front yard. A water fountain sat in the middle of the lawn. Totally out of place to the rest of the house. Jack stared at it, wondering how it got there. A memory sprang to mind. He'd lost his job with a landscaping company, and after a few drinks he'd decided to steal the fountain from the display center.

He forcibly shook off the sense of displacement – the memory wasn't his, yet it refused to budge. He decided to wander up to the sidewalk and look up and down the street.

"Honey," Mary-Ellen said nervously. "What are you doing?"

No vampires or zombies or masked monsters in sight, still, Jack sensed an unknown malevolence, so he told Caleb he could ride his bicycle on the driveway or not at all. He moved the station wagon out onto the street, and for the next hour he cursed his lack of physical fitness. His back ached from holding onto the seat of the bike. It turned out two slices of toast wasn't enough to give Caleb the muscle strength to turn the pedals.

A phone rang from somewhere inside the house. Mary-Ellen ducked inside and returned a few moments later carrying the handset.

"Jack. Call for you."

"Let's take a break," he told the kid. "I've got to talk on the phone."

"Aw, but I wanna ride my bike."

"Not by yourself."

"I'll push him," Mary-Ellen said.

"On the driveway only."

She laughed. "You're such a worrier."

Jack grabbed the phone and sank down onto the porch steps. He heard his back and legs creaking. I've gotten old, he thought as he lifted the handset to his ear.

"Yow, this is Jack."

Silence.

"Hello?"

Caleb squealed with delight, and an unexpected sense of resentment welled up inside Jack. Taking this call meant he'd missed out on a special moment in his son's life.

But I don't have a son.

Except that he did. Mary-Ellen was pushing the kid in question off the driveway and onto the sidewalk. Caleb held his legs up off the pedals. Mary-Ellen had a hold onto the seat. They were both laughing.

"Hello? Who's there?" Jack spoke sharply into the phone.

"Answer me."

Just then came a screech of tires.

Everything after the screeching tires happened quickly, yet it felt as if hours had passed. One second the white sedan car was on the road, the next it was on the sidewalk.

The car slammed into Mary-Ellen and Caleb and crunched into Jack's car parked on the street.

Jack bolted across the lawn. It took forever get there and his feet felt like they were stuck in mud. He found Caleb and Mary-Ellen wedged under the car. No amount of lifting helped budge it. Maybe the driver stepped out, or maybe it was a neighbor, Jack took little notice. He shouted for someone to lift the car off them. Then he shouted for Mary-Ellen and Caleb to get up.

Time may have sped up or slowed down or stopped altogether. He couldn't say exactly what happened after he grabbed a hold of their dead hands, not even when the ambulance and cop car arrived.

Someone pushed him out of the way, but he had a firm grip on their hands, willing them to squeeze back. A paramedic finally managed to pull him away and walked him over to the fountain. Lights flashed, people shouted, others sobbed.

A voice beside him spoke. "Is there anyone you'd like me to call? Family? Friends? Work colleagues?"

He formed words in his head but none come out. *This isn't real.*

A neighbor offered to go through his phone book and call relatives with the sad news. Did he have family?

"None of this is real," he said.

He let a stranger guide him back inside the house. The stranger said it would take time to sink in, then the stranger tried to coax him to bed. Jack refused to go. He gathered up all the photos off the walls and sat on the sofa, stroking the photos one by one, as if gathering up their memories so they wouldn't slip away.

***

An alarm clock buzzed. As Jack stirred awake, his dreams scattered like birds at the crack of gunfire, and he woke to the realization that his wife and son were dead.

I don't have a wife and son. This is just a game.

He opened his eyes. Mary-Ellen was in the bed with him. A startled cry burst out of his mouth.

Her eyelids flicked open. "You don't look so hot yourself."

"Mare? What's going on?" He sat up. "Caleb!"

She groaned. "Caleb will want to ride that damned bike all day. That's the last time we have the Kennedys over for dinner. They can drink as much as they like, they don't have a five-year-old who thinks dawn is 'up time'. I need coffee."

Jack shook his head to clear the remnants of the bad dream, then the bedroom door burst open. A young boy ran into the room. He crashed into the base of the bed, bouncing up and down like he either needed to go to the bathroom or evil clowns were chasing him.

"Mommy. Daddy. It's my birthday. Guess what? I'm five."

Mary-Ellen propped herself on her elbows. She showered Caleb with a smile that could have lit up a city.

"Wow, you're five," she said. "I never would have guessed."

Jack was scared.

"Can I open my present now?" Caleb asked, bobbing up and down.

Birthdays were always the happiest day of any kid's life, or at least they should have been. Jack sensed the foreboding of gloom hovering over this one.

Mary-Ellen lightly punched Jack in the leg. "Your son wants to open his present."

Caleb's eyes latch onto his. He jumped up and down on the spot. "Can I, Daddy? Can I?"

"I don't know, buddy," Jack said nervously. "Maybe we should go to the mall and get you something else. You're so... frail."

As Caleb's eyes welled with tears, Mary-Ellen scowled. "Seriously? You know he frets about his size. Besides, it's a little late to change your mind." She showered Caleb with her motherly smile. "Honey, Daddy told a fib and he will put one dollar in the fibbing jar. You are big and strong, now go to the garage but don't—"

"—open it till we get there," Jack said, finishing her sentence. He was starting to get an idea of how this day was going to pan out.

With a groan, Mary-Ellen pushed herself up off the bed and slipped into the dressing gown she'd lifted off the floor. She walked toward the door; at the end of the bed she yelped out in pain.

"Ah, Christ, I've stubbed my toe. Jeez, that hurts. I swear I need to walk around the house in combat boots. Haven't you moved this bed yet like I asked you to?"

Jack reluctantly rolled out of bed and followed Mary-Ellen as she hobbled to the garage. There, in the middle sat an object covered in wrapping paper. Caleb clapped his hands together like he wasn't fooled by the disguise for a second.

A sense of déjà vu invaded Jack and it caused his stomach to drop. Maybe what he'd foreseen wasn't a dream. Maybe it was a premonition. He made the decision to dodge the karma bus.

"We'll go to the park," he said.

Caleb and Mary-Ellen loved the idea of going for a ride in the park. She packed half the house into the beaten-up station wagon that sat in the driveway, and before Jack slipped into the driver's side he noticed the fountain in the middle of the front yard. It sat there like an omen, as if karma had conspired against him for stealing it. As he pulled out of the driveway he told himself that he'd dig it up and return it as soon as he got home.

He still had no idea about his surroundings. Some suburb in the middle of some county, and it could have been anywhere; the cars on the street were parked on the right hand side and a house on the corner displayed an American flag so he guessed not another country. It only made him more homesick.

It also meant he had no idea where he'd locate a park for Caleb to ride around, but he eventually found a place called Cascade Gardens near a strip mall. After hours of pushing around his son – he was starting to get used to the idea of family, and it wasn't *that* horrible –his back needed a rest. It was easy to entice Caleb off the bike with ice cream. Caleb must've been tired, because two minutes later Jack was storing the bike in the back of the wagon. Ten minutes later they were at Willow's Ice Cream, Willow Creek. Jack had never heard of the town. He didn't particularly hate the place.

The three of them walked into the ice cream parlor holding hands. The fridges hummed but otherwise it was quiet. Two customers stood off to the side, two staff members were behind the counter, yet there wasn't a happy face amongst the lot of them. Jack was happy enough for everyone. He paid for three ice creams. Outside, Mary-Ellen reached for his hand. He didn't particularly hate that either.

"This is nice," she said. "We should do more family things."

Jack nodded. "Why don't we?'

Her remote gaze fell on Caleb whose tongue was devouring the ice cream with the gusto of a Labrador.

"You're always either working or bowling," she said.

"I bowl?" Jack laughed out loud. Actually it was more like a snort and he was embarrassed when ice cream sprayed out of his nose. "Since when?"

"Since forever. Are you all right? You're acting weird today."

Caleb managed to lick the ice cream right off his cone. A tri-colored glob sat on the pavement. He burst out crying.

"Aw, jeez." Mary-Ellen performed one of her Mommy-miracles by producing a handful of tissues from out of nowhere. "Don't cry. It's just ice cream. Here, have Mommy's. Now stand still while I clean you up."

Already Jack was rummaging around in his pockets to buy the kid another treat. He still had a few dollars left. Not much, but enough to cheer up a sad little boy.

"I'll get him another one, Mare."

"It's all right," she said. "I was done anyway."

An armored truck pulled up across the road out the front of the Willow Creek bank. Jack's stomach tightened. In a flash he realized why everyone inside the ice cream shop had worn unfriendly faces. They were being held against their will.

Mary-Ellen had finished wiping Caleb's hands, but the two of them now stood facing the bank to stare at the truck. Caleb waved to the guards.

Jack called to them. "Mare. Caleb. Come here. Quick."

The threat of danger didn't come from the guards. It came from the two men who'd stepped out of the ice cream shop waving rifles in the air. They opened fire on the guards. Before Jack could bridge the ten-feet gap between himself and Mary-Ellen, one guard fell, blood pooling on the ground. The second guard raised his gun and returned fired. The two gunmen dodged, but the bullets found secondary targets. Collateral damage it was called.

Mary-Ellen and Caleb fell to the ground. The gun fight lasted all of three seconds, yet a millennium passed before Jack's reflexes kicked in.

He dropped to the ground. People screamed. He barely heard; his ears pounded with loud booms. He crawled towards Mary-Ellen and Caleb. They weren't moving. Still, he held onto their hands and squeezed tightly, despite knowing they couldn't squeeze back.

He pressed his head against Mary-Ellen's. "I love you. I've always loved you."

He kept holding their hands until a member of the Willow Creek Police force pried him away and guided him to a nearby bench. The cop asked if there was family or friends he could call. Numbness kept Jack mute.

"Not even someone from work?" the cop asked. "Someone you go fishing or bowling with?"

"I don't bowl," he said quietly. "I don't fish. I don't have a wife and kid. Because none of this is real."

"I'll get the shrink," the cop said.

"It won't help."

***

An alarm clock buzzed. As Jack stirred awake, his dreams scattered like birds at the crack of gunfire, and he woke to the realization that he must have bought a handful of tickets to the funny farm because Mary-Ellen was curled up in bed beside him.

He jumped out of bed and pointed at her. Wickedly, cruelly, too stunned to utter a curse to return her back to hell, but the implication was there.

"I look that bad, huh?" she said, dragging her black hair out of her eyes. "That's the last time we invite the Kennedys over for dinner. They can drink as much as they like, they don't have a five-year-old who thinks dawn is 'up time'."

"Mary-Ellen. You should be... Caleb!"

Jack sprinted out of the bedroom, almost running over the small boy.

"Daddy," the boy sang out, jumping up and down. "It's my birthday. Guess—"

"Yeah, I know, you're five." He ran down the hall and shouted over his shoulder. "Your present's in the garage. Knock yourself out."

He almost tore the front door from the hinges, then he sprinted across the lawn. Coming to a halt at the sidewalk, he turned, once clockwise, once anti-clockwise, scanning for a camera crew. *This can't be happening?* When he turned full circle he saw that Caleb was in the doorway bouncing on his toes.

"Daddy, can I open my present now?"

Something was wrong. He'd woken up two days in a row to witness Mary-Ellen and Caleb die. He shook his head to clear the muddled thoughts. This was a game. Pandora was messing with him. And he wouldn't stay around to watch them die again. No amount of simulated apocalyptic games could prepare a person to witness the death of loved ones.

Loved ones? I hardly know these people.

They were strangers sent to test his sanity, but a remnant of sanity prevailed, telling him that he should at least get out of his pajamas. He bolted back inside the house just as Mary-Ellen charged past him into the garage.

"Don't open that till Daddy... Aw Caleb, I said wait... Jack, what are you doing telling him he can open it?"

He ignored her tirade. He ignored Caleb's tears. In the bedroom, he scooped a handful of clothing off the floor, not caring about stench or stain or whether anything matched. Mary-Ellen glared at him as he pushed his feet into the first pair of shoes he grabbed.

"What the hell has gotten into you, Jack?"

THE APOCALYPSE GAMES - PANDORA

"Not now, Mare."

He tried to push past her but she was strong. She baled him up with an arm across the doorway.

"Where the hell do you think you're going? It's your son's birthday!"

He couldn't tell her why he needed to put as much distance between him and the house. The curse obviously sat with him. He ducked under her arm and ran out the house, then he ran down the street, running until his untied runners slid off his feet. He looked up to see that he'd stopped in front of Lacey's Bar. His wallet was in the pocket of his jeans. It contained about twenty dollars in small bills. He usually kept about a hundred dollars in his wallet.

This was just another insight into the future he'd have been granted if he'd gone home with Mary-Ellen that night in college.

As he stared through the glass window, he saw a reflection of his body hooked up to wires. He was lying inside a glass coffin, except it was standing upright. In this vision, his eyes were closed, his arms folded across his chest, and his face was deathly pale.

An out-of-body experience would explain everything. It also meant he was dead.

He shook his head. This was just more of Pandora's mind games. *Who the hell was Pandora?*

The phone in his pocket buzzed. It was Mary-Ellen. Jack didn't want to deal with her right now; he shoved the phone back into his pocket. She could yell all she liked. At least she was alive.

He couldn't go home. Home was a place where his past sat waiting to torment him. But he also couldn't get on a plane and fly away considering he only had twenty dollars in his wallet. So he decided he'd spend the day inside Lacey's Bar. Just for a few hours, until he could make sense of why his wife and son were senselessly dying over and over.

Except, I don't have a wife and son.

He looked in his wallet. All identification stated that he lived in a house in Willow Heights. He was certain he lived in a city apartment. He had a friend, he had a sister, parents, yet their names escaped him. He recalled something about a virtual game. Something about him getting shot in the game and now he was having a death dream. Whatever that meant.

Twenty dollars was not enough to numb his insides or make the fog clear. A sly smile made it to his lips. He could run up a bar tab. It wouldn't matter what the bar staff did to him at the end of the night – they could call the cops, beat him senseless, make him wash dishes – this was Jack Minnow's own version of Groundhog Day. He wouldn't be around tomorrow to repay the debt.

Tomorrow was supposed to be another day, but tomorrow he'd wake up in bed beside a woman who refused to stay dead. His version of Groundhog Day sucked.

The window reflected his haggard face and disheveled appearance. He might get served in the bar, but there was no way they'd let him run up a tab looking like crap. He spied a gas station across the road and headed over to use their rest room. After buying mints for his breath in order to get the restroom key, he freshened up and somehow he knew – though he couldn't tell you how – that running up a bar tab took a certain level of mastery in order to convince the staff you were good for the money. He walked confidently inside and gave the bartender a cheery wave. She gave him a casual glance and then he settled into a stool closest to the TV.

The phone in his pocket buzzed. This time there was a message.

Where the hell are you? Caleb is crying. Come home now!!!!!

"What can I get you?" the bartender asked.

"Beer please."

"Anything in particular?"

"Surprise me."

While she poured, he tried to recall if Caleb had cried when the car had hit him, or if he'd cried when the gunman had shot him. If not, he was one tough little guy. So Mary-Ellen must have been lying when she'd texted that Caleb was crying now. At least that was how he justified drinking beer instead of heading straight home.

The TV above the bar was turned down low. He'd have liked it to be loud enough to block out the memories: the screech of tires, their screams as their bodies were crushed, bullets firing, screams as flesh and bone were torn apart. He couldn't rid the sounds from his head.

The phone buzzed again just as the bartender placed the beer on the counter. "Someone sure is trying to get your attention."

"My agent," he said. If she thought he was a VIP and good for the money, she'd let him stay. She walked away without collecting money from him. He could now stay here all night drinking.

He didn't know why he checked the messages but it had to be done.

Are you all right?

You'd better be all right cos I'll kick your ass for making Caleb cry.

You son of a bitch GET BACK HERE!

You don't care about us.

Four little reminders that if he wasn't already in hell, he was going there soon.

By noon he was delightfully drunk. But he desperately needed to pee. If he could make it to the men's room without staggering, then

THE APOCALYPSE GAMES - PANDORA

the bartender wouldn't kick him out. As he forced himself to walk straight, it occurred to him that the few hours he'd given himself to prepare for going home had come and gone. Yet, he still couldn't leave.

A few games of pool helped slow up the drinking, and his efforts won him twenty dollars. He stuffed two five dollar bills in the bartender's tip jar and she poured him another beer.

At two o'clock, she said, "Haven't you got anywhere to be?"

His phone buzzed. "Not till tomorrow."

By three o'clock, alcohol-fueled love kicked in and he was desperate to hear Mary-Ellen's voice. Checking the messages on his cell phone turned out to be the Pompeii of disasters. The desperation in Mary-Ellen's voice made him wish for the ground to open up and swallow him whole.

"*Jack where are you? Why did you run off? Come home. It's Caleb's birthday.*"

"*Listen, you sorry piece of shit. You get home now or we're leaving. You hear me? Aw screw that, I'm not leaving this house. I'm not letting you make me and your son homeless. You either come home now or don't come home at all.*"

"*Jack, I'm putting Caleb on the phone. You want to hear your son crying? Do you?*" The sound of sobbing. "*You piece of shit.*"

Just like passers-by had trouble stealing their gaze away from a car crash, Jack couldn't stop from listening. None of her insults upset him; he deserved them. But it wouldn't make him leave the bar. Instead, he switched off the phone.

At six p.m., the evening news came on the TV. A reporter stood on the sidewalk in front of a house. There was a fountain in the background.

"I know that house," he said, a slur in his speech. "Turn it up please."

The bartender pressed the remote and volume increased.

The reporter said, "Neighbors called the fire department after they saw flames coming from inside the house. But when the fire department arrived, it was too late to save the residents. Caught in the fire were a twenty-eight-year-old mother and her five-year-old son. In a sad twist, it was the boy's birthday today. Police are searching for the husband for questioning. He wasn't in the house at the time of the fire."

Bile rose up in Jack's throat. While the phone started up, he begged for there to be no messages. There was only one.

"*Jack! Oh my god, the house is on fire. Jack! We're trapped. The smoke alarms didn't go off. Did you change the batteries like I asked...*" Coughing. "*...Oh my god we can't get out.*" Caleb crying. "*I* *don't know where Daddy is, Caleb. Jack where are you? Help us. Please. We're trapped—"*

The message ended abruptly.

"You all right?" the bartender asked. "You look a little pale."

He held the phone in his hands, staring at it, numb from his head to his toes. What had he done?

The bartender pointed to the back of the bar. "If you're gonna throw up—"

I can hear their screams. I can smell the fire.

The restrooms were too far away and he was too drunk to care. He threw up all over his shoes.

***

An alarm clock buzzed, and as Jack stirred awake, his dreams scattered like birds at the crack of gunfire. He woke to the realization that he'd lost his mind. The wife and son he didn't have had died three days in a row. It was enough to send a man to the funny farm. He'd have gone except it wouldn't have made any difference. At least he hadn't watched them die last night, though the notion gave him little comfort.

Mary-Ellen was curled up in bed beside him. "You really are beautiful," he said.

Her green eyes watched him beneath long lashes. She blushed, wiped a stray piece of hair from her face. "Be serious, Jack. I look like crap."

"I am serious. You're the most beautiful woman in the world. The best thing to happen to me. Did I tell you how much I loved you? I should have told you every day. I wish I had."

She propped herself up on her elbow. A nervous smile twitched at her lips. "Are you dying or something? Am *I* dying?"

Jack pulled her toward him. "I love you. I've always loved you."

"I love you too. But can you please stop talking in past tense?"

He let out a sigh as he stroked her hip. "My life wouldn't have been so bad."

"Stop." She sat up and her dark curls danced about sending Jack wild with desire. "You're not making sense. You've insulted me somehow. Are you still hung over from last night?"

He drew her back onto the bed and pressed his head against hers.

"Mare, I've got to tell you something."

Her body stiffened.

"Any second now Caleb is going to run in here and say 'Mommy.

Daddy. It's my birthday'."

Her body relaxed. "He said the same thing last year."

Caleb burst into the room and crashed into the base of the bed. He bounced up and down like he either needed to go to the bathroom or evil clowns chased him.

"Mommy. Daddy," he sang out. "It's my birthday. Guess what? I'm five."

Mary-Ellen groaned, but this time she groaned because Jack had slid his hands down inside her pajama bottoms. He was overcome with the urgent need to make love to her, but more importantly to drown in the essence of her life. If he drowned in her love and died, maybe the curse would be undone and she would live.

"Can I open my present now?" Caleb cried.

Mary-Ellen moaned. "Jack. Caleb wants to open his present."

Caleb's eyes latched onto his. "Can I, Daddy? Can I?"

"Sure," Jack said. "It's in the garage, buddy. Why don't you go ahead and find it?"

Caleb bolted out of the room. Jack's breathing increased, matching Mary-Ellen's.

"Don't open it until we get there," Mary-Ellen said in a weak voice. She licked her lips. "Make it quick. He'll want us there to watch him open his bicycle."

Jack kissed her throat as she wriggled free of her clothes. She was even more stunning than he remembered.

"Hurry, Jack," she whispered, though the urgency had left her voice.

"I don't want to hurry." His voice rumbled against her throat. "I want to stay like this forever."

"Oh, Jack. Keep talking like that and I might just forget about everything."

It was what he was hoping for.

He moved against her with a possessive need. It was over too quickly, but just the way she wanted. Then he held onto to her afterwards, not daring to let her go.

"Mare, I've got to tell you something and you're going to think it's weird but I have to say it."

"Oh." She squirmed beneath him and rolled away.

"It's not what you think."

"Really? How do you know what I think?"

"I'm having déjà vu or visions, or... I don't know. Something weird is going on. I keep reliving the same day over and over."

She sat up and slipped her dressing gown on. Her shoulders were slumped. "Jack, I know it feels like you're living the same day over and over—"

"It's not a feeling, it's actually happening. I'll prove it. In a few seconds you're going to stub your toe on the end of the bed."

She stood up and wrapped her gown tightly around her. He couldn't blame her for being angry. He was proving to be a lousy husband and father.

With a raised eyebrow she stormed across the floor toward the door, purposely avoiding the end of the bed. She turned and smiled smugly at him. Her eyes were the saddest he'd ever seen.

"See," she said. "No snubbed toe." As she spun to exit the door, he heard the *crack* as she banged her toe against the doorframe. "Ah, Christ, that hurt. I swear I need to walk around the house in combat boots."

He jumped out of bed and rummaged around for clothes. "I told you. And that's not all that's going to happen today."

"Caleb's waiting to open his present," she said. "Whatever you have to tell me can wait till after."

"I didn't deserve to have someone as great as you in my life."

She frowned, then tore off down the hall. Jack dressed quickly and followed. Standing in the garage, a lump formed in his throat as he watched Caleb tug at the paper wrapping the bike. Naturally, Caleb wanted to ride it, but Jack wasn't taking any chances. He carried the bike out to the back yard.

"You can ride it around here, buddy." He slipped a five dollar bill into the basket. "Gas money. Now go fill up and ride your bike till it runs out of gas. I need to talk to your mom."

Mary-Ellen looked frightened as she ducked inside the house. And because Jack didn't want to let Caleb out of his sight, he waited on the back porch for her to return.

She came outside carrying two mugs of coffee. Her eyes were wet with tears.

"Mare, I'm not going to tell you I'm leaving you or that I'm seeing someone else. In a way, it would be easier than trying to convince you that I'm reliving this day over and over."

Her face twisted as she grappled with her emotions. "I know this isn't the life you always dreamed of, but it's the life you got. Stop using me and Caleb as a metaphor for your insecurities. I'm sorry you think your life is screwed up because you had to leave college. I'm sorry you're stuck here in Boringsville with me and Caleb. I had to give up college too. I had to give up on my dreams. You think I don't want a better life for us?"

"Come here. Let me explain."

He patted his knee and she obliged. When she leaned into his chest, she was shaking.

"I wish it *was* insecurities, Mare. It's something bigger. I can't explain it, but every day I wake up and it's the same day as the day before and the day before that. It's always Caleb's birthday, but it always goes horribly wrong. I lose you and Caleb. I keep losing you and it's driving me crazy."

"You lose us?" Her tears stemmed and she gave a gentle laugh. "Like at the mall or something?"

"Mare, I'm serious. Every day I watch you both die."

"So this dream you have." She pushed herself out of his embrace and busied herself with picking up Caleb's toys from around the porch. "How do we die?"

In his mind, he heard their screams as the car crashed into them. He smelled the flames that engulfed the house. He saw the holes from the bullet wounds.

"I'd rather not say."

Holding the toys only made her appear more vulnerable. And the more vulnerable she appeared, the more useless Jack felt. He wasn't Superman. Never had been. He'd never really saved anybody or anything in his life. And no amount of trying would change it.

"Just tell me what happens to us," she said.

Jack glanced around to make sure Caleb was out of hearing range. "You get run over by a car. You get shot by bank robbers. You die in a house fire."

She screwed up her face. Fresh tears trickled down her cheeks. "Oh my god, you really *do* you want us out of your life."

"No! I don't want you out of my life. Don't ever think that. I love you two more than you realize." More than even *he* realized. "I'm just telling you what's going on at the moment. I'm going crazy. I don't know how to stop the nightmares."

"What have you done so far?"

Her question hovered there like the echo of a slap. He hadn't actually done anything, and he was immediately awash with shame that he'd spent the previous day in the bar while they'd suffered.

"I took you and Caleb away from the house, and you died. I left the house, and you died."

She angrily scooped up more toys. "That sounds like the Jack Minnow I know. Never actually fixing the problem."

It sounded *nothing* like the Jack Minnow he knew. His whole life had been spent trying to fix things, save everyone, make everything right again. Or so he'd thought. He couldn't quite remember anything prior to waking up a few days ago.

"What am I supposed to do?" he said.

She shrugged. "I don't know. Something. Fight for our lives. Fight for *your* life. Find out why it's happening."

Even if the answer was to have revenge exacted upon him?

Because it felt as if this recurring tragedy was payback for something he'd done to her in the past.

"We'll spend the day at home today," he said. "No going out near the road. I'll check all the power outlets. Caleb can play in the back yard."

"So you're not really doing anything except avoiding the issue?"

Mary-Ellen shook her head and made a series of *tut-tuts*. It wasn't fair that a figment of his imagination should mock him.

Caleb called out that he'd run out of gas. Jack took turns with Mary-Ellen to push him around the yard on his bike. Near lunchtime, Jack suggested a picnic lunch and Mary-Ellen's mood softened. She raced inside to make sandwiches while Jack kept an eye on Caleb. Maybe keeping them apart was the key, Jack thought. He told himself that he'd try a different approach tomorrow. For now he wanted to enjoy this special family time.

Guilt made his mouth dry; he was already preparing for their deaths.

Mary-Ellen strolled out of the house with sandwiches, potato chips, and fruit that she'd cut up into the shapes of squares and triangles.

"This is nice," Jack said. He meant it. Such a simple meal and he was enjoying himself.

"Yummy," Caleb said as he devoured his ham and cheese sandwich. He'd gorged it so quickly, Jack worried that he might choke. But the boy swallowed his food without incident then he hurried over to his bike.

"We should do this more often," Mary-Ellen said dreamily.

The second the words were out of her mouth, a dark cloud appeared overhead.

"Grab Caleb," Jack said.

Mary-Ellen didn't argue. She sprinted across the lawn and swept the boy up in her arms then high-tailed it for the porch. Jack was on their heels, but Mary-Ellen was quicker, running the way a mother does when she senses danger.

The three of them burst through the back door together. Only Mary-Ellen screamed.

The front door was wide open. In the middle of the living room stood a grizzly bear, it must have been over ten foot tall. Its jaws were wide open.

Jack pulled Mary-Ellen and Caleb so they were behind him.

"Get into the bedroom," he shouted. "Now."

"What about you?" Mary-Ellen cried out.

"It's not after me. Go!"

The grizzly landed on its front paws with a *thud* which knocked over a lamp. It ran towards Jack and swiped at his chest. Its claws slashed off flesh, and blood oozed down his shirt. Jack bit down on the pain; he wasn't about to let the grizzly attack his wife and son.

"Climb out the window," he shouted, throwing himself in front of the bear. "Get up on the roof. Use the ladder."

The bear swept Jack aside with one paw, knocking him to the ground. Then it charged down the hall.

"Run, Mare. Run!"

***

An alarm clock buzzed, and Jack awoke to the realization that no law existed that said bawl-your-lungs-out sessions were the exclusive behavior of children and heartbroken women. He could scream all he wanted and as loudly as his lung capacity allowed. Except that he didn't want to scream. He wanted to know why Mary-Ellen wouldn't stay dead. She was curled up in bed with him, and when she opened her eyes, a lazy smile tickled at her lips. Her black hair fell in big waves around her face. Her moss-green eyes had stripped Jack of the will to speak.

The bedroom door burst open. Caleb ran in and crashed into the base of the bed. He bounced up and down. "Mommy. Daddy. It's my birthday. Guess what? I'm five."

Mary-Ellen groaned as she pulled herself up into a sitting position. Her hair stuck to her face. She swiped at it and groaned again.

I know what's going to happen and I can't stop any of it.

This time, Jack wasn't seeing Mary-Ellen as she looked now. He saw her as she'd looked in college. Younger, longer hair, bigger smile, not a care in the world. He'd met her in his business management class. It was love, except he hadn't known it at the time, and he'd been terrified of losing her to another man, so he'd pushed her away. Straight into a taxi. It was the last time he saw her alive.

As he lay in bed, he cursed Pandora for forcing him to think about Mary-Ellen. But nothing stayed buried forever, so maybe this recurring nightmare was his own doing. He'd pushed the memory down into the dark recesses of his mind rather than admit that her death was on his hands. He hadn't been there when the taxi had run off the road, but he'd killed her just the same.

Jack didn't get out of bed all day. It didn't matter.

Mary-Ellen and Caleb still died.

16

Jack

Waking up to relive the same day over and over was taking its toll on Jack's mental state, yet his physical self wore the burden just as badly. He no longer showered. His eyes were permanently red from crying. His hands shook like jackhammers. Holding onto a coffee cup was an impossible feat. He couldn't drink it anyway. The only thing he could keep down was beer and bourbon. He'd stay in bed, drinking beer and bourbon, ignoring Mary-Ellen who yelled at him to get up. Caleb cried non-stop because Mary-Ellen yelled non-stop. And Jack passively waited for them to die.

Mary-Ellen cursed him, but he'd become accustomed to tuning out her insults. In the end, he welcomed them. At least while she was cussing, she was living and breathing.

On one particular day, he rose out of bed only because he'd run out of beer. Mary-Ellen refused to go to the store and buy more. In no shape to drive, he did so anyway and returned in time to witness two intruders break into his house and cut down his family with large knives. One of the intruders snarled at him and said, "This is your lucky day." The intruder let Jack live. Jack didn't feel lucky.

The next morning, he got out of bed and hid in the bathroom. He stayed there for hours until he heard their agonizing screams. He poked his head out the window to witness wild dogs tearing them apart in the back yard.

This went on and on. Some days he stayed by their sides while their bodies were ravished by a deadly fever. Other mornings he would usher them into the car, drive to the airport and use their savings to buy tickets to another state. One time the plane went down and he was the only survivor. Another time a small explosion punctured a hole in the hull and sucked them out of their seats. Only them.

Always Jack survived. Always they did not.

He got so used to their deaths that he sat in the living room watching TV and eating cereal or popcorn or potato chips, while they died on the floor in front of him from electrocution or choking or the roof caving in. Sometimes he went for walks to avoid hearing their screams, only to be attacked by the echoes of their horrific deaths upon opening the front door. This became his routine for the daytime. Nighttime was worse. In the dark, he would lie in bed and stroke the empty spot beside him, breathing in Mary-Ellen's scent. Or he would squeeze into Caleb's tiny racecar bed and cry himself to sleep. There were nights he drank till he fell into a messy heap. He delved into drugs, mixing randomly, mixing strategically. But drunk, stoned, or sober, the mornings always brought them back to life. The eternal resurrection of a loved one should have been consoling. Instead, he wished for his own death. But it never came.

Jumping in front of the bullets and knives meant for his wife and son never worked. His grief grew so bad that he tried to drown himself in the bathtub. He managed only to prune his fingers and toes.

Mary-Ellen's earlier words haunted him: *"What have you done so far?"*

Well, he'd buckled up and let the crazy ride carry him along all seven stages of grief – shock and denial; pain and guilt; anger and bargaining; depression, reflection, loneliness; the upward turn; reconstruction and working through; acceptance and hope. Sometimes he experienced these all in the same day.

One night, it could have been a Tuesday or Friday they were all the same now, the unanswered search for the residual memory of his real life struck him down with such anguish that he fell off the stool at Lacey's Bar. The waitress ordered him home. Rather than do that, he strolled the streets of his real/false town. His real/false world had to be a pretense for something else. But what?

His brain was fogged over. Maybe from madness.

Could anyone blame him?

He stumbled across a cinema playing *The Apocalypse Games.* The name triggered a memory. A virtual reality game.

Schizophrenics were burdened with voices but sometimes those voices stopped. Silence invaded Jack and he was instantly aware.

This was a game. But real lives were at stake. Not just dream lives or virtual lives. His life. The lives of Reis, Kelly, Douglas, Ash, Neil.

Hundreds of players had stepped out of their cars that warm autumn day and entered a simulation pod that would plunge him or her into a fantasy world. But the game had malfunctioned and trapped the players.

There had been no contact from the outside world. Why hadn't they rescued them? Was anybody out there? What had stopped the game?

***

The day the sinkhole opened up in the garage and took Mary-Ellen and Caleb down into the bowels of hell, Jack decided enough was enough. He went to the library to find answers. Of particular interest were books on déjà vu. They stated hallucinations brought on by illness or drugs could bring a heightened awareness that could be confused with déjà vu. But this opened up more questions. What if the pods not only emitted nutrients to keep them fed and hydrated, what if the machines they were hooked up to were slipping in trace amounts of hallucinatory drugs?

He dismissed the notion that his visions were due to reincarnation. But he didn't dismiss the notion that his false memories might be caused by schizophrenia. In fact, he placed schizophrenia at the top of the list. As well, déjà vu occurred in people who suffered anxiety and depression. He also placed these high up on the list of symptoms. What upbeat emotions could a person trapped inside a virtual game possibly feel?

He read about biological déjà vu associated with temporal lobe epilepsy. Just before having a seizure, a person experienced a strong sense of déjà vu. More questions. What if his body was having a seizure inside the pod? Right now. Or, what if this nightmare state was attributed to the chemicals leeching inside the pod?

He had many questions. Zero answers.

Then he read that delusions were different to hallucinations in that a hallucination affected a person's senses, where delusions had to do with a person's thoughts. Neither explanation helped. He suffered from both.

He even read about temporal loops. If he could correct a past mistake or recognize some key truth, the loop might stop. But the thing was that Mary-Ellen had altered *her* life, not Jack's. She was the one who got in the taxi and died. Sure, she wouldn't have gotten in if Jack hadn't acted like a jerk, but it wasn't like he had driven the car.

***

The day he placed one hundred candles on Caleb's birthday cake was the day he dragged their stiffening bodies into the car and drove it off the cliff. But all that experience taught him was that the family that died together, stayed together. At least until the morning.

***

Nothing in the books taught Jack Minnow how to stop reliving the same day. He took to watching movies about time loops, as if Hollywood had figured out the secret and hidden it within the plot. They hadn't.

He read as many science-fiction novels as he could cram into twenty-four hours, sometimes diving straight to the final chapters, as if the authors had secretly encoded the answer to reverse a time loop into the pages. They hadn't.

He fixed things around the house. The broken clothes dryer. The cracked tiles in the bathroom. A door that needed re-hanging. New batteries in the smoke alarms. He moved the bed two inches to the left so Mary-Ellen wouldn't stub her toe every morning. He did these things, as if correcting past laziness was the key to unlocking the loop. It wasn't.

He turned to prayer, walking around the house carrying rosary beads and muttering words he'd made up because even though he had the time to learn Latin he didn't have the inclination.

The day he sprayed holy water around the yard, Mary-Ellen called a psychiatrist. For kicks Jack allowed the doctor to ask him dozens of questions. He even took the pills the doctor gave him and had the prescription filled immediately. Take with meals, the bottle said. No time to make a sandwich. Down the hatch. Take it with beer. Warm buzz. Go to sleep. Miss all the fun.

He still saw them die.

He prayed to the gods, to the demi-gods, to demons, to angels, to evangelists, even to Leprechauns. Drunk and standing atop the fountain in the front yard wearing only his underwear, he prayed loudly. A neighbor videotaped it; when he searched on the internet the next day, it was as if the moment had never happened.

Jack purchased Bibles and wedged them into every nook in the house and yard. He hung crucifixes on the walls – right side up, wrong side up, it made no difference. He went to church. Sometimes twice in the same day. He dug up the fountain and returned it to the landscape yard, as if karma was the cause of his predicament. The fountain stood on display in the front yard the next morning.

His life wasn't all doom and gloom. Many, many wonderful moments happened before it all went to hell. There were mornings when he made love to Mary-Ellen with a tenderness he never knew he possessed. There were days where he sat Caleb in front of the TV and they screwed their brains out all day, the way they had in college. Some mornings they snuggled and slept in till noon.

Other days, they went on family picnics, and they once visited the zoo, though watching them fall into the lion's pit hadn't done Jack's state of mind any good. Some days they hired paddleboats, bicycles, go carts. They fed ducks and flew kites. Any day where they left the house and returned intact was considered a great day. A day worth celebrating.

Some of their happiest days came from trips to the mall where they accumulated an inordinate amount of debt. Watching Caleb run through the toy store squealing with childhood glee repeatedly drove Jack to tears. But denying Caleb these moments, no matter how short-lived, gave him greater pain. On these celebratory days, he took them to fancy restaurants purely to invite more debt, as if spite was the key to breaking the loop. He told Mary-Ellen he'd received a bonus so she wouldn't worry over the cost of the meals. She tried the lobster and always complained it was overrated. She was often dead by dawn from food poisoning.

Sometimes he dragged Mary-Ellen and Caleb to the library with him so they could also read books about out-of-body experiences, déjà vu, time loops, astral projection, butterfly effects, eternal returns.

By Jack's recollection, he had suffered over three hundred days of watching his private re-runs of hell. None of the theories told him how to stop it happening.

**

The night Mary-Ellen shot Caleb before taking her own life, Jack walked out the back door and sat in the middle of the lawn. He cracked open a beer and gazed up at the stars. As he lifted the beer to the sky, tears gushed down his face. Clarity often pursued disaster, taunting him with the name of his tormentor. And it wasn't just a computer named Pandora.

"I know what you're trying to tell me," he yelled at the night sky. "It's my fault Mary-Ellen died. But that's not what this is about, is it? You're digging deep. You're good. Very good." He choked back a sob. "The night Mary-Ellen died she was going to tell me about Caleb."

Jack and Mary-Ellen had dated for two months, at a time when

Reis was away on holiday. It was love, though Jack hadn't realized it until he'd opened the email from Reis. His friend was ending his holiday early. Jack's world would come crashing down the moment Mary-Ellen met Reis. It always did. He couldn't let it happen this time. So he'd decided to save himself for once.

Jack and Mary-Ellen had gone to a party. He'd been distant, hardly touching the free beers on offer, hardly talking to anyone.

"What's wrong?" Mary-Ellen had asked him.

He'd gazed into her moss-green eyes and willed himself to look away. She acted like she cared, but they never really did. How could they say they loved him one minute, then want his friend's number the next?

Mary-Ellen had placed the drink she'd toyed with all night on the railing. "Jack, I need to tell you something."

His body had stiffened. Here it comes, he'd thought. She's going to dump me. And then I'll see her strolling through the campus chasing after Reis. And while his friend had never once shown any interest in Jack's ex-dates, jealousy still drove a spike in his heart at the mere thought of it. Enough to convince him that he was doing the right thing by dumping Mary-Ellen first.

"Now's not a good time," he'd said. "I've got exams tomorrow. I don't want my head clogged with anything."

"I love you."

His heart had soared and then it'd taken a steep dive. He'd heard it before.

"Look, Mare. I've got a lot of stuff going on at the moment. And some of the guys are talking about heading into the city after the party."

"I can't go into the city." Her lips had trembled. He'd wanted to kiss them. "I have to get home."

She always had to get home. It wasn't an issue that she lived with her parents, so did he, but she'd never invited him to her place. How much could she love him if she didn't want him to meet her family?

"That's okay," he'd said. "You can head on home."

Just then a taxi had pulled up out the front of the house. Jack had run down to the couple getting in and asked if they could drop Mary-Ellen home. He'd thought he'd dodged a bullet and escaped the inevitable break up. But he'd found out the next morning that the taxi had dropped the couple off, and on the way to driving Mary-Ellen home the car's brakes had failed. On an dangerous stretch of road, the vehicle had slammed into a tree, killing the passenger and driver instantly.

***

The memory hit Jack hard, like a punch in the face and stomach. It clawed at his insides, and he cried like he'd never cried before. Mary-Ellen had wanted to tell him that she had a son, Caleb. An accidental pregnancy that her parents had supported. They'd looked after the kid while she went to college.

Mary-Ellen had been ready to let Jack into her world, and he'd callously blown her off. Worse, he'd gotten her killed. It was at the funeral that Mary-Ellen's parents had told him about the boy. And Jack remembered thinking that maybe he should have felt obligated to do something, but at the time he was twenty-three and the idea of fatherhood had terrified him.

Now, as he sat in the back yard of his fake home in Willow Heights and cried for the loss of his college sweetheart, he wondered if there was a road to redemption for a person who thought that another person's death was akin to dodging a bullet.

***

An alarm buzzed. Jack opened one eye first, then the other. The spot in the bed beside him was empty. He sat upright and swept his gaze around the room. He waited a few minutes for Mary-Ellen to wander out of the bathroom. He waited a few minutes for Caleb to come bursting through the door. Neither event happened. Didn't mean they weren't already dead. He'd fallen for that ruse before.

He counted to one hundred like this was a game of hide and seek. Then he swung his legs over the edge of the bed and listened for sounds of activity. Nothing. Still, he tiptoed around the house, although he didn't bother to search for a weapon in defense of an attack; he'd never once been the target of any mischief. But sometimes if he came across the wrong type of intruder, they made him watch.

Mary-Ellen and Caleb weren't anywhere in the house.

He checked the yard. Stepping onto the back porch, he was met by a perfect blue sky. Always a perfect blue sky looked down on him. He prayed they weren't outside. Dead in the yard usually meant playing hide and seek with dismembered limbs. But the yard appeared devoid of corpses. They weren't in the garden shed either. He peered over the fences into the neighbor's yards. Nothing.

The front yard was equally corpse free, so he walked along the path and past a few houses. Nothing out of the ordinary in the neighbor's yards. He kept walking. His plod turned into a brisk walk, a brisk walk into a jog, a jog turned into a sprint. He ran until he could no longer breathe, not allowing himself to believe this nightmare was over. It might not have been. He hadn't checked the roof.

He returned home to check the roof. They weren't there. Crazed from trauma, he had enough sense to place the ladder back in the garage; the last time he'd left it lying around Caleb had climbed up on the roof and Mary-Ellen had gone after him. Both had fallen off and died. That death had occurred around day eighty of this nightmare.

He went inside, sank into the sofa, and switched on the TV. Ten a.m. rolled around. Then eleven a.m. greeted him. The hours continued to tick over. Blue sky turned to gray, gray to black. Ten p.m. Eleven p.m. Still no signs of their deaths. No screams. No explosions. No trucks bursting through the front wall. Didn't mean a thing. He'd been tricked before. He hadn't checked under the bed.

***

The alarm went off. Jack slowly opened his eyes. The spot in the bed beside him was empty. At first he didn't believe it. It had to be a trick. A person didn't spend years locked inside a delusional world and exit without believing that what he saw with his own two eyes was merely another delusion.

He lay perfectly still, waiting for the truth to crawl up his leg like a spider. At least he knew why Pandora was messing with him. She was trying to get him to accept culpability. He'd played a part in the death of a woman, through apathy, jealousy, fear. He'd pushed Mary-Ellen away when he should've begged her to stay. She'd only wanted to talk to him. Since then, he'd run around saving imaginary people and dogs.

Superman possessed the good fortune to be separated from those he saved through true alienation – he wasn't from Earth. Jack was.

Superman also had the added luxury of not having a world to return to. Sooner or later Jack would have to return to his.

At last, Jack got out of bed and stumbled around the house, searching for something to dull the pain. The drugs were gone. So was the booze. So was every sign that a woman and child had lived in this house. Maybe he'd dreamed it. Maybe they had never existed at all.

If only absolution was as easy as closing your eyes.

**

By now, Jack realized he'd escaped the nightmare, yet a wave of sadness washed over him that, for over three hundred and something days, he'd never told Mary-Ellen how sorry he was that he'd let her go. Not once. It wasn't like he hadn't had ample opportunity. He'd also wanted to tell her that it was wrong to think he'd dodged a bullet when she'd died. If she would come back for real, he'd take care of her and her boy.

Regret never went away. He knew that now. A person could dig a deep hole and bury it, but it never went away. Jack wanted to hang up his superhero costume – he didn't deserve it – and he wanted to pick up a shovel instead. Dig a pit and bury himself. He could become a different type of superhero. His name could be Grave Digger. His super power was that he got people killed.

He walked out of the house, resembling the zombies he'd once mocked. Across the road he spied a food joint called the Sip N Dip. The fact that it existed surprised him. He knew the town of Willow Heights very well. He'd never seen a Sip N Dip. Something new didn't mean something good.

It felt as if years had passed while he'd been stuck in this limbo land, and years probably had, though not in a way he recognized. He staggered across the road to the Sip N Dip and sat in a booth by the window. The sign above the counter said the place served nachos and soda. Nobody came to take his order. It was no use asking anyone either; the place was deserted. His best option was to sit and wait, and hope Reis and Kelly found him. They always managed to. They had to find him now, before he became lost again.

His mind was rambling but he couldn't stop it.

Waiting was something he'd gotten good at, didn't mean he liked it. In the quiet of the Sip N Dip he heard the echoes of their screams, smelt the smoke, the blood, the stench of loosened bowels. He heard the reverberations of their laughter from the good days. He saw the ghosts of their faces from the bad days.

Jack missed Mary-Ellen. He'd never met Caleb in real life – the kid had been a baby – but he missed him too. Perhaps if things had gone differently in college, perhaps if Mary-Ellen hadn't died, they might have had a life together.

Perhaps once he escaped the game he'd look up her parents. Tell them he was sorry. Tell them that if he hadn't pushed her away she'd be alive.

"Can I get some service?" he yelled out, because the silence irked him. "I want to see the manager."

He'd have given anything to see Mary-Ellen and Caleb walk into the Sip N Dip. Salvation wouldn't come easy, but he hoped it *would* come. Everyone deserved to be saved. Even the damned were innocent once.

INSIDE THE SIMULATION POD

WELCOME TO THE APOCALYPSE HOME PAGE

Welcome to the SMART simulation survival center.
The apocalypse you have chosen to survive is…

Resource depletion apocalypse.

INSIDE THE SIMULATION POD

PRESENTATION BY
COMMAND LEADERS JONAS BARRETT AND STEPHANIE GEY

Command Leader Jonas Barrett:
Greetings players.

If you are watching this presentation, humanity is at threat of extinction due to global resource depletion. It is likely human survivors are hunters of their own kind and will stop at nothing to get what they need.

There are three contributing factors to a resource depletion apocalypse. Number one: overpopulation. Number two: lack of available resources. And number three: drastically out of aligned wealth distribution.

Command Leader Stephanie Gey:
In some expert opinions, wealth inequity will be the blame for the downfall of civilization because the world's resources will be controlled and consumed by the wealthy. It is predicated this inequity will lead to the collapse of the common class followed by the eventual decline of the wealthy elite.

Command Leader Jonas Barrett:
Other expert opinions claim an exhaustion of resources will signal the end of mankind. On a global scale, civilization relies on available minerals, water, and arable land for agriculture. Climate change is also playing a part in the natural depletion of resources, and it is predicted that human economic activities will cause further climate change due to the increasing population requiring even more resources to be processed. This production gets distributed into the environment as pollution. The chain of cause and effect will continue.

As with all apocalypses, proceed with caution.

Command Leader Stephanie Gey:
If you find yourself in the midst of a resource depletion apocalypse you will need to prepare a panic bag before making your way to the

nearest safe zone.

Your panic bag should contain the following items:

Torch and spare batteries. Energy shortages are a constant threat. Boxes of matches, fire lighters, and newspaper to burn. Temperatures in the world affected by climate change are unpredictable.

A first aid kit, antibiotics, other medicines. Hospitals, if there are any left, are a considerable distance away and so overcrowded you might not get in.

Good walking shoes. Oil is depleted so transport is mostly on foot. Despite advances in solar technology, all batteries used to operate and recharge solar vehicles were accumulated to power electricity for the cities until their dying minutes.

Sleeping bags or blankets for nights that drop below freezing.

The ready to eat meals such as the type used by the military and campers are preferred, as freeze dried foods require water to rehydrate. For example, freeze dried eggs can be shelf stable for up to twenty-five years.

Command Leader Jonas Barrett:
More items you'll need to survive are:

Tools to fix things that break down, tools to unlock doors, tools to tap into water systems, tools to obtain spare parts for machines you manage to get working.

Water purifying tablets and a small pot to boil water. Perhaps a small portable stove if you can find one.

Anti malaria tablets, anti fungal creams, disinfectants and soap to ward off infection as a result of diminished energy sources.

Seeds to grow food supplies. Choose quick growing herbs and vegetables to plant if you establish a community.

Fuel and a vehicle if you can secure them safely.

We at Simulated Military And Recreational Training have designed this program because we are committed to the survival of the human race.

Command Leader Stephanie Gey:
And because we are serious, we have put together the following tips for players encountering a resource depletion apocalypse.

The tips for survival are as follows:

Be sure to boil all water for cooking and drinking. Most pathogens will be killed off during the boiling process, but not all. The combined use of activated charcoal adsorption and boiling can neutralize most pathogens and pollutants.

Be ready to be mobile. Travel light and don't display your possessions or allow others to view them.

Be opportunistic and willing to trade items you have for other resources. Dispense with sentimentality as this is a wasted emotion.

Be wary of everyone you meet. They could be friend, thief, decoy or enemy.

Be careful around fuel stations as these are bound to be booby-trapped. Alternative fuel was a fallacy created by the Cornucopians who placed all their faith in technology. Peak Oil hit and derailed industry around the globe.

Command Leader Jonas Barrett:
Good luck and stay alive!

Command Leader Stephanie Gey:
I haven't finished, Jonas. I have more tips:

Avoid going it alone to water wells and pumps as these will be heavily guarded.

Stay active, alert, and healthy. Electricity will probably be gone. So there is nothing to distract someone from hunting you for your stockpile of resources.

Gather materials to make a shelter for longer periods of time to allow you to possibly grow foods and raise chickens.

Weapons can be comforting in times of major disaster, however your weapon can be used on you. Keep it hidden.

Money has no place in this world. Yet humans will always covet expensive things so if you can find anything of considerable value, its best to be on the safe side and take it.

Command Leader Jonas Barrett:
Good luck and stay alive.

Command Leader Stephanie Gey:
Come on, Jonas, you can do better than that. I'm yawning at your level at enthusiasm.

Command Leader Jonas Barrett:
(Sighing) Players. Welcome to the apocalypse!

17

Kelly

Kelly's mother, Kim Minnow, worked at a florist and drank the occasional glass of wine with dinner. Her father, Daniel, worked in a bank and twice a year went hunting and fishing with a group of friends from college. They rotated weekend barbeques with the neighbors, had taken their children to Disneyland annually, and now waited for grandkids to be born so they could take up the tradition again. They never fought, gambled, took drugs, hit their kids, hit each other, nor did they do anything to plant and foster the misanthropy that ate at Kelly's core.

She could tell you countless symptoms of her condition – crime, rape, cruelty, greed – but she couldn't tell you what had triggered this condition because none of these crimes had happened to her. Just like the mouse or the bird that had never done anything to earn the scorn of the cat, the condition still existed.

In a way, she viewed Matt's death as the justification she sought to hate the world. But she didn't want to insult his memory by blaming him for her dislike, since it'd existed long before she'd met him. Besides, Matt's death was senseless. To change her views now meant that his death served a purpose, and nothing in her heart and soul could convince her of this. So as she watched the game presentation and cheered for the end of the world, she wondered if this made her a bad person.

The presentation ended, and with a jolt Kelly landed in the game. The result of her misanthropy was that she believed suffering would bring solace. She belonged with this group of misfits who wanted to challenge the status quo by surviving the end of the world. Since her world was already over, the game was a picnic in comparison. Bring on the real apocalypse, she thought.

In this apocalypse, she wore ski pants and a thick jacket. It was cold. She surveyed the land on all sides. Electricity power lines ran

ahead and behind her. Rocks dug into her hiking boots; they were
worn at the soles. She now noticed that her ski jacket and pants
didn't match, and she got the sense she was lucky to be wearing
them at all.

Dust kicked up when she took a step. This was a cold, dry, barren
land; already her throat ached as if she was getting a cold. *Suffering
would bring solace. Matt's death served no purpose.*

There was a flash to her right and Reis appeared to drop from
three feet above the ground. She scanned the area for Jack; she
hadn't seen him since he'd driven off to battle the frogspawns. When
she discovered Reis was watching her, she turned away. It didn't
make sense that she could look at him and have her insides flutter.
Her heart was dead, cured lava, petrified wood, ashes and dust. She
shouldn't have feelings for him. It was too soon. She blamed her
fluttering insides on the malfunctioning simulation pod, the lack of
oxygen, and the lack of food.

Reis was scowling as he looked up at the sky. "The presentation
said to avoid the storm clouds."

"We have to wait for Jack."

She waited two minutes, but when there was no sign of her
brother, she accepted that she and Reis were on their own for this
game. She began walking away from the storm clouds, and Reis fell
into step with her. They'd once been good friends, but she suddenly
found she didn't know what to say to him. Every conversation in her
head lead to another conversation she didn't want to have. Asking
how *he* was holding up in the game led to him asking *her* how she
was holding up. She missed her parents and she worried that they
worried. Her friends might think she'd gone on a spiritual journey
like in the movies. Her boss would keep her job open for her as he'd
done the past year, but eventually he'd have to hire someone who
showed up for work. Talking about Reis's death dream where he was
going to marry Casey would lead to memories of her own wedding.
And the memories came.

It had been beautiful. Matt's parent's had a house on a lake.
They'd made a weekend of it. Fifty guests. Matt's mother had
planted poppies in the ground early so they'd be flowering for the
day. Followed by a honeymoon in Hawaii.

After Matt's death, Kelly had lain in bed for three straight days
with her album of wedding photos. Perhaps she'd do that again
when she got home.

She was surprised this idea could cause a bounce in her step.

She supposed she could ask Reis about his job, but that could
lead him to ask why she no longer accompanied him and Jack to test
the activities for Quest. He might ask why she'd stopped being his

friend.

They came to a rise. Down below, a dirt road led to a diner and not much else. The surroundings were as still as a painting. Balls of dust hung in the air, frozen in time. No cry of birds, no distant barking of dogs. Nothing lived here, and if it did it wasn't comfortably.

She headed for the diner, sensing in her gut that she'd locate Jack there. Pretty soon, she and Reis stood in the parking lot of a diner called the Sip N Dip. It had cracked and faded paint, cracked concrete, broken doors and windows. Time had stripped this place of the stench of decayed food. Kelly saw Jack sitting in a booth with his head in his hands. He appeared to be talking to someone.

She pushed open the door and sat in the booth opposite him. He was alone. When he looked up, he seemed startled by her appearance. His face was pale, his eyes were red. Kelly recognized the look of sorrow; it was a look that greeted her every day in the mirror.

"Are you all right?" she asked him.

He turned to stare out the window but said nothing. Kelly reached for his hands. They were cold, wouldn't stop shaking. This wasn't a good sign. Jack was usually tough, infallible, a freaking superhero.

"You're freezing," she said, noticing that he wore a shirt and jeans, not equipped for the coldness that had settled in with this particular apocalypse.

"I want to go home," he said. "Mom and Dad will be worried."

"I'll get right on it." She didn't sound convincing. Rescue from the outside seemed like a fairy tale. But she was sick of waiting for rescue; it was time she put her energy into doing something about getting out.

"We were right to call the computer Pandora," Jack said, still staring out the window. "She unleashes evil."

"Tell me what happened."

"It was a nightmare I couldn't wake up from." He pulled his hands out of her grip and wedged them under his thighs. He refused to look at her.

"Jack. Talk to me."

He said nothing.

"Look at me."

Finally, his gaze rested on hers. "In my nightmare, Mary-Ellen and I were married."

Pandora's ability to force two stoic bachelors into matrimony might have been commendable had the experience not left visible scars.

"In this nightmare," Jack said, "Mary-Ellen and I had a five-year-old boy, Caleb. And before you ask, no, we didn't have a child together. When I first woke up it was confusing, but nice." His voice caught in his throat. "It's always Caleb's fifth birthday. I can't even remember how long it was before they died on that first day. It happened so long ago. Mid-morning, I think."

Kelly felt the temperature in the diner drop. The storm was getting closer; the presentation said players should seek shelter because the rain forced pollution down from the chemical-filled atmosphere. This rundown diner would have to serve as shelter because she couldn't leave Jack's side. He'd stuck by hers when she'd needed it the most. She was grateful to be able to return the kindness.

"We got him a bike for his birthday," Jack said. "Why did it have to be his birthday? The poor little guy."

Jack paused, she waited for him to add more but it seemed as if he'd said enough.

"You know it wasn't real," she said.

Jack's eyes were moist and red. "It doesn't hurt any less. I don't even know why it hurts at all, to be honest. We only dated for two months."

"You said the first day they died. How many times..." Her voice caught, talking about death was still a sore point.

Jack's face drained of all color.

"That many," she said. "I'm so sorry."

And just like that she'd uttered the words that so many had uttered to her, words she'd described as hollow, but it was all she could say to express her empathy. Immediately afterward, a barb of shame impaled her stomach. She'd mistaken the kind words others had spoken as 'hollow' simply because there was a hole in her chest that nothing could fill.

Reis reached for her hand and gave it a squeeze. She choked down on her grief. This was Jack's time. Not hers. But she was grateful for his support.

"They didn't die just once," Jack said. His voice was husky and full of sorrow. "They died every day, over and over, for about a year. Maybe longer."

On closer inspection, he looked as if he'd aged ten years.

"You were only gone a few hours," Reis said.

Jack shook his head. "Feels like decades."

Death had a way of stealing years. Kelly studied Jack's messy brown hair for gray streaks. She found none. Since the player's bodies were in stasis chambers, their physical bodies would not age, but mentally... she was only now beginning to grasp the implications of this untested facility.

"How did they die?" Reis asked.

Jack scoffed. "How *didn't* they die? Shot. Stabbed. Eaten by a bear. Eaten by dogs. A sink hole took them god knows where. You name it. They experienced it."

"Who is Mary-Ellen?" asked Kelly. Her suspicions that Jack had never settled down because he'd never met the right girl were now unfounded. Obviously Mary-Ellen meant something to him.

"Just some woman I dated in college," Jack said.

His voice belied his words. He certainly looked like he was grieving. Red eyes, dark circles beneath, unable to look at her when he spoke, shaking hands. The real telltale was the constant sighing, as if his lungs fanned the hell fires in his stomach.

She flicked her gaze between the two men; Reis looked just as fatigued and Kelly hadn't checked her reflection in a mirror in a long while, but she wondered if there were dark circles under her eyes. There must have been, which meant their virtual images must be mimicking their physical bodies. There went her theory that she was fine as long as she stayed in her simulation pod.

***

There was a polite cough to their right, and Kelly turned to find someone standing near the kitchen. Swathed in snow gear, she didn't recognize the woman, but she was short and slender with dark features and hair. The woman introduced herself as Reekha Soodi. Then her gaze immediately locked onto Jack.

"Forgive me," she said, "but I overheard you talking. Outside in the real world I study memories, how they're formed, how they're stored, how they're retrieved. I also study sleep deprivation and emotional trauma."

A bubble of laughter escaped Jack. "You've come to the right place for a test subject."

"Don't I know it?" A worried expression flickered across her face. "The more stressed or tired you are, the more likely you are to experience déjà vu. Although some researchers believe the opposite is true. Obviously, the jury is still out, but from what you've said I'm leaning towards stress being a major factor."

"It wasn't déjà vu," Jack said. "It was karma."

Reekha went to sit inside the booth but Reis held up a hand.

"I don't want to seem rude," he said, "but can you show us your player pass? We seriously don't have the energy to invest in a non-player character."

Reekha bit her lower lip. "I'm a player like you. But I've lost my pass."

"You can't lose it," Reis said. "It's coded into your biometric pattern."

"Well, I lost mine."

Reis shuffled over to block her entry. "We're in the middle of a private conversation."

"Let her stay," Jack said.

Reekha sighed. "I'm not a *registered* player. My husband and I stowed away in one of the pods."

"Why would you do that?" Kelly asked.

"I guess it can't hurt telling you since none of us will make it out alive. My husband and I were hiding out."

"You're criminals?" Kelly's blood chilled. She'd always suspected that deviants and perverts would enter this game to get their thrills killing men, women, and children. Players could do anything in the game without any risk of being convicted of war crimes. The only true injury was to their moral compass, and that was easy to override and becoming easier when each new day brought another horror to survive. Rescue now seemed the furthest thing from some player's minds.

"Nobody knows what I'm about to tell you," Reekha said. "My husband and I were hired to conduct trials around false memories. Naresh and I didn't realize it at the time, but the organization we worked for had just completed building a virtual world. We overheard a meeting that spoke about kidnapping world leaders and placing them inside a virtual world exactly like their own world. And then doppelgangers would run the real world in their place."

"Nice concept," Reis said derisively. "But even in light of the current situation, it's still pretty far-fetched."

Reekha glared at him. "Far-fetched or not, it's what I heard."

"What's the name of the organization?"

"Fehlberg Enterprises."

Kelly noticed Reis mentally checking if he recognized this business. His father might even be on its board, but Reis shook his head.

"I'm sure it's just a front," Reekha said. "Naresh and I were working late one night when a group of people showed up for a meeting. We'd earlier installed listening devices in the meeting room. Naresh didn't trust the program directors. He didn't trust a lot of people. And he was right not to. We overheard the group talking about the virtual world. These people asked if it was ready. I recognized one voice, the guy we knew as Fehlberg. He said it was ready but it should be tested first. And he said he'd devised a way to test it. He'd built the perfect program. I believe *The Apocalypse Games* is the testing program he spoke about."

Kelly fidgeted in her seat. The launch was the first time this giant machine had been switched on. She'd known this of course, but she'd been too riddled with grief to question if it was *ready* to be switched on.

"I love conspiracies as much as the next guy," Reis said, "especially world domination conspiracies—"

Reekha held up her hand. "Let me finish, please. The day after the meeting, Naresh and I were followed. They must have watched security footage of us leaving the building. We didn't go home. Instead, we drove around until we were sure we'd lost them. Then we took buses and trains and hired a car. We had no place to go, so we hid in the most obvious place. We hid inside the very facility that this secret group was planning on using as a testing ground." Reekha's lower lip trembled. "The worst part is that they'll suspect I've blabbed, so if they find me, they'll kill me."

"If they find you they'll find us," said Jack.

Kelly's insides began to quiver with the anticipation that perhaps rescue was coming after all. Yet, Reekha's confession was making accomplices out of anyone she told. Reekha wore a sheepish expression, as if she realized this.

Reekha turned her attention back to Jack. "I believe you experienced hallucinations from staying inside the pod for too long. Symptoms will be major psychiatric disorders, including anxiety, depression, dissociative disorders and schizophrenia."

"I've got all those," Jack said.

"Plus, there have been studies of chronic déjà vu which scientists believe are due to a damaged temporal lobe. The circuits that are activated when you remember something get stuck in the 'on' position, creating false memories."

"In other words, death dreams," said Reis.

"Can the death dreams be dangerous?" Kelly asked.

"Are they dangerous *physically*?" Reekha shrugged her shoulders. "I'm not sure, though I imagine they have psychological impacts. Naresh was killed on the first day, in the first hour, and he hasn't moved since."

"Players are supposed to transmit straight back into the game a certain number of times," Kelly said. "My husband worked for CyberNexis. He told me that the computer would override re-entry if it considered a player to be mentally fatigued. It would place the player into a virtual waiting room. But it's meant to be pleasant."

"Did he tell you how to exit the game got stuck?" Reekha asked.

"No."

"If Naresh is going through what I went through..." Jack said, but he left the rest unsaid.

"Storm's coming." Reekha stared out the window. "I have to leave now if I'm to make it back to the power station. You're welcome to come with me. I'd appreciate any help. In the game *and* in getting Naresh to wake up."

Reekha headed for the kitchen and the others made an unspoken unanimous decision to help her.

Outside, despite the band of angry storm clouds that greeted them, the air tasted like dust. If they stayed ahead of the storm they'd make it to the power station. But what would be waiting for them?

***

Kelly's clothes were a dismal reminder of her imprisonment. Regardless of how stained or torn her clothing was, at the start of each apocalypse she entered the game looking fresh and clean. She was relieved to be walking in ski clothes, regardless of whether they matched or not. When she noticed that Reis had stopped to tie up the laces to his hiking boots, she decided to hang back. Hundreds of questions danced in the air and she plucked one that seemed to be dancing the craziest.

"Reis, do you know why Jack would dream of a woman and child dying over and over?"

"He's got nothing to feel guilty about." Reis pulled his jeans over his boots and stood up. "He and Mary-Ellen dated in college, like he said for two months. I don't get why he imagined they had a child."

"He's never mentioned her before. At all." From the day she'd met Matt she hadn't been able to shut up about him, telling everyone who had ears that she was in love. Matt this. Matt that. When people grew annoyed she'd accused them of being jealous. True love made you crazy with joy. Yet Jack had said nothing about this woman who obviously meant something to him.

Reis kept his gaze on the horizon. "I didn't think it was anything serious. Kelly, I'm not sure you should try to dig deeper. I think he's repressed a painful memory. Not everyone benefits from opening wounds."

His jaw tightened, as if this was a warning, but she took it as a challenge.

"He must have loved her for it to affect him this badly. And if he loved her, why did he break up with her?"

"He didn't break up with her. She died."

This news came like a punch in the stomach. Kelly had pictured her brother as the hero who'd flown in to rescue her. She'd no idea that he'd mourned the death of someone he cared about. No wonder he'd known all the right things to say and do; he'd been there and done that. Except he'd suffered alone.

"Why didn't he tell me?" She found herself glaring at Reis, resentment welling up that he would know things about her brother that she ought to have known.

Reis lifted his lips into a sneer. "He didn't tell me either. Not right away. And he didn't make a big deal out of it. I'm not keeping secrets from you. If I'd have known he was this troubled I'd have told you. I know you guys are close."

Kelly laughed. "Close? He's kept this a secret for almost ten years."

"Pandora is messing with him. I've been to enough shrinks to know how guilt operates. He feels responsible for her death so it has manifested in his head that she was the love of his life. They barely knew one another."

"That's an awful thing to say. When you meet The One, you just know."

"Exactly my point. Mary-Ellen didn't hold a special place in his heart until *after* her death."

***

Jack was almost back to his usual self by the time Kelly and Reis caught up to him. "Reekha told me she has been in this game before," he said.

This was a new turn of events. Kelly hadn't heard of players repeating a game, at least no-one on her team had. And she would have slit her own throat if she'd had to repeat the biological disaster game. She shuddered as she recalled how a soldier had strapped her to the table, then a doctor had tried to forcibly impregnate her.

"This game is played out near two power stations," Reekha explained. "Scientists have always theorized the end of civilization will come about from two opposing theories. One side is the Cornucopians. They believe increased population means more brains to think up new technology to overcome the issues around resource depletion. Thus technology will provide. So they keep trying to invent new things such as a pill that hydrates you or a pill that feeds you for two weeks, or how to recycle urine for drinking water. That sort of thing. They're in the station on the left."

Drinking urine for water sounded like a thing Kelly could die never having tried and die happy.

"The Malthusians are the pessimists," Reekha continued. "They believe the downfall will come from the basic need for food. The greater the population, the more mouths there are to feed. The more mouths to feed, the more resources are depleted. This group will stockpile and try to wait out the depletion. They'll try to grow crops but the soil will be tainted and rain will hardly fall. What rain *does* fall is too polluted for crops. And there's no way they could produce enough food even if the conditions were ideal. In essence, for humanity to survive in this scenario, most everyone has to die."

At the top of a small rise, the tall chimney of the power station came into view. They all stopped to stare. The clouds were fast on their tail. Whatever Reekha's motives, she'd led them to a possible means of escape. Listening to talk of technology and inventions had caused an idea to pop into Kelly's head. A power station might have residual power.

"Could we use the generators to over surge the mainframe computer?" Kelly asked.

"Both stations are tapped out. Or so they tell me." Reekha gave them a wicked smile. "The Cornucopians have a piece of technology I think might help set us free, though I suspect it requires a registered player to activate it. I'd give it a try, but if I die in the game, I might end up like Naresh."

A smaller power station sat next to the larger one. Reekha took the path that led the group towards the smaller power station. Time and disuse had taken its toll on its cooling tower and the chimney stack. Kelly's hope of finding residual power to use dropped.

When they arrived at a door, Reekha pressed a buzzer, and a few minutes later came the sound of metal on metal. The door opened and they entered.

"This place looks deserted," said Reekha. "But they're watching our every move." She walked directly towards a room about ten foot wide that in the past might have housed a couple of office desks. Now it housed a few beaten up sofas and out-of-shape bookshelves. On the floor lay a body, curled up as if sleeping. He didn't appear to have sustained any injuries to explain his state.

"We emerged in this game," Reekha said. "We didn't choose it. How could we? We landed a few miles down the road, and when we got here, Naresh just dropped to the ground." She knelt down and stroked his cheek. "He's been this way ever since. But I don't always transmit into this game. I was terrified when I entered vampire game. Not because I was scared of vampires, but I couldn't find Naresh's body. It took me all night to locate him."

Jack knelt down beside Naresh. "I had nightmares of my wife and child dying over and over. For his sake, I hope he is dead. It's better than having a death dream."

"You never told me how you woke up," Reekha said.

"Enlightenment."

"I'm from a Hindu culture. Enlightenment is many things, but a death dream breaker?"

"We used astral projection to drag Reis out of his death dream," Kelly said.

"Ash shot me point blank with a rifle," Reis said with a harsh glint to his eyes.

So that explained the animosity between the two, Kelly thought.

"We should plan to get the power station back up and running," she said. "There's a strong chance it'll do something to at least send a message to those on the outside when they see the spike in electricity."

"This place is heavily guarded," Reekha said.

"Why would it be heavily guarded if it's tapped out?" Kelly began pacing. "Doesn't make sense. Pandora *wants* us to start the generator. Why else would she send us here? She wants us to play."

As she paced, she realized many of the players had given up, through fatigue and heartache. Who could blame them? But seeing Jack in his current state spiked her determination to escape this mess.

"Jack should stay here to watch over Naresh's body," Kelly said. "He needs a break from all this craziness. Reis and I will work on getting the power plant operational. You're welcome to come with us, Reekha."

Reekha stood up and moved over to the window. "They'll get suspicious if you start sneaking around the plant. I'll try to think up a diversion."

At that moment, Reis fell to the floor, clutching his stomach and moaning.

"Good plan," Kelly said. "Pretend to drop dead. But you should do that where others can see you."

He didn't get up. Instead, he gasped for breath. His face turned blue.

Kelly nudged him with her shoe. "Reis. Stop joking around."

Reekha dropped to the ground and felt for a pulse. "I'll get a doctor." She ran outside and shouted for help. Footsteps sounded and Kelly was pushed aside as a young man lifted Reis's eyelids and flashed a small light into his eyes.

"He's slipping in and out of consciousness," the man said. "Let's get him to the infirmary."

A couple of people slipped Reis onto a stretcher and carried him out of the room.

"Kilian's the doctor here," Reekha explained.

"But we're not *here*," Kelly whispered.

"Kilian will explain," she said, and together they followed the doctor into a room with three metal tables. Nothing looked clean or sterilized. It didn't matter since this wasn't real, she told herself. Except when Kilian pressed down on Reis's stomach, and when Reis screamed in pain, it felt real enough.

Kilian gave Reis a jab of pink liquid from a dispenser. "This is the third case in two days. I've given him a neural suppressant. We were developing it as a way to treat a range of illnesses, instead I've used up most of my prototype on you *players*."

He spat out the word 'players', and Kelly was surprised that he'd used the term.

"I know who you are," he said. "Some of you are having issues with the simulation pods. My condolences on being trapped with us non-life forms."

The NPCs weren't supposed to be aware of their existence as an NPC. Kelly turned to look at Reekha who shrugged her shoulders and said, "I sort of let it slip. What can I say? My defenses were down."

It was hard to stay angry; really, it was only a matter of time before the scope of the virtual world and the players were exposed.

"Do you know anything about the pods?" Kelly asked Kilian.

He shook his head. "No, but I've discovered that small charges of electricity ease the patient's pain. You need to understand that if he's deteriorating in the game, chances are he's deteriorating for real. There isn't anything I can do inside here."

Kilian excused himself, saying he would replicate more of the neural suppressant, and the rest of the NPCs exited with him. That left Jack, Reekha, and Kelly to stand over Reis's body. Kelly had to turn away, unable to face the possibility that Reis might been dying inside his pod, which was so close yet so far away it could easily have been on Mars.

"Anyone know how to start a generator?" Kelly asked.

"No," Reekha said. "But I have an idea on how someone might get that information *and* gain entry into the heavily guarded plant. The night I told Kilian that he was a virtual character, we were drinking. I can't explain how alcohol affects us inside this world. Kilian tried to understand the concept, and while experimenting, he told me about his work. He designed an implant chip to improve human function. He called this an amplification implant, or 'amplant' for short. The amplant tells the body not to *think*, but *to do*. It picks up on a person's strengths and amplifies them. Basically it can turn a person into a superhuman."

"What does that have to do with the generator?"

"The amplant not only works on physical attributes, but on mental ones. It amplifies a person's ability to receive information. It hasn't been tested. I think Kilian wanted to trial it on himself but this was before he discovered he wasn't real. He now suspects it won't work on him. But it should work on a player."

"Why would it work on a player if it won't work on him?"

"Because players are meant to be able to control what happens in the game. Not a lot, but enough to tweak an environment. We're able to imagine any outfit we like and enter the game wearing it."

Jack shook his head. "I've tried it. For kicks I imagined a superhero costume."

"Hello," Reekha said raising her eyebrows. "Our bodies are inside glass domes wearing tight-fitting body suits with wires and cables poking out of them. Are any of you dressed like a CGI geek at a comic book convention? Trust me, you have control of the environment. You just don't know how to use it."

She made a good point. Their real bodies were not wearing regular clothes. Of course they had control over the environment.

Kelly shook her head. "It might be too dangerous. We're all scared, miserable, tired. It's likely to amplify this negativity and send one of us on a huge killing spree."

"I'll do it," Jack said.

"No, you won't." Kelly waved a finger at him. "You're in worse condition than me. I'll do it."

"Don't I get a say?" Reekha asked.

Kelly looked over her shoulder. Naresh was lying on the floor in the office. "If this works, you'll want to get him immediate medical help. Where is this amplant?"

"In Kilian's office. Down the hall. Last door on the right. He keeps it in his desk drawer."

Kelly nodded. "How do I get the amplant to work?"

"It has a trigger gun which you press against your arm, and the device will find its way to your neural core. But brace yourself, it will hurt."

Jack grabbed her arm as she walked toward the door. "I won't let you do this. It's too dangerous. What if something happens?"

"Jack, let me save you for once. Please."

"Once it's injected," Reekha said, "you should know how to operate the generator. And do me a favor."

"What's that."
"Succeed."

***

Jack insisted on accompanying Kelly, and she was glad for the support. She had to admit that she might not be the best person for the task; her own personality was likely to see the world destroyed, not saved.

"You do realize the game is playing *us*," Jack said.

Kelly found the dispenser that contained the amplant exactly where Reekha had said it would be. "I know. But our best chance at surviving is to play along."

She took the amplant out of the drawer. Last chance to find a better person for the job, she told herself. That person should have been Jack, but he was too fragile at the moment. Reis might have been a good contender, but he was out of action. Strange that his potential death should tug at her chest. She guessed all death would affect her from now on.

"Let me do it, Kell," said Jack. "I'm begging you."

"No." She pressed the dispenser against her arm. She felt a sharp prick, like the NADs during the symbiotic hook-up. It burned for a few seconds, and then the pain was gone.

"Am I supposed to feel differently?" she asked.

"I'd imagine so," Jack said.

After waiting a few minutes, she still felt her usual self. "What if it needs something to activate it?"

"I'll try to attack you," Jack said. "And you defend yourself."

He swung an arm at her and she blocked it then grabbed his shirt. Next, she picked him up and threw him across the room. She laughed as Jack slid down the wall into a heap.

He also laughed. "Just like old times when we used to wrestle as kids."

A voice came from the doorway. "I wish you hadn't done that."

Kelly looked up to see Kilian standing in the doorway. He had a gun aimed at Jack but he spoke to Kelly. "I can't kill you, you're too strong,. But I can kill him and send him into cyberspace."

The knowledge to overpower Kilian came within an instant of time. One second she was standing midway inside the room, and the next she had flung Kilian back into the hallway and now stood over him, pointing his gun at him. The impulse to shoot him in the head was strong. He had threatened her brother's life, and that was a crime in her world.

"Don't do it, Kelly," Jack shouted. "Don't let it take over you. Dammit, I knew I shouldn't have let you do this."

Jack's voice switched the impulse to shoot Kilian into shutdown mode, but she kept a hold of the gun as she ran down the corridor. She ran past the office where Naresh was sleeping. Reekha's face was pressed up to the small window in a look of surprise.

Outside, light rain fell, forming a large pool of water on the ground. Kelly had to control her breathing to conquer the urge to shoot everything in sight. The amplant heightened her sense of taste and smell.. The rain tasted foul. Filthy. Everyone deserved to die.

She saw the schematic layout of the power station in her mind's eye. At the rear of the complex sat the cooling tower, the generator was located twenty feet inside the room. The fact that it was guarded brought a smile to her face. Running across the ground, the scenery rushed by in a blur. The amplant gave her incredible strength and knowledge. Flashing into her brain was a set of instructions on how to operate the generator, how to adjust the voltage output without upsetting the system, and the instructions on trouble-shooting electrical and mechanical systems.

Except, she didn't want to fix potential problems. She wanted to create them.

***

Two men guarded the generator. Without warning, Kelly fired off two quick rounds and their bodies fell to the ground. The gunshots attracted shouts and Kelly disposed of four more men. 'Kill or be killed' was the premise of the game, and she was a model player right now. Lock and load. Shoot first. Everyone deserved to die.

The amplant was pumping adrenalin through her veins; she reckoned she could have stuck a finger in a power socket and lit up Las Vegas. The device made her fast, strong, and knowledgeable. She viewed more schematics and operating manuals in her mind. There were twenty-seven major components to this power station. The amplant gave her the names of the parts. Cooling tower. Low pressure turbine. Boiler feed pump. High pressure turbine. Superheater. Generator. Pylon. Precipitator.

She would kill anyone who attempted to stop her from blowing up the power plant.

More importantly, she would kill anyone who attempted to remove the amplant. She'd never felt so alive.

The plant ran on eight boilers and four turbines. The boilers used a circulated fluidized bed compulsion system, making it efficient and environmentally friendly. These improvements didn't make a lick of difference in saving the planet; it had still burned out.

Not yet used to the amplant, she surprised herself when she gripped the large metal door and it soared through the air behind her. *Relax Kelly. Let the amplant do its work.* After that, she took orders only from the amplant. It told her a guard waited inside. He noticed Kelly, then he licked his lips and rubbed his groin, indicating what he'd do to her. Bad move. She hated rapists. This scum of the earth deserved to die slowly.

She shot him in the balls and laughed as she stepped over his bleeding body.

The generator was easy to locate. It was the size of a small house and pale-green. The implant told Kelly it rotated and converted mechanical power into electrical power. It created relative motion between a magnetic field and a conductor. As least it hadn't been torn apart and salvaged for scrap metal. The keypad wouldn't operate without electricity, yet there was a backup hand crank. Ordinarily, Kelly Lawrence would never have attempted to turn over anything more powerful than a kitchen tap, but with her powers, she turned the hand crank as easily as a door handle.

She heard a *click* behind her. Clever was the person who could creep up on her, she thought. And stupid. They would be dead within seconds. But she would like to see the face of the person who tried to stop her.

Kilian had a gun pointed at her. "I can't let you blow up the generator. I have a right to exist."

"You're nothing but blips on a screen."

"I'm blips now. But if you destroy the mainframe then I'll be nothing."

"You have no right to exist anymore than I do," she said. "But my brother does."

She moved with lightning speed and tore the gun out of Kilian's hands. In a moment of clarity, her inner voice screamed at her to not shoot the doctor. He was more than a non-player character, he was aware of his existence and he had a right to that existence. So she would let him live. For now.

The implant told her something surprising – the mainframe computer was running out of power. Pandora was trying to boot them out, and failing. This knowledge was swallowed up by her rage. She smacked the barrel of the gun on Kilian's temple and he went down. She should have been afraid of the amplant taking control. She had entered the game to extinguish the indistinguishable grief that burned in her veins. The amplant generated a light inside her that burned so bright she feared it would swallow her grief. And she didn't want it to stop.

It would never end and why should it. Everyone wanted her to get over his death, even she'd considered it. She missed Matt. She loved him. She wanted him to be alive. Why should she stop missing him and loving him and wanting him to be alive? There was no time limit on such things, and she resented that everyone kept trying to make one up.

As she stepped over Kilian's body, she pushed the urge to kill everyone to the back of her mind. Something else rose to the surface. She'd lost track of time. She started calculating back to when she'd entered the game. It had been a Saturday when they'd battled vampires. Sunday was zombie day. Monday was the cruelest of days with the biological disaster game. Tuesday was the next most alarming scenario, kids who were dying to be young, but Jack had seemed to think she'd had a death dream or had slipped into another game while she was unconscious in alien invasion. They must have battled aliens on Tuesday, but it could have been Wednesday. Even if she said Wednesday for the sake of it, then today, Thursday, was resource depletion apocalypse. Tomorrow was Friday. The day after that was the anniversary of Matt's death.

She had a mission, and it had nothing to do with the games or even saving Jack. She had to visit his gravesite. His parents would be there and she vowed she'd be there too.

She gave the hand crank one final spin. After a few clunks and clangs the shafts inside the generator began to rotate. Her mind ran through a mental checklist of the procedures to adjust the voltage output. The power generation and the electrical load had to be close to equal to avoid overloading the network. She set the power generation to maximum.

Next, she ran through the trouble-shooting processes to fix electrical and mechanical problems, and these she set to create problems. When the emergency procedures to shut down the plant flashed across her mind's eye, natural self-preservation kicked in and she bolted for the door.

Outside, the rain was steady and it smelled of oil and gasoline. The amplant had compensated for the intense odor and now the smells died away.

She stopped when a flash of light caught her attention. Her eyes tried to penetrate the electrical current of the virtual world to see *through* it. If she could locate the simulation pods, preferably hers, she could open it up and it would be Game Over.

Two figures came running towards her. She recognized Jack and

Reis. They stopped about twenty feet away. She lifted the gun. If they tried to stop her mission, then they deserved to die.

"You don't need to blow up the station," Jack said. "Reis is fine."

Kelly studied Reis. He didn't look fine. He was clutching a hand to his chest and he could barely stand up. Mist from the rain surrounded him, which reminded her of the auras she used to see when she stared at the sun for too long. He was beautiful in this light. Why had she never noticed this before about him?

"Put down the gun," Jack ordered.

"Can't do that."

"You've killed enough people."

"They deserved to die."

Years of pent up rage burned her insides. Matt had quenched this anger somewhat, but he was no longer here. She would start with destroying the power station. Then she would destroy all the Cornucopians for their arrogance that had led to resources being depleted. Then she would destroy all the Malthusians for their complacency that had led to resources being depleted.

That flash of light again. Only this time it was millions of colors swirling together.

"The amplant is amazing," Kelly said. "I can see into another dimension. The simulation pods are in my peripherals. I just have to focus."

Kelly poured all her energy into imagining the pods. To her right, something came into view. She saw part of a glass, domed lid. Wires. Cables. A hallway. Then she caught a glimpse of her body wearing a cyber suit and bashing her fists against a window.

"Jesus, Kell," she heard Jack say. "How are you doing that?"

She concentrated further and more images came into view, another simulation pod, cut in half with the fragment of dimensions.

The gun faltered in her hand. Her concentration was broken and Jack took a step towards her. Then the images disappeared and her grip on the gun strengthened.

"You've got to get away," she told Jack. "The plant is set to blow up."

"Power stations don't explode," Jack said. "They generate electricity which feeds along transmission lines. Most they'll do is blackout. It could be enough to do damage to the mainframe, but it won't kill everyone."

"I bypassed the fuses that prevent overload." The rain was coming down in big fat drops. She looked down to see the water, it was two inches deep. "Water is a conductor of electricity. This place will become energized as soon as the plant overloads. You have to go now. Save yourself, Jack. For once, put yourself first. Reis, get him out of here."

But Reis and Jack didn't flee. Instead they ran towards her and barreled into her, crashing onto the ground. Water splashed around as the air began to sizzle. Transmission lines that had lain dormant for hundreds of years now came alive with sparks.

The last thing she heard before it went dark was Reis's voice in her ear. "I'm here for you, Kelly. Whether you let me in or not."

18

Reis

Once upon a time a teenage boy and his best friend had played a prank on the best friend's little sister. They'd known the little sister feared monsters, but it was a particularly dreary day with not much else to do except torment cats and little sisters. The cat would have none of it and had zipped off to hide in a neighbor's yard. They'd coaxed the little sister into watching a horror movie with them, and because she was the kind of sister who always wanted to do whatever her brother and his friend did, she watched it. The little sister had survived watching the movie, even bravely declaring that it was stupid and pointing out all the flaws of the visual effects, and then she'd taken herself to bed. The two boys had decided it would be fun to dress up in clown costumes and creep into her bedroom.

***

Reis woke up in an apartment, made sure he was in *his* apartment by checking the electricity and phone bills – they were addressed to him – and then went into the living room to feed his pet turtle, Angus. When he heard screams outside, he poked his head out the window. On the street below, clowns with knives were terrorizing pedestrians and drivers. Rather than hurry down, he took a moment to soak up the ambience of home. He ached to curl up under the bedcovers and watch TV, but Pandora, tapped into his mind, *must* have known that Kelly hated clowns. Furthermore, she must have known that Reis was responsible for embellishing on this fear and scarring her for life. If he could've transported back in time he'd gladly have done so and tormented the cat instead. But what was done was done.

He rummaged inside his closet for his anti-abduction device – a

Browning 308 semi-automatic rifle that Stafford had given him for his twelfth birthday – then he grabbed his car keys and took the stairs down two flights. Kelly's house was close by. He was sure she'd appreciate rescue from the clowns.

It took four rounds to obliterate the clowns trying to steal his BMW. He drove quickly to Kelly's house. Out front, he stopped and peered up at the second story window. It had been a long time since he'd stopped at the front of her house. The last time he had, Matt had glared at him from behind a lacy curtain.

The front door was ajar. He pushed open the door just as a swathe of colored cloth disappeared up the stairs. Reis hurried to catch up and managed to catch sight of the clown's oversized show as it ducked into Kelly's bedroom.

"Kelly!" Reis shouted.

He burst through the doorway with his gun held out front. The clown was carrying a knife towards the bed where Kelly was tangled up in her bed sheets. The clown raised the knife and Reis fired the rifle and shot the clown in the back. A chunk of clown flesh splattered the wall. Kelly tossed aside the sheets and launched herself out of bed. In one airborne stride, she was in the hallway.

"You've got to be kidding me," she cried out.

Her hands were curled into fists and she wore a lacy nightgown. She gave Reis a heated stare and pointed at the clothes on the floor. He picked up a pair of jeans and t-shirt and tossed them her way. She turned her back to him while she dressed.

"Killer clowns," she said when they was in the hallway. "Killer *freakin'* clowns. You know I hate them."

He grabbed her by the arm and guided her down the stairs. At the bottom, she pulled her arm out of his. "Hang on a minute. You have some explaining to do. Just before the last game ended, you said you'd be here for me whether I wanted you to or not. What did you mean by that?"

"Can we talk about this later?"

The words had tumbled out his mouth when he'd thought they were all going to die. He couldn't take them back, he didn't want to take them back, however *now* wasn't the time to explain what he meant since he was barely trying to process it himself. There was no doubting that his feelings for her were growing, after years of lying dormant, yet was it the NADs causing these feelings or the closeness they'd experienced while trying to survive in this crazy world?

At the front door Kelly stopped and gazed back up the stairs. "It was nice to wake up in my bed for once. I could have stayed there all day."

Reis nodded. "We'll get home again. This has to be over soon."

He kept his rifle trained for anything moving. Outside, the porch light glowed enough to light the way to his BMW, which was once again blocked by hobo clowns with sad faces and tattered clothes. However, instead of holding balloons in the shape of animals, they were holding long-handled knives.

"I severely hate clowns," Kelly said.

"I'm sorry."

"Not entirely your fault. I hated clowns before you and Jack scared me."

The streets of Mission Valley, California were tree-lined. Reis couldn't tell how many more clowns might be hiding amongst the palms and bushes. He fired shots at those blocking his path, knocking the creatures to the ground, but they didn't stay dead for long. They twitched and opened their eyes and mouths. Not only were they dealing with killer clowns, these creatures wouldn't die.

Once in the car, Reis sped off with no destination in mind.

"Thanks for saving me," Kelly said.

"Least I could do."

Reis drove around the block. It used to be that he'd drop Kelly off at home and cop the angry stare from Matt. Then he'd drive around the corner and wait. Just in case she needed him. But she'd never called because Matt wasn't the monster he'd hoped would force Kelly into his arms. He'd never stopped praying for the call though.

Reis returned his attention to the road. He could sense Kelly studying him and he fought to keep his face impassive.

"Are you okay?" she asked. "You collapsed at the power station. The doctor claimed something was happening to your body for real in the simulation pod. He gave you a shot of electricity. And you recovered."

The collapse was difficult to explain. A searing pain had overwhelmed him, as if shutting down his neural system. He couldn't see, smell, speak, hear.

"I'm fine now," he said. "Must have been a glitch."

"That's my point." She sighed. "I thought it would work. I saw a glimpse of the pods. They were *there*, they were *right there*. I gave the computer a massive jolt of electricity when I blew up the power station and it didn't work."

"You should be proud of yourself. It's the closest we've come to the outside world. How did you do it?"

"I believed I could do it. The amplant supercharged every living fiber inside me, including my confidence. A little bit of it remains in me, because I need to believe that we will get out of here. Today. This has to be the last day. I can't take it anymore."

Right before the power station blew up, an image had appeared in the corner of Reis's gaze, of a glass coffin and a long corridor, but he'd dismissed this image as an effect of his collapse. If Kelly had caused it, then was it really a case of mind over matter?

"I miss our conversations," she said. "You used to tell me stuff all the time, like what you were doing on the weekend, how much you paid for a jacket, what Stafford had done to make you mad."

"I miss them too," he said, his back stiffening. Her random question had all the markings of a calculated one. He could sense manipulation a mile away. Growing up with Jewel and Stafford would turn even the most gullible man into a cynic.

"Why don't we have them anymore?" she asked.

"I don't know."

"I think you do."

He scanned the road for killer clowns. Anything was preferable to admitting the truth. That her husband had stopped by his office a few week's into their marriage and demanded Reis stop spending time with her. Reis had ignored the threat, since Kelly was a grownup who could do as she pleased, yet through the natural course of things she'd drifted away on her own.

"Is that what's really bothering you?" he asked.

"Reis. Answer the question."

"You got married."

She fidgeted in her seat. "But that shouldn't have mattered. We should have been able to stay friends."

"No, Kelly. It would have been impossible to stay friends because Matt had every right to glare down at me through the window in a jealous rage. He had every right to want to keep you away from me."

"Oh."

Reis tightened his grip on the wheel, and he might've turned around and taken her home except that killer clowns were probably trying on her makeup.

"We should find Jack," Reis said. "Check the glove compartment for my phone."

Kelly found it and handed it to Reis, who plugged it into the car's hands-free cradle. He punched in Jack's number. It rang and rang. He got voicemail and hung up without leaving a message. Reis drove through a set of red lights, because stopping could lead to an ambush. Homeland Security had provided him with lessons on survival; Jewel would be pleased he was finally using them.

Kelly said, "So Matt was jealous. I can understand why you'd avoid me then. It doesn't explain why you haven't spoken to me for the past year."

Reis floored the pedal and took the corner too fast. It felt good to be driving his car again. He knew these streets and he pushed the car like it was Stafford's and he wanted to return it broken. He drove as if he could avoid the conversation by losing control of the car. But Kelly wasn't swayed.

"It doesn't explain why you're not talking to me now," she said.

The metaphors about his life weren't lost on him. He pushed people away to escape getting hurt by them. His beloved pet was a turtle that could retreat into its shell when he didn't want to face the world. He lived a pedestrian life because money could buy you anything except the thing you wanted most.

"Reis!" She slapped the dash. "Why won't you talk to me?"

He slammed on the brakes and the car came to a screeching halt in the middle of the road. He got out and stared up at the sky, not caring about being ambushed by clowns. That was a thousand times more preferable to being ambushed by a woman.

Star gazing usually calmed him, but not this time. Kelly touched him on the arm and he almost jumped. He didn't believe in psychic connections, but every time she was close, he sensed her sadness, as if it were a ghost hovering beside her. Her touch almost drove him to fall to his knees and weep.

He stepped away from her. He closed his eyes. Not quick enough to escape the glimpse of the sorrow on her face.

"You should have married me," he finally said. "I wouldn't have died and you wouldn't be sad all the time. And now it's too late because you'll never get over Matt. No man can compete with a ghost."

"That's unfair," she whispered.

When he next opened his eyes, Kelly was pacing around in a circle. Her arms were wrapped around her body. She would stop to gaze off into the distance then begin pacing again. At last she stopped and looked him in the eye. "It's unfair because you had a chance to ask me out and you never did."

"You called me an emotionless robot."

"When?"

"That time we went to Mexican Joe's and did tequila shots. You were drunk and crashed on my sofa."

"Oh my god." Kelly threw her hands into the air. "That was, what, seven years ago. You're holding me accountable for something I said when I was shattered. I can't believe you've hung onto this." She shook her head. She seemed speechless, confused. "Really? That's what your cool and distant act is all about?"

He was cool and distant because he had to be. His emotions were best stored under the skin where nobody could play with them, ransom them, knead them like dough. Kelly's words had struck a nerve because they were the truth. He couldn't survive in his parent's world by displaying his feelings. He couldn't survive in Kelly's world either. He was a misfit, like the Zombie Girl who wasn't quite mindless creature and not quite happy teenager. He didn't belong anywhere except in a shell.

"You're not an emotionless robot," Kelly said. Her eyes softened and she gave him a rare smile. "Did I really say that?"

"It doesn't matter."

She raised an eyebrow. "Obviously it does." She rubbed her hands along her arms. "Can we get out of here? I have a bad feeling."

He sensed it too. As if a malevolent creature with a curly wig and oversized shoes was watching them from amidst the shadows. Back in the car, Reis drove towards town, dialing Jack's cell number, but it kept ringing out. In town, the carnage was noticeable. Cars sat on the side of the road, body parts were strewn on the sidewalk. Chunks of buildings were gone, indicating the military had swept through town. Maybe they'd evacuated everyone safely. Maybe Kelly and Reis were all that was left to face the end of the world. He wouldn't have minded at all, he even supposed he'd learn to put up with Matt's ghost, the way he'd learned to put up with the man.

From the beginning, Reis had wanted to dislike Matt, but he was smart, funny, and he'd ended up doing the graphic design for Quest. He genuinely liked the guy. Watching Matt and Kelly together had become uncomfortable, so Reis had handballed the graphics and marketing to Jack, made Jack the General Manager and given himself the title of Creative Manager. It was around this time that Matt took up the habit of watching him from the second story window whenever Reis dropped Kelly home. Two years later the guy had been killed in a car crash. Reis would give anything to see Kelly smiling again, even if it meant he'd have to step out of the picture.

Reis cleared his throat. "You never told me if you found Matt in the game."

"I found him."

"And?"

"And I'd rather not talk about it."

"Did seeing him make you happy?" He tried hard to keep the disapproval out of his voice.

She stared down at her hands. "Happy. And sad. I have to get out of the game."

"I know."

She shook her head like he didn't.

His phone rang. Jack's number was on the screen. In the hands-free cradle it was automatically on speaker.

"Jack," Kelly said. The relief in her voice was evident. "I was worried about you. Where are you?"

"La Mesa."

Kelly turned to Reis. "That's where we're going."

"Wrong," Jack said over the phone. "Not sure if you've encountered any supernatural clowns—"

"We have."

"Well, I need you to follow a lead for me. I'm stuck here for a bit. I'll get there when I can. There's a guy in town runs a store, *Clarence's Props and Costumes*. He's a friend of mine. If anyone knows how to stop the clowns, it'll be him."

The call ended, and Kelly and Reis exchanged glances. Reis suspected a trap, or worse, that Pandora was leading them astray. It wouldn't be the first time. He hoped it would be the last, yet somehow he doubted it.

Kelly thumped her fist on the dash. "Another clue. Another quest. Another delay. Why won't this end?"

"Have you ever considered that if this really is mind over matter, there are more players who want to stay than want to leave?"

"Are you one of the players who wants to stay?"

"It's better than outside. Easier rules to follow."

"What rules? There are no rules?"

"That's why they're easy to follow. It's also easier to identify the enemy. My mind's already screwed up anyway, Pandora doesn't stand a chance of doing any further damage."

Just then, a silver sedan sped down the street and didn't appear to be stopping. It headed directly for them and Reis had to pull the wheel tightly to the right to avoid a collision. He heard tires screeching. Looking in the rearview mirror, he saw the sedan turn around.

"Reis, it's coming for us."

"I can see that."

The sedan came up on their left, too fast to have been an ordinary car because the BMW had been hundreds of yards away when it had passed by. The mind over matter theory had merit. But maybe it was the enemy who'd gained control over the game.

The clown rolled down the window. It lifted its hands off the steering wheel and screamed, and then it grabbed the wheel and wiped its brow. It did this a few times and Reis realized it was a comedy routine. Then the clown's face twisted from a smile into a snarl. He flipped Reis the middle finger then rammed the car into the side of his BMW.

Kelly screamed when the cars collided.

"Learn to drive," Reis yelled.

Clowns trying to kill him, zombies trying to eat him, vampires trying to tear his head off his body. These things he could deal with.

But ramming his beautiful European car into a beaten up Toyota almost broke his heart.

The clown now had a pistol in his hand. He fired a shot and it hit the front fender.

Reis rammed his car into the sedan. He had his Browning rifle but he couldn't drive and fire the weapon at the same time. When the clown fired a second shot, Reis slammed his foot onto the brake and the sedan sailed by. He hurried out of the car and stood in the middle of the road with his gun aimed at the sedan. But just then another vehicle entered the road, and the clown took off after it.

"You drive," Reis said. "Unless you'd rather shoot at the clowns."

Kelly shook her head and they switched places. Reis asked his phone to search for the phone number for *Clarence's Props and Costumes.*

After the fifth ring, someone answered.

"Clarence," Reis said. "I'm calling about your store. You deal with the paranormal."

"That's not quite right. I deal with *costumes and props* of the paranormal."

"I think you *do* deal with the paranormal. Specifically supernatural clowns."

"I can't help you right now. I'm having a little crisis of my own."

"So you know what's going on," Reis said.

"Yes, yes, clowns are coming to life and killing people. But like I said, I'm a little tied up right now."

"Please, Clarence. You know more about this than we do," Kelly said. "Can you help us?"

Clarence went quiet. Reis wondered if the call had been disconnected.

"Clarence?" she asked.

A sigh down the line. "If you come right away I'll tell you what I know about clowns. But hurry, I don't know how long I have."

"Hang on. We'll be there in ten minutes." Reis told Kelly to turn the car around and head south to National City.

***

Reis had imagined 'I don't know how long I have' to mean that clowns were banging down Clarence's doors, and he and Kelly would have to battle their way past supernatural creatures to get inside. However, they walked in through the front door of *Clarence's Props and Costumes* like it was a normal day.

A voice called out from within the store. "Come on through."

The store was blazingly lit up by ceiling lights and desk lamps. As Reis charged through the store, he took in the dozens of racks containing monster masks. There was a section of Roman statues. Shelves displayed animal heads. As he stepped around a glass case, a mannequin wearing a Star Trek uniform startled him.

It was the mirrors that caught his attention the most. Reis would have expected a prop store to contain them, but not this many. And they were all stacked against the walls so it felt like walking through a fun house.

Kelly appeared at his side. "I can't believe Jack is obsessed with this stuff. And what's with all the mirrors?"

A short man with wild black hair appeared at the end of the aisle. "Are you the couple who called earlier?"

Reis nodded.

"You're lucky I'm here. I'm doing stock take." Clarence turned and waddled down the aisle. Reis had to jog to catch up. At the end of the aisle, Clarence climbed up a ladder and peered into boxes. Over his shoulder he said, "A number of my props up and left when the invasion started. It's bad for business not knowing exactly what stock is on hand. Not that my customers will want to hire clown costumes anymore."

He climbed down from the ladder and moved off to another shelf, almost disappearing into a box marked CIRCUS GEAR. He emerged and marked things off his clipboard. Reis watched in growing annoyance as Clarence repeated this step along the rest of the aisle.

Finally, Clarence stopped at a spot where two giant toy soldiers stood guard. "Some experts suggest the bad clown image is overused," he said. "So maybe I'm not so worried the blasted things have left me. Sales were dropping anyway. Everybody wants to be a zombie these days."

"Can you tell us about the clown apocalypse?" Reis asked.

"Yes, I can. We're in the middle of one." He leaned in close. "The clown is a living caricature. A mockery of humanity if you wish. That's the reason for the mirrors. Mirrors make the clown see beyond the mask to the humanity within. They've avoided this place since I set up the mirrors."

"So we can just hang here," said Kelly.

"Until they adapt," said Clarence. "Which is why they must be stopped. They're probably alive due to a curse. Guns and knives and even rocket launchers won't stop them. You'll have to track down the source of the curse and break the spell."

"Who? Us?" Kelly took a step backward. "I'm not going out there."

"Pandora sent you to me for a reason," Clarence said.

"What do you know about Pandora?" Reis asked.

"I know she wants you out of the pods. She can't keep you all alive for much longer. Her systems are staring to fail."

"Did she tell you why she trapped us here?" Kelly asked.

Clarence shook his head. "Something happened to the outside world. She's not picking up signals from satellites or the internet cables, and the air readings are off kilter. She's not exactly sure, but her best guess is heavy cloud is covering the earth. She needs you to get out of her mind. You're killing her."

Reis said, "If Pandora wants us out of here she'd do something about it."

"Pandora is a computer." Clarence tapped the side of his head. "Mind over matter is the key to getting out. You did it once, Kelly. Do it again."

How could this man know that Kelly had caused images of the simulation pods to appear, unless he'd been watching?

Reis scanned the store for CCTV cameras. Was this really just an elaborate reality TV show?

"How do we stop the curse?" Kelly asked him.

"Find the source." Clarence reached into his jacket and withdrew a silver knife. "Take this. Most supernatural beings are repelled by silver."

Kelly snatched the blade and pressed it against her chest.

Clarence said, "You have my phone number. Call me if you get stuck. I think I'll be here all night, despite my endeavors to get out of here and head home. Lock the door on your way out, if you wouldn't mind."

It took Reis and Kelly a while to find their way back to the front door. Instead of locking the door, Reis left it wide open.

"In case his damned clowns return home," he said with a grimace.

Kelly scowled at him. "Lock the door."

"You've got to admit he deserves to be killed by his own props."

"Nobody deserves to be killed by their props."

"He's setting us up," Reis said after he locked the door. "This whole thing is set up. Pandora is just messing with us."

"Maybe, but we have to give it a try. You might want to stay in the game, but I have to get out of here."

Kelly drove while Reis kept his rifle ready to fire. He punched Jack's number into the cell phone and it was answered on the second ring.

"How did you go with Clarence?" Jack asked.

"We're driving from National City, heading north," Kelly said.

"Clarence says the clowns are cursed and we need to find the source. But we're coming to get you."

Reis glanced at Kelly. Moments ago she'd said she wanted to find the source, and now she was ignoring her own order and going to find Jack. He'd never figure her out.

"Find the source of the curse," Jack said. "I have to stay here for a while. I ran into a woman and her kid, well, not literally. I ran her car off the road. The least I could do was see them get home safe. But I've learned one thing. The clowns came to life and started attacking people a week ago. Exactly one week ago. I need you to check something else out and follow the trail to break this curse."

Kelly mouthed the words, "It's a set up."

Reis nodded. While Reis understood that Jack would feel obliged to help someone he'd run off the road, this conversation sounded exactly like Pandora was sending them on a quest.

"Where in Claremont did you say you were?" Reis asked.

"I didn't. I told you I'm in La Mesa. I'm not a decoy, if that's what you're thinking."

Which was exactly what a decoy would say, Reis thought.

"I'm reading an article about a guy named Victor Steiner," Jack said. "He had problems with a clown exactly one week ago. Victor lives in City Heights." Jack gave Reis the address. "If you go there now, I'll come as soon as I'm done here."

The call ended.

"This stinks of Pandora," Reis said.

"Agreed. But what else can we do?"

Kelly drove with steely conviction, despite witnessing clowns chasing men, women, and children with knives, chains, rocks. She turned her head when a clown lifted a park bench over his head and slammed it down on a trapped man.

"Don't look at them," Reis urged. "They're not real."

"I'm fine."

He knew she was lying. He guessed that she'd never become accustomed to the senseless violence, and the truth was, he didn't want her to.

***

Kelly stopped the car outside a single story stucco house but left the engine running in case clowns burst out from behind the jasmine bushes. Strings of lights showed a tidy appearance and manicured lawn, indicating someone other than a guy who created curses to bring evil clowns to life occupied the home.

"You sure this is the place?" Kelly asked.

"Pandora wouldn't send us here otherwise."

"True."

They got out of the car and walked up the path.

"Victor Steiner," Kelly sang out as she banged on the front door. "Open up. We know you're in there." The door opened a crack. "Are you Victor Steiner?"

A single bloodshot eye glared at them. "Who are you?"

"I'm Kelly Lawrence and this is Reis Anderson. We'd like to talk to you about the clowns."

"Not interested."

"We're not reporters. We just want to talk to you."

"Why?"

Because you're a crazy clown man responsible for the death of millions of people and we've come to kill you, Reis thought. There were times when biting one's tongue was called for. He had to curl his hands into fists to resist the urge to beat the guy senseless. He couldn't show Kelly his anger; it might scare her away and they'd become close again.

"You're the number one expert on clowns," Kelly said.

"Well, I can't argue with that."

The door opened and Victor spun on his heels and sashayed into the house without inviting them, but he didn't say they couldn't come inside, either. The man wore a dressing gown and slippers and had more stubble on his face than Reis. He also staggered and stank as if he was drunk. Kelly and Reis followed Victor into a small foyer and then into an entertaining area. The place was decorated with good quality dark furniture, framed prints of Hollywood icons on the walls, it had a slate tiled floor, a bar, and pool table. The place had a musty, sweat sock smell as if the guy hadn't left the house for a while – perhaps exactly one week. The article said Victor manufactured toy clowns, but he obviously didn't put them on display in his home.

Reis could sense Kelly jumping at every noise and shadow. Given her phobia of clowns, she was doing better than expected.

A TV was mounted on the wall; it was switched on but the sound was muted. Images of clowns attacking people and the resulting carnage flashed across the screen. Victor headed for the bar and poured himself a drink. Pappy Van Winkle, twenty-year-old family reserve whiskey, and Stafford's favorite. Victor lived in a modest home but he must've made a decent income if he could afford to drink Pappy's. Otherwise he was keeping this one bottle for an important occasion, such as the end of the world. Since he didn't offer them any, Reis suspected it was the latter.

"The newspaper said something happened to you a week ago," Reis said to Victor. "Can you tell us about it? We think what happened to you might be connected with all the crazy clown stuff."

"I don't see how." Victor threw back a shot and poured a second. "Can I offer you a drink?"

"Sure."

Victor placed the cap on Pappy's and reached for a regular bottle of whiskey which he poured into two glasses. His gaze flicked toward the TV briefly, but he kept his head facing the rear deck, which he started walking towards.

"Like I told the reporters, I import clowns," Victor said. "Clown radios, lamps, dolls, costumes, wigs, pictures, bed covers, sheets, absolutely anything featuring a clown. It's not an obsession, just a business decision. I sell them online. My warehouse is out back. You want to see it?"

Kelly almost dropped her glass. "No. I believe you."

As she backed up close to the wall, Reis noticed that a piece of cloth was hung over an object. He could see the reflective edges of a gold framed mirror. *Why would this guy cover an object capable of saving his life?* Unless he didn't know that mirrors warded off the clowns.

Victor carried the bottle of Pappy's and beckoned for Reis and Kelly to follow him through a set of French doors out onto the deck. Victor leaned on the railing and stared out into his yard. Lights hung from a tree. Moonlight shimmered on a pond. The warm breeze tickled Reis's face. He had to hand it to Pandora; she was great at creating illusions. It was easy to accept that this was the real world.

"It started a month ago," said Victor. "A kid reported to his school teacher that one of my clown dolls bit him. The teacher decided to write a letter to the newspaper. The reporter decided I was flavor of the month and tracked down my past. 'Ex-con sells toys to kids' read the headline. She made it sound like I was a pedophile. I forged checks and got caught, that's all. Nothing sordid like she suggested."

"So the kid created an urban legend and everyone bought it," Reis said. "Doesn't explain how the clowns turned into killers."

Victor twisted his body until he was leaning with his back against the railing. He reached inside his robe pocket and produced a cigarette. He lit it, blew out a plume of smoke. Reis got the impression that Victor was either stalling or enjoying his moment under the spotlight.

"The article humiliated me. In a fit of rage I shouted, 'I wish clowns ruled the world'. And here we are." Victor flicked his gaze inside to the living room. "Lady Clown normally stands in that corner. She's a statue I found at the back of this place I worked at straight out of prison. Broken arms and missing a leg, nobody wanted her, so I took her home and fixed her up. Oh, I didn't live here then, I lived in a trailer. She became my only friend. Then I got the idea to go into business for myself."

Victor walked back inside and topped up his glass, overlooking the bottle in his arms. Reis found his attention was riveted to the spot where Lady Clown should be standing. A covered mirror. A missing clown statue. This was sounding more like a mystery to be solved than an apocalypse to survive. Kid's stuff.

"The beauty of online retailing," Victor said returning to the deck with a second bottle of booze, "is that people have to pay upfront. I only needed to purchase the goods after I was paid for them. I eventually raised enough capital to import goods and sell them directly from my trailer. Customers appreciate fast delivery. Anyway I made enough money to buy this place."

"And Lady Clown is the inspiration behind the dream," Reis said.

Victor sighed, gazing back inside the house. "Lady Clown is something else. She's... magical."

Reis turned around to discover Kelly was standing at the spot where Lady Clown used to stand. His chest squeezed. He felt the malevolent presence again.

"Is she out on the streets killing people?" he asked.

Victor almost choked on his whiskey. "Good lord, no. Lady Clown is my protector."

A door slammed, and into the living room strode a clown who was six foot tall and wearing the checkered body suit of a Harlequin clown. In its hand was a sword.

***

Lady Clown charged out onto the deck. She swung her sword at Reis but he moved out of the way with lightning speed. The sword dug into the railing, giving him a chance to dash inside. Lady Clown followed. So did Victor, but only to saunter over to the bar where he opened another bottle.

"Stop the curse," Reis shouted at Victor.

"You assume I haven't tried." From the corner of Reis's eye he saw Victor take another swig from the bottle. "She won't even let me leave the house. What happens when I run out of whiskey?"

Something was thrown at Lady Clown's head. A lamp. It hit the clown dead on, but the creature merely twisted her neck sharply to glare at Kelly; if the clown were human, her neck would have broken.

Lady Clown laughed and squeezed the flower on her chest. Reis watched in horror as liquid squirted in Kelly's face. Kelly screamed and scratched at her eyes.

Lady Clown advanced on Reis, swinging the sword, tauntingly. She lunged at him, and they danced around the room for a bit. Reis tossed everything within reach at her. Lady Clown easily deflected pool balls, empty bottles, wall hangings, art deco. While he panted from the exertion, the clown was hardly affected by the battle. Reis didn't know how much longer he could last against a supernatural monster.

He heard noises as Kelly blindly crashed into furniture. She cried out when she banged into the wall. Reis quickly flicked his gaze her way to make sure she was okay, and she had managed to pull down the cloth that covered the mirror. The image Reis saw in the reflection wasn't that of Lady Clown.

"Kelly, the knife," Reis shouted.

The cursed creature snarled and ran toward Kelly. Reis ran at Lady Clown and tackled her around the ankles. She kicked at his head. From his peripheral he saw Victor standing at the bar. Reis kicked and punched at Lady Clown to escape her grasp. He jumped up and looked into the mirror. Then he turned again to look at Victor.

Clarence had said the mirror revealed the true clown. It did, and it wasn't this come-to-life statue.

Lady Clown had a fierce look on her face as she picked up her sword. By now Reis had made his way to Kelly and he grabbed the silver knife out of her hand.

"Undo the curse," Reis shouted at Victor, even though he knew Victor would never do it. But he wanted to give the guy one last chance.

"She'll kill me before I can utter a word," Victor said with a groan.

Lady Clown lifted her sword above her head. Reis charged at Victor, ducked when the clown swung the sword, and stuck the knife in Victor's chest.

Lady Clown stopped moving. She became as still as a statue, positioned with the sword slicing through the air. Victor lay on the floor with a dagger sticking out of his chest.

They were both frozen. The danger was gone, but Kelly was still wiping at her eyes, so Reis ran into the kitchen and returned with a wet cloth.

"Are you okay?" he asked her.

"I think so. What happened? How did you stop the curse?"

"When you pulled the cloth down from the mirror, I saw Victor in his true form. He didn't create the curse. He *was* the curse."

Before their eyes, Victor transformed into a man with white paint on his muzzle and eyes. He had black eyebrows, a red nose, and a red upside-down smile. His clothes had transformed too. A tattered vest over a short-sleeved shirt. Baggy pants with holes. Big shoes.

Reis led Kelly into the kitchen to run her face under the faucet. Then he searched for a first aid kit and popped open the tubes of saline and poured the liquid into her eyes until the sting was gone.

"You're cut," he said tenderly.

Kelly lifted her arm and there was blood on her sleeve. She peeled back a piece of fabric to expose a slash in her flesh. Reis guided her to the dining table so he could wash away the blood and tend to the wound using cream and bandages from the medical kit. They'd won. It should be Game Over. And for the first time, he was ready to face the outside world. He was ready to go home.

***

Once Kelly was sorted, Reis grabbed four beers from the fridge. He drained the first bottle in a few gulps then opened a second.

Kelly was toying with hers. "What are we doing here, Reis? I know I said we had nothing else to do, but why are we playing this stupid game? And I don't mean just this one."

"It's actually not a stupid game." He pulled one of the dining chairs so that he could face her. "It's just going about things in a stupid way."

"I'm not sure I follow."

Reis took a sip of beer to delay what he was about to tell Kelly. It was something he'd never told anyone. He took a long swig and drained half the bottle.

"I thought the premise of the game was 'kill or be killed'," he said. "But it's not. You can't pick and choose which rules you obey and which ones you ignore. When it all goes to hell, the thing that gets you through the chaos is order."

Kelly peeled at the label on the bottle, and when Reis looked down he noticed he was doing the same. He placed the bottle on the table.

"These games are a lesson," said Reis. "In survival, I'm guessing. And Pandora is a cruel teacher."

"Reis, I'm tired and confused, you'll have to be clearer."

"Jewel's biggest fear when I was born was that I would get

kidnapped. She wasn't worried about paying the ransom, but she was terrified that if something went wrong, I'd be killed. Somehow she planted the idea in her head that I should know how to survive a kidnapping attempt."

Although the beer was fresh from the fridge, it now began to leave a bad taste in his mouth. But there was no backing out. He had to start living his life, start trusting people, open the door to let them in, and in order to do those things he would have to expose his fears and scars.

"I was kidnapped when I was five," he said.

19

Reis

Reis had never spoken to anyone about the day someone had grabbed him and stuffed him in the trunk of a car. He didn't want to talk about now. He'd never seen the appeal of confession; there was nothing therapeutic about it. If anything it twisted his insides into knots and made him want to throw up.

"My kidnapper taunted me every minute. He'd say things like, 'When I look into your eyes, what do you do?' I couldn't believe he expected an answer. I can't even remember what I said. But if it was the answer he liked, then he'd smile and pat me on the cheek."

"And if you gave him the wrong answer?"

His throat was dry. The beer wasn't helping. "If it was the wrong answer, he'd make his fingers into a gun, and say, 'you're dead, kiddo'."

Kelly gasped. "My god, Reis. That's awful."

He nodded. "This went on for six hours. He'd ask all kinds of questions. What should I do if the door was left open? What should I say to the kidnapper? Should I talk politely or yell at him? What should I tell them about the ransom money? He'd make me memorize every detail of the kidnappers and the location and repeat it to him with my eyes closed. I was so frightened. I peed my pants and threw up probably ten times."

Staring down at the bottle, he heard the chair scrape against the floor, then he felt Kelly's hand press against his thigh. After a minute, Reis reached for her hand. She didn't flinch or take it away.

"So there I was," he said. "Tied up to a chair in a dark room and this guy asked me what I had done to try to escape. I was five years old and scared out of my wits. I was crying, telling him I wanted to go home, and he slapped me. Told me to toughen up. Asked me what I'd done while I was in the trunk of the car. Had I tried to smash the rear taillights? Had I tried to get out of the binds? Had I taken notice of the turns, the length of time I was in the trunk?"

Kelly's hand went to her mouth. "I apologize for every mean thought I ever had about you. It's a wonder you can walk around and function like a normal person."

He chuckled. "I'm flattered you think I'm normal. But I'm not. I don't trust anybody. Aside from Jack, my only friend is a turtle. Women get close and I dump them. I can't open up about my feelings to anyone. I'm always suspecting the worst."

"I don't know what to say." A tear trailed down her cheek. "I'm sorry. I'm shocked. Does Jack know?"

He shook his head. "Nobody knows. I'd erased it from my mind, vowed to myself that I wouldn't let it ruin my life."

"Did it work?"

He shook his head.

"Nothing is ever truly erased, Reis. And how could you *not* let it affect you?" She squeezed his hand. He held onto it as tightly as if she was a life raft and he was floating off the edge of a waterfall.

"That's not the worst of it," he said. "One day Jewel let it slip that she and Stafford had arranged the whole thing. They'd paid a guy to kidnap me so I would learn from the experience." He felt his anger rising. No matter how hard he'd tried to keep this memory locked in a vault, it was stronger and more willing to slip out through the cracks. And there were plenty of cracks for it to find.

A sob escaped Kelly. Reis kept his gaze averted, because he'd never wanted pity. Never expected it either. Nobody ever truly pitied the rich, Jewel had told him that. Why he listened to anything she said he'd no idea. But in a way, she was right. All his life, nobody could muster up sympathy for the kid who got chauffeured to school, or the kid who lived in the mansion, or the kid who snapped his fingers and got whatever he wanted. He hadn't asked for that life, he didn't want it, and nobody believed that about him, either.

"Surviving a never ending apocalypse is a piece of piss," Reis said at last. "It's what's outside waiting for me that I can't deal with."

Kelly nodded. "After Matt's death, I thought I was surviving, but I merely existed. There's a difference. And you might be right that this game is a lesson. I'm not sure what use it'll be to know how to beat zombies, but I feel more alive than I have for a long time."

"Me too," Reis said. "And yet, more dead at the same time."

Her voice came out hoarse. "I've also never felt more guilty than I do now. I'm scared that one day my heart will beat strong and loud, and it'll mean that I don't miss Matt anymore. Maybe I'll never stop missing him. I'm only saying this because I want you to hear it. I don't know if I'll ever be ready to love again."

He'd always known this, but it still hurt to hear.

***

Reis stood up and grabbed four more beers from the well-stocked fridge, then he beckoned Kelly to follow him outside to the deck. She drank her beer down fast and asked for another.

"I have to get out of here," she said. Then she shook her head. "Not just because this place is driving me crazy. But it'll be one year tomorrow. Matt's parents will show up at the gravesite and they'll think I've forgotten about him."

"No, they won't," said Reis. "They'll call your folks who will have already called the police. They'll check your computer and your emails and they'll realize you're at CyberNexis in Arizona. I'll bet there's a bunch of law enforcement officers and emergency personnel, maybe the military right now using the jaws of life to pry us out of our pods."

"So why aren't we out already?"

"Unhooking us from the pod is a delicate process. You can't just unplug us like you would a printer or a toaster. The wires are hooked into our neural networks, hooked into our brain, our nervous system. Someone is coming to rescue us, Kelly."

"I knew his anniversary was coming," she said in a quiet voice. "I thought I'd be prepared for it. But, there's a small part of me that's glad I'm here. Visiting Matt's gravesite tomorrow is going to hurt. A lot."

Reis stared up at the sky. It could have been any night in San Diego. Above, the sky was faded black from all the city lights. There was a breeze which brought the scent of jasmine in from the front yard. It was the jasmine that made Reis think about his parents. He missed Jewel and Stafford. They were screwed up, but they were all he had.

The Minnows were *like* family but they *weren't* family. Plus they were busy living their own lives, and for the past year they'd rallied around Kelly to the point of excluding Reis from the daily routine he'd grown accustomed to. Ever since he was a little boy, he'd wanted everyone to leave him alone, and now it seemed they were. He wanted them back in his life. Which meant returning to the real world where he'd be forced to deal with the issues of his life – a mother who didn't have a maternal bone in her body, a father who wanted him to enter politics, an ex-girlfriend who wanted some easy cash.

If Kelly could handle life in the real world, so could he. And maybe they'd rekindle their friendship.

Kelly laughed, surprising Reis with how easily she could switch moods. "I can't believe there's a dead body inside and I'm out here drinking beer. If my bosses heard about this, they'd fire me for sure."

"What do you care? You don't even like your job."

"That's not true. I love my job. It's criminals I don't like. I also don't like that for every drop of goodness carried out on this planet there are a million acts of badness. If the goodness is a counterweight, then the scales are too broken to make an impact. We have laws to protect children *because* people abuse them. We have laws to stop industry polluting the waterways *because* industries pollute the waterways."

"You sound like Stafford. Only you mean it."

"I'm glad we're talking like old times. I just wish it hadn't happened under these circumstances." She slipped her hand into his and dragged him across the deck. He would have let her lead him off a cliff, but she only wanted to guide him onto the lawn. She stared up at the skies above. "Let's make a wish."

"It's not first star."

"Doesn't matter. Just make a wish. Any wish at all."

"Do I have to keep it a secret?"

"Yes. Actually, no. You tell me your wish and *I'll* keep it a secret. And you can keep mine."

A secret meant trust. Perhaps something good could come out of being stuck in this virtual world after all.

"I wish I could hate my parents," he said.

Kelly tilted her head. "How could you not?"

"Jewel did what she thought was the right thing to do. Apparently I had gotten lost at the mall when I was four and I'd disappeared for a few minutes. In her mind I'd been kidnapped and tortured. She'd panicked and decided to protect me the only way she knew how."

Kelly nodded. "I always wondered why you called your parents by their first names. Makes sense that you'd want to place a wedge between you and them."

"I don't call them Mom and Dad because they don't act like parents. They act like parole officers. On any given day, one of them, sometimes both, will find an excuse to call me, or they'll make something up just to talk to me. Jewel will accuse Stafford of cheating, which he'd never do. Stafford will threaten to disinherit me if I don't come home, which he might do. Believe me, the threat is enough to keep me awake at night. Or he'll demand I give up my nonsense business and enter politics, which is definitely a reason to keep me awake at night."

He didn't add that sometimes the phone would rang at two in the morning and the only sound he'd hear would be Jewel crying. It would tear at his heart, but he'd never hang up on her. He'd just let her cry. Eventually she'd feel better, tell him goodnight, and hang up.

"They'll make up any excuse to speak to me at least once a day," he added.

"How can you even stand speaking to them? If my parents had done something so horrific to me..."

"Jewel has unresolved issues from her own childhood. They're not mine to divulge." He even felt bad for revealing this much about her. She was a private person who didn't like to pry because she didn't like others to pry. "You can imagine whatever scenario you like. Anyway, she'll be worried sick that she hasn't been able to speak to me for five days now. That's why I wish I could hate them, so I could cut them out of my lives and get on with mine. So there you go. Rich kid problems. So now it's your turn to make a wish."

Kelly tilted her head up to gaze at the stars. "Nothing I wish for will take away your pain. Or mine. Besides, none of my wishes ever come true."

"That's not true. You and Matt got married."

Kelly sighed. "I never planned on it, not the way some women dream about marrying the perfect man and living the perfect life. So it's not really a wish come true. More like a bonus."

Reis was overcome with the urge to slip an arm around her waist. He did so and gently pulled her towards him. She didn't fight him. Her head fell against his chest. He felt his heart beating, and then he felt her heart beating, and finally their two hearts beat in unison. It was tragic and it was cliché but Reis didn't care. Even though he also didn't believe that wishes came true, he took the wish Kelly had abandoned and used it to hope that she could learn to forget about Matt. And then he took it back, because it wouldn't be fair to deny Kelly this chance to let go.

She needed to hold onto her pain as much as he needed to let go of his.

"I'm sorry," he said.

"You didn't do anything," she whispered. "But I like what you're doing now."

INSIDE THE SIMULATION POD

PRESENTATION BY
COMMAND LEADERS JONAS BARRETT AND STEPHANIE GEY

Command Leader Jonas Barrett:
Thank you for joining us in the studio. What a remarkable day for a remarkable event. For those of you who've been living under a rock or on another planet, GEMS is the Global Emergency Monitoring System which is about to launch simultaneously all around the world.

The GEMS Project started after an earthquake struck without warning and the fourteen-year-old son of Reginald Kincaid, a multi-billionaire in the running for presidential election, was killed. Kincaid promised to pour billions of dollars into the development of an advanced early earthquake system.

Command Leader Stephanie Gey:
An investigation by Kincaid's team discovered that the majority of time lost in emergencies resulted from a range of systems communicating with one another, or in reality mis-communication. The firewalls installed in thousands of networks designed to stop hackers was found to ultimately impede communication.

Kincaid wanted to design a computer program that would eliminate the need for humans to enter passwords. Many resistors initially considered Kincaid's program would leave their networks open to hackers who would then have access to secure files, however Kincaid said his system would not retrieve or record personal information, thus eliminating any criminal interests. It would be designed to provide information only. This investigation led others to invest in the scheme and Project GEMS was established.

Command Leader Jonas Barrett:
The GEMS project mission is to provide information in an emergency such as hurricane warnings, tsunami and earthquake warnings, and evacuations plans for an entire town. In the past, casualties resulted when people did not have access to or understand emergency procedures. GEMS is designed to detect a natural disaster and broadcast into people's homes, businesses,

cars, or planes. Wherever you are, GEMS offers the evacuation plan to suit your situation and save your life. GEMS is also designed to provide information on how to treat heart attacks, drowning victims, car crash victims. Helpful information like this can save lives until the paramedics arrive.

Command Leader Stephanie Gey:
This extraordinary system doesn't stop there. It has full monitoring capability to allow it to detect crime in progress and contact the closest police vehicle, not just the dispatch, but the nearest vehicle. Kincaid says such a feature can save minutes off a response time. It can also direct an ambulance to a hospital with fewer casualties, because there are times when the closest hospital may not be the one with the most staff on hand to handle the emergency.

Command Leader Jonas Barrett:
Now, the role of GEMS isn't to replace human functionality. It's to simply cut down on response time and provide early detection in natural disasters. And maybe iron my shirts.

Command Leader Stephanie Gey:
It doesn't iron shirts. I already inquired. The global launch of GEMS is set for thirty minutes time. It'll be the most watched event in television history since the 1969 moon landing. Anyone who had their eyes glued to the TV set that day would no doubt remember what they were doing and where they were at the time of the NASA launch.

Command Leader Jonas Barrett:
And if they don't remember the moon landing they'd have no idea where they were or what they were doing.

Command Leader Stephanie Gey:
That is how memory works, Jonas. In less than thirty minutes, the world as we know it will change forever. People all over the world will be storing this day into their memories so they can tell their grandkids where they were the day GEMS launched.

20

Jack

The phone on Jack's desk rang. "Spider Web Designs," he said.

Only in California could pets have their own chat room, and this caller wanted Jack to create one for her cat. He took the details down on a scrap of paper and promised to email her a quote as soon as possible.

"Might not be till tomorrow," he told the client. "Computers are down for the GEMs interface."

GEMS was the acronym for the Global Emergency Monitoring System that was going online around the world in a few hours. The benefits of the system that reported on emergencies such as tsunamis, earthquakes, burglaries, house fires, heart attacks, was supposed to far outweigh the inconvenience of no power and no internet, but so far Jack wasn't convinced. What was he supposed to do all day? Without the internet, his computer was just an expensive word processor. Without power he couldn't even watch TV.

He found a deck of playing cards and tossed them one by one at a trash can. Seated next to the window with sunlight streaming in, he read a newspaper he'd found in the kitchen, even though it was a year old. Finally, the hands on the clock that ran on battery power sat at one and twelve. No wonder his stomach grumbled.

Reis still hadn't shown up for work, so Jack grabbed his jacket and headed out to lunch by himself. He headed for Stella's because it had an outdoor eating area as well as big windows on three sides to catch the Californian sun. It would be affected by the power outage but he could at least grab a bag of potato chips. By the time Jack arrived, the outdoor tables were already filled with patrons eating pre-made food, so he moved inside, where it was unusually packed and warm. Without power, Stella's air conditioning units were inoperable.

The waitress stood behind the counter waving her arms in the air. "Sorry, folks," she cried out. "We've been informed the blackout will last another hour or so. You can blame the integration of GEMS for the inconvenience."

"It's technology gone crazy," a man in running gear said.

"I got caught in a bushfire last year," a man in a suit said. "It took an hour for the fire trucks to arrive. I'm glad we'll have an early detection system."

The crowd provided their opinions to whoever would listen, but Jack agreed with the runner. He relied on his computer to store and retrieve data, and it was an invaluable piece of equipment when hooked up the worldwide web, but he wouldn't trust it in a life or death situation.

The crowd was starting to grumble louder, which caused the waitress to ring the counter bell.

"I shouldn't even be keeping my doors open," she said. "But I have pies, muffins, salads, sandwiches. Some that have to go now, which I'll sell for half price. If you want something special made up, you'll have to wait for power to return."

Jack's stomach rumbled, but since he wasn't in any hurry to return to the office and sit at a desk in the dark, he shuffled into a table by the window to read today's newspaper. The first five pages were dedicated to the launch of GEMS. The headline on the front page read NERD RAPTURE:

Some have called singularity nerd rapture. The world's experts on artificial intelligence have waited for this day for decades, yet many claim this is one more step to replacing humans with robots.

"Our jobs are already becoming too computerized," said a worker at a San Diego glass factory. "I used to fabricate the window frames and glass door sliders, but now a machine does it. Not only that, a machine supervises my lunch breaks."

Claims that GEMS, which is the acronym of Global Emergency Monitoring System, heralds the rise of the robots are not taken seriously by GEMS project creator, Reginald Kincaid.

"Granted, we live in a world reliant on technology, but we do not live in a world of robots."

Despite these claims, IBM's Watson who easily beat two contestants on the game show Jeopardy! in 2011 is being sent off to medical school. And the fact is machines now do legal research and creative jobs, so while the idea of robots taking over is scoffed at, what isn't a joke is the notion that singularity will lead to accelerated human thinking by the means of artificial intelligence implants. And if that's the case, it won't be a matter of robots rising up against humans, the threat will come from computer enhanced humans, commonly referred to as cyborgs. Ultimately, humanity's thirst for technology could be its biggest threat.

By the time Jack had finished reading the rest of the newspaper the lights and power had returned, yet he had to wait till the waitress had served all the customers before she wandered over to take his order. He ordered his usual. Chili dog, fries, and Coke.

"It'll be about twenty minutes to get the fryer hot again," she said.

"I've got nowhere else to be."

"Where's your friend?"

It was Friday, so Reis was probably at the music store. The waitress would probably enjoy hearing that Reis played an instrument, and since Jack secretly resented Reis's popularity, he told her a lie.

"Probably at the casino gambling away his grandfather's life savings."

Twenty minutes later she brought over Jack's meal and she also placed a slice of cherry pie on the table.

"On the house," she said with a wink.

He suspected it was a casualty of the power outage, but free pie was free pie. The waitress busied herself filling up the napkin dispensers, and Jack ate his meal while he re-read the newspaper.

The headline on page 2 read: WHERE WERE YOU ON THIS DAY?

The article asked its readers to log into their website and share what they were doing at the moment of the GEMS launch. Jack laughed at the irony. The internet was down for the GEMS launch. How long would people's attention last after it was back up. They'd have forgotten where they were because they hadn't immediately captured it on Facebook or Twitter. But the newspaper was giving away a holiday to Niagara Falls for the most interesting comment, so he tore off a section of the paper and stuffed it into his pocket. He wouldn't admit that he'd spent the day alone in his darkened office tossing cards at a waste basket before eating a lunch of chili dog and fries. No. He'd make something up. Maybe he'd ask Reis what he'd done during the launch and use that as his entry.

Thinking about Reis's exciting life made Jack's lunch taste as bitter as his resentment. But he chewed it down, swallowing the negative thoughts the way his mother had taught him – one bite at a time.

It was almost two hours after leaving the office when he'd finished eating. There seemed no point returning. The loss of power and internet seemed to be forcing Jack to communicate the old fashioned way. In person. So he headed to Axl's Music Store.

Jack pushed open the door and heavy metal music assaulted him. He had to shout to be heard. "Hey, Axl. Is Reis here?"

Axl pointed at the back of the store. Reis was in the booth and plugged into a Fender amplifier. He was responsible for the music. Twelve years of private tutoring meant Reis could play any style of guitar – classical, flamenco, jazz, blues. He'd once told Jack that he'd mastered the noisiest style – heavy metal – for the sole purpose of pissing off his parents.

The lights in the store suddenly went out.

Reis popped his head out of the booth. "Sorry, Axl."

"Wasn't you caused the outage," Axl said. "Power's gone out all over the block."

"Again?" Jack said.

"Been like this all day."

"Must be the GEMS program integration," Fox said, a regular at the store who had a habit of appearing out of nowhere. Fox was always buying drumsticks despite not owning a drum kit. But Jack wasn't sure how he knew this; he also had a feeling he'd never met the guy before.

"How could I forget about GEMS?" Reis slipped the guitar from around his neck and placed it on the stand. "It's only the most important event for mankind since the moon landing."

Axl rolled his eyes. "Pl-ease. They faked the moon landing."

"I was being sarcastic," Reis said.

Fox laughed. "I heard they're running a competition for the most creative entry for what you were doing the day GEMS launched."

"Don't look at me," Axl said. "The question won't be where you were the day GEMS launched. It'll be where were you when it went ape-shit and took over the planet?"

Jack joined Reis who had moved to the front of the store to stare out the window. People up and down the street were standing on the sidewalks with their necks craned up at the sky, as if the cause of the blackouts hovered above. The hairs on the back of Jack's neck tickled. He imagined a spaceship, yet the sky remained devoid of silver orbs. By some universal code, any attacking alien spaceships would be hovering over Los Angeles or the White House anyway, not Axl's Music Store in downtown San Diego.

"I'm telling you it's the end of the world," Axl said. "Our government should never have gotten involved with GEMS. Who do you reckon is behind it? Koreans? Russians?"

"Pakistanis?" Fox asked.

"Maybe it's our own government," Jack said. Riling these two up was one of his favorite pastimes. "After all, GEMS *is* the brainchild of Reginald Kincaid? He's one of us."

"Maybe he's one of them." Axl shifted his gaze to the sky.

Reis shook his head. "Now you've done it, Jack. Here come all the conspiracy theories."

"You won't be so cynical or so cocky after today," Fox said. "They'll hear every word you say, see everything you do, smell your every crap."

"I'm sure they already hear us," Axl said.

"It's true." Fox nodded his head vigorously. "Billy got picked up last week for speaking out against the GEMS project."

Axl snorted. "Billy got done for possession."

"That's what they'll have you believe." Fox tapped his finger against the side of his nose.

Reis leaned in close to Jack. "I should kill you for getting them started."

The lights started to flicker and hum, and pretty soon the store was lit up and the guitar was screeching because Reis had left it lying face down against the amplifier.

Then the room began to shake and Jack thought an earthquake had struck. He didn't realize he'd fainted until he saw the faces of Reis, Axl, and Fox hovering over him.

"Dude, you passed out," Axl said.

They helped Jack up, but the room began to spin once more. This time he saw the floor coming up to greet him.

INSIDE THE SIMULATION POD

PRESENTATION BY
COMMAND LEADERS JONAS BARRETT AND STEPHANIE GEY

Command Leader Jonas Barrett:
Well, Stephanie, GEMS has been live for four hours and already the program is getting good reports. In the Californian area, ten heart attack victims were saved when GEMS provided tips to family members via their home computers. GEMS reported two child abductions to police and the criminals were apprehended and in police custody within ten minutes using traffic cameras as evidence. GEMS also gave an early warning to a small village in the South Pacific saving hundreds of people. It looks as if GEMS is a true gem.

Command Leader Stephanie Gey:
Yes, only four hours since it launched and GEMS has saved thousands of lives around the globe. There were people who questioned the cost of such a program, but how can you put a price on the life of a loved one.

Command Leader Jonas Barrett:
What about claims by people that the machines will rise up against us?

Command Leader Stephanie Gey:
I doubt an uprising will happen, Jonas. I tell my computer to print and half the time it just doesn't respond. Sits there blinking at me. And as for downloading anything off the internet. Forget it. I'm sure I'll be able to outrun a machine simply by telling it to download something. It once took my computer forty—

INSIDE THE SIMULATION POD

PRESENTATION BY
GAME CREATOR MAX WINTERDOM

Players, I'm interrupting this program to bring you an emergency broadcast. The Apocalypse Games is experiencing a mainframe malfunction due to an outside disturbance, possibly from an impact event. There is a Union Bank built into every setting so please make your way to the nearest Union Bank. Make your way as soon as you can and await further instructions.

I repeat. There is a malfunction with the game's mainframe computer due to an external disaster. It is imperative that all players make their way to the town center immediately. When this presentation ends you will have full consciousness and the temporary world you have experienced so far will cease to exist. Over and out.

21

Jack

"Jack. Are you okay?"

Axl and Fox stared down at him. Reis was trying to lift him up. Jack felt split in two. He recognized their faces, yet he didn't at the same time. He pulled himself up and hurried out the store, ignoring their shouts. He expected the streets to be chaotic. Instead, a typical autumn day in California greeted him. Cars drove by. People poked faces against store windows. Why had he expected to see carnage? Why had he expected to find people equipped with bug-out backpacks or at least holding THE END IS HERE placards? Everyone was behaving as they normally would.

Reis came running from the music store.

"That was weird," Reis said. "I was standing there watching the presentation like there was an invisible TV in front of me."

"We've got to get Kelly," Jack said.

"My car is around the corner."

Jack followed Reis to his BMW. One hundred and five players should have received the call to the town centre, so essentially everyone who was carrying a coffee cup or pushing a pram or carrying a briefcase was part of the game. But the NPCs had been acting like players lately, so it could be difficult to tell them apart.

Reis floored the gas pedal. "Kelly could be at home or at the courthouse."

"Try the courthouse," Jack said. "It's closer."

Reis drove through an amber traffic light while Jack dialed Kelly's cell phone. He got no response.

"She'll be hysterical," Jack said. "You know what today is?"

"I do *now*."

Jack studied his friend. For reasons of jealousy he'd wanted Reis and Kelly together. And while he'd considered that emotions were involved, Reis had always been aloof and Kelly was comatose emotionally, so it hadn't really sunk in that pushing them together might have had consequences. Hadn't Pandora highlighted to Jack, in no uncertain terms, the results of what happened when Jack acted on his jealousy and ignored consequences?

Yet, this wasn't an act of jealousy anymore. He felt in his gut that these two needed each other. So if his meddling made them happy, then he was happy to meddle.

Jack let his mind dwell on the possibility that someone had noticed they hadn't come home and had reported it. He also let his mind dwell on the possibility that a rescue team was right now breaking into the pods. Rightly so, they had to be careful and not open the pods in a rush. Such a task needed to be done slowly, the way deep sea divers needed to return to the surface slowly. Otherwise the players might suffer the bends. He had convinced himself that rescue was coming by the time he saw Kelly sitting on the steps of the courthouse.

Reis parked in a no-parking zone. Together they walked up to the steps, Reis sat on her left and Jack on her right.

"You okay, Kell?" Jack asked.

She sighed. "No, but thanks for coming to get me."

"We don't have to go to the Union Bank," Reis said. "You want to drive around for a bit?"

"The cemetery isn't far," Jack said.

She nodded. They huddled towards the car, and Jack sat in back with Kelly while Reis drove. Jack held his sister's hand and she leaned her head against his shoulder. She was calmer than he thought she'd be. Calmer than he was. His hands were shaking.

Kelly squeezed his hand. "How long since you visited Mary-Ellen's gravesite?" she asked.

"Not since the funeral."

"Then it's just as well we're heading to the same place."

A wave of shame nestled into Jack. He couldn't even remember which cemetery she was buried in. He reached for his phone as if the answer was stored in there somewhere, and instead he found the piece of newspaper he'd torn out while at the diner. Where was he the day GEMS launched? On his way to redemption, he hoped.

***

Cemeteries always gave Jack the chills. Beautifully manicured lawns and perfectly sculptured gardens; this one had rolling hills and magnificent views, as if the dead had need of such things. Reis stopped the car at the bottom of a hill. Jack had no idea where he'd find Mary-Ellen's gravesite, or if she was even here, or where Matt's gravesite was for that matter. He'd just followed the crowd at both funerals.

"Matt is this way," Kelly said. "Where is Mary-Ellen?"

He shrugged, suddenly lost for words. If he opened his mouth he might cry, and this was Kelly's day, not his.

Reis took out his phone and called the office. "She's in the Evergreen section," he said when he hung up.

"Go with Kelly," Jack told Reis. "I need to do this on my own. Meet back here when we're done."

He watched them walk away. Reis had his hands in his pockets. Kelly slipped her arm through his until finally Reis removed his hand slipped it into Kelly's. His sister deserved to be happy and in love. Matt would understand.

Only after they'd disappeared from view did Jack start down the path to the Evergreen section. At each step, his heart grew heavier. He had so much to say and none of the courage to say it. Perhaps the reason they kept the grounds so lovely was to act as a conversation starter.

He located Mary Ellen's grave. A simple granite stone in the ground. Name. Date of birth. Date of death. The words IN LOVING MEMORY were carved into the stone. He felt bad that he hadn't brought flowers, so he snapped off a handful of daisies from a nearby garden and stood with them in his hands. He bent down to place them on the ground. Then stood up again. He didn't like the way the flowers obscured her name so he bent down and moved them a few inches to the right. Then he stood up again to stare down at the grave. No matter the angle, the words were lost to him.

At last he cleared his throat and said, "I'm sorry."

The words acted like a dam bursting. His chest tightened. He squeezed his eyes. With his eyes closed, he pictured that night:

After Mary-Ellen had slipped into the taxi, she'd stared at him through the window. Downturned smile. Sad eyes. He'd wanted to avoid a broken heart yet she'd broken it anyway by dying. If he'd fought off the jealously, she'd be alive. Even if she had become infatuated with Reis, she'd be alive.

The cemetery could do with seats, thought Jack looking around. So he sat down on the ground, filled with the sudden need to be close to her.

"I'm sorry, and you don't have to forgive me. I don't deserve it. What I deserve is exactly what's happening right now. I'm stuck in a computer, reliving a nightmare over and over. I should be angry that I'm trapped, but the truth is I'm glad it happened. If it wasn't for Pandora poking around in my head, you'd have stayed locked inside.

But I'd like to go home now. Please."

A breeze picked up and swept the daisies to tumble through the air. He was too cynical to imagine it had anything to do with the ghost of Mary-Ellen. He scooped them up and dug a hole in the grass with his finger, and then he tore off the stem off a rose on the gravesite next to Mary-Ellen's. He placed the flower into the hole. It looked lonely. So he dug a second hole and added another rose. It still looked incomplete so he added a third.

"Pandora showed me an alternate reality," he said. "Funny thing is, I didn't hate it. If that's how things would've turned out, it wouldn't have been so bad. But we never got the chance. I blew it, for you mostly. Soon as I get out of here I'm going to tell your parents that I put you in the taxi that night. I never told them that. I said I didn't know what happened. And I'll offer to do what I can to help raise Caleb. If he's anything like the kid in my dreams, he's a great kid. I'll be like his Uncle Jack."

He noticed a few people standing at other gravesites. They appeared to be studying him, as if Pandora had sent her minions to steer him to where he ought to be. He'd lost all interest in surviving apocalypses. He only wanted to make it up to Mary-Ellen and her parents.

And that meant finishing this game, because he now believed it was on a cycle that wouldn't end till it'd run its course. He said goodbye to his college sweetheart and strolled back to the car. He arrived just as Reis and Kelly began their trudge down the hill. The drive out of the cemetery was short and quiet. Kelly sat in the front and stared out the passenger window. Jack stared out the side window from the back seat. Reis kept his focus on the road ahead.

Jack was desperate to check how Kelly was doing, but she could ask him the same and he wasn't ready to answer.

As soon as they drove onto the main street, the Union Bank popped into view. Reis stopped the car a hundred yards away. Out the front of the bank mingled fifty or so players.

"It's just another ruse," Jack said.

Reis nodded. "But what if it isn't?"

They watched intently as a CGI woman stepped out of the bank. She was tall with white features, wearing a white gown, with snow-white hair that she wore down to her waist. Jack expected to see a vapor trail behind her, but she wasn't a ghost; she was as real as he was inside this world. More all-white women appeared, all dressed in similarly yet different ghostly attire. They began to usher players inside the bank.

"We should at least check it out," Reis said.

Jack had to agree, but once inside the crowded building he

became separated from his friends. He decided to survey the crowd for Douglas, since his chat at Mary-Ellen's gravesite had sparked a renewed sense of responsibility to look after the kid. As he scanned the crowd, someone bumped into him and he turned to find Neil Cooney beside him. Neil was dressed in his civilian clothes – a Hawaiian shirt and cargo pants. Jack hadn't seen the doomsday prepper since the battle of the frogspawns. He'd signed on with Reis as a teammate, but if there was any other player he could choose to team up with, it would be Neil.

"What do you make of this?" Jack asked him.

Neil scoffed. "It's a trap. I only came here to get something."

A high pitched noise like the feedback of a microphone put a halt to further conversation. It had come from the rear of the bank where a large screen hung over the wall of the bank manager's office. On the screen appeared the head of a Nordic looking man. In the background was a lot of computer and office equipment.

"Greetings players," the man on the screen said. "I'm Max Winterdom. I apologize for the malfunctions with The Apocalypse Games. I assure you that we're working on fixing them. Meanwhile, be assured the simulation pods are designed for lengthy periods in stasis, and nutrients and oxygen are continually pumped inside. As well, we are administering electric shock therapy to ward off muscle dystrophy. I'm sorry to bore you with the medical details, but it's my belief the truth isn't something we should be afraid of saying or hearing."

"The truth is you suck," someone from the crowd yelled, and a round of cheers erupted across the room.

Max didn't flinch. "I wish I knew the cause of the malfunction, but it's too early to tell. Some of you might think this is ironic that I'm appearing during the technological singularity apocalypse, but I assure you this is not part of the game."

Jack turned his attention away from the crowd and onto the interior of the bank. Max's speech could have been pre-recorded. Or he could have hooked himself up to the computer and this could be a live feed. The hairs on Jack's arms rose. Maybe rescue *was* imminent.

"We're doing all we can," Max said.

"You're not doing enough," someone shouted. "I've been in the game for a week now. I haven't slept, I haven't eaten—"

Max smiled. "Nutrients have continued to pump into the pod."

"I want real food," one player shouted.

"I've got kids, a job, a wife who's gonna think I ran off," another shouted.

"Please calm down," a nearby operator said. Suddenly a wall of them appeared. Sometime during Max's speech, dozens of these creepy CGI women had skulked their way into the crowd, and they now appeared robotic and sinister. Jack grew nervous.

"We're doing all we can," a second operator said. "Please calm down and await further instructions."

But the crowd didn't calm down. They wanted to know what was being done to unhook them from the pods.

"Witness the true human reaction to the end of the world," Neil shouted in Jack's ear. "It's chaos and confusion. And asking these cyber-bitches for help is like asking an ATM to stop the bank from charging you fees."

An explosion outside knocked the glass out of the front doors. Angry shouts turned to injured screams. A military tank had stopped out the front of the bank, and its gun now swiveled to follow the fleeing crowd.

"Let's get out of here," Neil said.

The tank fired and half the back wall was blown apart. The presentation screen was sliced in two and it floated down to the ground on the dusty air. The bank alarms had been triggered and were deafening. Anti-burglary shields came crashing down over the teller counters. They exploded and sent shrapnel through the air. Smoke set the fire sprinklers off and water rained down from the ceiling. People screamed as the crowd rushed toward the rear of the bank to escape the armed military tank. It fired another shot, taking out the ceiling; chunks fell down, people screamed. Jack could barely hear his own thoughts. Water gushed down as if a dam had broken; the gun fire tore apart the water tanks feeding the sprinkler system. Players fell over one another as they scrambled out of the way.

Jack looked around for Kelly but he couldn't see her. He caught sight of Neil's brightly-colored shirt and watched as Neil ducked inside an office. Jack decided to follow him.

"What are you doing?" he shouted at Neil. "That tank is gonna kill us."

"Get down. The tank will move on when it sees that everyone has fled. And then I'll get what I came here for."

Jack squeezed in under the desk beside Neil. "Do you mind telling me what you're after?"

"You'll find out soon enough. A few of us have been in this game before and we think we know a way to win."

"Okay." Jack could hear explosions outside. "But how is the tank even operating?"

"This is the future. Military has gone full robotics. GEMS has gone rogue."

It seemed to take forever for the noise outside to die down, but as Neil had predicted, the players had fled and the tank had moved on.

They emerged from the office, carefully stepping over rubble as they headed into the destroyed building. The operators were standing inside the bank.

"Why didn't they flee?" Jack asked Neil.

"They're part of GEMS. They have no reason to flee."

Neil picked through discarded items: a shoe, a brochure stand, a bag of money. He stopped beside a sheet of metal, a piece of the teller security shield with a body lying beneath it. Jack was relieved when he didn't recognize the face. Neil beckoned for the nearest CGI woman to come over and help him. Dripping wet with her white gown clinging to her curves, she stepped over the rubble and grabbed onto the metal.

"Not there. Come and take this side."

She did as he asked and as soon as she was beside Neil, he grabbed her around the wrist. She twisted but he held her tight. He pulled her close to his body and pressed a gun against her temple.

"These creatures are the key to winning this game," Neil said with a sneer. "Only they refuse to tell us because they *are* the game."

"Which means they can't die," Jack said.

"This isn't an ordinary gun. It's a polarity gun." Neil pressed the nozzle up into her chin. "The thing about *this* apocalypse is that it's geared around technology. We landed back into our old lives, but not in our old time."

"Help me." The captured CGI woman's eyes searched Jack's. "Please."

His stomach did a back flip. He hadn't been raised to treat any woman – real or not – like this. From the corner of his eye he saw the other women circling.

"Only you can save me, Jack," she said. Then her lips lifted into a wicked smile.

"Get out of my head, Pandora," he whispered.

The operator began to laugh. "Or you can let me die, Jack. It's up to you."

Neil tightened his grip around her neck. "She's messing with you. Help me get her out back. A truck is waiting."

Indecision gripped Jack. This was the line that soldiers in a war faced every day. Protect the innocent and risk injury or death to you and your team. Or say screw the consequences and complete the mission.

"I can't do that," Jack said, his humanitarian side winning.

Neil began to drag the woman towards the back. One of the operators lunged at Neil; he fired his gun at her and she shattered into a million particles. A few more operators charged at Neil and he made them disintegrate too. The others must have decided to let him escape with his hostage because they stayed well clear of the gun.

"Jack. Help me get her out back."

"No. It's wrong."

"We need one of them alive to short out the GEMS computer."

"I won't do it."

An old man appeared behind Neil. His salt-and-peppered hair was messy, he wore jeans and an army-green t-shirt. He took a quick look at the scene then fired a weapon at the women, who shattered into glittering dust. A stray bullet hit Jack and it felt like a tiny electric shock had hit him.

When the assault was over, the old man came up to Jack and said, "It had to be done, son. They're not what they appear to be."

"Then what are they?"

"You'll see. Come with us if you want to survive this game."

The old man removed another gun – a different type Jack saw – from his belt which he fired at Neil's captive. She fell to the floor in a heap. Neil struggled to hang onto her.

"A little help," he said.

Jack shook his head. He'd have no part of this atrocity.

"She isn't a real woman," the old man said. "She's a... hologram is the only way I can describe it. This is the only way to win this war."

"What war?"

"GEMS has declared war against humanity. This game is nothing like the others. We get annihilated."

Neil said, "Capturing a cyber bitch is the only way to survive."

"Don't call her a bitch."

"Fine, capturing a member of the GEMS army is paramount to the survival of the human race. And that is the real premise of the game. So are you gonna help me or not?"

By now the bank was empty of players. Everyone had fled. The ground was piled high with rubble and dead bodies. The alarms had stopped. So had the fire sprinklers. Jack had expected emergency vehicles to arrive, but they were integrated into the GEMS program, so if GEMS was at war with humans, it wouldn't send anyone to help them.

"No, you're right," Neil said. "Let's wait here for reinforcements. And when humanity burns to the ground, we'll blame you because you did nothing to prevent it."

***

Blame was something Jack didn't want any more of, so he helped Neil carry the unconscious operator outside where a school bus waited. The old man ran on ahead, and as they neared the bus its engine revved like it was ready to take off. They'd just managed to make it on board.

The inside of the bus had been converted to accommodate computers and weapons. Seats were ripped out, and tables, beds, and benches took their place. Neil pointed to a bench and Jack helped him lift their captive up onto it. The old man immediately began plugging her into a series of wires which then fed into a series of laptops.

"Jack Minnow," Neil said, "meet Gordon Talbert. Gordon has had the pleasure of reliving this particular game seven times. He knows what's coming. He's building up his defenses."

"Does Gordon know how to get out of the game?" Jack asked.

"The CGI women are the key," Gordon said.

Lying on a bench, the captive appeared to be sleeping. "Looks are deceiving," Neil said. "She's part of the GEMS army."

"I still don't see why you have to torture her," Jack said. "Aren't we supposed to operate with some level of decency? Just because this isn't real, doesn't mean we can do whatever the hell we like."

"We need to trick the computer into thinking it's been beaten," Gordon said. "Are you aware of the digital law that doubles the power of technology roughly every eighteen months?"

Jack had a college degree in technology. Of course he knew.

"In ten years, our devices will be one hundred times more powerful. In twenty, they'll be ten thousand times more powerful. In thirty years, a million times more powerful. Futurists predict that before humans can reach the limits of our progress, artificial minds will be able to think faster than us. And this is the point known as singularity."

"Also referred to as the point of no return," Neil said.

"The launch of GEMS happened at the point of no return," Gordon said. "In order to trick the computer into thinking it has been beaten, we need to win this game. I'm sorry about taking a prisoner, but you'll see soon enough that she isn't what she appears to be."

"But we always win the game," Jack said. "It's the whole point. Why would someone pay five thousand bucks to have their ass kicked?"

"We never win this one." Gordon's lips were set in a grim line. "I've done seven rounds with GEMS so far and we've always lost.

Right down to the last man on Earth."

This isn't real. Jack reminded himself. But separating fantasy from reality was twisting his insides to see the woman lying on the bench. He regretted the part he'd played in this war crime. Nothing could redeem him. Not in here.

A convoy of fire trucks and ambulances tore past them down the street. Neil shook his head. "GEMS is sending emergency vehicles out to the wrong addresses. Meanwhile buildings burn and people die of a heart attack or from car crash injuries. The emergencies the system is supposed to prevent are happening."

"That's a slow way to kill people," Jack said.

"It *is* a slow way to kill people. One computer has got to do a lot of work to kill six billion people one plane at a time. But don't fret, you'll see plenty of carnage before the day is out."

"Why would I fret?"

"It's not like humans are stupid," Gordon said. "GEMS forces planes to crash. Man stops flying. GEMS forces disruptions to traffic. Man stops driving."

"By the way, we're driving a truck built before the computer age," Neil said proudly. "Otherwise GEMS would find a way to turn Old Yeller into the WMD of her design."

"Old Yeller is your bug-out bus in the real world, isn't it?" Jack asked.

Neil nodded. He got a whimsical look on his face. "I spent years converting her into this thing of beauty to protect my family. If Pandora is tapping into my mind, then she knows where I'm storing food and supplies. But we're not battling Pandora today so I don't need to give away the tricks up my sleeve."

"GEMS has a trick up her sleeve," Gordon said.

Jack caught the exchange between Gordon and Neil, making his feel left out. He couldn't blame them, since all he'd done so far was argue with their methods.

The woman on the bench cried out and her body contorted. Jack wanted very much to release her but he was sure Neil or Gordon would shoot him with any of the dozens of guns in their arsenal. There were dozens of guns in holsters on their belts, guns hanging on the walls, guns lying on benches. All just out of Jack's reach.

The woman settled back down and the bus continued to drive along the back streets of San Diego. At one point, Jack looked out to see people inside a Pancake House banging on doors to get out.

Neil shook his head. "GEMS is linked into the building's alarm system which means it can lock doors, disable safety switches on elevators—"

"Launch nuclear missiles," Jack said.

"You catch on quick."

"So the presentation back there. You came to the bank even though you knew it was a trap. Even though you knew all the players would arrive and you did nothing to alert them. Players died, Neil."

"That was unfortunate. I hadn't anticipated the tank showing up when it did."

Neil and Gordon exchanged another brief look.

"What?" Jack demanded. "Tell me what's going on."

Gordon nodded. "You know how I said GEMS has a trick up her sleeve? I'm about to show it to you." One of the laptops beeped. "I've fixed one the computers so it's running free of the GEMS interference. Come and watch this."

Gordon turned the laptop so it faced Jack. On the screen were dozens of all-white CGI women, standing next to metal tables in a room that looked like a laboratory. Men and women were strapped down to the tables. They didn't move, but Jack suspected they were alive. On the screen, a woman opened a metal ball the size of a basketball, and inside the ball was a spider-like device. This device crawled up to the head of the man on the table and it attached itself to his face. Immediately, the body thrashed on the table. After almost a minute, the spider lifted itself off and half of the man's face was coated in liquid silver. The operator fixed a device that resembled a camera lens into the cybernetic face while the spider moved down the body to work on the chest. Then the player's head was lifted up and a silver helmet slipped over to protect the brain.

After the spider had completed its conversion, in place of the human chest was a metal plate, designed to protect the heart. The spider then moved down to the left hand, and after much thrashing about by machine and man, the hand was covered in the same silver goo which the woman placed into a square box. After about five seconds, she lifted the player's hand out of the box. The hand was transformed into a gun.

The entire process had taken ten minutes.

"*That's* Pandora's trick up the sleeve," Neil said.

"They're making cyborgs," Gordon explained. "It's what happens to players who die in this game. They're now the enemy."

"Jesus." Jack felt as if he would throw up. There had been a lot of dead bodies back at the bank. And they were now lying on the tables, converted into cyborgs.

"This game doesn't have many rules," Jack said. "But it has one that so far everyone has obeyed. Players aren't supposed to kill other players."

Neil pointed at the screen. "They're no longer players."

"You've played this game seven times?" Jack said to Gordon.

Gordon clenched his teeth. "The efficiency with which GEMS and the cyber women work together means the apocalypses have become more brutal in a shorter span of time. If you want to know how I know all this, I was killed a few games ago and became a cyborg. In fact, I've been killed a few times. Let me tell you, I am well and truly cured of my fascination with androids and robots."

Jack could understand that, what he couldn't understand was the design of *this* game. "I operate a tour business," he said. "And this is where it doesn't make sense to me. Let's say you choose to enter this game first, but you die and get converted into a cyborg. This is still a game. The entry fee is five thousand dollars. The clients would get pissed and demand a refund. No way would CyberNexis program a game in favor of the computer."

Gordon sat down and stared at Jack like he was about to give him a fatherly lecture on the dynamics of sexual relations. "I didn't choose this game. In fact, I don't think this game exists on the menu."

***

Gordon went to the fridge and took out a couple of beers and handed them around. He even gave one to the driver. "It's not like the cops are around to book us," he said with a shrug. Then he sat near the front but didn't open his beer. He just stared at it.

"You okay?" Jack asked him.

"I miss my grandkids. When this is over, I'm taking them on a vacation. Maybe an island where there's no chance of war breaking out and technology turning me into a cyborg. But I'll probably take them back to my home country, Germany. They should know their heritage." He finally opened the beer and took a long swig. Then he began to tap away at the keyboard. Neil busied himself with getting weapons ready.

"Can I do anything?" Jack asked Gordon, suddenly feeling useless.

"Keep an old man company. Where you from, Jack?"

"San Diego."

"I live in Alaska now. Retired. I used to be in IT." The way he worked the computer, Jack reckoned he still was. "I moved to Alaska to be closer to the grandkids after I got diagnosed with cancer." Gordon waved the beer bottle absently around. "Don't be sorry if that's what you're inclined to say. I've come to terms with it. Anyway, the eldest grandchild told me to write a bucket list." The old man chuckled and smiled fondly. "Emily's thirteen. Has a huge chip on her shoulder and thinks I'm a simpleton. She explained how a bucket list works, and instead of me telling her how my generation invented the concept, I let her help me write one. What I wouldn't give to spend the afternoon having her make fun of my dreams and wishes." His smile faltered. "Sorry, I got a little carried away."

"It's okay. And you're right. We should do whatever it takes to get out of this situation."

Gordon paused with his beer halfway to his mouth. "No, *you're* right. We should operate within boundaries. It's what defines us as humans."

"There are people who love us on the outside," Jack said. "They'll come looking for us."

Gordon nodded, took a swig of beer, then he placed a laptop on the table in front of Jack. "Since you're from San Diego, and we happen to be playing the game in your hometown, take a look at this footage and tell me if you recognize any of the landmarks."

The footage was grainy. A building popped into view but it disappeared before Jack could recognize it. More grainy images appeared. Then a series of images popped up – a tree, a road, a café, a bridge.

"Recognize anything yet?" Gordon asked.

"Not yet."

"By the way," Gordon said, "that's Cookie, the driver. He's an NPC but he's on our side."

Cookie lifted a hand in a wave and Jack hesitantly did the same.

"Where is this footage coming from?" Jack asked Gordon. "I thought GEMS controlled everything."

"It's her SOS signal. She's sending it back to the mainframe. Thankfully our guest isn't capable of giving away our location. We've jammed all incoming transmissions."

Gordon used to be in IT and Jack suspected it hadn't been in a corporate environment. More likely the guy had worked for NASA or the CIA.

"Remind me to improve my computer skills when we get outside," Jack said.

"Why wait." Gordon explained how he'd hooked up the operator to the laptops then used a radio jammer, which he also explained was illegal in America but readily available. He then explained how the frequency was tuned to the point of 'subtle jamming' where no sound was heard at the receiving end. Otherwise GEMS would have detected the radio jammer and instructed a plane to fall out of the sky and land on Old Yeller. Apparently this was a simple operation if you knew what you were doing.

Jack studied the images on the laptop but he still didn't understand why he was seeing landmarks. He said as much.

"We've converted her digital image into analogue," Gordon added. "So GEMS can't use satellite to track us. Right now our guest is sending information back to the mainframe. It's like looking at the radio wave as it runs along a television or telephone cable. The signal pops into view every time it jumps from the ground to a pole, so every ten or so seconds an image pops up of a landmark."

"And GEMS can't trace this signal?"

"Correct. It'll receive it, but it can't trace it back. GEMS relies solely on the digital airwave." A distracted expression settled on Gordon's face. "The oddest thing about this virtual world is that every symptom of my cancer is gone. When the doctors gave me six months to live, I could hardly walk ten feet. But in here, I've battled cyborgs, cyber creatures, outrun tanks, dodged bullets. Well mostly, dodged bullets. It's like I'm invincible."

"But if you're dying out there and invincible in here, why would you want to escape?"

"Because nobody I love is in here."

An image flashed across the laptop, once Jack recognized. He pointed at the screen. "I know this place. That's the bell tower at the University of California in Riverside. The thing's over a hundred foot tall."

"GEMS must be located inside the tower." Gordon called out for Neil to grab a map. He told them what Jack had discovered.

"How far away is it?" Neil asked.

"A little over an hour's drive. Will this bus get us there?"

"She's as strong as a tank," Neil said. "And we'll need her to be. California has about thirty military bases. Army. Marines. Navy. Air Force. Before the day is out, GEMS will turn our own systems against us."

***

The bug-out bus was equipped with a train's cow-catcher attached to the front. The fire-engine-red, V-shaped wedge was designed to push obstacles off the railroad track. It looked dangerous enough to punch through solid brick walls. Or in this case, the walls of the bell tower. Jack helped prepare the weapons while the ghostly pale woman on the bench continued to twitch and send her signal.

Neil looked up from where a pile of rifles sat at his feet. "To tell

THE APOCALYPSE GAMES - PANDORA

the truth," he said, "I'm glad I'm finally getting to use these skills. Practice is one thing, but a real bug-out with real variables, now that's something to get excited about."

A loud boom rocked the bus and halted any conversation. They were all deathly quiet as they looked out the window. There was a plane on the interstate, crumpled and on fire. Black smoke poured from the carcass. Nobody could have survived the impact.

"Just wait till the missiles start firing," Gordon said. "You haven't seen fireworks till then."

The operator was now staring up at the ceiling without expression. Her lips twitched but otherwise she didn't move. In every aspect she appeared human, and Jack still had trouble forcing himself to believe she wasn't. But he'd seen the evidence of what her kind did to aid the GEMS war; she would turn him into a cyborg the moment she was freed of the restraints.

"Sorry it has to be this way," Gordon said to the CGI creature, "but you have information we need."

"I hope it helps," Neil said. "GEMS seems to *always* know when we plan an attack."

"Not this time," Gordon said.

In the sky, a plane made a steep and fatal descent. Jack watched as people ran up and down the street. Some wore prison uniforms because GEMS had obviously released them in order to create more chaos. Stores were on fire.

When people ran toward the bus, Cookie just drove faster.

Gordon sighed. "Another player just got killed."

Jack had had enough of watching the carnage outside. He went over to sit beside Gordon. On the laptop, he saw a person stretched out on a table.

"What's going to happen to him?" Jack asked.

"He'll become a cyborg."

The image cleared up and he recognized the player. "That's Reis."

Reis was restrained on a table as the woman opened a case. A silver spider crawled out. It scurried across Reis's legs and abdomen and landed on his face. Jack couldn't bear watching as the body jerked and pulled at the restraints. It must have hurt. But he also couldn't *not* look. It took ten minutes for the device to strip every inch of humanity from his best friend. After the operation, Reis pushed his metal body up off the table and allowed the woman to guide him to a platform. She hooked him into a computer and his body finally went rigid.

"He's just gone into the mainframe," Gordon said. "He's now the enemy. I'm sorry."

"I don't see Kelly."

"She may have been lucky and escaped."

"I should have stayed with her," he said. His intention to allow Reis and Kelly some alone time may have backfired.

"Then you'd be a cyborg," Gordon said. "And we'd have to hunt you down and kill you. Look, we can save your friend by winning this game. But I can't do it without your help. You need to focus. The operator we've captured is still sending out her SOS, but I don't know how long before GEMS realizes we've targeted her location."

Jack stared at the laptop until he was convinced his sister was not amongst the conversion crew. If he couldn't save Kelly or Reis at least he could save the world. That had to count for something in the way of redemption.

By now, Neil's bug-out bus had reached the university. Cookie drove into the empty grounds; normally thousands of students were wandering around on their way to and from classes. The bell tower was situated in the middle of a park. Cookie drove over the lawn but stopped short of the tower by two hundred feet. A fence had been erected around the tower and it was patrolled by men carrying guns. Using a set of binoculars, Jack counted about fifty men. Part of the GEMS army; the players would have been killed and converted into cyborgs, but Jack didn't see any of them.

He handed the binoculars to Gordon. "I'd say this lot are just part of the special effects. NPCs. No real threat and no point shooting them. We should just focus on killing the enemy."

"I don't see signs of either," Neil said.

"Maybe we're in luck." Though the way Jack's luck was going, he doubted it.

Neil scoffed. "Luck is for losers. I'm for blowing up the tower with the rocket launcher. Just get it over and done with and end Pandora's reign here and now. We all watched the footage. We can't afford to be shot and end up as cyborgs. We'll turn on one another and I don't want to have to shoot any of you. And make no mistakes about it, I will shoot you."

Just then the bell in the tower rang loudly, and hundreds of white-haired, white-faced creatures poured out from the doors and spilled out onto the grounds. They headed straight for the bus. These were not the nice type of operator from the CyberNexis launch who'd flirted with players during the symbiotic hook up. These creatures were nasty looking things, all leathery flesh and bone, looking more like skinned ferrets. They carried guns and fired at the bus. When the first round of *pings* hit the metal, Jack ducked behind a cabinet.

Neil scoffed. "You reckon I'd prepare for the end of the world and *not* bullet proof my ride? I'm insulted by your lack of confidence."

Then he stormed to the rear of the bus and lifted up a mattress where he retrieved a rocket launcher. "The only problem is the range is best at around one hundred feet. We'll have to drive the bus right up to the tower."

Cookie put the bus in gear. "Not a problem. Next stop GEMS mainframe."

As the bus gathered speed, so did the creatures. They fired at the bus windows and the exterior walls. When the bullets ricocheted off the enforced metal, they shot at the tires.

"Just keep driving, Cookie," Neil shouted. "Old Yeller has a set of steel rims on the inside of each wheel. It'll be a bumpy ride but we'll make it."

Gordon grabbed a polarity gun and slipped the barrel through a small hole in the window, no doubt designed for this purpose. He blasted two creatures into shimmering atoms. Next, cyborgs started running from within the tower, heading for the bus. Jack grabbed a rifle and slipped the barrel into a pre-drilled hole in the front windshield. It didn't leave much room to maneuver the rifle, but with the bus aimed directly at the cyborgs, he managed to shoot a few to the ground.

"Aim for their legs," Neil shouted.

"Brace yourselves," Cookie yelled.

The bus slammed into the fence. But none of the passengers were prepared for the abrupt stop. The bus plowed through but stopped abruptly when it became tangled up in the wire mesh. Bodies were tossed around. Jack was thrown against the windshield, landing on his back. A searing pain snaked through his shoulder. He was positive he'd dislocated it. It took a few seconds for the pain to subside and a few more for the strength in his shoulder to return to normal.

He stood up. The GEMS army vastly outnumbered theirs.

"We've got to take out the tower," he shouted.

Neil hefted the rocket launcher onto his shoulder. "Cookie, open the damned window and get out of the way before I blow you to pieces."

Cookie slid the driver window open and Gordon dragged Jack away from the line of fire. Neil wedged the barrel of the rocket launcher in the opening.

What was he doing setting the thing off from in here?

"Not in here, you idiot," Jack yelled, but Neil didn't hear. Or if he did, he'd purposely chosen to ignore the warning.

Neil pressed the trigger. The backblast shook the bus and knocked items off the counters. Jack pressed his hands to his ears, momentarily deafened. He could tell that people were screaming but no sound entered his deafened canals.

Jack spun in time to see one of them opening the window. He staggered back, directly into the CGI hostage, who sat up and ripped the wires and cables out of her body. She reached for a gun and pointed it at Jack. Before she could fire off a round, she disappeared into a million fragments. Jack spun to see Gordon holding a polarizing gun in his hand. He then shot more creatures, but for each one he destroyed, more filled their place, multiplying with each fragmentation. Jack ignored the ringing in his ears and picked up the polarity gun that Gordon had tossed at him. He was firing blindly, creatures were morphing into mist, but he couldn't be certain of what he was hitting, if he was hitting anything at all; the ringing in his ears had left him off balance.

When a second backblast rocked the bus, Jack almost shot Neil just to stop him from making his deafness permanent. Inside the confines of the cabin the weapon was as dangerous as the enemy. But deaf was better than dead.

Smoke and flames emerged from the tower. Creatures crawled down from the walls like spiders. Cyborgs appeared from out of nowhere and immediately charged toward the bus.

Cookie drove the bus forward and dragged the fence along with it. He managed to sweep a few cyborgs out of the way with the cow-catcher. Everyone inside the bus was shooting at the enemy. Yet, each time a soldier of the GEMS army went down, more replaced it.

"We can't keep doing this," Jack shouted. "They're multiplying."

Neil loaded a third missile and said, "Third time is the charm."

He fired the missile at the tower. The top half exploded and pieces of it toppled to the ground. Yet still the enemy came.

A cyborg bashed a metal fist at a window until it shattered.

"Board it up," Neil shouted.

Gordon and Jack hurried over to place a mattress over the opening. Outside, cyborgs threw themselves at the bus to get inside. Jack looked down and saw blood on his arm. He bit down on the pain as he helped secure the mattress.

Neil tossed the rocket launcher to the side. "That had better do it 'cos I'm out of missiles."

The bottom section of the tower began to shake on its foundations. It was weakening, but not fast enough. Creatures continued to pour out of every crevice and the rubble. No humans would survive this massacre.

From what Gordon had said, Jack guessed no human was supposed to.

***

The cyborgs started tearing at the reinforced metal shell of the bus. As easy as opening a soda can.

"Get us out of here," Neil shouted to Cookie.

Cookie slammed the bus into reverse but the cow-catcher was tangled up with the fence and wouldn't let the bus free. A white body jumped up onto the bus; through the window she shot at Cookie who slumped into the seat. Neil shot at the creature with the polarizer before scrambling over the bodies and the seats, then he grabbed a hold of Cookie's body and dragged him along the floor. Neil lifted up a hatch and pushed Cookie down the hole.

Jack had stood mute the whole time. His feet wouldn't move. This was the end and he was doing nothing to save himself. Guess he needed someone else to save for his superhero powers to kick in.

He noticed the shine in Neil's eye. Not madness, but sorrow. Neil had expected to win this time.

Neil jumped in behind the driver's seat and tried to reverse the bus. It was stuck. They were outnumbered and trapped.

A cyborg shot Neil and his body fell to the floor. Gordon looked at Jack in shock. Jack knew what the old man was thinking. Out of all of them, Neil was the least likely to get himself killed.

"Get him out of the bus," Gordon said. "Otherwise he'll return as one of them."

Gordon dragged Neil to the hatch, but the cyborgs had discovered the opening and they lay in waiting. A cyborg shot Gordon. He fell out the bottom of the bus. More creatures were clambering in through the window while cyborgs were crawling up through the hatch.

Everyone was dead. Jack was the last man on earth, and he would not survive either.

Just then, the ground started to shake violently. Jack grabbed onto the bench and stared in horror out the front window. A mushroom cloud appeared. The stem grew till it was almost out of the atmosphere. The bell of radioactive cloud hung in the sky that glowed black and orange. The deafening *boom* followed.

This was game over.

He closed his eyes, waiting for the blast wave of the explosion to reach him. He must have been a safe distance because his flesh didn't peel off.

When he finally opened his eyes, the bell tower had exploded into millions of pieces. GEMS, having lost control of her army, severed the link and their enemy dropped to the ground like ragdolls.

The mushroom cloud had developed a button-shaped ring at the top, like a flying-saucer shaped hat.

Maybe not game over. Maybe new game. Survive the nuclear fallout.

He didn't relish dying of radiation poisoning, so he got off the bus and started jogging until he couldn't run anymore. Then he walked until his feet blistered, only looking forward, never behind. Pandora had unleashed evil upon mankind, but when the jar was finally closed all that remained inside was hope. It wasn't over, wasn't ever going to be over, but Jack needed to believe it was possible.

22

Kelly

"She's crying. She's alive. Kelly! Wake up."

The voice cut through her dream. She didn't want to wake up. In her dream, Matt was beside her. She tried to move and found she couldn't. Like a weight was pressed down on her chest. A soldier's boot. A vampire. Maybe in this new game she was a survivor of a nuclear apocalypse and someone was stealing her boots.

"Her brainwaves are registering," a woman's voice said.

"She's experiencing sleep paralysis," a male voice said. "It'll last about thirty seconds."

If the weight kept pressing down on her chest, she would be dead before the thirty seconds was up. She almost laughed. Who was she kidding? If only she *could* die.

"Kelly. Wake up!"

The scenery began to fade until it was gone altogether.

A woman's face popped into view. Kelly squinted. The woman had hazel eyes and freckles over pale skin. Her reddish-brown hair was clipped tightly to her skull. She wore a gray shirt with a patch on her chest. REYNOLDS. Beside her, a thin black man wearing glasses stared down at Kelly without expression. His name badge read AUSTIN.

"You're awake," Austin said.

"Where am I?" Kelly was surprised her voice was sore and dry.

"Houston, Texas."

"How did I get here?"

"The pods were transported to a NASA facility so you could be safely unhooked from them."

Kelly Lawrence wanted to weep with joy. Instead she lay inside a glass coffin, no longer scared that her handsome prince was never going to rescue her. She no longer needed saving. Her house might be empty of life, but it was alive with memories and love.

"Home," she said. "I want to go home."

Reynolds and Austin exchanged a worried look.

"What's wrong?" Kelly tried to sit up, found she could hardly move.

"Where's home?" Reynolds asked.

"San Diego."

That worried look again. "What's wrong?"

"Nothing."

"Tell me what happened."

Reynolds shook her head. "The shock might cause a reaction and I just don't know enough about the residual effects of neural stimulators to risk giving you the bad news. Not yet. I shouldn't have said anything.

"It's that bad, huh?"

Reynolds nodded. "It's that bad."

Kelly tried to sit up but the cables kept her restrained. "Untie me."

"You're not tied in. It's muscular dystrophy. Don't try to move. You'll fall down."

"Great. I'm paralyzed and you won't tell me the bad news. Why the hell did you bother to unhook me?"

Kelly forced the tears away. She'd survived the worst of the worst. Gone to hell and back, gotten knocked down and back up again. There wasn't anything these two could say that would frighten her.

The feeling returned to Kelly's hand, which she clenched into tight fists. "It's supposed to be over," she said.

"It *is* over," said Austin. "You're out of the game."

One door closed. Another stood before her. If her time in The Apocalypse Games had taught her anything, it was that you never knew what lay behind any door. You could stare at a closed door as long as you liked and mentally will it to stay closed, but all doors opened eventually. Sometimes, you were better off not knowing what lay ahead.

Now wasn't that time.

"Tell me why the game malfunctioned."

Reynolds nodded. "Yellowstone erupted. The eruption triggered a chain of earthquakes. Half the towns along the fault line are gone. It cut power to the facility and the back-up power failed, clogged by the ash. All over the country, power is out. Communication is out. Volcanic ash is covering most of the country and blocking out the sun. The ash has ruined crops, muddied drinking water. There may be no home left for you to go to. Not for any of us."

Kelly began laughing. At first, a chuckle, which grew into a loud roar. Eventually tears streamed down her face.

"We're not lying," said Reynolds.

That only made Kelly laugh harder.

"Why are you laughing?" Austin asked.

"Because if what you're saying is true, it's hardly Game Over. It's more like Game On."

"So why is that funny?"

It wasn't. But what else could she do? It was either laugh in the face of death, or let death laugh in her face. And Kelly Lawrence wasn't about to let death win. Not anymore.

EPILOGUE

"Once upon a time a teenage boy and his best friend played a prank on the best friend's little sister. They'd known the little sister feared monsters, but it was a particularly dreary day with not much else to do except torment cats and little sisters. The cat would have none of it and had zipped off to hide in a neighbor's yard. They'd coaxed the little sister into watching a horror movie with them, and because she was the kind of sister who always wanted to do whatever her brother and his friend did, she watched it. The little sister had survived watching the movie, even bravely declaring that it was stupid and pointing out all the flaws of the visual effects, and then she'd taken herself to bed. The two boys had decided it would be fun to dress up in clown costumes and creep into her bedroom."

Kelly sat on a plastic chair in a circle of chairs inside a room devoid of all other furniture, like this was an Alcoholic Anonymous meeting. Except there was only one other person seated in the circle of chairs.

She glanced up from the notepad. She had written these words down after they had floated into her mind while sleeping. She'd heard them inside the pod.

"You do understand it was a game," a man named Kardinski said. He was the space doctor in charge when the world had gone to hell. Qualified to deal with cyber sickness, he was now in charge of everyone's mental health.

"But someone designed that game," Kelly replied.

"Obviously."

She tried to focus, but it was getting harder to decipher real memory from implanted memory.

"CyberNexis," she said at last. "They built the pods, the game, they did this to us."

"Kelly, I know you want to blame someone for what happened. We all want things to fit conveniently into boxes. Your husband's death, that was fifteen months ago."

"Twelve," Kelly said.

Kardinski shook his head.

"Oh, fifteen. I still can't believe we were trapped in those pods for three months. Where is everyone else?"

Kardinski sighed. He rubbed his eyes. "We've gone over this before."

"Sorry if I can't remember."

"It's the drugs."

"I didn't take any drugs."

He glanced up to the corner of the room, and that was when she realized that someone was watching this session through a video camera. She also realized that she had lost movement in her body. Her arms wouldn't move.

"Where am I?"

Kardinski picked a small recording device out of his pocket. "The patient is exhibiting signs of amnesia. She keeps slipping in and out of lucidity. Remind me to report the designers of this game to the government."

"CyberNexis," Kelly said. "They did something to me. I can feel it."

"Why don't you save your strength for your recovery. You're out of the simulation pods. You'll be back on solid foods by this evening."

"I want to go home."

"This is home now."

"CyberNexis," she said. "They did something to me. I can feel it."

Kardinski stood up and walked to the window. "Take her back to bed. She's in no condition yet to talk about what happened."

"I want to go home. Please, let me go home."

"This is your home now."

Tears coursed down her cheeks. "Why won't you let me go?"

In two strides, Dr Kardinski was kneeling in front of her. "Read your story again. Tell me about the boy who tormented his sister. Because she defeated those monsters. Didn't she? That's the part of the story you left out. She defeated the monsters. Focus on that Kelly. She defeated the monsters."

Kelly's mind was already someplace else, thinking about the monsters. She'd defeated them. But they were coming for her. She could feel that too.

Kardinski's voice drifted away. Then she was floating.

"It's the drugs," she heard a distant voice say.

But she hadn't taken any drugs. They'd done something to her. She could feel it.

THE END.

FOR NOW...

OUT NOW

THE APOCALYPSE GAMES
CYBERNEXIS (BOOK 2)

THE APOCALYPSE GAMES
CHRYSALIS (BOOK 3)

Read sample chapters of Book 2

Chapter One: Kelly

The internet always crashed at home. Without fail, a quick search for a recipe turned into an epic battle, lasting longer than the Napoleonic War. However long that was; Kelly Lawrence didn't actually know because the computer had crashed the day she'd tried to find out.

The cause of her aggravation was not the plastic box and silicone chips that housed the data. The culprit was a non-sentient thing, capable of wreaking more havoc than a sugared-up toddler in a china shop. The culprit was cyberspace. Littered with viruses, worms, malwares, and Trojans.

Why had she placed her life in the hands of a something prone to collapse?

Because it was meant to be a game.

It was also meant to be fail proof.

Someone was whispering in her ear. "It's over. You're safe."

No such thing as safe, she told herself, tuning out the voice floating to her from a corridor that could only lead to her darkest nightmares. She'd had enough of nightmares that charged towards her with blind fury, sending fiery sparks that stung like ant bites and always heralded another battle with monsters that wanted her dead.

"She's slipping away," the faraway voice said. "Come on, Kelly. Fight it."

Some people were born fighters. Others learned the skill. But always, even when you won you lost something.

"Stay with me," the voice beckoned. "I'm not gonna lose you."

What was the point of fighting? Pandora was never going to let her go. Yes, they'd given their cybernetic nemesis a name. Over one hundred people had entered simulation pods to escape reality. When it'd gone horribly wrong, it'd made sense to name their enemy after a goddess who'd unleashed hell upon mankind. All they'd had left was hope.

Even that was gone now.

Kelly let the darkness drag her away.

***

Kelly opened her eyes and was taken aback for a second. Seated opposite her was her late husband, Matt. Her heart lifted a little. He'd found her. Or had she found him? It seemed she recalled, hazily as if under the influence of a drug, that she'd gone in search of him inside the game, and here he was. He looked exactly as she remembered, with his dirty-blond hair that refused to stay out of his eyes, wearing a green shirt that melded to his body with adoration. He'd be almost thirty-one if he was alive. She was on the downhill side of twenty-six. These details should have mattered.

Instead, something akin to fear grew inside her, building the way a tornado does until she knew that whatever was heading her way could only be dangerous. Like a shipwreck survivor adrift in the ocean, Kelly slapped at the surging darkness to grab hold of the faraway voice. It was gone. She was alone with the ghost of her dead husband.

"The pursuit of happiness is a sink," Matt said, stabbing a slice of toast into the runny yoke of a boiled egg. "You fill the bowl with things that make you happy; shopping, drinking, smoking, eating. Whatever. Then you wake up the next morning to discover that the sink has a hole in it and the bowl is empty. What do you do?"

Too tired to take the bait to an argument so old it could only be interpreted with a hieroglyphics manual, she let her shoulders slump. She cast her gaze around the cafe where she and Matt had spent most Sunday mornings. The rustic decor of copper pipes converted into bookshelves, wine barrels made into tables, old jam jars used as drink glasses...these decorative items had once fascinated her. Now they terrified her. Only Matt could have replicated this virtual world. A world that both touched and saddened her heart at the same time, for this world was a glimpse through a window. Memories were all that were on offer in this cafe.

And yet, the past could only haunt a person if they let it, so why was she?

"Kelly?" Matt was scowling at her with a furious look in his eyes. The real Matt only ever scowled in fierce concentration, never in anger. "What do you do?"

"My addled brain sports neither concern nor clue," she said, quoting her dead husband who'd once spent a month talking like a Shakespearean actor while working on a Mediaeval cosplay website. This version stared at her blankly. Proof that he wasn't real.

"I just want to go home," she said.

The moment the words left her mouth she felt the air shift. The cafe faded and in its place was a war zone. Buildings were on fire, guns were being fired, smoke filled her nostrils.

The window beside her smashed, glass flew into the plate of eggs, and someone — no something — jumped through the opening.

There wasn't anything human about this creature. It had matted hair that was encrusted with dirt and blood. It carried knives in both hands and the hide of a deer was wrapped around its back. Bones hung around its neck and when it caught Kelly's gaze, it growled. The spell was broken. Her reflexes sprang into action. She ran out of the cafe.

Whatever happens next, she told herself, just keep running.

The beast matched her pace, running beside her with its wild hair trailing like a horse's mane. It turned its head and smiled, revealing yellow teeth. In her head she heard a voice yelling at her to go left, and so she did. But she ran straight into another creature.

It held a knife above its head. Staring at it, she noticed it was too small to be knife. A syringe! The beast swung the syringe down into her neck.

Except it wasn't a syringe, it was a computer cable.

Chapter Two: Jack

"Player twenty-one is about to enter the game."

Orange atoms flashed in front of Jack Minnow's eyes and he felt the lurch of his stomach as if plummeting from a great height, and he thought to himself, *I didn't choose a game.*

These atoms flashed, sparking as if alive with energy, until finally the show was over and the display vanished. Jack noticed his surroundings had shifted from the bright colors of the pod to the dull grays of a hospital room. Rows of beds were situated along two walls and a desk sat at the far end of the room. About twenty beds. No windows in the room. No flowers either, or fruit baskets or visitors for that matter. But the bitter smell of disinfectant and lost hope was abundant.

Other than the overhead vent humming and his sneakers squeaking on the floor, the room gave off no noise. Patients lay in the beds, as still as corpses with tubes sticking out of their arms and mouths. Alive but sedated, giving him a glimpse of what his body looked like from outside of the virtual reality simulation pod.

Impressions didn't count for anything in this world. Bodies being used for medical or science projects wouldn't be out of character. They might not be human. Androids. Whatever. Pandora wasn't offering up any clue as to why he stood in a hospital ward holding a patient chart.

He looked over the notes, although he'd never studied medicine so he had no idea what the illegible scrawls meant. Hearing a noise, he looked up and braced himself for a fight. Instead of the enemy, a woman in a nurse's uniform stepped into the room. Her deadpan stare traveled around the room. It landed on Jack and hovered there like a wary cat eyeing a rabid dog.

He tried to smile. "I take it from the confused look on your face, you're a player."

"Lucky me." She ripped the cap off her head and sauntered her way into the room. Her short red hair fell to just below her chin. Jack was instantly attracted to her.

"We should stick together," he said, his mood lifting. "Until we can figure out what's going on."

"Sounds good to me." She held out her hand. "I'm Sasha Vaness."

"Jack Minnow."

She waved at finger at his chest. "Actually, you're Dr. Jack Minnow and I'm Nurse Vaness." Her smile turned into a scowl.

"Can't believe this game is sexist. I'm a woman so I have to be the nurse."

Jack handed her the chart. "You can be the doctor. I have no idea what it says."

She took the chart and read it. "It says the patient came in with pneumonia. She has asthma." Sasha tossed the chart on the floor. "The cold conditions have exacerbated her illness. Who cares, I say. She's one of *them*."

Jack stared down at the patient. "One of who?"

"A non-player character. I'm sick of wasting my energy on them. They can't help me."

"I don't think they're supposed to."

From behind, someone coughed and Jack turned to see a short man wearing an orderly's uniform standing in the doorway. He wheeled a mobile medical cart into the room. Another non-player character — NPC — that Sasha wouldn't waste her energy on, but Jack still wanted to know what they were dealing with.

"Where are we?" he asked the orderly. "What world are we in?"

The orderly gave him a queer look. "Look, I'm just here to change the sheets."

Jack had never harbored any notion of obtaining a medical degree anyway, so he and Sasha let the orderly do his work while they wandered along the corridors.

Jack said, "Did the presentation tell you what we're meant to do or what we're up against? I doubt it's as innocuous as the common cold."

"Could be a pandemic outbreak."

A muffled cry, followed by a crash, came from the room they'd just exited. Jack stepped back to peer through the glass panel. The orderly was pressing a pillow down onto the patient's face.

His reflexes kicked in and he burst through the door. He surprised the orderly, who lifted the pillow off the patient's face, giving Jack the opportunity to charge at him. The guy was short and thin, and frail like a stern word could topple him over, but when Jack charged, the frailty was replaced with a snarling monster who produced a knife. Slashing wildly, he drove Jack backwards.

The orderly kept coming and he would have sliced Jack in half if Sasha hadn't appeared, smashing a bed pan across the guy's face.

Blood splattered onto the bed. Bones crunched. The guy went down and Sasha continued to strike the bed pan at his head with the force of a professional thug. She lifted the bedpan over her head for a final strike, but the orderly grabbed her around the ankles, toppling her to the floor.

Jack rushed to help Sasha and the orderly fled.

She jumped up and pushed him aside. "I wasn't finished." She burst through the door and Jack had to run to catch up. But the assailant had vanished.

"I don't think he'll be back," Jack said. Not if the guy had any sense.

The metal bed pan was dented and the bent fold of metal made it a dangerous weapon. He was mildly impressed, and also mildly scared of the woman.

"You handled yourself well," he said, deciding to get on her good side.

She gave him a sly look. "I come from a badass neighborhood. Okay, you may have a point about knowing what we're up against. Let's check on our patient. She might be able to tell us why someone wants her dead."

Chapter Three: Reis

Landing in a new game always came with one, or all, of three things: the rush of adrenalin brought on by the fight or flight response activated in the brain; the brilliant orange, yellow, and red fireworks display on the heads-up unit; and/or a jolt like an elevator stopping abruptly. Reis Anderson experienced none of these things. Instead, he felt as if he were floating. That wasn't quite right either. Floating usually involved a gentle sideways motion and right now he felt like he was buried under a car.

He opened his eyes to find circles of lights shining down on him. Somewhere a clock ticked and a full minute passed by incredibly slowly, in which time he pondered the absence of feeling in his body. He couldn't move, couldn't even turn his head, but there was motion in his peripheral vision.

He began to hyperventilate.

Then, berating himself for panicking, he closed his eyes as if willpower alone could reboot his brain and return his settings to normal.

Nothing is crushing me. Nothing is restraining me. This is all in my head.

"It's the side effects making your body feel heavy," said a male voice to his right. "There's nothing wrong with you."

"Then why can't I move?" This voice came from the left.

Sounds of shuffling followed and then people in all directions started coughing. Reis kept his eyes closed. Playing possum seemed a plausible tactic, something he'd learned as a boy when Homeland Security had taught him how to stay alive.

Curiosity got the better of him and he fought the invisible weight to lift his head a few inches off the bed. He wasn't alone. In the room, there were men and women lying on army-style, fold-up beds that sat two feet off the ground. Those who were tending to the patients had to kneel down or stoop. Other patients lounged in armchairs that were haphazardly placed in the available nooks.

Reis became fixated on the black-and-white photographs of rocks on the wall. Someone sure liked rocks.

He caught a whiff of vomit and looked down at his chest. Not his. But he noticed that he was wearing cotton drawstring pants and a loose-fitting t-shirt. His feet were bare so he wiggled his toes, expecting to hear the jiggle of metal restraints. He heard nothing, but he still couldn't lift his leg.

He tried to move his hands. Still no movement there.

Of all the nightmares he'd faced in The Apocalypse Games, waking up in a public hospital, a breeding pool of germs, with the inability to get up and walk away, ranked the worst of the worst.

A green light over the door blinked. After a minute, the door opened and a man with a pale-complexion stepped into the room. He wore a blue shirt with brown slacks. A pair of reading glasses hung from a chain around his neck.

His gaze quickly surveyed the patients.

"I'm Dr. Roger Kardinski," he said, addressing nobody in particular. "I'm the medical officer for the Life Sciences Division at NASA. I'm what you call a space doctor."

He paused as if waiting for people to show their admiration, but everyone was sick and numb and couldn't manage anything except a contemptuous stare for the man who was clearly denying them the drugs that'd ease their illness.

"I specialize in keeping our astronauts fit in space and rehabilitating them back on Earth," the doctor said. "You are currently situated in the old site of the Lunar Receiving Laboratory in the Johnson Space Center. You're in the old crew recovery room where NASA used to quarantine astronauts returning from space."

"We're under quarantine?" said a man in the next bed.

The doctor looked annoyed. "There's no reason to quarantine you. You have muscle dystrophy and cyber sickness. The symptoms are similar to space flights. Therefore, you'll experience light-headedness when you stand up, dizziness when you move, and you may even feel as if the world is spinning while you're lying still. On the plus side, we have a few lunar rocks that I'd be happy to show you once you're well enough" He began to rock back and forth on the balls of his feet. "Seeing the rocks used to boost the astronauts' spirits."

The doctor's pep talk had the desired effect. Heads lifted, chatter flourished, and those who were coughing tried their best to suppress it. All because of a few rocks that he claimed had come from the moon.

Reis never held much stock in the genuineness of the Moon landing. So it was with skepticism that he watched the doctor's gaze as it traveled over the group, searching for a particular patient. Despite his words, the doctor wasn't here to boost their morale.

"I've done preliminary examinations on each of you," said the doctor, again to nobody in particular. "I'll now do follow up examinations in alphabetical order." He consulted a chart. "Reis Anderson. You're the lucky first."

The doctor's gaze swept around the room and Reis wasn't sure he wanted to be this guy's guinea pig.

"When are you gonna tell us our scores?" said a burly white man propped up in a wheelchair. He had dark circles under his eyes and red blemishes on his face as if infected. He resembled a junkie. On closer inspection, so did everyone in the room.

The doctor consulted his chart. "Bran Tucker, isn't it? I'm a busy man with a lot of patients. Alphabetical is the fairest way to visit all the patients, so I'll be with you shortly."

"But I want the scores for the game," Bran said. "I need to know this rash ain't for nothing."

"Yes, you developed an allergic reaction to the bodysuit. I've given you medication to contain the itch and the infection. Other than the rash, you're in perfect health."

"My team and I entered the game for the prize money. What are the scores, Doc? We need to know who won."

Won, thought Reis. They'd all been lucky to come out of this episode with their lives. Who cared about winning?

But of course, as a gambling man, Reis did. Right now he wanted Bran to shut up and stop taking the doctor's attention off *his* recovery.

"My only concern is the health of my patients," said the doctor. "Which you're delaying. If you'll excuse me."

The doctor headed towards Reis, but it seemed the soldiers had their own agenda.

"There was a twenty grand first prize for most kills," said another player, a blonde woman. She was hanging her head over the side of the bed and dry retching. "We need to know the scores."

"Eileen Bakersfield," said the doctor, once more consulting his chart. "I'll get to you next. Please, everyone. We're not a medical facility. We only have a few staff who can attend to you. Actually, we have one qualified staff member. Me."

"Call me Dodge," said the woman. "Only my mother calls me Eileen. And if you're not a medical facility, what are you?"

Kardinski sighed. "Homesick. Listen, Dodge, I'll do your checkup when I'm consulting the D patients. Okay?"

She slumped onto the bed and Reis grew curious about the prize money. The money didn't interest him, but his competitive streak meant he might not have spent all his time playing the white knight to a woman who clearly didn't want his help. He might have fed his gambling addiction instead.

Strange that this was the first time he'd ever considered himself an addict.

He managed to lift his head all the way up, though it hurt his neck muscles. He couldn't see Kelly or Jack in the room. He also still couldn't open his mouth to speak.

Two people entered the room and Dr. Kardinski deviated from his path to confer with them for a few minutes. Meanwhile, Reis wanted to fill the room with his impatient screams but his vocals chords were locked.

The doctor finally made it to his bedside, and he used a stethoscope to check Reis's lungs, a neuro hammer to test his reflexes, took his blood pressure with the Sphygmomanometer, his body temperature with a thermometer, and finished his examination by shining a tiny flashlight into Reis's eyes.

Reis hadn't moved or resisted any part of the inspection. Simply because he couldn't.

"How are you feeling?" Kardinski asked, slipping the instruments onto a metal tray.

Reis finally found his voice. "Like...I'm paralyzed."

"Well, you're not. You need to tell your body you're not. It still senses that it's hooked up to the simulation pod. We've given you valium to combat the anxiety you'd ordinarily experience at waking up with little or no sensation."

"What can you...tell me about the pods?"

"NASA designed them. Someone else built them. Two of our engineers did most of the design work and they analyzed the computer files and video footage. "

"Footage?"

Kardinski nodded. "The rescue crew gathered what they needed in order for me to unhook you. Our guys were impressed with the technology. Some of it was more developed than what they'd originally designed." Kardinski scowled. "CyberNexis spent a bucket load of military funds on building that facility. What the hell were you doing in the pods anyway?"

"Playing a game."

"Such a flagrant misuse of property. Those pods were designed for space travel. I'll bet you're glad to be out of them at least."

"Depends where I am."

The doctor was smiling like a proud father when he said, "NASA, Houston."

"Right. Houston. How convenient."

Kardinski's smile faltered. "You're in the old Lunar Receiving Laboratory. There's a collection of rocks from outer space—"

"Of course NASA has space rocks." It seemed as if Reis's voice had fully returned. "What I don't get is why NASA moved the pods from Arizona to Texas. And why can't I remember anything of the trip?"

"Calm down. I haven't got any answers. I was working in my lab when the front doorbell rang and a truck arrived. You were carried in on stretchers. The men stayed long enough to help set up beds and reload our supplies. Then they left. That's all I know."

"What happened to our bodysuits?"

"I've told you everything I know." The doctor busied himself with thermometers and flashlights and other medical gadgets.

Reis scowled. "I don't believe you. This is just another one of Pandora's games—"

"Yes, yes, I'm hearing that name quite a bit. Except nobody will explain to me who Pandora is." Kardinski's level gaze landed on Reis. "Or should I say what? I'm assuming Pandora is the computer. No need to be embarrassed. NASA gives everything a name."

"Pandora became an expert in messing with our minds. You'll understand why we don't believe you."

A wry smile crept onto the doctor's face. "Then how about if I tell you something that the computer could not possibly know."

Reis waited.

"Do you think the computer would tell you the actual length of your stay in the pods? It isn't two weeks like you believe."

"How long?"

"Three months."

"That can't be right." Reis's mouth went dry. "Three months?"

"Yes. By NASA standards you'd be one month away from landing on Mars."

Reis rubbed his fingers against his face. He'd have expected a full beard after three months. This was just another one of Pandora's games.

The doctor waved a hand in Reis's direction. "You were in a state of suspended animation, hence the slow growth of your facial hair. I'll prove this is real once you're well enough to leave the ward."

"We played a few games, but not three month's worth." Reis tried to keep the tremor out of his voice.

"It's likely you didn't play any more than one game. When the brain has a near death experience, or goes into a deep sleep or undergoes anesthesia, the unconscious brain pieces together an alternate world."

"Now you're telling me I dreamed all those scenarios. That we *all* dreamed the same dream."

Reis struggled to sit up. Most of the people in the makeshift hospital ward were unfamiliar, but he recognized William Rush, the actor hired to play one of the command leaders in the presentations. He now sat in the corner leaning over a bucket. The older man looked over and gave Reis a weak smile and a half-hearted thumbs up.

Maybe this *was* real. Everyone seemed too sick for it to be fantasy.

"Where's Kelly and Jack?" Reis asked Kardinski.

The doctor shook his head. "I'm not familiar with everyone here. Are you experiencing dizziness?"

"My head aches like a lumberjack is using it to store an axe."

"The pain will go away."

"Seems a lot of pain and sickness for someone who was dreaming."

"Your brain was asleep, almost shut down. The technical term in a sopor, and you were in a deliberately induced sopor. You'll also have to recover from addiction to the drugs they fed you. Plus you've suffered an incredible amount of trauma. Astronauts suffer less."

Reis had trouble understanding the doctor because everything was going in and out of focus. Vertigo was setting in, making the room spin. His skin was starting to itch.

"Reis, are you okay?" asked the doctor.

"I'm fine." Except for the ringing in his ears and the crawling sensation on his flesh. Then the strangeness passed, leaving him more confused than ever.

"What can you tell me about your time hooked up to the game?" the doctor asked.

"Nothing. I don't remember much."

Kardinski nodded. "That's to be expected. I'm certain your amnesia isn't permanent. Your brain won't be affected since you didn't suffer an injury, so you'll regain full consciousness. And you'll recover the memories in due course. You're lucky to be alive. Your pod showed signs of stress. If they hadn't found you..."

"Who did find us?"

"The military. What's left of them. Government has tried to control the surviving population including their armed forces, but if you don't pay people, they don't want to do any work."

"*You're* not collecting a wage."

"I work for NASA, not the military. I'm here because science will see us out of this predicament."

Reis was afraid to ask. "The military has their own doctors," he said. "Why transport us to Texas?"

"You're asking a lot of questions that I can't answer. And I have many patients to see."

"Who *can* answer them?"

Kardinski considered this while clicking with the flashlight's on/off switch. "That would be Joan Reynolds. She's the most senior person in this building."

Kardinski turned to walk away.

"I have one last question," said Reis.

Kardinski stopped.

"How many players didn't survive?"

"I don't have the authority to give you that information."

"That's bullshit. Tell me what happened to my friends."

"You need to recover, Reis. The evacuation transport is due in less than a week."

Then the doctor moved off to examine another player.

***

Scraps of memories returned to Reis and they weren't pleasant. He saw decayed bodies inside the pods. Faces that were unrecognizable. He saw remnants of the laminated passes the players had worn around their necks and his hand reached for his chest in search of his. He was surprised when he touched the pass, certain that it would have been removed. Its presence loaned merit to his theory that Pandora was still in control.

A series of dry retches attacked Reis, blocking the oxygen to his brain. He held onto the side of the bed for support and a thin black man wearing glasses and a baseball shirt ambled over to the bed and gave him a cup of water.

"I'm Derek Austin," the guy said. "Head of robotics."

"Build me a robot to take me out of here," said Reis.

"I'll get right on it. You think you can hop out of bed and into a shower?" Austin asked.

Anything to get out of the hospital bed, even embarrassing himself by allowing Austin to help him into a wheelchair.

"Astronauts always want a shower first thing," said Austin. "Can't blame them, stuck in their spacesuits for months on end. Most of them said they wanted a hot shower over sex."

"A hot shower sounds good." Actually, it sounded like heaven.

Austin pushed Reis along the corridor. The wheels *click-click-clicked* and echoed. Somewhere in the distance Reis heard the hum of machines.

"It can take astronauts months to recover from space travel," said Austin. "We can't know for sure how long it'll take you'all to recover fully. This is a unique situation. Technically, you weren't in space."

Reis fidgeted in the chair. "Do me a favor and stop pretending this is real."

Austin chuckled. "You'll accept it soon enough. Especially when you discover the pipes to the showers are frozen over and food is whatever NASA can squeeze into a tube. But hey, it's better than what you were fed in the stasis pod. Right?"

"Says who?"

"People talk. Is it true you battled machines? Cyborgs and CGI soldiers, now that's something I'd have liked to have taken a look at."

Images came to Reis of tanks running on autopilot, rolling down the streets annihilating everything in sight, crushing buildings, people, and roads. Cyborgs had gone on a rampage killing everything in their path. Cyber creatures had swarmed buildings and vehicles and pulled people out into the open for the machines to destroy. Nowhere had been safe for humans when the machines had turned on them.

No matter the carnage, people like Austin would always find them fascinating, the way an arsonist finds a charred corpse fascinating, he supposed. Hell, it'd be people like Austin who would start the cyber wars.

"You must have learned something in the game," Austin said, unconcerned about Reis's silence. "Tell me something. Anything. No matter how insignificant you think it is, it'll be music to my ears."

"I learned to keep my mouth shut," Reis said.

Did you enjoy reading The Apocalypse Games - Pandora?
You might like to leave a review at your favourite online store.

You might also like these other books by
D L Richardson:

SCIENCE FICTION
Earth Quarantined
Earth Arrested
Earth Reclaimed – coming soon

YOUNG ADULT
The Bird with the Broken Wing
Resident Spy
One Little Spell

.

About the Author

D L Richardson is the author of character-driven science fiction for adults and paranormal fiction books for teens.

Whether DL is writing about ghosts, magic, the end of the world, alien invasion, curses, or guardian angels, all her books feature strong character development and lots of twists.

You won't find the usual tropes in her books. These are unique stories about regular characters who find themselves in difficult situations. And yes, lots of twists.

When she's not writing, she can be found, watching back-to-back episodes on Netflix, playing her piano or guitar, curled up on the couch reading a book, or walking the dog.

Stay up to date with new releases:
Sign up to the author newsletter for new releases, updates, special offers, and giveaways.

Details on the website
www.dlrichardson.com

Printed in Great Britain
by Amazon

73248230R00177